GREENHOUSE SUMMER

GREENHOUSE SUMMER

NORMAN SPINRAD

TOR®

A TOM DOHERTY ASSOCIATES BOOK
NEW YORK

GREENHOUSE SUMMER

This book is printed on acid-free paper.

Edited by David G. Hartwell

A Tor Book
Published by Tom Doherty Associates, LLC
175 Fifth Avenue
New York, NY 10010

www.tor.com

Tor® is a registered trademark of Tom Doherty
Associates, LLC.

Book design by Scott Levine

  Library of Congress Cataloging-in-Publication Data

Spinrad, Norman.
    Greenhouse summer / Norman Spinrad. — 1st ed.
      p.   cm.
    ISBN 0-312-86799-9 (acid-free paper)
    I. Title.
  PS3569.P55G74   1999
  813'.54—dc21   99-37457
                                                      CIP

First Edition: November 1999

Printed in the United States of America

0 9 8 7 6 5 4 3 2 1

Pour le peuple et l'exception française.
Merci pour votre compréhension.

GREENHOUSE SUMMER

TRUE BLUE BLUES

PART ONE

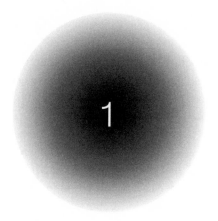

1

"TO BREAD & CIRCUSES," SAID MERVIN Appelbaum, toasting her with one final glass of first-class champagne as the Right Stuff flight from Tripoli came out of the holding stack, through the cloud deck, and turned on final toward Newark International.

"To the Gardens of Allah," Monique Calhoun replied, fixing a virtual grin on her face as she hoisted a virtual glass.

Little did her client know that the tag she had hung on the project was a snide reference to a seedy motel in twentieth-century Hollywood wherein famous literary lions like Fitzgerald and Faulkner had cranked out film scripts for corporate capitalist dream factories under the morally anesthetizing influence of oceans of booze.

It's people like you who make this job disgusting, Mervin, she restrained herself from saying.

While I, of course, am as pure as the natural snow.

Not that Bread & Circuses' charter didn't provide its citizen-shareholders with a moral rationale along with the dividends and fringes.

The Hypocritic Oath, as it was sometimes referred to in B&C circles.

Just as it was the professional duty of a legal syndic to represent the interests of any person or legal entity accused of a crime in any jurisdiction, so was it the professional duty of an interface syndic and its citizen-shareholders to represent the *client's* agenda to the *client's* satisfaction, not its or their own.

As Monique had once again so admirably done.

Mervin Appelbaum was a vice-president in charge of marketing the services of a corporate dinosaur calling itself Advanced Projects Associates.

APA seemed to consist of a suite in a fancy office building in London, a pool of funds or perhaps merely credit lines, and the e-dresses of actual construction syndics to fulfill its contracts. In the hoary old corporate capitalist tradition, it made the deals, skimmed the cream, and did nothing of work-unit value itself.

The deal in question, if not the outfit, had *seemed* idealistically Blue up front. Back in the twentieth-century, Muammar Qaddafi, a Libyan generalissimo given to bizarre costumes and financing extravagant projects with his desert jurisdiction's oil riches, had caused the construction of a massive series of tunnels to bring the waters of interior oases to the cities and towns of the coastal plain where most of the population resided.

As with the earlier and even more grandiosely naive damming of the Nile at Aswan and many later such ill-conceived climatech projects up to the present day, it had seemed like a good idea at the time.

But just as the Aswan Dam had destroyed the fertility of the Nile Valley by ending the annual flooding that maintained it, the Libyan Water Authority had by now long since sucked the oasis aquifers dry.

And while a simple nuclear device might have sufficed to take out the Aswan Dam, drain Lake Nasser, and get what was left of the central African silt flowing back down the Nile, something a bit more sophisticated than a Blue terrorist bomb would be needed to convert a tunnel network leading from dried-up oases to what was left of the flooded littoral population centers into an asset again.

This Advanced Projects Associates proposed to achieve at a handsome profit by building desalinization plants at the coast, blasting large craters at the sites of the defunct oases, and reversing the original direction of the pumping operation to fill them, thus creating large artificial lakes surrounded by newly valuable primo real estate. It had seemed like a good idea when Giorgio Kang had handed her the assignment. But once again, what had seemed True Blue in Giorgio's air-conditioned office in New York turned out to be something else again on the ground in the Lands of the Lost.

The flight had been approaching Newark International from the east, over the seafood farms and dismal mosquito-infested swamplands of southern Long Island, where once New York's main airhub had been sited, back when the Island was a lot wider than it was today.

But when the Dutch engineers had presented their estimates, even an idiot who was not a savant could have calculated that saving JFK International Airport would not be remotely cost-effective. Indeed, even diking-in Manhattan was going to keep the property holders and renters thereof paying off the bonds for the next several hundred years.

Now they were coming down across the Apple itself, Manhattan Island, girded by its seawall, its non-alabaster towers, if not exactly undimmed by human tears, then at least soaring far above the level of the otherwise encroaching greenhouse tide.

One could take this as a metaphor for the Apple's iron determination to triumph over its natural ration of planetary disaster and remain on the side that was winning by sheer act of economic will, especially if Bread & Circuses was being paid to put such a Green triumphalist spin on it, and the extra expenditure for keeping the Statue of Liberty from going the way of JFK was a typical insouciant New York touch.

Coming down the glidepath into Tripoli, on the other hand, had left Monique no doubt that she was once again approaching the Lands of the Lost.

That same familiar sinking sensation somewhere between her stomach and her conscience. That same nagging twinge of outraged True Blue righteousness. That same guilty but grateful Green thankfulness that while this was going to be another terrible place to visit, she and her client would be ensconced in an air-conditioned first-class hotel, so that she wouldn't even have to endure living there while she was living there.

For all Monique knew, Tripoli might once have been an Arabian Nights fantasy facing an azure sea over a golden strand. Now, however, the Mediterranean had long since flooded the Libyan littoral, past what must have once been the Tripoli waterfront, so that what the flight approached over an endless waste of mudflats, tide pools, and half-submerged ruins was a typical "second growth" Land of the Lost seacoast metropolis.

Cheapjack office towers and cheaper apartment blocks surrounded by shanties and, in this case, tents. Only government buildings, mosques, and housing for the rich built atop high artificial hilltops proclaimed any investment in a local future much past next Tuesday, and they were a testament only to conspicuous architectural consumption.

Who knew how far the oceans would rise before the sea level stabilized? The northern ice cap and the Antarctic ice shelves might be just about gone, but would the cloud-cover generators *really* halt the melting of the Antarctic continental cap itself? Who would invest in anything built to last when no one knew if or when or how far the city would have to be pulled back again?

As per the drill to which Monique was accustomed, an air-conditioned jetway conveyed her and Mervin Appelbaum into the air-conditioned terminal, where a Water Authority functionaire slid them through VIP customs and directly into an air-conditioned limo, which whisked them through the squalor into their air-conditioned hotel.

The only contact with the local atmosphere that they were forced to endure was while covering the few meters between the limo and the hotel, a full ninety seconds of searing dry heat and merciless actinic solar glare that had Appelbaum bitching and moaning about sleazebag hotels that failed to provide proper entry through an air-conditioned garage.

Monique had managed to restrain herself from pointing out that the unfortunate local populace enjoyed no such respite, that billions of humans in the Lands of the Lost endured such toxic climate and worse for their entire short lives.

She arrived in her standard VIP air-conditioned room fuming and cursing to herself, and stood there before the standard sealed window staring down and out over the scene below with her standard case of the True Blue blues.

In her capacity as a Bread & Circuses VIP-services operative, Monique all too frequently found herself shepherding said Very Important Persons on deal-making trips to the Lands of the Lost, found herself all too frequently in a clone of this room, looking down from on air-conditioned high upon the malarial coastal mangrove swamps of China or Brazil or Texas, the refugee barge-huts of Nouméa or Perth or Hokkaido, the favelas of Athens or Ankara or Nairobi, the patchwork Bedouin tents and shacks of Tripoli, whatever, feeling like one of those colonial overseers in the historical pix, lacking only a servile native in a red organ-grinder monkey suit delivering a room-service mint julep to make her guilty wallow complete.

The sad song that the True Blue sang was that despite the manifest increase of the biomass, the warming had produced more losers than winners, or at least the losers had lost more than the winners had won, and that the planet should therefore somehow be restored to the status quo ante, as God or the greatest good for the greatest number or the local self-interest intended.

Monique's ramblings through the Lands of the Lost had convinced her that they at least had a point. The interior deserts of North America, Asia, and Africa might as well have been another planet, upon whose surface un-air-conditioned humans could not hope to survive. What was left of Japan clung precariously to upland earthquake zones. The Great Mississippi Estuary drowned what had been some of the best farmland in the world. The entire Pacific Rim festered with refugees from Polynesia and the Southeastern Asian littoral.

One would have to have a heart of stone not to feel sympathy for the desperate dispossessed billions of the Lands of the Lost.

One would have to have a brain of similar density not to thank fortune that one was not one of them.

One would have to have the saintliness of a Gandhi or a Diana to contemplate trading the newly balmy green lands of Northern Europe and America and Siberia, delivered from the gray glooms of winter at their expense, in order to rescue them.

And so, Monique Calhoun, inhabitant of the Apple, daughter of Greenhouse Europe, discontented herself with her Green guilt and consoled herself with the thought that projects like the one Bread & Circuses had been hired to help peddle to the Libyan Water Authority at least served to ameliorate the catastrophe.

Nor was Mervin Appelbaum the worst of clients. Gray, balding, cherubically pink and chubby, decked out in the sort of loose-fitting short-sleeved tan pantaloon suit recommended by Saville for such climes, a proud grandfather, unlike certain Very Important Ass-Pinchers who had also been more than old enough to be her father, Appelbaum kept his hands and his suggestive suggestions to himself.

He even displayed a reasonable simulation of idealistic enthusiasm as he delivered the intro to the son et lumière that Bread & Circuses had prepared to Muammar Al Fawzi, chairman of the Libyan Water Authority.

"The Gardens of Allah will fulfill the great dream of your illustrious namesake, Sheik Al Fawzi, if not exactly in the manner he intended, and with a little creative financing, at a price you can easily afford," he burbled as Monique booted up the holodeck and loaded the chip.

"Naming me after the Clotheshorse of the Desert was my father's idea, not mine, Mr. Appelbaum," Al Fawzi said dryly. He himself wore a plain white robe, a short black beard, and a tired sardonic expression that seemed permanently engraved on his sallow leathery face.

"I only meant—"

"Nor is 'sheik' a title recognized in postmodern Libya, and believe me, things being what they are, there is no such thing as a price we can easily afford."

"Ready," Monique announced posthaste.

"Let the show go on," Al Fawzi drawled with a negligent wave of his hand, a take on both an impresario and a fictional Oriental potentate that Monique found somehow endearing.

Al Fawzi's nondescript office filled with the S&L that Bread & Circuses' imageers and spinners had prepared, and with no little creative conflict, Monique was given to understand.

THE GARDENS OF ALLAH!

Flowing green letters floated before them as they soared over an azure sea toward a mercifully vague and distant shore.

Someone had suggested opening with an actual muezzin's chant of "Allah Akbar," but this had quickly been scotched as dangerously and offensively obvious in favor of an electronic bass line mimicking the rhythm thereof and an ululating tenor delivery of the title mirroring the phrasing.

The style of the lettering was supposed to suggest Arabic script, though to Monique it appeared more reminiscent of classic twentieth-century graffiti. Green was the sigil color of Islam, but since it also had a political implication that didn't exactly play well in the Lands of the Lost, it was thought best to balance it with a simultaneous blaze of True Blue.

Of such finely spun cultural and motivational details was the syndic's typical S&L crafted. Bread & Circuses. Though what bread had to do with it was something Monique had yet to comprehend.

The basic sell was the client's climatech scheme, but the deep sell was what the tag Monique had hung on the project was meant to imply to an Islamic and Arabic demography unlikely to be intimately familiar with early-twentieth-century Hollywood folklore.

The Garden was the specific Koranic image of paradise and the Oasis its incarnation in real estate to which the faithful might aspire, an image that keyed into feelings of both wealth and virtue. To create or re-create oases, to bring gardens to the desert, was, therefore, both the professed socioeconomic ideal of Arabic governance of whatever system, and the mystical utopian vision of doing the work of Allah by bringing a piece of His paradise down to the Earth. Which, it would seem, was why green was the holy color.

What this translated to in terms of the S&L specifics was a quick overflight of washed-out low-saturation dun-colored desert wastes stripped away to reveal schematics of the now-dry and useless tunnel system that the Clotheshorse of the Desert had proclaimed "the Great Man-Made River" while a dry cost accountant's voice detailed the failure thereof, followed by a much more lengthy virtual tour of the virtual future glowing with supersaturated greens as a throaty houri crooned a seductive description of the Paradise that Advanced Projects Associates proposed to bring to the parched Libyan earth while an Arabized version of Ravel's *Bolero* built behind her.

Monique studied Muammar Al Fawzi's reaction out of the corner of her eye as nuclear desalinization plants arose on the latter-day coast, as preternaturally blue waters poured down the dry tunnels of the

Great Man-Made River, as small, clean, nuclear charges blasted out lake beds, as foaming fountains filled them, as palm trees and vast green lawns sprang into being around them, as the music began to approach its triumphal orgasmic climax.

Oh yes it was kitschy, oh yes it was as obvious as the *Bolero* bedroom sell had been for a couple of centuries or so, and oh yes she could see him fighting it. The chairman of the Water Authority was a sophisticated cynic who no doubt was as aware of the nature of the sell as all those maidens, callow and otherwise, who had nevertheless succumbed to Ravel's make-out music down through the years.

It was the *deep sell* that got them. There was a level on which Al Fawzi was about as immune to the wiles of the Bread & Circuses spinners as a fifteen-year-old girl would be to the biorhythmic proto-plasmic seduction of this music. For a couple of centuries, there probably hadn't been a female in the West who didn't know just what a guy was up to when he played her *Bolero*. Nevertheless, it still worked.

And indeed, by the time the S&L concluded with a speeded-up flowering explosion of the desert wastes into riotous solarized green timed to the musical orgasm, from the look on his face, Muammar Al Fawzi, had the sell been sex rather than an irrigation project, would have had his hand in his pants. If he had been wearing pants.

"Very entertaining . . ." he said, as he came blinking out of it. A certain edge returned to his demeanor. "Quite a little . . . magical mystery tour," he drawled, as if to let them know he was no raghead bumpkin.

Appelbaum slid a chip and a printout from his briefcase and handed them over to him. "The plans and the financial details," he said. "As you'll see, there's no magic, it's all simple off-the-shelf technology. And no mystery about the financing, you put up forty percent and we have interests who will pick up the rest." He flashed Al Fawzi a winning foxy grandpa smile, seemed almost about to wink. "Not a loan bearing interest, but for a percentage of the real estate proceeds, in the approved Islamic manner."

"Indeed?" said Al Fawzi. "No magic to the technology? No mystery to the financing? Then shall we proceed to the tour of the real estate?"

This turned out to be a long, slow, broiling, gut-wrenching cruise southeast across the Sahara in a Libyan blimp. The gasbag was in the form of an enormous wing, the better to maximize the surface area of the solar-cell array that powered the propellers, at the cost of a certain increased susceptibility to the roller-coaster dips of the up-and-down drafts, of which there were plenty. Whether the Water Authority had sprung for helium, or whether the balloon-wing was filled with cheap but explosive hydrogen, was something Monique did not care to contemplate.

The landscape below, however, was something she could hardly avoid contemplating, and the more she did, the more harebrained the "Gardens of Allah" scheme seemed.

The deep Sahara had been a largely uninhabitable waste long before the hand of man had sent its borders creeping south and its temperature soaring upward. Now the moaning air conditioner of the gondola was hard put to maintain an interior temperature below forty degrees centigrade as the blimp flapped like an overweight manta ray through an ocean of air at least twenty degrees hotter than that at a humidity of approximately zero.

Dunes of sand and rocky wastes searing under a pitiless and cloudless sky bleached to near-whiteness by a sadistic sun. No mirages from this aerial vantage, but the sun, and the whited-out sky, and the heat waves pulsing up off the shadeless surface into the superheated atmosphere, turned the horizon into a silvery microwave shimmer, abstracted the landscape below into an unreal and unearthly glare.

If the Earth ever really succumbed to Condition Venus, surely the runaway effect would begin here, in the Sahara, a vast deadland stretching from the drowned littoral of the Mediterranean shore deep into the withering heart of Africa, which, as far as supporting the lifeforms of the Gaian biosphere was concerned, was no longer part of this world already.

Pump water into craters here and it would steam into the atmosphere like soup boiling on a stove. It was so hot and dry that not even local cloud cover would form. It would be like opening the windows of this gondola so the air conditioner could attempt to cool down the whole planet.

Oases? Palm trees? Crops? Gardens? People?

Water or not, nothing could live in that heat, under that sun.

Surely Advanced Projects Associates had to know that.

Nor did Muammar Al Fawzi impress Monique as a world-class idiot.

So what was APA really up to?

And why had Al Fawzi dragooned them into this torturous inspection of the brutally obvious?

The answer to the second question turned out to be that Muammar Al Fawzi's local version of a Bread & Circuses S&L sell, or rather anti-sell, was his sardonic way of getting down to the down and dirty of extracting a straight answer to the first.

At length, at considerably more length than Monique would have liked, after hours of this grand tour of the lifeless broiling void, after she had long since become well basted with her own sweat and Appelbaum was panting like a beached Mississippi manatee, Al Fawzi finally verbalized the point he had long since made, at least as far as she was concerned.

"So you see, Sheik Appelbaum," he began as if the bazaar haggling had been going on for some time already, "the notion of re-establishing oases in what the Sahara has become lacks, shall we say, a certain practical cost-effective credibility."

"Perhaps if the tunnel system hadn't already been built," said Appelbaum. "But as it is, it's simply a matter of a few cookie-cutter nuclear desalinization plants thrown up by the low bidder, pumping stations we can acquire from any number of dried-up oil fields for a song, and a few nukes readily available on the open market."

Al Fawzi gave him the look of a Bedouin of old regarding a spavined and scrofulous camel. "By that logic, we would have only to defrost a bit of the polar permafrost and pump the water into a few selected craters to turn the Moon into the Garden of Eden."

"The atmosphere out there is perfectly breathable."

"Perhaps then you would like us to leave you out there for a few hours to breathe it as an experiment . . . ? With all the water your metabolism might require?"

Appelbaum's eyes became carefully hooded. If he weren't soaked already, he would've started sweating. Somehow Monique found herself beginning to enjoy this.

"Mr. Appelbaum, I remind you that my position requires a certain modest expertise in climatech engineering. While it may be true that you can pump water out here at a rate that could keep up with the evaporation, it would not lower the ambient temperature by a single degree or raise the humidity an iota. You would need to construct thousands of such artificial oases in order to create cloud cover significant enough to make the area even remotely habitable or arable.

While you're at it, why not dam the Strait of Gibraltar and the Bosporus and pump enough of the Mediterranean into the Sahara to reclaim the former shorelines and turn the desert into an African version of the Siberian savanna?"

"This is a serious proposal, Mr. Al Fawzi," Appelbaum snapped irritably.

"Then suppose we get down to serious business."

Mervin Appelbaum finally did, and that was when Monique's enjoyment of the conversational fencing match began to evaporate as swiftly as a dewdrop in the desert sun.

"Fuller domes with controllable albedo over the lakes and surrounding farmland," Appelbaum said. "Standard Israeli prefab."

"At considerable extra cost."

"Our . . . financial backers will absorb the overage."

"Will they now? And toward what end?"

"Agriculture."

"Hardly a cost-effective means of growing cucumbers and oranges."

"That's not quite what they had in mind. They would plant crops chosen to maximize the financial yield per acre."

"*They* would not happen to be Bad Boys, now would they . . . ?" Al Fawzi ventured.

"You have a problem with that?" said Appelbaum.

"Nothing personal," said Al Fawzi. "But there is a certain humorless conservative point of view here that does not quite comprehend that that which calls itself Bad Boys is a righteous syndic of citizen-shareholders rather than a revenant criminal triad."

"They strictly observe the local ordinances of all jurisdictions in which they operate," Appelbaum pointed out.

"Or cause them to be modified when inconvenient."

"Be that as it may, the cultivation of marijuana *is* legal in this one."

"You are saying that no legal adjustments would be required?"

"Coca *is* an even more lucrative crop in terms of financial yield per acre," Appelbaum opined. "Strictly for export, of course, and taxed at an attractive rate."

"Opium poppies would be even more profitable," Al Fawzi suggested sardonically.

"Even Bad Boys draw the line somewhere," Appelbaum huffed indignantly.

"How nice to know . . ."

Speak for yourself, Monique thought sourly.

Not that she had anything in particular against cannabic confections, eptified cocaine, or for that matter the Bad Boys syndic, which, after all, was no more a capitalist wage-slaver than Bread & Circuses.

What made the blimp ride back to Tripoli even more disagreeable than the trip out was not so much the deal that Appelbaum and Al Fawzi worked out between them along the way, as the entirely correct expectation that Bread & Circuses, and she herself as its representative, would do their professional duty to sell this particular icebox to the local Eskimos.

Even at the thirty percent that Al Fawzi got Appelbaum down to, the Libyan Water Authority was still going to be pouring funds into this scheme which would have to come from somewhere, and whether through taxes or water-rate raises, there was no place for them to come from but the parched and threadbare hides of the local populace.

Winners and losers.

Bad Boys would have a large cost-effective supply of cannabis and cocaine. Advanced Projects Associates would make out like bandits just by putting the deal together. The subcontractors would do well even after APA dipped its wick. B&C would get the lucrative interfacing contract. The Water Authority or some other Libyan entity would collect considerable taxes. And all along the line mucho baksheesh would pass along from one hand washing the other.

The Libyan citizens, however, who, as was common in these Land of the Lost jurisdictions, were not shareholders in even what was left of the oil revenues, would get little more than a thorough hosing. Bad Boys' syndic charter might require them to grant citizen-shareholder status to a few thousand field hands, but those servicing the workers and their families would be on their own as wage slaves. The desert would not bloom. The "Gardens of Allah" would be sealed terrariums. They might as well be on the Moon or the bottom of the Mariana Trench.

Winners and losers.

Bread & Circuses would earn its hefty fee from the former for selling this scam to the latter, if not exactly what Monique could call honestly then certainly not without strenuous labor.

In some elusive way, the unfortunate roll of the climatological dice always seemed to lead to even more bad karma in the Lands of the Lost. In some less than elusive way, with the truest of Blue sentiments, Monique could not avoid adding to it.

First-class and supersonic though it was, the flight back to New York had been too long and the movie too short for Monique to avoid conversing with Mervin Appelbaum, nor did the unlimited champagne with which she sought to ameliorate the experience do much to enhance her taciturnity.

Besides which, she was, after all, in VIP services, and it was her self-interested professional duty as a citizen-shareholder in B&C to not only keep the client happy and represent his agenda but to do so creatively and at least simulate enthusiasm.

And while she was no spinner or imageer, wittingly or not, she knew damn well she had been all too creative when she had tagged the project "The Gardens of Allah."

Appelbaum had at least had the grace not to get down to the down and dirty until they were well into the Strawberries Romanoff. "We may have a bit of a problem selling the project to the local electorate," he ventured, a gross understatement by Monique's lights.

Nevertheless, she chose to play the ingenue. "As I understand it, there isn't exactly any such thing as a Libyan electorate," she said. "And even if there was, the Water Authority is a trans-sovereign entity. . . ."

"Call it public opinion then. I mean, the tunnel network is fairly vulnerable to sabotage, the desalinization plants even more so. Nothing that a good security syndic like Road Warriors or the Legion couldn't handle, but they don't work cheap, and even low-grade terrorism would eat into the profit margin."

"You would like the Libyan populace to love Big Brother."

Appelbaum gave her a blank look.

"To love the Gardens of Allah . . ."

"Right. How do we sell it to the raghead masses?"

"Not on the economic benefits to their standard of living, that's for sure. We have to deep sell it."

"We are not paying Bread & Circuses to tell us the obvious, Ms. Calhoun."

"But it *is* obvious, Mr. Appelbaum, and thanks to my brilliance, we're halfway there already," Monique found herself blurting. "We deep sell the Gardens of Allah as the Gardens of Allah."

"En inglés, por favor."

Shit. Now she was going to have to lay it out for him. Well, it had to happen sooner or later.

"We do what we did with the industrial S&L writ large. Commercials. Billboards. Popular songs. Graffiti. Endorsements by mullahs if we can swing it. Key it into Koranic verses. Paint it all green. The heroic and righteous Libyan people are virtuously following the Word of the Prophet and fulfilling the Will of Allah by building his Gardens in the desert."

Monique found herself gagging, and not on her final strawberry. "That should get your infrastructure built without any undue restlessness on the part of the natives."

"And once they see what they hath wrought?"

Mercifully, the cabin lights dimmed for the movie.

"Let me get back to you on that," Monique said. "I want to see this."

This, as kismet and the nature of the flight would have it, was an erotic remake of a classic Disney animation called *Aladdin*, with the original songs re-recorded by the Silicon Wayfarers and a seamless combination of computer decor and fantasy creatures with live actors. The Arabian Nights as a lavishly over-the-top porn opera.

Aladdin? Disney? Arabian Nights?

Shit.

Halfway through the film, Monique realized that she had it. By the time the lights went up, she had convinced herself to lay it on Appelbaum.

"You build a *real* Garden of Allah first, make sure it's finished before you build anything else, and you keep it the biggest and the best. The biggest lake in the biggest oasis. An artificial tropical reef. Glass-bottom boats. Scuba. The world's greatest botanical gardens. Tiled pathways through them. Fountains filling the air with multicolored mists—"

"Are you out of your mind—"

"A museum of Islamic art! A museum of Islamic culture! A mighty modern mosque! The whole thing designed in consultation with top-drawer mullahs and Islamic scholars!"

"It's insane!" Appelbaum cried. "Why, it'd cost as much as a minor disneyworld—"

He brought himself up short.

"Oh," he said.

"An *Islamic* disneyworld," said Monique with a creamy smile. "The one and the only. A billion Muslims worldwide. Bring the wives, bring the kiddies, bring the whole harem, 'cause it's certified kosher . . . er, halal, by the highest religious authorities, who distribute ten percent of the profits to Islamic charities. And the Libyan populace becomes citizen-shareholders in another twenty percent, which also entitles them to one free entry per family per year."

"Ten percent."

"Whatever. You really think there's going to be any unseemly noise over whatever else you do with the rest of the property after that?"

And Appelbaum would have grinned from ear to ear had that been physically possible. "Bread & Circuses!" he had exclaimed in delight.

"At what we do," Monique had told him quite sincerely, "we . . . are . . . *the Greatest!*"

"I would say this calls for more champagne, Ms. Calhoun!" Mervin Appelbaum had declared, snapping his fingers imperiously for the steward's attention.

After that, there had been no need for more than small talk, and no need for the steward to have to be summoned to keep their glasses filled.

As the wheels dropped, and the flaps opened, and the plane crossed the sprawl of tacky hotels, antique malls, crumbling warehouses, and industrial bric-a-brac that formed the usual airport accretion disc around Newark International and touched down on the runway, Monique consoled her True Blue conscience with the thought that she had at least salvaged *something* for the Libyan citizenry out of this sleazy deal.

Thanks to her, they would at least be *citizen-shareholders* in *something*, which was more than could be said for most of the unfortunate denizens of the Lands of the Lost, politically dominated by generalissimos military and otherwise, incompetent retrosocialist dreamers, or nepotic monarchies, economically dominated by the last of the corporate capitalist dinosaurs when anyone cared to have anything economic to do with them at all.

True, also thanks to her, Bread & Circuses would make out like the other bandits on this one. At least for the next few weeks, she would be the fair-haired girl with Giorgio Kang and the syndic board. There might even be some extra shares for her in it. There damn well *should* be. She certainly deserved it.

And there you have me, Monique Calhoun thought as the plane taxied to the terminal. Think Blue, live Green, as befits the granddaughter of Cajun refugees from Lost Louisianne and a Franco-American marriage born in Siberia the Golden.

Which made her, even by her own lights, the perfect Bread & Circuses VIP operative for these Land of the Lost ventures by the Mervin Appelbaums of the world.

For while B&C was a modern postcapitalist syndic and therefore by definition and economic self-interest a creature of the Green climes, the Lands of the Winners, where the money was, a good portion of its billing was racked up by outfits like Advanced Projects Associates and, worse, dedicated to further enriching the greedy at the expense of the needy.

Who better to serve as an interface between than someone who was Blue on the inside, Green on the outside.

Or was it the other way around?

How did that old riddle go?

Is a zebra a white animal with black stripes or a black animal with white stripes?

Well, there might be no zebras left in the wild these days, but Monique reckoned that there were plenty of animals like her still running free who fit the modern answer to the old riddle.

A Monique Calhoun was no-colored animal with blue *and* green stripes.

It was a balmy March afternoon in Paris, no more than 28° C, humidity no more than fifty percent, and the breezes that had cooled down the heat and unsogged the atmosphere had also cleansed the air of pollution and turned the sky a cerulean blue.

These same breezes blowing through the bamboo forest in the Tuileries Gardens set the stems waving and clattering against each other, sending the skittish parrots flying, but providing Eric Esterhazy with the musical accompaniment of nature's own marimba band as he stalked his quarry.

Nevertheless, Prince Eric was less than content. It just did not seem right. Entirely lacking in class. He could not even dignify the device he had been instructed to use by thinking of it as a weapon.

In the outside right pocket of his yellow linen jacket was a cylinder of compressed air that so ruined the line of the garment that he had been constrained to fill the left pocket with pebbles just to avoid looking deformed. A prince, even a phony prince, should not have to appear in public as if his tailor had draped him with prêt-à-porter straight off the rack at Galleries Lafayette.

Less obtrusive but still annoying was the tube that snaked through a hole in the pocket-lining seam up his right sleeve to the . . . instrument he palmed in his right hand.

He could hardly think of it as a gun. It fired hair-thin projectiles of hardened gel containing a gene-tailored toxin. They felt like insect bites going in, dissolved into the bloodstream, and caused the target to expire of a massive cerebral hemorrhage approximately forty-eight hours later, leaving no chemical signature.

By Eric's lights, this was no more a proper hit than the wimpish American practice of dispatching felons with "lethal injections" as if it were some kind of medical procedure, an honest execution.

"Not only that, Mom, it reminds me of the old Bulgarian umbrella trick that went out with Todor Zhivkov," he had complained. "Tacky, really tacky."

"Whaddya wanna do, Eric, fill him fulla holes with an antique tommy gun and dump da stiff out of a black Citroën in the middle of the Place Maubert?"

"It would at least make a statement."

"You weren't such a wise guy when you made ya bones, I seem ta remember," Mom had reminded him, then mercifully dropped out of the Prohibition-gun-moll act, which only she found so amusing. "If memory serves, Prince Charming, your main concern was to keep from shitting in your pants."

This had been enough to end the discussion on Mom's terms, an indulgence she was accustomed to enjoying one way or another, whether speaking on behalf of the syndic or not. Though as Eric remembered it, it hadn't been fear that had made him reticent so much as a certain moral reluctance that he dimly seemed to remember having had in those days.

Mom had had the last word then too.

"Maintaining civilization's *always* been a dirty job involving a certain amount of wetwork, kid," she told him, "and since *someone's* got to get rich doing it, it might as well be you."

"You're talking about mur—"

Mom stopped him with a finger to his lips. "Think of it as an initiation ceremony, think of it as a corporate discorporation," she advised him. "Of a blue-balled capitalist son of a bitch standing in the way of a sweet deal to liberate the wage slaves of the Appalachian coffee plantations from durance vile and make them citizen-shareholders in a new coca syndic highly sympathetic to the financial interest of all citizen-shareholders in Bad Boys. Think of it as a service to humanity."

"Well, uh . . ."

"Look, Eric, you wanna be a gopher for the Big Boys in Bad Boys all your life, or you want them to make you a prince? Well call them hopeless romantics, but they don't hand out goodies like that to green kids who won't prove their seriousness by making their bones."

"Well, when you put it that way, Mom . . ."

She always *did* have a way of putting it that got him to see things her way, whether by appeal to his romantic idealism or his bottom-line survival instincts, and more often than not by convincing him that with a little imagination he could come to see them as one and the same.

"Your father had all the survival instincts of a lemming," she had told him when she finally made their dire situation clear to her callow twenty-one-year-old son. "His way of handling a tight corner was to exit down the toilet bowl, leaving *us* to negotiate with people who are not in the charitable business of writing off debts to be kind to widows and orphans."

Eric Esterhazy's paternal line had been Balkan hustlers, their modest horse-thieving origins drifting back well into the era of the Emperor Franz Josef in that general area where Hungary, Romania, Poland, and Ukraine interfaced uneasily behind flexible borders that could change Romanians to Hungarians and Poles to Ukrainians any given week and usually did.

This did not inspire atavistic ethnic loyalties, especially since the family stew contained its measure of Jews and Gypsies, rendering the Esterhazys well prepared for survival in the postnational world.

During the collapse of Communism, Eric's grandfather had snake-danced his way out of Romania and into France, where he survived by the usual low-grade scams until the warming turned formerly worthless Carpathian real estate that *his* father had been conned into accepting to settle an otherwise uncollectable debt into a primo mountainside marijuana plantation.

So Eric's father grew up in the swank spots of Europe and Siberia as the rich-kid scion of former refugee scum who had struck it rich, and made an appropriate marriage to an *American* refugee, a former Floridian, who spoke as little as possible about her previous means of support while adventuring through the high life and low spots of the Green world's playgrounds.

Eric, too, enjoyed this palmy lifestyle, until the age of nineteen, when a consortium of Ukrainian wheat syndics got together the financing to purchase a string of cloud-cover generators in an attempt to restore the viability of their farmlands.

This was moderately successful from the point of view of the Ukrainian wheat syndics, but the usual unforeseen side effects elsewhere, in this case a lowering of the temperature and a return of snowfall to certain parts of the Carpathians, were disastrous to the Esterhazy family fortune.

Dad's way of dealing with this altered economic reality was to drink enough booze and do enough drugs—toward the end on credit—to insure that he wouldn't be around to face the eventual music.

Leaving Mom and Eric with a small mountain of debt to some less than sympatico people.

But Mom was a survivor. Mom was not about to give up her lifestyle. Mom had connections. Mom could get a twenty-year-old with no apparent marketable skills work.

Mom, it turned out when push came to shove, was an honorably inactivated citizen-shareholder in Bad Boys, and with old lovers well placed in the syndic.

Well placed enough to get her son in.

Chez Mom, Bad Boys may have been formed by elements of the Russian and Italian mafias, Oriental triads, Colombian and Mexican drug cartels, and assorted other less than punctiliously legal operations, but under a righteous syndic charter that not only required that all its enterprises now be legal within the sovereignty in which they were practiced, but that forbade the hiring of wage slaves and granted all Bad Boys operatives down to the lowliest field hand in a coca plantation citizen-shareholder status.

Bad Boys was no more "Bad" than the "Boys" who ran it were callow adolescents. Indeed, according to possibly apocryphal syndic lore, the name in the original draft of the syndic charter had been "Wild Boys" until a literarily sophisticated citizen-shareholder who had read the twentieth-century novel had pointed out that this had certain undesirable homoerotic references.

Many Bad Boys enterprises were no shadier than high-risk, high-profit operations that required pocket politicians, legislative adjustments, and forceful persuasion to succeed. Much of the rest involved the marketing of goods and services—produced in small sovereignties where they had been made legal—in major markets where they were not, well, not exactly, well, we wouldn't be the Bad Boys if we didn't bend our charter a little when necessary. . . .

Bad Boys wasn't some gang ruled by cigar-smoking godfathers or a predatory capitalist corporation owned by cigar-chomping plutocrats; it was a proper syndicalist democracy with a board of directors elected by its citizen-shareholders.

And, moreover, the syndic was as Green as it got; if they knew how, Bad Boys would turn the whole planet into one big endless tropical summer playground for the enjoyment of everyone, since, after all, most of their profits came from some sort of leisure trade.

"The godsons of Robin Hood and Jesse James and the Buccaneers, crusading against evil nationalism and revenant capitalism and for this balmy green lifestyle as we would like to continue to know it, now wouldn't we, Eric?" Mom told him when he seemed less than entirely enthused. "Or maybe you got a better idea, kiddo?"

Well, this certainly had its romantic appeal to a kid whose alternatives were nothing he cared to contemplate, and so Eric signed the Bad Boys charter, accepted his shares, and began his career at the bottom, gophering for middle management around Europe.

After a while, no doubt under the prodding of Mom, the powers that be were given to realize that Eric's family Eurotrash background gave him easy access to certain pretentious circles where they were still considered social pariahs.

Thus the deal to make him a prince.

Once he had made his bones, no problem.

There was hardly a sovereignty in which it was illegal to *call* yourself a prince, and plenty competing to sell you a title at cut-rate prices. Bread & Circuses handled the launch, and once a staple of the society gossip forums and spa circuit, Prince Eric Esterhazy was a nice name to have fronting a casino in Lille or a whorehouse in Amsterdam.

Prince Eric strolled with apparently aimless indolence through the bamboo grove, now gaining on Gauldier, now losing ground, now heading toward him, now away, approaching him in an indirect manner, so that the momentary crossing of their trajectories would seem like a random event, both to the target and to any observer who might chance to see the hit.

Nor was he the only faux boulevardier engaging in this sort of charade on such a sunny afternoon, the Tuileries Bamboo Boudoir being a well-known venue for reasonably priced but not entirely uncomely or tastelessly costumed whores of various genders, promenading about displaying their wares for the custom of an equally varied potential clientele pretending not to be inspecting the merchandise.

Pierre Gauldier was a known regular in the Bamboo Boudoir, all too well known by those who plied their trade therein as a cheap chiseler who used his position as a prefect in Force Flic to extract freebies, often after the fact of the act. Indeed, the word from the birds was that playing the corrupt cop extorting free fucks in the nearest thicket from honest working girls was the nature of his pervo game.

The solo entrepreneurs in the Bamboo Boudoir were not citizen-shareholders in Bad Boys, and the relationship between Bad Boys and the Parisian police syndic was in general admirably symbiotic, so in the ordinary course of events dealing with a pest like Pierre Gauldier on their behalf would have been a contract that the syndic would have found it prudent to refuse.

M. Gauldier, however, had of late taken to the running of similar freelance extortions of funds rather than fucks from certain enterprises, which, though not actual Bad Boys operations—no one was stupid enough to try that—had purchased insurance contracts from the syndic.

Serendipitously, the whores of the Bamboo Boudoir had gotten up a collection to secure Gauldier's removal and had offered the contract to Bad Boys at about the same time that Bad Boys had begun remonstrating with Force Flic about his violation of their cozy concordat.

Relations between Bad Boys and Force Flic being what they were, and this, after all, still being France at least in a cultural sense, the response was a Gallic shrug, and a suggestion that gallantry indeed required Bad Boys to come to the rescue of these Ladies of the Evening in distress. But do not be so obvious about it as to force us to investigate such a public service. Which we would be compelled to do for the sake of our own morale if it appeared that a police official had actually been murdered.

Thus had Prince Eric Esterhazy been offered the opportunity to do the good deed and been provided with the ridiculous instrument presently distending the drape of his jacket in such an unfortunate manner.

Contrary to hoary folklore, this had not been an offer he could not refuse. As a citizen-shareholder in Bad Boys, one might enhance one's career progress and secure large bonuses in return for occasional special services rendered.

Well, actually one.

Alas, the time had not yet passed when the removal of certain recalcitrant individuals was essential to the fiduciary health of the syndic cause. But the syndic charter forbade wage employment, and granting citizen-shareholder status to full-time professional killers did not seem like a swift idea.

Much better to be able to call upon citizen-shareholders engaged in other full-time occupations to perform the occasional special service.

Once or twice a year at the most, Eric. And you can refuse any contract you feel violates your moral or political principles with no hard feelings, we can always give it to someone who would find it more fulfilling. No more than one hit a year had ever been required of him, and when he turned down the occasional contract on moral or esthetic grounds, there were indeed no unpleasant repercussions.

So it might fairly be said that because the esthetics of the manner in which he was constrained to fulfill this one left so much to be desired, preventing the dishonorable and odious M. Gauldier from further disturbing the commerce of this fair pleasure garden and the harmonious relationship between Bad Boys and Force Flic would be an act of righteous self-sacrifice.

Noblesse oblige.

He was, after all, a prince, was he not?

2

MONIQUE CALHOUN TOOK THE ELEVATOR DOWN
and strode through the lobby out onto Seawall Avenue, the boulevard
atop the dikework that ran around Manhattan, the only real New
York, the city she hated to love and loved to hate.

This, of course, made her a true New Yorker.

This in itself was part of the *attitude*.

Her cramped studio apartment on the eleventh floor of a Seawall
Avenue tower might hardly be a candidate for anyone but a New
Yorker's object of affection, but those favored by a crepuscular rendezvous therein, who didn't have to live there, seldom failed to express
their envy.

For the westward view through the picture window at sunset was
heart stoppingly glorious on a good day, the blazing ball of the sun
bronzed by the haze over the New Jersey shore as it sank majestically
behind the silhouetted filigreed fairyland landscape of the Palisades,
painting the sky mauve and purple and orange, turning the Hudson
River into a brilliant mirror of rippling light.

The cold cruel light of morning at seawall level, however, presented a somewhat less romantic vista. The Palisades skyline was

starkly revealed as a hodgepodge of factories, apartment blocks, windmills, tank farms, and solar arrays.

Houseboats, barges, sampans, and fishing boat docks, with their connecting chaotic network of rotting gangways, formed an amoeboid floating favela outside the seawall, spreading five hundred meters and more out across the Hudson along as much of the length of Manhattan as the eye could see. And while from the eleventh floor she didn't get much of the smell, even with the sun just beginning to steam the aroma off River City, she got a good dose of cookfire smoke and frying fish and better-you-don't-ask from here.

If the Paris of her girlhood was favored by fortune and the Lands of the Lost of Monique Calhoun's guilty professional day-tripping were the victims of the roll of the climatological dice, New York was somehow both Blue and Green and yet neither.

New York was energized by its perfect winters, the clear blue skies, the tangy air just a shade too warm to be called brisk. New York basked in its golden tropical springs and autumns, when it wasn't being drenched with their monsoon rains.

New York broasted in its horrendous summers, when you could fry an egg on the pavement and steam one in the supersaturated air if you could keep the mosquitoes and flies from devouring it first, when orbital mirrors had to burn away the inversion layer every other day to keep the air more or less breathable.

The swamping of so much of the shorelines of Brooklyn and the Bronx and Long Island might have provided the breeding grounds for vast hordes of mosquitoes, flies, and swamp rats—and alligators and water moccasins and cockroaches the size of cats or so the legends went—but it had also created the habitat for the rich profusion of crabs, lobsters, shrimp, crayfish, catfish, carp, and shellfish which made seafood so cheap locally and had created the aquaculture and fishing industry in which, one way or another, most of the refugees from the Southeast Asian littorals and Pacific islands found gainful employ.

Are we Blue? Are we Green?

The Hot and Cold War? Which side are we on?

On *our* side, whose else, buster?

And we intend to keep it the side that's winning.

In place of politics, New York had *attitude*.

Winners and losers?

Do what it takes.

Ocean rising gonna drown the Apple?

So hire the Dutch to dike it in.

It's gonna cost a bundle.

So tough shit.

Brooklyn and the Bronx and Long Island gone to feed the fishes? So eat as much as you can digest of lobster Newburg and bouillabaisse and linguine marinara and peddle what's left to the rubes west of the Hudson at fancy prices.

Attitude.

Monique just didn't get it when she arrived in New York as a college freshman straight off the plane from Paris and into a city that seemed to be on another planet.

Paris might not exactly be the bargain-basement capital of Europe, but not even Novosibirsk or Zekograd could have prepared her for the prices here. Building the seawall that had saved New York from an ocean of water had inundated the city in an ocean of bond debt, the result being that there were sky-high taxes on everything, including, it would seem, taxes on taxes. As a result, the prices in the shopwindows were unreal, and what would rent you a decent forty meters in Paris got you the equivalent of a maid's room here. The metro had long since been inundated, the trams were expensive and unreliable, the motorized taxis were only for the rich.

How do people *live* here?

What am I *doing* here?

New York speedily enough taught Monique its answer to the first question. You did not waste time and energy bitching and moaning about taxes or the climate or the injustice of it all or your crappy broom closet of an apartment except when you had the leisure to indulge in New York's favorite parlor game.

You survived.

Columbia University had dormitory studios students could afford at three per room. The street food was plentiful and varied and cheap. The gray-market pedicabs and rickshaws got you around at cut-rate untaxed prices to be negotiated. Tax-free secondhand machine-made or first-hand-crafted clothing was inexpensive once you developed the street smarts to find the black markets. You wore a mosquito repeller in the summer and sprung for sonic cockroach guard and air-conditioning no matter what it took.

You developed the *attitude*.

Or else.

It took a bit longer for New York to teach her to fully appreciate the irony of the answer to the second question, though she had known it even before she left Paris.

Monique had been dispatched to New York to develop a True Blue social conscience. It had been a negotiated compromise to bring about a truce in the familial Hot and Cold War.

Mother had grown up in balmy palmy Paris as the daughter of Cajun refugees who ran a restaurant in the Marais called Bayous et Magnolias.

Father was the son of a French architect who had made his pile building mansions for the movers and shapers of booming Siberia and the American public-relations consultant he had met there doing likewise with their rough-and-ready images. Having made their fortune in the Wild East, they had repaired to Paris to enjoy it.

In Paris, however, an American PR lady with limited French hardly commanded the salary to which she had become accustomed in Siberia the Golden. Nor was an architect who had specialized in neo-Las Vegas mansions for the Siberian *nouveau* plutocracy in hot demand in the City of Halogen Light.

So by the time Monique's father married her mother, her paternal grandparents had been constrained to sell off their Paris apartment and retire to a farmstead in Var, where they could afford to live off their capital and from which reduced economic vantage they could not afford to look down their noses at the daughter of modest restaurateurs as economically below their son's station.

The Blue and the Green of it, however, was a cat-and-dog matter.

Mother's family wore their Blue on their sleeves, not to mention the decor and menu of their restaurant. Pining for Lost Louisianne was their stock-in-trade, and you couldn't eat oysters bienville and crayfish gumbo from their kitchen without a dripping garnish of Spanish moss and True Blue climatological revanchism.

Father's folks, on the other hand, having been enriched by the warming of Siberia and the consequent boom times to the point of being able to live off it through decades of permanent midcareer crisis, had their own class self-interest in viewing the brave and balmy new world through Green-colored glasses.

Nor was the conflict ameliorated when Father—under the baleful Blue influence of Mother and her family, or so *his* family saw it— chose the career of climatech engineer, spiting one's parents and impressing one's girlfriend by declaring oneself an enemy of their class being a youthful mode never likely to go out of fashion.

Thus, when Monique's two sets of grandparents *did* speak to each other, they did it at the top of their lungs, and often enough with the destiny of their darling granddaughter as the dialectical shuttlecock.

Given this girlhood, it was not without her own enthusiastic consent that Monique's parents, when the time came, decided to extract her from this ideological battleground by sending her to university in America. Nor was it without political cunning.

Her maternal grandparents approved on nostalgic Blue grounds and recommended Tulane, which had been re-established on suitably muggy swampland in bayou suburbs of St. Louis.

Her paternal grandparents concurred on practical career grounds— an Anglophone higher education was essential, even the mighty Siberians were constrained to interface with the rest of the world in English—but assumed it would be Berkeley or Stanford or one of those Newer Age universities endowed by the major syndics headquartered in the lotus land of the Pacific Northwest.

Instead, it was Columbia, in New York, a city whose political hue was ambiguous enough to leave both sets of grandparents equally dissatisfied. A city far more hard-edged than climatologically blessed Paris, where, or so her parents hoped, Monique would herself gain a keener appreciation of the unfortunate fact that there were people for whom the warming was not all palm trees and long golden afternoons in the Jardin des Plantes without being exiled to durance vile and a third-rate education in some truly grim Land of the Lost metropolis.

Monique shuddered a little inside as she began to descend the stairs leading down to the pedicab stand on West End Avenue. She knew it was irrational, but she also knew it would be unnatural ever to get used to *this*.

Seawall Avenue was about five meters above the Hudson, and from this perspective, when she looked west, the surface of the river seemed more or less at eye level. But West End Avenue was not just east of Seawall Avenue, it was *down*.

Ten meters down.

Meaning that halfway down the staircase the surface of the river was *above her head*. The dormitory studio she had been assigned as a student had been on the first floor. This had not seemed significant until the first time she had stood atop Seawall Avenue to catch the view over the river and then looked east and back whence she had come and realized the awful truth.

The place she lived in was *below sea level*. Every night she slept with a threatening ocean towering over her head. Even now, up on the eleventh floor, she still had the occasional nightmare about it.

That had been what the Third Force mystics called the satori. If her parents had sent her to New York to develop a True Blue social conscience, that had been the moment they had succeeded. That was when Monique had gotten the big picture.

Living down there in the city below the waterline, dreaming at night of tidal waves washing over her, slogging her way through the chronically flooded streets, impoverished by the sky-high survival taxes, shoulder-to-shoulder, cheek-by-jowl, nose-to-armpit with the refugees who had managed to make it this far and their displaced descendants, she did indeed feel for the washed-over masses of the drowned isles and lost littorals, and in the greenhouse summer, when temperature and humidity exceeded even her grandparents' tallest stories of lost New Orleans and vast clouds of giant mosquitoes invaded the nights, she felt at one with the survivors in the jungle fringes of the Amazon Sea.

That was the Blue of it.

The Green of it was that a girl who had grown up in sunny sultry Paris would have had to be a saint in a crown of thorns and a hair shirt to trade such environs, which the gods of chance had greened, for the modulated surcease of the agonies of the Lands of the Lost.

A no-colored animal with Green and Blue stripes.

Which, upon graduation, as it turned out, made her a valuable recruit for Bread & Circuses, and made the syndic culture thereof an offer she couldn't refuse.

Monique's pedicab dropped her off at Thirty-fourth Street, where Bread & Circuses' headquarters occupied a modest four floors atop the Empire State Building. This second-most-prominent visual icon of the Apple had had its ups and downs during the two centuries that it had been to New York what the Eiffel Tower was to Paris, and when Bread & Circuses had moved in, it was going through one of its seedy epochs.

As far as B&C was concerned, since the Statue of Liberty was unavailable, this made the deal perfect. The syndic bought the top thirty floors at a distressed price, renovated the exterior tower and the lobby, lit it up like a halogen and laser Christmas tree, redid the top four floors as its headquarters, and then sold off the twenty-six floors below, one by one, at ever-increasing prices, to chic entertainment, couture, travel, and resort syndics.

This resulted not only in a handsome profit to its citizen-shareholders but in soaring property values in the rest of the skyscraper and the consequent renovation of the whole building's decor and prestige, leaving Bread & Circuses sitting high, wide, and handsome atop the city's reborn signature edifice.

That is, the crowning monument to New York's mighty edifice complex, Monique could never refrain from thinking, despite the tired awfulness of the pun, every time she stared up the gargantuan gray length of the Empire State Building, capped by a rounded and gleaming silvery tower, from which B&C had caused the antenna to be removed in order to enhance the phallic effect.

Deliberate?

Believe it!

Advertising, public relations, lobbying, putting on events, promoting causes, however the client wished to interface with the public, B&C could handle it for a price.

But Bread & Circuses wasn't content to be just the world's *leading* public interface syndic, it intended to be *the* public interface syndic for all practical purposes, and nesting atop this ultimate totem pole to the potency of the deep sell image was not the sort of thing B&C did without full consciousness of the effect it was achieving.

Nor, she had to admit, without a syndic sense of humor.

Of which, she hoped, she was not about to become the hapless object.

Bread & Circuses had a private express elevator to its suite of offices, and Monique took it to middle-management country, where Giorgio Kang's lair was located.

Giorgio had been humorously appreciative of how she had not only been instrumental in closing the Gardens of Allah project for the client, but had done so in a manner likely to garner B&C a lagniappe larger that the original deal in the form of a long-term interfacing contract from the projected Islamic disneyworld.

But while Giorgio handed her her assignments, he was only a supervising account executive, far below the board level, and a long lateral distance from the accounting department too.

So when an immediate bonus of additional shares had not been forthcoming from on high, she took Giorgio's assurance that this was merely a bureaucratic hang-up as less than definitive.

"Don't worry, Monique, once we get the Gardens of Allah interfacing contract, you'll see at least a hundred shares out of it."

"And if we don't?"

"Be real, cara mia, with something of this magnitude, who else is there?"

True enough, but in the meantime, they had kept her spinning her wheels doing inconsequential this and that around town for six weeks, waiting more and more nervously for her next assignment.

And leaving her with a little too much time to think.

B&C's syndic charter called for it to serve the custom of any and all paying comers; Green, Blue, Bad Boys, the tourists boards of central African disaster areas, or unreconstructed capitalist predators, whatever.

Thus a good portion of its billing was racked up by wicked old corporate dinosaurs like Advanced Projects Associates selling their services to the flotsam and jetsam desperately trying to cool down the planet—or at least their little corner of it.

And Monique's True Blue spirit allowed her to work better than most Green-tinged Bread & Circuses operatives for just such clients. As she had just once more proven.

This, she was beginning to worry, had its downside, as well as its more obvious upside.

The upside being that this was what had interested Bread & Circuses in her in the first place and was why her career had progressed so rapidly into VIP services, the cushiest posting in the syndic since it dealt with fulfilling the requirements of honchos and honchas and had the appropriate budgets with which to do so while traveling in the appropriate grand manner.

The downside was where Monique generally found herself when she got there. Namely, more often than not in the Lands of the Lost. In which, she now realized to her dismay, she had unwittingly made herself something of a specialist. And by turning a routine operation in Libya into a potential bonanza for Bread & Circuses, she had hammered the point home.

So when Giorgio Kang told her on the phone that he had finally "stuck in his thumb and pulled out a plum," Monique earnestly hoped that she had misread the irony she thought she had heard in his voice, that the syndic hadn't heard the old one about how no good deed goes unpunished.

Giorgio's standard-issue office was decorated in pseudo-Italianate chic as befitted his adopted pseudo-Italianate persona—sleekly curved pink marbline desk, chairs and couch off some fantasy Venetian deco spaceship, and as its centerpiece, the Coffee Monster, a huge gleaming chromed coffee machine that could produce every variety of the beverage known to man simultaneously while doing a fair imitation of "O Sole Mio" as played by a steam calliope.

Giorgio himself wore a tightly tailored powder-blue cotton suit with enormous lapels, a white dress shirt open down to his breastbone, and swept-back semi-mirror-shades in titanium frames. His sleek black hair seemed sculptured into a helmet.

Giorgio's family were Vietnamese Chinese fisherfolk who had migrated to New York to work the South Bronx marshes and still had a string of shrimp boats. He had been born George. Why he had gone Italian was something Monique never quite got. De gustibus non, or however they said it in Milano.

Giorgio produced two anisette-laced double espressos, strong enough to raise the dead and propel a mirrorsat into orbit.

"How would you like to represent the syndic in Paris?" he said.

"The one in France, or the ghost town in the Texas desert?" replied Monique, looking the gift horse in the mouth and counting its teeth.

"Seriously," said Giorgio. "The Gardens of Allah deal went through. The board was impressed and grateful. This is your reward."

"I'd rather have my bonus shares."

Giorgio waved his hand in a fair take on Roman insouciance. "That too, cara mia," said. "Not my department, but I've been told there's a hundred and fifty making their way down the pipeline. What do you know about UNACOCS?"

"Unacocks? Is that a straight line to a dirty joke?"

Giorgio displayed his perfect smile. "It has been in the past, in a manner of speaking. The United Nations Annual Conference On Climate Stabilization. UNACOCS to its friends, assuming it has any. Surely you've heard of it."

"Something to do with Condition Venus . . . ?"

Giorgio nodded.

Right.

The typical UN response to the Condition Venus scare of a few years back.

As Monique remembered it, one Dr. Allison Larabee had produced a climate model purporting to demonstrate that if the warming wasn't stopped, at a certain point it could suddenly go exponential, converting the Earth into a six-hundred-degree clone of Venus within the theoretical lifetimes of children already born, though of course they wouldn't survive to see it.

Since such dire Blue climate models were chronically produced by the score and no climate model of whatever color had ever proven itself usefully reliable and Larabee had not enlisted the services of Bread & Circuses, the loud Blue screams resulting therefrom had been pretty much confined to the professional journals and the science sites.

Had B&C been given the contract, they surely would have broken the story out into the front pages of the general news sites and press by keying into Larabee's claim that her model showed that the endless tinkering with world-level climate effects by every two-bit sovereignty and demi-sovereignty and syndic was about to trigger Condition Venus *right now.*

As it turned out, the sudden terminal fragmenting of the north polar ice cap a year or two later had broken the story anyway, producing banner tabloid shrieks that it was too late already and Holy Rolling panic that the End Was Nigh.

So the UN had decided that Something Had To Be Done.

Or at least it had to look that way.

So, what else, they established these annual conferences.

And while they hadn't succeeded in coordinating worldwide climate-engineering efforts according to True Blue planetary goals, they *had* succeeded in pushing Condition Venus into the back pages and end files of the news syndics, and turning these conferences into easily ignorable yawners.

"There've been how many of these things, four?"

"Five," said Giorgio. "This is number six."

Something here did not add up. The United Nations had long since become a threadbare, toothless, and flatulent forum for the whinings and mendications of the plethora of impoverished and atavistic full sovereignties of the Lands of the Lost who dominated it numerically.

And . . .

"*Paris?* But haven't these things always been held in cheap locales in the Lands of the Lost?"

"Brasília, Damascus, Nairobi, Tijuana, Colombo . . ."

"So why Paris?"

Giorgio's shrug was more Gallic than Italian, though perhaps you had to be a Parisian to notice. "Why not? No doubt those in charge finally decided on a city with world-class restaurants."

"And they've hired Bread & Circuses? To do what?"

"What we do so well, cara, give their event cachet, brio, a touch of class."

Monique eyed Giorgio narrowly. "They've never hired us before, have they. . . ?"

Giorgio gave her the nod and the smile at the same time. "And as a consequence, UNACOCS has always had a tawdry image, lacked a certain credibility. . . ."

The odor of Giorgio's familial enterprise was beginning to waft off this. "Not to mention sufficient financing to put on an event like this in a city like Paris," Monique said. "Or afford our services."

"For which," said Giorgio, beaming, "they have therefore paid in advance."

"Why do I get the feeling there's something you're not telling me, Giorgio?"

For a moment, Giorgio Kang dropped the whole act. For a moment, Giorgio actually became sincere. "Because," he said, "I don't know. The financial end of it makes no more sense to me than it does to you."

Then the mask went up again, the silky mediated mafia don this time. "This is not an offer you can't refuse, Monique," he said out of the side of his mouth, flicking ash off a phantom cigar. He smiled with massive fatuity. "If you don't want to run VIP services for us in Paris, France, I *can* offer you an alternative assignment . . ."

Monique did not deign to feed him the straight line.

"The one in Texas," Giorgio said.

The sun was sliding down the sky, the shadows were lengthening in the Bamboo Boudoir of the Tuileries Gardens, and Prince Eric Esterhazy had more important and satisfying tasks awaiting him.

Up ahead, in a shadowed grove beside the path, the odious M. Pierre Gauldier had struck up a conversation with a Polynesian whore in a brief crushed-silk semblance of a grass skirt and a minimal mylar halter that left barely enough to the imagination but more than enough to be completely holding his pop-eyed attention.

Time to get it over with.

Eric sauntered slowly up the path toward this less than romantic rendezvous, not even making a moment of eye contact with his target, indeed not even breaking stride as he reached up with his right hand to smooth back his long blond hair, an entirely natural gesture given the breeze, did so, and, passing behind Gauldier just as he dropped his arm back to his side, pointed the nozzle concealed in his palm at the back of the miscreant's neck en passant, squeezed the trigger, and walked on by.

C'est tout.

Gauldier hardly even noticed the poisoned gel needle that would kill him, only started to reach up to scratch at the "insect bite," apparently more akin to that of a gnat than to that of an angry bee or a formidable Seine mosquito, paused, then returned his full attention to the whore's décolletage.

Eric found the whole thing unpleasantly clinical, unmanly even, to the point that while his sympathy for the likes of a weasel like Pierre Gauldier was minimal, he briefly entertained the notion of a beau geste, of somehow providing him with an ovenighter tomorrow so that he could die, as it were, in the saddle.

But contemplating the ire of his syndic should they learn that he had actually done such a recklessly stupid thing was enough to banish this gallant fantasy, and the whole affair left Eric in a peckish mood entirely inappropriate to such a golden afternoon. So to lighten his spirits, he decided to do something kitschily amusing, totally touristique.

Rather than strolling north through the Tuileries up to the Rue de Rivoli and taking an ordinary taxi, he went south, to the Seine, to the Quai des Tuileries, and took a gondola instead.

The drowning of Venice had left the gondoliers' syndic unemployed and had rendered their boats redundant. Some had migrated to Amsterdam, where Dutch engineering had preserved a canal system of the appropriate scale, some had tried their luck in St. Petersburg or Los Angeles, but more of them than not had figured that it would be the Seine that would provide the richest tourist pickings.

In that they were not mistaken, but the Seine was not the Grand Canal. The Seine, despite its enclosure by man-made quais throughout its passage through Paris, was in fact a real river, with a strong westward current and heavy motorized boat traffic, touristic and even commercial, and singing gondoliers in silly costumes trying to navigate it under paddle power swiftly proved helpless hazards to the river traffic, their naive tourist passengers, and themselves.

After a short period of utter chaos, the Syndique de la Seine decreed that the gondolas must become motorized, nor were the hapless transplanted Venetians about to argue once the solution had been suggested.

So the gondola that Eric boarded—while replete with rococo scrollwork on its recurved prow and stern and gondolier in traditional costume seemingly paddling and steering the thing with a single long oar—was actually a disney, powered by a discreet electric water jet, steered by hidden foot pedals.

"*La Reine de la Seine*," Eric told the gondolier, for he need say no more, except, that is, that musical accompaniment would not be required, and the gondola headed out into the river, westward and Left-Bank-ward, toward the Port de la Bourdonnais, where, as even the rudest Siberian tourist knew, the Queen of the River would, at this hour, be anchored.

The Seine was bustling with river traffic, most of it touristic at this waning afternoon hour: gondolas, great faux Polynesian outrigger canoes replete with nonfunctional oarsmen in full island drag, dragon-boat disneys, and the old-model bateaux mouches, many of the great glassed-in monstrosities pathetically attempting to ape *La Reine* herself with paddle wheels, white-painted scrollwork, tour guides in white ice-cream suits, vile Louisiana cuisine straight from the microwave.

Though truth be told—which it wasn't, since Bad Boys did not at all subscribe to the bizarre notion that honesty was always the best policy—it was *La Reine* that had drawn its inspiration from this superficial tarting up of the bateaux mouches in Mississippi riverboat nostalgia during the Lost Louisianne craze which had come and gone years before her launching.

Well, not entirely gone. These modes of the moment might become déclassé swiftly enough, but no such ersatz vogue ever seemed to quite fade away in Paris. Tourists still flocked to Montmartre, where the tacky illusion of the twentieth-century Hollywood version of nineteenth-century Paris was yet maintained, replete with sidewalk painters in berets, quaint clochards passed out in the gutters, whores in can-can outfits, can-can versions of happy hookers, and pickpockets done up as teams of apache dancers. The Rue des Rosiers still pretended to be a street in an old Eastern European ghetto, though certain unpleasantnesses with Israeli expatriates had caused Force Flic to stop providing the quartier with cops done up as Cossacks. Dressing all in black, growing scraggly beards, and hanging out in Latin Quarter cafés flocked with old newspapers, Soviet flags, and antique Che Guevara posters was still a workable strategy for picking up wide-eyed girls from Siberia looking for existentialist action.

The Lost Louisianne vogue, however, had been, and in attenuated form still was, not yet another virtual fossil laid on by the City of Light for the seduction of tourists, but a spontaneous growth—like the Spanish moss draped from the cypress trees overhanging the quais surrounding the Ile St. Louis or the palm trees that had sprung up in the Luxembourg gardens, or the alligators of the Seine—that had ensnared the inner romantic souls of the Parisiens themselves, as had a similar syrupy version of an imaginary Vienna in a bygone century, marzipan pastry and Strauss waltzes rather than oysters bienville and Dixieland jazz.

Paris yet nursed an atavistic sense of francophone solidarity, and so the Louisianian diaspora had touched the heart of the city. As New Orleans slowly sank, decaying and dripping vertigris, into the marshlands whence it had arisen, the waves of refugees had been welcomed with open arms as a long-lost tribe of France, no matter that no more than a tenth of them had been true Cajuns, less than half of those had arrived speaking French, and that a patois that was incomprehensible.

Then too, Paris had always had a taste for jazz, the more safely out-of-date the better, and however unauthentic the watered-down Cajun dishes and peppered-up Creole fare that generally passed for La Cuisine Louisianne might be, it tasted of an exoticism with a French accent, and indeed its influence added a certain something to the art of several two-star chefs, foremost among them Anton Dubrey, whom, after much pleasurable auditioning, Prince Eric had chosen to preside over the dining salon of *La Reine de la Seine*.

No doubt the climate also had something to do with this attempt to re-create New Orleans on the Seine, and certainly with its visual persistence long after Lost Louisianne chic had faded into kitsch.

Mercifully, the greenhouse warming had not inflicted upon Paris the hideous saturation humidity of a classic New Orleans summer, but no one could exactly complain about desert desiccation, and the balmy spring and fall temperature range was quite similar, the summers thoroughly tropical, and the winters nonexistent, so that the flora and fauna which had one way or another arrived with the human refugees from Lost Louisianne not only thrived but had proven virtually impossible to eradicate.

Eric took care not to thoughtlessly dangle his hand in the water as his gondola took him past the mossy stones of the Quai Anatole-France, as absentminded tourists occasionally did to the delectation of the alligators. Ultrasonic mosquito repellers were de rigueur anywhere near the Seine at most seasons, and he had activated his long before reaching the river.

It was hard for Eric to imagine what this languid glide down the lazy boat-filled river would've been like in dim days gone by. When the quais had not been overgrown with encrustations of lush green ivy and fragrant honeysuckle and morning glory perfuming the waning afternoon with an erotic tropical boudoir sweetness. How much graver the office towers and Hausmannian housing blocks of the Avenues New York and Kennedy must have been without the tall palms and even taller eucalyptus. How stark the Musée d'Orsay must have seemed when the river face of the old railway station did not rise behind its great hedge of weeping willows, branches sweeping near to water level, brightly colored African finches singing in the moss, toucans and flocks of parakeets screeching from its rooftop and parapet.

The gondola passed under the greened stonework of the Pont d'Alma, then the Pont Debilly, as it edged closer to the Left Bank, rounding the gentle bend in the river that gave onto the sudden dramatic vista that was surely *the* scenic signature of Paris.

On the Right Bank was Trocadéro, a concrete wedding cake that might have been confected by Benito Mussolini on lysergic acid, its balconies latter-day Hanging Gardens of Babylon, the plaza between it and the river a tropical garden of palmettos, palms, brightly colored hedges of South Seas exotics.

On the Left Bank, across the Pont d'Iéna from Trocadéro, the Eiffel Tower rose out of the tangle of morning glory, honeysuckle, ivy, and bougainvillea climbing its pillars like a mighty cast-iron tree soaring up from a rain forest undergrowth. From the river, through its legs, Eric could see the awesome leafy corridor of giant live oaks marching down the Champ-de-Mars, though admittedly a white and pillared

Georgian plantation house would've looked better as the architectural light at the end of the tunnel than the square squat profile of the École-Militaire.

On the riverbank just east of the Eiffel Tower, a sector of the Quai Branly was done up as a levee, complete with re-created horse carriages, an elaborately detailed dockside warehouse stocked with high-end tourist junk, themed fast-food emporiums, and strolling black minstrels in straw hats playing banjos.

At a discreet distance from this tacky spectacle and walled off from its clientele by black iron fencing and a screen of high topiary hedging was a low white embarkation pavilion tastefully and subtly reminiscent of a sort of riverside gazebo set in a copse of magnolia trees now coming into full blossom. Moored before it was *La Reine de la Seine.*

La Reine was half again as long as the largest of the bateau mouche tourist boats that had plied the Seine for a century and more but not much wider, since these ungainly glassed-in flatboats had been de-signed to pack in the maximum number of tourists per trip, meaning that nothing much wider would fit through the smallest central arches of the many bridges spanning the river and anything approaching twice as long would have difficulty negotiating the 180-degree turn around the Ile St. Louis.

But since the bateaux mouches drew less water than the old Seine freighters and their houseboat conversions, *The Queen of the River could* have a full deck below the waterline, which she needed, since the height of the lowest bridge arches pretty much limited the design to two decks above.

As Prince Eric's gondola approached, what he beheld was a full-sized and then some replica of a classic Mississippi steam-powered riverboat straight out of Mark Twain lore. The lower deck sported an open promenade at the bow and a roofed one at the fantail, connected by a covered porchway that encircled its cabin. The upper deck was an open pavilion with the casino cabin at its center and the wheel-house up front. There were great paddle wheels amidships, port and starboard. The railings of the promenades and the pavilion were wooden scrollwork carved to be somehow reminiscent of both Geor-gian plantation-house columns and the iron railings of New Orleans

French Quarter balconies. Anything that wasn't gleaming white was polished brass.

The only things missing to complete the image were tall twin smokestacks puffing clouds of steam and soot as the crew fired up the boilers. They would not make their appearance until *La Reine de la Seine* was under way.

Passengers for the evening's cruise were already assembling in the embarkation pavilion as he arrived at the dock, but no one was allowed on board or on the quai until Prince Eric Esterhazy stood at the top of the gangway to greet them. Nor could he perform his duties dressed like this.

Unlike the real thing, which had carried passengers the length of the mighty Mississip, *La Reine de la Seine*, which never went farther than the endless round trip between the Eiffel Tower and the Ile St. Louis or on certain occasions the Port de Bercy, had no staterooms or cabins.

Well, not exactly. Belowdecks, along with the engine room and the galley, there *were* a dozen fantasy boudoirs of assorted flavors, not designed to be endurable over the days between New Orleans and St. Louis, but pleasant enough for a few hours' erotic idyll.

Eric had appropriated one of them as a wardrobe and dressing-room hideaway, and there he repaired immediately upon boarding to don his Prince suit for the night. These outfits were not quite costumes and not quite uniforms, but one could not exactly feel at ease wearing them in the Métro either.

Upon reflection, he chose a royal blue velvet ensemble tailored to suggest a riverboat gambler's suit pushed toward the deco, set off with a more authentic ruffled white shirt and simple black snakeskin string tie, secured with a turquoise squash-blossom clip. The color of the suit went well with his long blond hair, though he wondered if the greenish hue of the tie clip should have been pushed a bit more to the blue so as not to clash with it. On the other hand, a subtle note of discord here and there served as a statement of princely sartorial daring.

Thusly accoutered, Prince Eric Esterhazy repaired to the gangway entrance to greet his guests.

"It's been far too long, Madeleine, working too hard as usual. . . ."

"Boys' night out, Georges, or am I missing something?"

Admission to *La Reine* was by invitation only—though if you were on the list of invitables to begin with, you could request an invitation—and while the guest lists were compiled by other departments of Bad Boys, the pretense was that each and every patron was the personal guest of Prince Eric Esterhazy himself and Eric signed each invitation-ticket with an antique Mont Blanc fountain pen to maintain it.

"So nice to see you, Pierre. . . ."

"Lovely gown, Elvira, you look absolutely devastating in peach. . . ."

Each VIP, each mover and shaping, each whatever that Bad Boys for their own reasons wanted aboard, got a greeting by name thanks to the heads-up display on the contact lens in Eric's left eye, and since he *was* after all a prince, each, no matter how puissant, got the first-name treatment. Every human female got the gallant old Romanian hand-kiss, practiceable with a straight face only by those bred to it in their genes.

"Ah, Alicia, how lovely you look tonight. . . ."

"Mon Dieu, Antoine, you look as if you've been having a rather strenuous good time. . . ."

After crowning him Prince of Charming, Bad Boys had dispatched Eric to Amsterdam to front a modest bordello, promoted him to fronting a porn-opera palace in Baden and thence to a first-class casino in Lille, as a warm-up for fronting the launch and continued operation of *La Reine de la Seine*.

The nature of which was not quite what it might seem.

"Back from Zekograd at last, Ahmad . . ."

"Is it really true that the entire poppy crop got washed away, Gunter?"

The casino, the bars, the restaurant, the sexual services, might be priced outrageously enough to make the riverboat profitable, but *La Reine* was built with state-of-the-art surveillance equipment integrated into every nook and cranny, for the real raison d'être was information and special services, the moving and shaping of movers and shapers whom Bad Boys or their paying clients might wish to move and shape.

"Are those marriage rumors really true, Ian?"

"What ever *did* happen to the Napoleon opera project, Maxine? *I* thought it was a natural part for Boris."

Who better to front such an operation than Prince Eric Esterhazy? Prince Eric had the name, the social connections, the rep as just one more sleazy phony prince, which Bad Boys had carefully crafted for him.

He might know nothing about boats or navigation, and could not be trusted to supervise the accounting, but he had matured within the syndic well enough to run the commercial-intelligence end of the operation too.

Who better than a comic-opera prince whom no one could take seriously as more than a glorified doorman?

Once the evening's passengers were aboard and the gangway was up, Eric paraded through the grand salon and up the semicircular staircase to the upper-deck promenade and then forward to the wheelhouse to be seen presiding over the commencement of the voyage.

Theater it might be, but he *did* enjoy starring in it.

The captain of *La Reine*, Dominique Klein, though grandly costumed in white pantaloons and blue jacket and cap liberally festooned with gold braid, was a taciturn career Seine boatman and not much for center stage.

The "pilot," Eddie Warburton, might be dressed in a white suit as the elder Mark Twain and had even been persuaded to affect the hair and mustachios, but he knew about as much about steering a boat or the currents of the Seine as Eric did, being a virtuality-effects engineer hired away from a midsized traveling circus.

The wheelhouse might be a perfect simulacrum of the historic article, and yes, there was even a big ship's wheel with which one could at least in theory steer *La Reine* in the event of computer failure or an attack of lunacy, but the screens and keyboards and consoles between the wheel and the front windows were the real controls of the boat.

So Prince Eric was not entirely unjustified in strutting into the wheelhouse as if *La Reine* really *were* under his command. Not for a prince, after all, to master the grubby details, and indeed, should Captain Klein fall overboard and be eaten by the alligators, the riverboat's computer system was fully capable of guiding the rest of the evening's voyage.

"Evenin', Yer Highness," Warburton drawled.

"Ready, Captain?"

"Bien sûr, Monsieur Esterhazy."

"Light her up, Eddie!"

"Rock and roll!" said Warburton, and hit the appropriate function key.

Eric saw the effect live from the outside only when changes were being rehearsed, but he had seen the coverage and the pub often enough to see in his mind's eye just what they were seeing over at Trocadéro, on the Eiffel Tower, all along this stretch of the river, and phony prince or not, he had not yet become so jaded as to not share the thrill.

"Bah-*bah*-BAH! *BAH-BAH!!*"

A huge recorded full orchestral fanfare resounded over the Seine as the halogen tubes hidden in the woodwork lit up the great white riverboat in a blaze of glory, and two tall holographic virtual smokestacks sprouted amidships belching black clouds of virtual coal smoke and gouts of white virtual steam.

La Reine's lasers painted virtual fireworks across the purpling vault of the crepuscular sky as the paddle wheels began to churn. The band in the grand salon began to play "When the Saints Go Marching In" as she warped slowly away from the dock, and her speakers boomed it out over the river.

The band segued to "Rollin' on the River" as *La Reine de la Seine* reached the center of the channel, made a majestic right turn, and headed east at her leisurely top speed beneath her own virtual aurora borealis.

Eric Esterhazy, head tilted slightly upward, gazed out the front windows of the wheelhouse, an icon of lordly vision in which in this moment he more than half believed himself.

As they promenaded grandly up the Seine, the Left Bank, the Right Bank, lights beginning to come on before darkness had really fallen as if by grace of her passage, gondolas, canoes, dragon boats, even bateaux mouches pausing in midstream to allow their tourists to gape and cheer, the Eiffel Tower behind, the Musée d'Orsay approaching, *La Reine de la Seine* was indeed Queen of the River.

Was not her master therefore in a certain sense the real thing?

Was there a nobler domain than the City of Light?

Was not Eric Esterhazy truly Prince of the City?

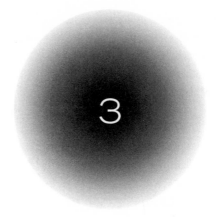

3

IT HAD BEEN A HECTIC AND RATHER MYSTIFYING
week in Paris for Monique Calhoun, and the United Nations Annual
Conference On Climate Stabilization hadn't even started yet.

She actually felt *relief*, dutifully guilty relief, but relief nonetheless,
that Father was halfway around the world working on some fore-
doomed project to desalinate the Hanoi marshlands and had taken
Mother with him.

Dining at Bayous et Magnolias would be familial duty enough
under the trying professional circumstances. The phone conversation
with her parents had made it all too clear what life would have been
like had they been in town and she been unable to escape living en
famille in her old room in the apartment on the Avenue Émile-Zola.

Out of town or not, they had felt thoroughly snubbed even at half
a world's remove when she had thanked them for their kind offer but
told them she'd be staying at the Hotel Ritz.

"The family home is no longer good enough for our woman of
the world?"

"Really, Mamam—"

"How on Earth can you afford a suite at the Ritz?"

"*I* can't, Father, no human can. Bread & Circuses is paying for it.

Do try to remember that this is *not* a vacation trip back home, I'm here on syndic business!"

"Still, Monique, wouldn't you feel more comfortable at home? You'd have the whole place to yourself."

"Of course I would, Mamam," Monique had lied. "But I need the suite at the Ritz for an *office*."

The latter was at least half true. Bread & Circuses' Paris branch had two floors in a converted Hausmannian apartment building right behind Trocadéro, she would be using their staff when necessary, and they could've found her office space there.

But she was here to run VIP services, which meant sticking close to her charges, most of whom would be put up at the Ritz or hotels like it. Besides which, she was authorized to rent herself a first-class suite on the expense account. It was a sweetheart of a job, but somebody had to get to do it.

The Ritz had been, well, *ritzy* enough for a couple or so centuries for the word to have passed into several languages, and Monique's suite, though by no means the top the hotel had to offer, had a bedroom approximately the size of her parents' living room, a salon approximately half the size of their entire apartment, and a bathroom larger than her studio apartment in New York.

The suite was decorated in a bizarre mélange of Louis-the-Something-or-Other Rococo and Retro-Deco. The bathroom was swirling chrome and black marble reminiscent of both the Chrysler Building and classic 1950s Harley-Davidson. The bedroom ran to burgundy-flocked walls with gilded sconces, an enormous bed canopied and braided in the same color scheme, a huge antique Bokhara rug, a halogenated crystal chandelier, Tiffany incidental lamps, and a ceiling whose fruit-salad moldings and central medallion had been carefully painted in full colors. The salon mirrored this style in royal blue and gold, with antique eighteenth-century couches and tables choc-a-bloc with Bauhaus chairs and a desk-cum-media-console stunningly packaged in abstractly carved mahogany inlaid with silver Yemenite filigree.

If the suite struck Monique as more than a tad over the top, well that was the point; this was, after all, to be the headquarters of VIP services, and therefore must make the point that the mistress thereof was herself a Very Important Personage.

It did seem to daunt Lars Bendsten when she invited the General Secretary of the United Nations Annual Conference On Climate Stabilization up to the suite for an introductory meeting.

Bendsten, as the impresario of the event, represented, and in a functional sense *was*, the client and she his subordinate, but he entered the suite as if summoned into The Presence.

He was a tall silver-haired man in a dark-blue UN diplomatic suit, the sort of Scandinavian professional that the United Nations had strategically reverted to in a attempt to counter its all-too-accurate image among the economic powers as a shrewish alms-seeking Land of the Lost debating society.

Bendsten had the standard manners and cool restraint, but Monique sensed something else beneath. Perhaps it had something to do with the way he had turned down her suave offer of champagne or sherry and requested a shot of ice-cold vodka straight up.

"Well, what can I do for you, Mr. General Secretary?" Monique said after these niceties had been concluded.

"Mr. Bendsten will do, Ms. Calhoun," he replied primly, whacking down a slug of vodka in a manner that suggested it was not his first of the day, even though it was not yet even a civilized British teatime. "At the moment, not very much, since the displays and exhibits are still being set up in the Grand Palais, and none of the . . . invitees have actually arrived yet."

"Displays . . . ? Exhibits . . . ? I was given to understand that UNACOCS was a scientific symposium."

Bendsten fidgeted nervously. "And indeed, so it is, Ms. Calhoun. But in order to stage it in Paris, where we . . . where it is hoped it will draw more serious media attention, and in order to afford the services of your syndic to accomplish that end, it was necessary to . . . go outside the United Nations appropriations budget to secure a bit of supplemental funding."

Come to think of it, renting the Grand Palais *did* seem like overbudget overkill for an event that had never needed much more than a fancy thousand-seat auditorium.

Curiouser and curiouser, Monique thought, giving him the silent stare.

"Nothing unseemly, you understand," Bendsten said, contemplating his vodka. "A few . . . educational exhibits . . . some . . . industrial displays . . . by organizations equally concerned with reestablishing a stable planetary climate . . ."

"Mmmmm . . ." Monique observed carefully.

"And of course, in return for these subsidies, our patrons desire an enlarged and enhanced image for UNACOCS and their participants' participation . . ."

"Hence Paris. Hence Bread & Circuses."

Bendsten smiled. More or less.

"Exactly, Ms. Calhoun," he said.

"Perhaps it might be a good idea for me to . . . look over the set while we both have time, before the principals start arriving."

"Excellent idea, Ms. Calhoun," said the General Secretary, smoothly slurping down the rest of his vodka as he stood to conclude the meeting. "I'd be delighted to show you around. Shall we say tomorrow at fifteen-thirty?"

As Monique trotted up the formal flight of stairs leading to the somewhat grandiose entrance to the Grand Palais, she found last night's dinner conversation with her grandparents coming back on her like an unbidden burp flavored with the taste of jambalaya and blackened redfish.

Her grandparents' Cajun restaurant in the Marais, like the district, no longer chic, had now retired to the merely quaint. The Marais had been Seineside swampland, then a rough-and-ready quartier populaire, then a gay nightlife district, and now a re-creation of the French Quarter of New Orleans, itself a vanished Louisianian re-creation of mythic Paris, to complete the strange karmic circle.

Bayous et Magnolias' entrance marquee still featured a holo riverboat incongruously gliding down an outsized bayou overhung with cyprus and weeping willow and the dining room was still the glassed-over interior courtyard of what had once been a sixteenth-century tenement.

The Grand Palais had originally been constructed in the nineteenth century as what it was now, an exhibition center, not a conference auditorium. The art-nouveau iron framework and crystal-palace ceiling had been retained and preserved during its several renovations, the ceiling glass smartened to provide variable tints of "natural" lighting, the ironwork rather garishly gilded and fitted with concealed halogen tubing, the lighting, sound, and computer systems updated to state-of-the-art. But it was still a single huge space far more suitable to carnivals, book fairs, and industrial exhibits than conferences.

An odd venue for a scientific symposium, Monique had made the mistake of mentioning to her grandparents by way of idle table talk last night. Why the Grand Palais?

Her grandparents had been stridently convinced that they had the True Blue answer.

Thanks to Monique's involvement, they had boned up on these conferences. Indeed they knew more about UNACOCS than Monique had felt she had a professional need to know herself.

Chez Grandma and Grandpa, the conferences had indeed been instituted as a ploy by the UN to be seen to be Doing Something about the Condition Venus threat so as to push the panic below the surface.

But the substance of the conferences was the continuation of a serious scientific quest, a quest whose beginnings went as far back as the closing years of the twentieth century—the search for a predictive planetary climate model that actually worked, the holy grail of climatologists ever since.

What had gotten her grandparents' old True Blue blood bubbling was that while previous UNACOCS had taken place out of media sight and mind in obscure locales, the United Nations had now moved the conference to *Paris*, had hired *Bread & Circuses* to bring it to the attention of the world.

Had rented the Grand Palais.

Ergo, something had obviously changed.

Grandma and Grandpa were sure it could only be one thing.

Someone was going to announce a planetary climate model that worked. And the UN wanted to present it to the world as loudly as possible. And that had to mean that it would prove what they already knew, namely that the planetary warming which had lost them Louis-ianne must be reversed or the biosphere was doomed.

Well, that had seemed a long chain of questionable assumptions last night, but what greeted her inside the Grand Palais certainly gave her an even more piquant aftertaste of last night's food for thought.

Lars Bendsten was there to meet her.

At the edge of considerable chaos.

A stage backed by a huge video screen had been set up at one end of the vast space, workmen were completing the installation of a semicircular amphitheater of temporary seating around it, other work-men were stringing lights, speakers, microphones, wiring. A circle of blue-painted fiberboard panels emblazoned with the white UN logo was in the process of going up, apparently to screen the conference auditorium from what was being set up in the rest of the Grand Palais.

Large-scale booths and industrial displays in various stages of erec-tion. Video screens. A scale model of an orbital mirror. A full-size plankton-seeding barge being hauled into place by a tractor. Cloud-cover generators. A silvery ovoid looking like a nuclear terrain-sculpting charge that Monique earnestly hoped was a replica. Cloud-seeding drones. Qwik-grow trees. Devices and bits and pieces of this and that being hauled around and put together that Monique couldn't identify. Kiosks. Signs. Holos. Banners.

"A bit of supplemental funding, Mr. Bendsten?"

Lars Bendsten gave Monique a smarmy smile. "We are fortunate to have secured the generous support of quite a few private entities seriously concerned with stabilizing the planetary climate," he admit-ted redundantly, as he led her across the bustle of the exhibition floor.

"At a profit to themselves, of course."

"They could hardly continue to operate without sufficient fund-ing," Bendsten pointed out.

"An unfortunate fact of life even in our postcapitalist world, as the United Nations and UNACOCS itself have annual cause to con-template."

"And of course, in return for their idealistic support of the con-ference, they hope to secure lucrative contracts for their goods and services. . . ."

"Enlightened self-interest must be a feature of any functional economic system, must it not?"

"Bien sûr . . ."

Something about this arch conversational fencing match was beginning to grate on Monique. She found herself giving the conference General Secretary her own version of smiling smarm.

"And of course, their enlightened self-interest will in no way impinge upon the intellectual or political content of the conference," she said. Maybe her grandparents had managed to get to her a bit after all.

"The United Nations takes no advocacy position on the optimum goal of planetary climatic stabilization."

"Meaning that this UNACOCS will no more reach a meaningful conclusion than the previous ones?" Monique found herself blurting. "Allowing these conferences to continue into the indefinite future?"

Lars Bendsten's fair Scandinavian complexion reddened. Other than that, UN professional that he was, he displayed no emotion.

"The United Nations provides the venue and the infrastructure for these scientific symposia," he said. "We would hope that a scientific consensus on planetary climate goals will be reached as soon as possible, of course, but we do not set the technical agenda or influence the content, nor do we seek to."

"Of course not, Mr. General Secretary," Monique said, backing off as she realized that she had gone too far. "No offense intended."

Bendsten's Caucasian flush remained, but his expression softened, became more personal, turning it into a sigil of embarrassment rather than anger, or so it seemed.

"None taken, Ms. Calhoun," he seemed to say almost sadly.

Monique found herself tuning out Bendsten's patter as he showed her around the temporary auditorium, the state-of-the-art media facilities, the lighting, as he went on about the coverage B&C's Paris branch had already secured. She found herself constantly looking back over her shoulder at the industrial display area, at what would seem to have become the real main event.

UNACOCS had somehow metamorphosed into a trade show. The main order of business was going to be business.

The climatic engineering business.

That much was obvious.

But something more seemed to be going on too.

Monique found herself reading the names on the kiosks and banners and holos going up and doing a nose count.

NASA. Erdewerke. Boeing. Bluepeace. ESA. Tupelov. Aerospaciale. Ocean Systems. Euromirror. BlueGenes. Smaller outfits. Scores of them in all shapes and sizes, and yes, Advanced Projects Associates, too.

What all these enterprises had in common was the sale of climatech services. Some of these outfits would be quite willing to set up cloud-cover generators for one sovereignty and then sell orbital mirrors to supposedly correct the mess they had made to the outraged neighbors.

But most of them were True Blue, most of them were in the business of reversing the effects of the warming, locally and globally: increasing albedo, lowering carbon dioxide, generating cloud cover, reforesting, restoring the status quo ante.

The sixth annual United Nations Conference On Climate Stabilization was being massively supported by the Big Blue Machine.

Lobby or trade organization, keiretsu or paradoxical syndic of corporate entities, the Big Blue Machine had neither formal charter nor legal existence in any jurisdiction.

Nevertheless, its nonexistent membership list was a matter of unofficial public record, and its nonexistent charter required all member entities to refuse any contract that would add greenhouse gases or calories to the atmosphere.

True Blue.

But Big Blue was far from an idealistic charitable organization. Most of its components were either unreconstructed or cosmetically reconstructed revenant capitalist corporations or semi-corporate arms of semi-sovereignties like NASA and Aerospaciale, and all of them were deeply interested in turning a profit.

True Blue climatech *mercenaries*.

Monique didn't get it.

For five years, these conferences had been held in Land of the Lost cities, and the Big Blue Machine's financing was nowhere to be seen, even though virtually all of its potential client base was there. And Big Blue, dependent upon said penurious Land of the Lost jurisdictions for its contracts, was itself not flush enough to have developed the habit of throwing money down black holes.

Yet now Big Blue was pouring funding into a UNACOCS.

In Paris.

Which they certainly wouldn't be doing if they hadn't *wanted* the conference here.

But *why?*

Ariel Mamoun gave her the old Gallic shrug when she asked him the same question later in the day over coffee in a sidewalk café close by Bread & Circuses' Paris offices.

"Do not look a fat contract in the mouth, Monique, is this not an American aphorism?"

"Gift horse," corrected Monique.

The director of the Paris branch gave her an owlish look. "In America, they are still in the habit of gifting each other with horses?"

"In New York at least, they are in the habit of counting the silverware *before* the guests leave, Ariel."

They laughed together.

Given that he was the head of a branch of B&C considered more of a sinecure than the cutting edge, there could've been bad blood between Mamoun and the young hotshot from headquarters sent in to take over VIP services on the biggest contract he had seen in years from his own staff.

But somehow the chemistry was right. After twenty minutes in his office, they were on a tu-toi basis in French and a first name basis in English.

Mamoun was pushing seventy, he had a wife, two children, and six grandchildren, he had a gentleman's farm in Jura, he had enough shares to live there comfortably for the rest of a long life on the two-thirds retirement dividends, he could not be more indifferent to matters of turf or pecking order.

"Seriously, Ariel, why do you imagine Big Blue is subsidizing this conference?"

Mamoun shrugged again. "I am perhaps too old to have the energy for imagining such things anymore."

"Come off the foxy grandpa act, Ariel."

"More comprehensible if considered not as the subsidizing of a conference, but the use of the conference as an element in an advertising and publicity campaign, Monique. I am given to understand that what is budgeted for Bread & Circuses far exceeds what they are spending on the conference itself."

"*What?* We're getting more than what it costs to set up that whole floor of exhibits?"

Mamoun laughed. "Unfortunately not," he said. "I refer to the much more modest largesse lavished upon the UN organizers to persuade them to move UNACOCS here. That, and what Bread & Circuses is receiving, is the advertising and promotional budget. The trade show, of course, is what is being advertised and promoted."

"A trade show is itself promotion, Ariel," Monique pointed out. "Figure that in the promotional budget, and it's huge. The question is, where's the payback?"

"Where else, Monique, but in selling what is being promoted?"

"Climatech, engineering services?"

"Bien sûr . . ."

"*Blue* climatech engineering services? Here? That's like trying to sell thermal underwear in the Nebraska desert!"

"Monique, Monique, Paris is the *set*, not the audience! The audience is the world, and we are being paid to command *its* attention. What better setting for a mega-commercial than the City of Light? Do you imagine our task would be made easier if we had to do it from Dacca or Tripoli?"

"Well we certainly *would* have a lot more trouble luring the world press with all-expense-paid junkets to fabulous Tripoli . . ." Monique was constrained to admit. "But still . . ."

"You are young, you are in Paris, you have a suite at the Ritz and a generous expense account, ma chérie, so relax and enjoy it, as any number of disreputable phallocratic jokes advise a lady in your position," Ariel Mamoun told her. "Do not complain if, as only the British could put it, there is no egg in your champagne."

"Beer," corrected Monique.

"Merde," said Mamoun. "Even more disgusting."

The restaurant to which she had been invited that night, La Cuisine Humaine, was anything but disgusting, though Monique imagined that if she had requested an egg in the Premier Cru that Avi Posner had ordered for aperitifs, the tuxedoed waiter wouldn't have blinked, but probably would have inquired as to whether she wished chicken, duck, goose, or quail.

La Cuisine Humaine was a converted Seine river freighter that moved around; currently it was docked on the Quai de La Tournelle right across from Notre Dame itself, the cathedral dripping fragrant honeysuckle and cunningly illuminated in subtle mauves and oranges so as to seem to inhabit its own eternal tropical sunset.

The decor of the restaurant was as retroconservative as its cuisine was avant garde. Rose-colored walls, white linen with full silver and crystal service, candles on the tables and in sconces on the walls, not a bit of electric lighting, staff in tuxes, a sommelier with an actual key on a ribbon around his neck, the works.

The leather folder of the menu, however, concealed a screen and keyboard upon which you could call up something like a hundred pages of dishes from all over the world, and, moreover, there were hyperlinks so that you could concoct your own cross-cultural adventures.

How the kitchen managed to pull this off was as mysterious to Monique as how anyone not on a major expense account could pick up a tab at these prices, which made a meal at the world-famous clipjoint Tour d'Argent seem like a quick kebab from a street stall.

Ergo, Avi Posner had such an expense account.

Bread & Circuses had its own VIP security department, but no one took it very seriously, and it was not unusual for the organizers of an event like UNACOCS to hire a separate security syndic like Mossad, reputed to be top-of-the-line.

Nor was it unusual for the security chief to wish to coordinate with the honcha of VIP services before their joint charges started arriving.

What *did* seem odd was for Avi Posner to have the budget to fête her in a place like this with no VIP in attendance.

Posner was short, muscular, and had shaved a receding hairline into gleaming virility rather than fight it; on the surface, much like the syndic he represented, which provided bodyguards to the well-heeled and security forces to major events.

But just as Mossad, which everyone knew had once been the Israeli intelligence agency, was reputed to supply more sophisticated services for more sophisticated prices, Posner, elegantly dressed in a well-tailored pearl-gray suit, seemed a lot more sophisticated than mere muscle.

The champagne he had ordered was no obvious Dom Pérignon but some obscure marque Monique had never heard of, just as expensive, but much better. He knew his way around this extremely complicated menu like a restaurant critic, better certainly than she did. The suggestions he made when she appeared a bit lost were excellent—corn and smoked-duck salad with walnuts in some complex mélange of oils with Mexican and Oriental spices, a tagine of lamb and prunes baked with lemon, onions, and almonds in a thick and complex curry paste. He then proceeded to work his own order around hers—a pasta with smoked salmon, pepper vodka sauce, sour cream and beluga caviar, medallions of wild boar in Szechuan pepper sauce—so that the same wines complemented both meals, beginning with an unusual rosé from Georgia, and then a powerful Premier Cru Pomerol.

If the idea was to enjoy the expense account for all that it was worth, he had royally succeeded. If the idea was to impress her with the self-evident fact that he and his commission were more than their official description, he wasn't doing too badly either.

"It's a scandal an indigent outfit like the United Nations is paying for all this," Monique ventured over the entree.

"The client is paying for it," said Posner.

"But UNACOCS *is* the client . . ." Monique said ingenuously.

Poser gave her a faux world-weary frown. "Young as you may be, surely you were not born yesterday, Ms. Calhoun," he said. "We are both professionals. We both know who the *real* client is."

"The source of our funding . . ."

"By definition . . ."

NORMAN SPINRAD ○ 69

"The Big Blue Machine . . ."

"Which," said Posner, "by definition does not quite exist."

"Which, therefore, by definition you do not quite represent."

Avi Posner favored her with a thin little smile, perhaps the first sincere expression Monique had seen on his face. "I think we will work well together . . . Monique, if I may."

He reached into a pocket and slid a ROM chip across the table. "This is the preliminary list of invited guests we will be jointly . . . handling," he said. "Those whose meals, accommodations, and entertainment expenses the client will be picking up."

"It's a bit unusual for *security* to be handing the VIP list to VIP services instead of the other way around."

Posner gave her a fish-eyed stare over the remains of the entrees. "You may add as many names to the list as you like, press, and so forth, but that comes out of the Bread & Circuses budget," he said.

A tuxedoed busboy cleared the table. The waiter arrived with the tagine and wild boar. The sommelier removed the rosé and its setups and poured the Pomerol.

"Now that we're finished with the entree," Posner said in quite another tone of voice, "shall we get down to the main course?"

"By all means."

"As you have surmised, I am here to provide a bit more than simple security, I am also your . . . shall we say *liaison* . . . with the client. . . . Are you following me, Monique?"

"Oh yes."

"I refer the VIPs to you for . . . servicing. I from time to time may specify certain special services. In return for which, you have a chance to earn certain special favors."

"Why do I not like the sound of that?"

"But you should."

"Should I?"

"May I be blunt with you, Monique? One professional to another?"

"I think I can live with it, Avi."

"You are not here by chance. Mossad was asked by the client to sort through the Bread & Circuses personnel according to certain parameters, and the Gardens of Allah deal popped your name out of the profiles. We then prevailed upon certain circles within B&C, and voilà, here you are in gay Paris!"

"What's the payback? Where are the strings attached?"

"Think of it as a courting gift from interests who wish to be your friend. Interests with the power to become even more friendly."

"How . . . friendly?"

"Friendly enough to secure you the position of head of Bread & Circuses' Paris branch. Friendly enough to gain your attention?"

Monique had already dropped her fork into her lamb tagine.

"Who do I have to kill?" she inquired.

"Not your department," Posner told her. "What you have to do is whatever you are called upon to do to make sure that the conference succeeds. The client wins, you win. All that's required of you is friendship to your own enlightened self-interest. Nothing sinister about that, now is there?"

The New Yorker in Monique finally came to the fore. "Look, Avi," she snapped, "you know damn well I'm interested, but I damn well have to know what I'm interested *in*, so let's cut the crap, shall we. The client wins, I win? Win what? And how? As near as I can see, the client is the Big Blue Machine, and the client is pouring money down a rathole. What the hell is going on?"

Posner shrugged. Strangely enough, he seemed rather relieved at this outburst.

"They don't tell us any more than they think we have a need to know either," he said in a harder voice. "And the fairy story is that they're desperate because their tech side is convinced that Condition Venus is right on the edge of starting and that the fate of the biosphere is in their hands. It might even be true."

"They've been saying that for years. . . ."

Posner nodded. "What we've found out ourselves is that their financial position really *is* desperate. They've pretty much already sucked the Lands of the Lost dry, meaning that they need new customers capable of paying their formidable fees. Thus their high-stakes gamble on UNACOCS. Thus Paris. Thus holding their fiscal breath and hiring Bread & Circuses. Where better to attract well-heeled syndics and sovereignties whose representatives would not be caught dead at a True Blue event like this in the Lands of the Lost? Where better to wine and dine, to win contracts and influence planetary destiny? Who better than Bread & Circuses to sell cream puffs to diabetics?"

Monique's jaw dropped.

"The purpose of UNACOCS is to get *Green* money to finance *Blue* projects?" she exclaimed. "After which, I suppose, we walk on water?"

"If they didn't think they had *some* chance of succeeding, would they have spent all this money?"

"But how?"

Posner just shrugged. He smiled fatuously at her. "Don't ask me," he said, "I'm only muscle. I do my job to the best of my ability, and you do yours."

"Which requires me to do exactly *what?*"

"Whatever special VIP services your friendly client desires. What friends do when called upon to advance the mutual interests of themselves and their benefactors."

If this sounded a tad open-ended to Monique's pragmatic side, the carrot being dangled in front of her certainly seemed juicy enough to justify it, and after all, in the service of VIPs, she had procured everything from ladies and gentlemen for the night to contraband substances, and was hardly an innocent.

And after all, it was all in the True Blue cause of planetary salvation, now wasn't it?

Wasn't it?

"You'll start with something easy," Posner said. He checked an antique stainless-steel-bodied Rolex. "Ah yes, it should be along just about now . . ." he said, nodding out the window in the direction of Notre Dame.

Here the Ile de la Cité, on which the cathedral stood, split the Seine into two channels, and westward, beyond the Pont de l'Archevêché, the sky was magically emblazoned with an impossible aurora borealis, sheets of neon green and lavender, moving toward the cathedral.

Then the bridge and the narrow channel leading to it were lit up by a mighty blaze of light, chiaroscuring the vines overgrowing the stonework of the quais, casting long shadows on the weeping willows overhanging the river, shadows that grew shorter and shorter as the source grew closer and closer. . . .

Even through the window glass, Monique heard it before she fully saw it, a mightily amplified acoustic Dixieland band playing "Sweet Georgia Brown."

And then, there it was, coming up the lazy river like a great white ghost ship, its smokestacks puffing steam and coal smoke, far too tall to pass under the bridge, and even though she knew it was a holo effect, Monique's breath caught for a beat as the riverboat passed under the Pont de l'Archevêché and the smokestacks passed *through* it.

And then the magical riverboat was passing right past La Cuisine Humaine, coruscating with lights under its own self-generated aurora, great paddle wheels churning white foam, its upper promenade deck thronged with revelers, music blaring, phantom fireworks proclaiming its glory, and Monique in that moment acknowledged the justice of its self-proclaimed title.

"*La Reine de la Seine*," said Avi Posner. "*The Queen of the River.* Rent it for the duration. Get it as cheaply as you can, of course, but the client is prepared to pay whatever it takes not to get no for an answer."

Prince Eric Esterhazy styled his apartment on the Quai de La Tour-nelle his "little bachelor pied-à-terre" when inviting ladies up for the first time. This uncharacteristic touch of princely modesty was a cunning piece of seductive reverse hype, and seldom failed to enhance the desired gasp.

For the said "little bachelor pad" was a penthouse atop the sixth floor overlooking Notre Dame across the Seine.

It had a fifty-meter living room the size of your average Parisian one-bedroom apartment decorated like an eighteenth-century noble-man's salon.

It had a large terrace overlooking the river, landscaped into a fair simulacrum of a lost South Seas paradise: palm trees, palmettos, brilliant floral exotics, a small saltwater pool with an ersatz coral reef and a precarious population of tropical fish.

It had a state-of-the-art robocuisine in which one might prepare a hands-on-gourmet dinner or, if one was as hopeless in the kitchen as Eric, leave it to the software to convince your guest that you had.

It had a bathroom featuring a small sauna and a giant marble bathtub with jacuzzi, leading directly, more often than not, into a bedroom equipped with bar, holowalls, polarizable picture window overlooking the cathedral, and, not at all incidentally, a large bed well equipped with electronic and mechanical enhancements.

It also had an office masquerading as a nineteenth-century Victorian English nobleman's library—ridiculously functional fireplace with elaborate mantel, walnut bookshelves filled with leather-bound titles, overstuffed burgundy-leather chairs, heavy walnut breakfront. And while one wall of books was the real thing, the other was a flat that slid open to reveal a computer, an outsized vidphone screen, a safe, and a small armory of a dozen tools of Eric's occasional alternate trade.

Right now, however, he was dealing with his main enterprise and unhappily refusing a large sum of money.

Their checkered paternal ethnic history in eastern Europe being what it had been, the Esterhazys had never been encumbered by a family religious tradition, but turning down major offers of money certainly violated it anyway.

"Look, we *are* willing to negotiate, so let's cut the fencing act and get to the bottom line . . . Prince Esterhazy," said the woman on the screen, expressing her willingness to up the offer a lot more facilely than she seemed willing to grant him the dignity of his title.

In fact *they*, whoever *they* were—the UNACOCS bureaucracy, the UN itself, Bread & Circuses, it was never quite clear—had been trying to rent *La Reine de la Seine* for the duration of their conference for over a week now.

Having failed thus far with unalloyed greed, they had now apparently decided to try upping the ante with a more alluring representative.

Alluring this Monique Calhoun was, or as alluring as any woman could be via vidphone without a glimpse of anything below the elegant neckline—that delicate yet somehow strong French nose and high cheekbones, that looser and easier anglophone-muscled mouth, those neat shell ears peeking out from a short bedroom tumble of black hair, those weasel-keen bright blue eyes—but there was also something annoying about her, too certain that the weight of Bread & Circuses behind her gave her a puissance no mere phony prince could resist.

On the other hand, Eric was forced to observe, his phallic alter ego seemed to be displaying a certain independence, taking it as a challenge, and rising manfully to it.

"*You* may address me as simply Prince Eric, Ms. Calhoun," he told her magnanimously.

"May Ah really?" she replied in an acid-tinged magnolia accent.

"Noblesse oblige, Ms. Calhoun."

"I'll bet you say that to all the girls . . . *Prince Eric.*"

"Only to the ones who meet my refined and sophisticated standards of beauty, Monique."

"*You* may address me as Ms. Calhoun, Your Highness," she said. "And you may also tell me what your real price is, because the chances are we are ready to meet it."

Eric hesitated. Eric grew more deeply unhappy. Eric didn't know quite what to say. Certainly the truth did not seem a palatable option.

Because the truth was that *La Reine* was not for rent to anyone at any price for any reason. And the truth was that this was Bad Boys policy set at levels to which he lacked even access, let alone the authority to overrule it. Nor was he permitted to violate the fiction that he was the lord and master of *La Reine de la Seine* by alluding to the syndic he fronted for. Thus the truth was something it would be both dangerous and galling to admit.

Doubly galling, somehow, to admit it to Ms. Monique Calhoun.

Although, perhaps, by arduous physical effort, she just might be able to extract an edited version from him. Or not. At least the poor girl should be given an opportunity to try.

"You are serious, Ms. Calhoun? I may simply set any price?"

"Within reason."

"I thought so," Eric said dryly. "Still, I suppose, I have nothing to lose by indulging you in a discussion of the nature of reason. A philosophical discussion, of course."

"Right . . ."

"Say this evening around four-thirty . . . ? At my office?"

"Where's that, on the boat?"

"Ashore, actually. On the Quai de La Tournelle. Attached to . . . my little pied-à-terre."

4

MONIQUE HAD PREPPED HERSELF WITH A QUICK netsearch on Prince Eric Esterhazy, which had yielded hundreds of items, but little useful information. Most of them were gossip file stuff, and most of that seemed professionally planted to her educated eye. The name was apparently real, but the dubious title had been purchased from the Grimaldis at the usual cut-rate price, and the pedigree swiftly peetered backward and eastward into a long line of undistinguished Austro-Hungarian-Romanian con artists.

Esterhazy had apparently traded on his title to obtain employ as glorified doorman to a series of casinos and whorehouses leading up to his current position as an upscale version on *La Reine de la Seine*. The famous riverboat itself appeared to be the property of a syndic whose citizen-shareholders included the crew, the chef and his team, the band, a score or so of onshore support workers, Esterhazy, and, strangely enough, his mother, who appeared to have only a token position as "booking agent."

Who had how many shares was not a matter of public record, but it did not appear that Esterhazy had a particularly dominant holding, or, given his previous employment record, could have been a serious financial contributor to the construction of *La Reine*.

A sleazy ersatz Eurotrash nobleman from nowhere in particular fronting the latest in a string of leisure palaces who had reached the top of his dubious profession.

But which turned out to seem to be a more lucrative one than Monique had supposed.

His apartment building, a six-floor eighteenth-century edifice last renovated in the twentieth by the look of it, seemed modest enough from the outside, though the Left Bank quaiside address was primo. The elevator was indeed the standard twentieth century Parisian retrofit, a tiny vertical coffin in a grillework cage squeezed into the central well of an ancient spiral staircase, and it deposited her in a small unprepossessing antechamber.

The door to Prince Eric Esterhazy's demesne, however, looked like something taken from an old church—anciently gray carved wood bound in well-greened bronze, set in a gothic stone archway—and it seemed genuine. When she raised and let fall the gargoyle-faced knocker, it triggered a full orchestral version of the four signature notes of Beethoven's Fifth Symphony.

The man who opened the door a perfect sixty seconds later *was* handsome enough to be a prince. Eric Esterhazy was tall, well built, with high dramatic Slavic cheekbones, an aquiline nose, clear green eyes, and a lovely mane of long blond hair. Only the smirky set of his full lips rescued his face from the blandness of fashion-model perfection. He wore a black velvet pajama suit just tightly enough tailored to display the goods to the maximum effect without getting obvious about it.

"Welcome to my humble abode, Ms. Calhoun," he said with only the slightest frisson of irony, and when he made with the Romanian hand-kissing act, he did it to four-star perfection, though Monique found herself counting her fingers afterward.

Esterhazy then turned with a flourish, and led her directly into a living room that fully matched hers at the Ritz for rococo glitz and was maybe twice the size. Bird's-egg-blue walls, rose wall-to-wall carpeting under four antique Oriental rugs, crystal chandelier, carved green marble fireplace, a warehouse full of eighteenth-century furniture, none of it looking particularly sittable, massive landscape paintings in ornate gilt frames, huge bouquets of flowers in porcelain Chinese vases.

The works.

Esterhazy gave her a carefully measured moment of goggle time.

"It's a bit cozier out on the balcony," he suggested.

The cozy "balcony" was a large fully landscaped terrace with a breathtaking view of the Seine, and Notre Dame, and the Right Bank beyond—the river traffic floating lazily through the green-encrusted stonework bayou, flocks of green and blue parakeets wheeling over the bronzed roof of the cathedral, the twin lines of tall palm trees marking the Champs-Élysées' long march from the lush landscapes of the Tuileries to the Arc de Triomphe bridging the reflecting pond in the center of the Place de l'Etoile gardens—all the way to the ghostly white Moorish mirage of Sacré Coeur floating atop the jungled hilltop of Montmartre at the far limit of vision.

At this afternoon hour, the sun was just coming down past the Eiffel Tower, sending lengthening shadows over the chiaroscuroed cityscape, beginning to purple the sky at the zenith, gilding the inversion layer haze over Paris to a romantic glow.

It was heartstoppingly lovely. It was the Paris of her heart's desire. It was so perfect that it would have been absolute kitsch had it not been real.

The *landscaping* of the terrace, on the other hand, was just the sort of disney that set Monique's True Blue teeth on edge.

Some urban interior decorator had confected his fatuous notion of a South Seas island paradise. Potted palms and palmettos. A dozen species of waxy-flowered plants forced into riotous colorful bloom. A pond done up as a phony miniature coral reef, complete with brightly colored tropical fish extinct in the wild and worth their weight in caviar. Rattan tables and great woven peacock chairs than on second look turned out to be crafted from weatherproof synthetics. In a silver ice bucket sat some tropical punch, heavily laced, no doubt, with rum or gin and probably both. The only thing missing was the grass skirts and slaveys with palm-frond fans.

A South Seas island.

As reconstructed from old twentieth-century advertising videos by someone who had never been there. Never seen the sere, desiccated scrub of what little remained above the waterline. Never broiled in the actinic sun. Never swum above the dead-white corpses of the reefs overrun with starveling starfish.

To Monique, who had seen and done these things in the grim line of duty, the landscaping of Prince Eric Esterhazy's terrace had all the charm of that hideous virtuality re-creation of the legendary Great Barrier Reef, replete with singing tropical fish and dancing sharks, that she had once been dragged to in downtown Sydney.

Esterhazy steered her to chairs beside the table holding the ice bucket, and poured her a tall drink that was somehow both blue and brownish. It was sickeningly sweet and unsubtly powerful. It was called a "zombie."

It somehow seemed perfect.

Monique sipped at it very gingerly indeed.

"Shall we get down to business . . . Prince Eric?" she said.

"That would be a waste of a lovely sunset, Ms. Calhoun," Eric Esterhazy said. "However, I will offer you one deal right now—I get to drop the Ms. Calhoun, and you get to drop the Prince." He gave her a smile that must've melted a thousand panties. "Have we got a quid pro quo . . . *Monique?*"

"It's a beginning, *Eric* . . . But as we say on the sunken sidewalks of New York, money talks, bullshit walks."

Esterhazy smiled right through it.

"Then I will not risk the latter by pretending that your last offer was a whisper in the wind," he said. "One million eight hundred and fifty thousand wu for ten days' rental speaks loud and clear. However . . ."

However, Monique thought, an arms dealer or a rug merchant or a camel trader never takes an offer, no matter how foolishly magnanimous it might be, until the customer is about to stomp out the door in outraged frustration.

And 185,000 work units a day, they both knew damn well, was more than a princely offer. *La Reine de la Seine*'s cash flow might not be public record, but its capacity was, and so were the prices on its menu and at the bar, nor was the little casino a serious high-roller operation, and a simple spreadsheet program easily enough revealed that 100,000 wu a day would probably be stretching it.

Posner hadn't told her to bargain hard or given her a limit, but this was already approaching the ridiculous and her own professional pride would not let her be taken for more than two million tops by the likes of Prince Smarming.

"However, not being a mathematician or computer-literate, you would find a somewhat rounder number easier to calculate?" Monique suggested. "Like one million nine?"

Esterhazy gave her a look that, like the zombie cocktail, seemed a clash of incongruous elements—one part suppressed amazement, one part greed, one part some kind of wistful regret—and hence entirely unreadable.

"Two million would be even rounder," he said larcenously, but sounding as if his heart wasn't in it.

"*Ten* million is a one followed by seven zeros," Monique snapped. "It doesn't get any rounder than that!"

"*You're serious?*"

"Are you?"

He flashed her a brilliant golden boy smile. "I was seriously interested in meeting you, Monique," he said.

"To do what? Pour me full of rum and gin and then carry me into your bedroom and make mad passionate love to me?"

Eric Esterhazy kept the smile, lidded his eyes to half-mast as he stared into hers. "If you were persistent enough," he said dryly, "I suppose in the end I could be persuaded. . . ."

"Are we talking about beds or boats here?"

Esterhazy shrugged, shoulders only, the smile fixed, the boudoir eyes inviting. "As I've already told you, my *boat* is unavailable," he said, then paused dramatically. "*However* . . ." he added, and let it dangle invitingly.

Monique was not amused. But she *was* confused. What was going on here? Was this character trying to use sexual repartee to up an already ridiculously overpriced 1,900,000 wu to two million? Or was he serious about *La Reine de la Seine* being unavailable at any price and sincerely interested only in getting her panties off? But if so, why in the world would he not snap up an offer that would double his enterprise's gross?

Then the only possible answer dawned on her.

The guy's employment record had been as a glorified maître d'. There was no evidence that he had ever really managed the business end of those whorehouses and casinos. Why assume that *La Reine de la Seine* was anything different?

"Are you . . . seriously considering my offer?" Esterhazy purred.

"Are you seriously considering mine . . . ?" Monique purred back.

Of course you are, she thought. Who wouldn't be? But you just don't have the authority to take it.

"*La Reine* is not for rent to outside parties," Esterhazy said with a great and entirely unconvincing show of aristocratic snottiness. "Not for royal weddings, not for papal coronations, not for the Second Coming of Jesus or Elvis, and not even for you, ma chérie."

Right, thought Monique, and just maybe you have the authority to change the color of the toilet paper.

But of course he couldn't admit it.

Nor would it be wise to force the issue.

Much better to give him a graceful way out.

"I *think* I can get the client to swallow two million wu, Eric, so let's leave it on the table overnight," she said, and then held up her hand to silence his reply, giving him her own version of the boudoir stare. "Let's not decide until we've . . . slept on it."

Prince Esterhazy gave her the full force of his bedroom charisma right back. "Well now," he oozed, "there's an offer that a gentleman can hardly refuse. It would be hard to deny that this conversation might go better over a champagne breakfast."

Monique was tempted. It wouldn't be the first time she had allowed herself a tactical fuck, and this one would no doubt be entirely enjoyable. For while Eric Esterhazy did not exactly have her idea of a great personality, he certainly was one beautiful male animal, and given his own obvious high opinion of himself as a seducer and the nature of his profession, it would be quite a surprise if he turned out to be less than a master cocksman.

Monique sighed inwardly, for no, it would be a highly counterproductive tactic. The whole point of letting him "sleep on it" was to let him have a private chat with whoever made the money decisions, who would surely accept the two million, and allow him the face-saving pretense that he had simply changed his mind. Which would not be possible if she stayed the night.

"Let's make it lunch instead," she said.

Eric smiled. "You intend to keep me up that late?" he said.

Monique found herself wondering if she could. Or if *he* could. But this was not the time to find out.

"Perchance in your dreams this night, sweet prince," she said dryly, rising. "Business before ... *pleasure*," she said cockteasingly. "New York girls never do it the other way around."

After his tantalizing and frustrating tête-à-tête with the sweet-and-sour Monique Calhoun, Eric Esterhazy was in no mood for an alternative romantic rendezvous and had an urgent desire to kick her insanely generous offer upstairs, so he called his mother and met her for a quick drink at an anonymous little café on his way to the boat.

"*Two million*, Mom!" he groaned. "Can you imagine what it felt like to say no to *two million wu?*"

"Can't say I've had the pleasure, Eric," Mom drawled.

"Some pleasure! About as pleasant as ... as ..."

Mom eyed him knowingly.

"A case of the blue balls?" she suggested.

"The *what* ... ?"

"Nuts in a vise, kiddo, non-coitus mucho interruptus."

Mom had become a devotee of these obscure American gangster-isms after Dad died, many of which had probably become obsolete a century or so before she was born. Freed from any need to conceal her previous identity and forced by necessity to come out of retirement and reactivate her citizen-shareholder status in Bad Boys, she amused herself by overplaying the out-of-date "gun moll."

Her present costume was typical. A black leather dress suit with an antique mannish white shirt and tie, a gray felt fedora cocked jauntily off center on her rather closely cropped iron-gray curls, and swept-back mirrored sunglasses hiding the wrinkles around her hard blue eyes.

"Foxy grandpa, your father never was," she liked to say with a lubricious wink, "but foxy grandma, that's me."

And indeed she seemed to be in the eyes of gentlemen of a certain age, and for sure in the La Fontainian sense. Eric was under no illusion that he would've gotten where he now was without what she called her "backdoor street smarts," and he needed them now.

"What's the problem, Eric?"

"I not only felt like an idiot turning her down, it made me feel, well . . . *impotent*. As if I were only some sort of . . . of . . ."

"Doorman in a fancy monkey suit?" Mom suggested.

Eric flushed. "I'm sure that's how I must've seemed to her."

"So whaddya want me to do, tell her you're really a tough guy who's made his bones?"

"I want you to call Eduardo. I want you to do it now."

Eduardo Ramirez was Eric's official non-official conduit to the Bad Boys board and Eric could just as well have called him himself. But Eduardo was also one of Mom's lovers and dealing with him through her gave her son a certain twisted leverage.

"And tell him what?"

"About Monique Calhoun's offer."

"Why?"

"*Why?* So he can authorize me to accept it."

"You've gotta be thinking with your dick, Eric, because your brain's gotta know it ain't gonna happen. *La Reine* is not for rent period, and you know why. An extra mil over ten days would be nice, but not worth the risk of compromising the real operation."

"Call Eduardo, Mom. Tell him the story. Sweet-talk him."

"I'll humor you as far as making the call, Eric," Mom told him. "But if and when and how I sweet-talk Eduardo is between him and me."

She pulled her mobile out of her purse, got up from the outdoor table, and walked a discreet distance away down the street before she used it.

Eric sat there drumming his fingers on the table for a good five minutes as he watched Mom talking to Eduardo Ramirez. When she finally finished, she turned, took off her sunglasses in a kind of a thoughtful gesture, and sauntered slowly back to the table with a bemused expression.

"Well?" Eric demanded.

"Well, Eduardo will meet us on the boat," Mom told him, shaking her head slightly. "He's very interested. He wants to have a serious talk about it."

Eric regarded her slyly. "Come on, Mom, how did you do it?" he wheedled. "What did you tell him to make it happen?"

Mom shrugged.

"Just the facts, ma'am," she said in a strange flat voice, no doubt another of her obscure gangster pix references.

Eric didn't get it.

And from the look on her face, it seemed that Mom didn't either.

La Reine de la Seine provided food, music, drink, drugs, sex, and gambling for her guests above deck, but not any prospect of privacy for Prince Eric Esterhazy, who spent two hours doing the usual—greeting guests as they came aboard, chatting at the bar and the baccarat and poker tables, pressing the flesh and massaging the ego—before he had a chance to slip below deck to more discreet environs.

Below the waterline, in addition to the engine room and the galley, were the boudoirs of assignation, Eric's dressing room, and a secure room keyed to his retina-print which housed the receiving end of the surveillance equipment.

The boudoirs were all occupied by paying guests, and Eric didn't want to hold a meeting with Eduardo Ramirez and his mother in what amounted to a clothes closet with a bed in it, so the computer room it was.

This was the heart of the real onboard business, and it was all business, no Lost Louisianne decor here. Plain gray bulkheads. A wall of video screens. A computer rig whose mundane appearance concealed powerful ten-rat meatware supporting a top-of-the-line AI program. Recording devices. Boxes of spare memory chips and cards. And only two swivel chairs, leaving Eric standing as Mom and Eduardo took them.

They made an odd couple sitting side by side, Mom in her black suit and Bogie fedora, Eduardo casually elegant as usual in blue-and-white seersucker slacks and a fawn-colored jacket sewn from the skin of a real fawn. About the only thing they appeared to have in common was how well they had aged, Mom still trim enough not to look ridiculous in her outfit, Eduardo, with his perfectly coiffed hair still black, his white ascot, and his affectation of gold-rimmed glasses, look-ing like an eminently successful director of cinema or theater or opera.

"So Eric, it is your considered opinion that we should make an exception to policy and rent out the boat?" Eduardo Ramirez said.

"An extra million wu for ten days' rental of *La Reine*? Why not? Fools and their money."

"Bread & Circuses is your idea of a ship of fools?" Mom drawled.

"The UN is and it's *their* money."

"Or so you assume," said Eduardo.

"Or so I assume?"

"The United Nations has been indigent to the point of chronic mendicancy for decades. Aren't you curious as to the source of their sudden major budget enhancement?"

"Loot first and ask questions later, as Mom would say. Who cares where it came from as long as we know it's coming to us?"

Eduardo affected the sinister leer of some godfather out of one of Mom's old gangster pix. This was hardly his style, but around Mom, he occasionally put it on to please her.

"I care," he said. "Because we know."

"Know what?"

"Where the money's coming from. It could be interesting to know why."

"And your little Miss Calhoun?" Mom chimed in. "Looks like her Bread & Circuses VIP services job may be a cover."

"Cover for *what*?"

"*That* is another question it might be in our interest to have an-swered," said Eduardo. "Which is why you are right about renting her *La Reine* after a fashion, if not for the right reason."

Eric regarded him in total confusion. "I am? It isn't? Would you mind telling me what I need to know?"

"What *you* need to know is that Monique Calhoun seemed to be merely one of Bread & Circuses' media mercenaries," Eduardo told him. "She first came to our attention when she went to Libya and appeared to come up with a brilliant ploy that sealed a deal to the mutual benefit of Advanced Projects Associates acting as agent for the Big Blue Machine, an Israeli construction syndic, and ourselves. Soon thereafter, she surfaced in Paris seemingly to run Bread & Circuses'

VIP services at UNACOCS, interfacing with the principal via Mossad. What does that suggest to you, Eric?"

Eric stared at him blankly.

"Use the old noodle!" Mom told him. "Little Miss Nobody supposedly pulls off a sweet deal in Libya for the Big Blue Machine and an Israeli syndic, and pow, bam, shows up here running B&C's VIP operation for Big Blue via their Mossad controller—"

"Wait a minute!" Eric exclaimed. *"The Big Blue Machine* is backing the conference?"

"No," said Mom, "the UN is getting its financing via flying saucers from Alpha Centauri."

"Duh . . ." said Eric.

"Exactly," said Eduardo.

It all fell into place. Both Mossad and the Israeli construction syndic might be semi-autonomous pieces of the former full sovereignty of Israel, but Israeli syndics tended to hire each other and scratch each other's backs.

So Occam's straight razor would indeed have it that a clever move in Libya to the benefit of an Israeli construction syndic and Big Blue would be more likely to have been designed in a wily Mossad think tank than by some low-level B&C operative.

Especially when she shows up soon thereafter way off her usual turf reporting to a Mossad controller in the employ of the Big Blue Machine.

But . . .

"But why is Big Blue financing a United Nations climate conference in a Green town like Paris? And who is Monique Calhoun working for? Bread & Circuses? Big Blue? Mossad? And why is whoever it is so willing to spend two million wu to rent out *La Reine* for the duration?"

Eduardo Ramirez smiled at Eric in the manner of a teacher pleased that a not-unintelligent student a bit slow on the uptake had finally gotten it.

"That," he said, "is what *we* need to know."

"So?"

"So, gallant gentleman that you are, you relent. Up to a point. For two million wu, she may indeed rent *La Reine de la Seine* for the duration of the conference, but on a nonexclusive basis. She controls half the guest list, but you retain control of the other half."

"For *two million wu?* She'll never do it. She'll cut the offer in half."

"Bargain the difference in ten percent intervals down to a million and a half."

"What makes you think they . . . whoever they are . . . will go even that high?" Eric asked.

"Because they would not have been willing to spend two million wu simply to wine and dine their favored guests in style," Eduardo told him. "Because in the waters in which both Bad Boys and Mossad swim, it would be *assumed* that we are running *La Reine* as an intelligence-gathering operation. Which is why they want to rent it in the first place. And why they will be willing to pay a million and a half, when, after much hard bargaining, you reluctantly allow Ms. Calhoun to use these surveillance facilities."

"*What?* Compromise the whole operation!"

"Better inside the tent pissing out than outside the tent pissing in, in the immortal words of Lyndon Johnson," Mom said cryptically. "Especially when it's *your* tent, and you're in control."

"Ms. Calhoun is not to be granted independent retina-print access to this control room," Eduardo elucidated. "She is not allowed in here alone. She is not allowed to bring anyone in with her. She most certainly is not allowed to know that Ignatz exists. All she is permitted to purchase is the raw data in realtime and the means to record it."

"A *disney*," said Eric, beginning to be amused.

"In a manner of speaking," said Eduardo.

"With you at her side the whole time to lead her by the clit through it," said Mom. "Get to her. Find out what's going on."

"Why . . . Mother, you're not suggesting that I . . . *seduce* the lady, are you?"

"It's a dirty job, Eric, but somehow I think you can . . . rise to the occasion, kiddo."

Avi Posner had cut Monique off after she told him that Eric Esterhazy had called to offer a rather unanticipated form of deal.

"*Never* assume that a phone is secure," Posner had told her. "But you can generally assume that the rooms in a hotel on the level of the Ritz are clean, because if anyone found a bug, the occupancy rate would swiftly approach zero as a limit. I'll be there in twenty minutes."

While she waited, Monique passed the time wondering whether Posner had ever been inside a suite at the Ritz, and if not, whether that, more than the security issue, had been his major motivation.

It took him only about fifteen minutes to arrive. She opened the door, ushered him in with a little ironic bow, observed his reaction as he surveyed the huge salon, running his eyes quickly and measuringly over the blue and gold flocking, the antique furniture, the rugs, the mahogany and silver-filigree media console, the mirrors, the chandelier, the paintings, like an insurance syndic appraiser.

"Bordel, as the French would say," he said. He finally cracked a small smile. "Or more accurately, perhaps, *bordello*."

So much for the pleasantries. Posner seated himself not very comfortably on the edge of a yellow and silver striped armchair.

"Well?" he said.

Monique sat down on a matching couch across a curvaceous marble coffee table.

"Well Esterhazy called late last night to tell me that I had charmed him into a change of heart and he was now willing to accept our offer to rent *La Reine* for two million work units."

"That was easy," Posner said suspiciously.

"There's a catch," Monique told him. "A rather large one."

"That's a relief," Posner said, and his body language seemed to tell Monique that he meant it.

"For two million wu, we get *half* the boat."

"Half the boat? How is that possible?"

"We get to control half the nightly guest list, but Esterhazy keeps control of the other half."

"Interesting . . ." Posner muttered. "Maybe better than anticipated. . . ." Then more sharply: "What did you tell him?"

"Half the guest list, half the money."

"And he said . . . ?"

"A million eight."

"And you said?"

"A million two. And he said, let's continue the haggling over lunch on *La Reine*. And I was mightily relieved to say okay." Monique shrugged. "Because I had no idea of whether you even want me to continue bargaining on this basis."

"Excellent!" Posner told her. "You've done very well."

"I have?"

Avi Posner bounced to his feet, began wearing a circle in an expensive rug as he spoke. "We now know that the amount of the rental fee is not a serious issue, and the policy level of Bad Boys have their own reasons to want *our* guests on *their* boat—"

"Bad Boys!" Monique exclaimed. "You never told me that *La Reine de la Seine* was a Bad Boys enterprise!"

Posner froze in his tracks, regarded her blankly. "This I had to tell you?" he said. "Esterhazy works as a front man for a series of casinos and whorehouses and then does likewise for *La Reine* and you imagine he is what, a citizen-shareholder in Moonlight & Roses?"

When it was pointed out to her in such a gentle manner, Monique did feel like a bit of a naif for not having seen the obvious. Indeed, the machinations of Avi Posner and whatever it was that he really represented were beginning to make her feel a good deal less the worldly sophisticate she had imagined herself to be in New York.

"So Bad Boys, or an entity employing Bad Boys, has an interest in *our client's interest* in UNACOCS," Posner continued in his previous mode as he resumed his pacing. "Else they would not propose *sharing* their data sponge with our operation—"

"*Data sponge?*"

Again Posner froze. Again he gave Monique a look that made her feel born yesterday. "Why do you imagine we were willing to overpay for the boat in the first place?"

"Uh . . . because it's the current ultimate in Parisian chic?"

Avi Posner rolled his eyes toward the rococo ceiling.

It would have been nice to have found something intelligent to say, but Monique's wits had failed her, for once again she found herself abruptly realizing that she was out of her depth.

"Bad Boys would never have missed the opportunity to thoroughly wire the boat, no inside information required to deduce that, one must merely assume that one is not dealing with morons," Posner said.

He sat down. He frowned.

"I had assumed in the end they would've simply agreed to give us access to the surveillance equipment if we made it a deal-breaker—"

"And tempted them with a big enough overpayment!"

Instead of the broad expression of approval she had hoped for, Monique got a mere nod of the head, which, she decided, she might as well take as a sign of professional acceptance.

"But now it appears that there's a player who *wishes* us to do just that," Posner muttered to himself. "Almost enough to have a rational man pondering Third Force dialectics . . ."

"Bad Boys themselves?" Monique suggested brightly.

"Maybe . . . maybe not . . ."

"But *why?*"

Avi Posner seemed to snap back into focus. "Those are indeed the operative questions," he said sharply. The smile he gave her was entirely mirthless.

"And it would be considered an act of friendship if you found out," he added, in a manner that indicated that what it would be considered an act of if she didn't was something she felt no current need to know.

"So, huh, how do you want me to deal with Esterhazy . . . ?" Monique asked nervously. "Do I make the deal? How high should I be prepared to go?"

"Oh, you make the deal all right," Posner said immediately, "and you go as high as you have to to do it."

He seemed to ponder some inner landscape for long moments.

"But you don't make it easy," he finally said. "And when you finally agree on a number, you tell him that access to the surveillance data is a deal-breaker."

"You think Esterhazy will really go for it?"

"*Esterhazy* would not have the authority to either accept it or turn it down," Posner told her.

"Therefore if he does either, it means that our move was anticipated in advance . . ."

Now Avi Posner finally did favor her with a genuine smile of approval, a virtual pat on the head. "Very good, Monique," he told her. "You're learning fast."

Monique's bask in Posner's approval was fleeting, however.

Oh, she was learning fast, all right.

The unsettling question was, learning *what*?

In order to reach *La Reine de la Seine*'s anchorage at the Quai Branly, Monique had to skirt the sorry sight of a low-end tourist pier crafted as a nineteenth-century New Orleans levee, the perfect tastelessness marred only by the fact that the strolling banjo-playing minstrels were real blacks, rather than whites in blackface.

Once she had passed through the fence surrounding *La Reine*'s private dock, this sleazy carnival was hidden from sight by a hedge, but while the embarkation pavilion, done up as an outsized, plantation house gazebo, might be a high-budget version, it still impressed her as yet another disney.

Tied up at the dock shorn of its light shows and holoed smokestacks, the great white riverboat itself seemed a shadow of the grande dame she had beheld from the dining room of La Cuisine Humaine promenading down the river under full son et lumière and virtual steam.

Prince Eric Esterhazy himself met her at the gangway, wearing what was probably his notion of informal attire, a brightly patterned red, yellow, and brown short-sleeved African leisure suit, which in some perverse manner made him a figure inversely reminiscent of the minstrels in straw hats and peppermint-stick suits she had just seen on the tourist pier.

"Welcome aboard *The Queen of the River*, oh Queen of my Heart," he oozed, kissing her hand, but with a sardonic edge that cut the goose-grease and made it *almost* charming.

"I'll give you the grand tour myself," he told her as he led her around the roofed passageway that surrounded the cabin of the lower deck like a plantation house portico. "There's usually no one on board at this hour, but I've prevailed upon our chef to prepare a few snacks which we'll have al fresco."

Once aboard, Monique had to freely admit that *La Reine* was impressive, even in empty repose, and more grudgingly that its splendor was rather tasteful.

The abundant brasswork was the real thing, down to the nautical fittings and the nails that secured the genuine teak decking. The restaurant-cum-cabaret that occupied the lion's share of the lower-deck cabin was classical elegance—plain white walls set off with brass fittings, round tables with napery in white and blue, not so much gold braid as to be obtrusive, some nineteenth-century paintings of Mississippi River scenes of a tasteful size on the walls, but no garish murals.

Toward the bow end of the dining room was a saloon with a big mirrored bar and stools and cushy leather chairs around low tables. Sternward was another bar, this one entered via a closed door in a wall. It was smaller, and it gave out onto a small open area under a roof over the stern, but it was otherwise similarly appointed.

"The main bar is public," Esterhazy told her. "This one we can close off and turn into a private club you can use for meetings."

Back in the cabin, Esterhazy led her up a brass-and-teak spiral staircase, which led directly into the upper-deck casino. There were a low stage and bandstand to port and a bar without seating to starboard. The ceiling was painted a deep green and from it depended a mirror ball, quiescent now, whose glass facets had been smoked to a deep bronze. The walls were white paneling framed by a profusion of oiled oak.

There were roulette and craps and baccarat tables in the middle of the room, but most of it was occupied by small round tables suitable for poker or blackjack or bridge, all of which were covered in green pool-table felt.

The effect was perversely peculiar. "There should be a word for this," Monique said. "It's a kind of reverse-disney, isn't it? Designed to be *less* sleazy than the real thing!"

Eric Esterhazy gave her a narrow appraising look, the most intelligent expression Monique had yet seen on his theatrically handsome face.

"The sort of clientele we favor isn't interested in gambling frenzy," he said. "Or rather, we don't want that sort of clientele."

Monique went over to one of the small tables, ran her hand teasingly over the felt surface, the edges, underneath, not really expecting to find anything obvious. "Better the sort of clientele who relax over a few drinks and a few wagers to loosen each other up for a little discreet and frank conversation . . . ?"

For a moment, they locked eyes, Esterhazy's face as carefully blank as that of a male model in a fashion photo. "Why surely, Monique, you're not suggesting that we would be so crass as to *bug* this pleasure dome?"

"Wah Prince Eric, wherever would a nice girl lahk me get an evil idea lahk that?" Monique drawled at him, dripping Spanish moss, but giving him the cold deadpan back.

The casino was surrounded by an open unroofed promenade with white garden tables at the bow and at the fantail, where one of them had been laid with a white tablecloth, blue china, silver cutlery, crystal, and a silver ice bucket containing a dry white Burgundy rather than champagne.

Esterhazy ushered her to the chair facing sternward, affording Monique a gorgeous view of the Eiffel Tower through a screen of palms and bougainvillea, and across the river, the great arc of the Trocadéro, stonework gleaming in the bright noonday sun where it peeked through the overgrowing foliage, bright green and red and blue parrots screeching and gabbling in the riotous blooms of the tropical gardens.

"Impressive," Monique was constrained to admit.

"Bien sûr," said Prince Eric, clinking glasses. "And only fitting, for after all, are we not two impressive people?"

One of whom is obviously more impressed with himself than with anyone else on the planet, Monique thought, but it was a toast it was impossible not to drink to anyway.

The "few little snacks" to which Eric had alluded in a reverse English sell worthy of Bread & Circuses proved to be impressive too. Oysters, mercifully non-bienville, but taken raw from their shells and served in cups crafted from fried saffron noodles. Not Mediterranean langoustine, but of all things, tiny tails of crayfish, imported, amusingly enough, from New York, stir-fried briefly in walnut oil with whole slices of fresh ginger, endive and red onions, and served over a cold salad of mango, papaya, coconut, lime slices, and whole leaves of fresh basil.

Impressive enough that Monique felt it would have been jejune to get down to the down-and-dirty before the dessert of peaches and apricots poached in rum and cinnamon over a cold champagne mousse.

Laying it on with a trowel, perhaps, but a girl could sure get used to it. But if she knew what was good for what was going to turn into an ongoing working relationship with Eric Esterhazy, not to mention her waistline, she had better retain her edge and equilibrium.

Prince Eric Esterhazy was growing bored with this pecuniary pavane and he had the feeling that Monique Calhoun was fecklessly dancing around the bottom line too.

"A million three . . ."

Her turn to curtsy.

"A million seven . . ."

My turn to bow.

And while what he now knew about the fetching Ms. Calhoun did not include hard information on who or what she was fetching *for*, it was enough to convince him that the current four-hundred-million wu difference between their positions was hardly of the essence of what this haggling was really about.

"Shall we cut to the chase?" he suggested.

"Why Eric, I thought this *was* the chase," she purred.

"Don't you find all this number-crunching a bit unseemly? Better left to accountants, wouldn't you say, Monique?" He gave her his best bedroom smile. "After all, what's four hundred thousand wu between people who would like to be friends?"

"Four hundred thousand here, four hundred thousand there," she said deadpan, "after a while, it adds up to real money."

Eric couldn't help laughing. "By my calculations, half of four hundred million is two hundred million, which, either added to a million three or subtracted from a million seven, comes out to the same million five. . . ."

He swirled the remains of the wine in his glass, leaning back in his chair. "So," he said, "we can either waltz slowly closer to the figure we both know we are going to reach in tedious ten-thousand-wu increments, or consider the difference split and go on to something more amusing. What do you say, Monique?"

"I say I'm ready to drink to a million and a half," she told him, clinking glasses. She brought her glass to her lips, but paused teasingly before drinking. "Provided we can reach an agreement on exactly what my principal is paying a million and a half *for*."

"Your principal being . . . ?" Eric drawled speculatively, neither expecting a useful answer or receiving one.

"Why UNACOCS, the United Nations, of course," Monique said sweetly. "Which, as we both know, is not exactly in a position to piss away money. And, as we both know, a hundred and fifty thousand wu a day is rather grossly overpriced for . . . a mere party-boat rental."

The new dance had begun. This one at least promised to be more entertaining. Who knew where it might end? Perhaps ultimately in one of the belowdecks boudoirs1 . . . ?

"*La Reine de la Seine* is the finest party boat in Paris, after all. . . ." Eric ventured.

"So I've heard. . . . I hear it has certain . . . clandestine enhancements. . . ."

"Ah yes, our belowdecks boudoirs of assignation," Eric said suavely, giving her the eye. "There are a dozen of them, each with a different decor. You'd like to try one out perhaps? I'd be happy to provide a suitable demonstration."

"I'm sure you would, Eric," Monique Calhoun said dryly. Then, more promisingly: "And I believe you could. And at some point . . ."

She let it dangle, put down her glass. "But not just yet," she said sharply. "You say you're bored by all this waltzing around? Well so am I. We both know why I'm willing to overpay for *La Reine*. We both know what I really want, now don't we?"

"I have my fantasies," Eric said superciliously.

Monique frowned. The endgame was definitely at hand.

"All right," Eric said in a harder tone, "so why don't you tell me?"

"Why Eric, I thought you'd never ask . . ."

"No you didn't."

"Probably not, so shall we cut the crap, and cut as you say to the chase, which is to say the bottom line. Which is that for a million and a half for a guest list share, we have to have access to the surveillance equipment, or there's no deal."

"Surveillance equipment? Why whatever—"

Monique Calhoun bolted to her feet. "Nice not knowing you, Prince Charming," she snapped.

"Wait a minute!"

She froze. "For what? The coffee and after-dinner mints? More moonbeams and malarkey?"

Eric made a great show of sighing in reluctant resignation. "All right, all right," he said. "You win. You can't blame me for trying."

"Depends on *what* game you're trying to play, now doesn't it?" she said, but in much softer tones, and giving him a seductive smile whose sincerity was seriously in question. "And now I'd like to inspect the facilities, if you don't mind—"

"My pleasure. Shall we go below—"

"And I don't mean the boudoirs!"

"Oh yes, you do!"

"Oh no, I don't!"

"Come with me, ma chérie, and I shall elucidate," Eric told her.

And Ignatz shall obfuscate.

Monique did not exactly consider herself an expert on surveillance equipment, but by her technologically naive standards at least, *La Reine de la Seine* had been constructed as a data sponge with a thoroughness verging on the obsessive.

Chez Prince Eric, there was not a cubic centimeter of the boat not covered by cameras and microphones, down to the stalls in the toilets.

The cameras and mikes were tiny, powerful, and redundantly profuse. They were secreted in obvious places like the casino mirror ball, the restaurant chandelier, and behind every mirror on the boat. They were camouflaged as everything from nail heads to rococo swirls in gilt picture frames, to the screws connecting toilet-paper dispensers to the walls.

This Eric explained while pointing out an example here and there on their way through the casino, down the spiral staircase to the restaurant deck, and down a gangway to belowdecks country.

Down here, *La Reine* was strictly functional from amidships sternward: the galley and its larders, the engine room and the fuel tanks, the paddle-wheel gearing.

Amidships was a transverse corridor with Oriental-design carpeting, golden-glowing ersatz candles in brass sconces, and walls painted a shade of rose verging perilously on the vulval. A series of doors ran along the bow-ward side of the corridor. Eric Esterhazy displayed what lay behind them for Monique's delectation.

Some of these boudoirs were what she would've expected. An Arabian Nights harem, a Summer of Love hippie pad, a flaming pink honeymoon suite, were of course de rigueur in an operation like this. The simulated tree house was unexpectedly imaginative, as was the Indian erotic temple room. The dungeon with the straw floor and assorted manacles was something she cared not to contemplate. The soft-screen room that could turn into a disney of anything was a modern touch. The eighteenth-century Sun King bedroom was far too kitschy for Monique's taste. The palace of pure light was weird. The schoolroom was unsettling. The sauna seemed wholesome enough.

"All thoroughly bugged, I presume?"

"Every nook and cranny," Eric told her.

"You could make a fortune recording what goes on and selling the. . . ." Monique paused. "You *don't*, do you. . . ?"

"Would I tell you if we did? Would the sort of people allowed down here let me get away with it?"

"Probably not. But it might give you a certain leverage, now mightn't it?"

"No comment. What kind of person do you think I am anyway?"

"No comment," replied Monique. "What's this one, the Marquis de Sade's playpen?" she said, opening the final door before Eric could stop her.

Inside was a cross between a backstage theatrical dressing room and an outsized clothes closet. There was a bed against the far wall. Tidy, it wasn't.

Monique gave Eric a quizzical look.

Eric smiled weakly back. "My own little onboard lair," he said. He winked at her lugubriously. "For future reference, one of only two places on the boat blind to the surveillance equipment, if you're the shy type."

"The other being . . . ?"

"Not nearly as cozy . . . the computer room on the receiving end of the data stream, of course . . ."

Eric Esterhazy did not know much about computers and that which dwelled within them, but he knew what he liked. And Ignatz had been designed to be liked by the likes of him.

The problem with the data stream from the cameras and microphones permeating *La Reine* was that there was so much of it. Close to a thousand camera and mike pairs. Operating about eight hours a night. Eight thousand hours a day of video and sound recordings, most of which was not only useless but boring, and some of which, such as the toilet footage and all too much of what went on in the boudoirs, was disgusting as well.

With modern technology, storing it all on chips was no problem, but filtering and sorting and searching it before it dated into worthlessness—meaning as close to realtime as possible—was quite literally an inhuman task.

Hence Ignatz.

Eric's comprehension of such technical arcana might be vague, but he did understand the difference between hardware—or in this case meatware—and software. Ignatz was a program. Ignatz could be removed from *La Reine*'s computer and installed elsewhere. Ignatz could be duplicated.

Ignatz could be preprogrammed to follow individual guests throughout the night, or combinations of guests, or combinations of guests linked to keywords, and display the edited results in realtime on the screens. Or sift through the night's recordings retrospectively for same in a few seconds. Ignatz could also alter the atmospheres in the boudoirs by direct command or inject psychotropics according to preselected word and/or guest-identity triggers.

Ignatz operated by voice command. Ignatz was an Artificial Intelligence sophisticated enough to be commanded in plain or colloquial English, French, Russian, Spanish, or German by the likes of technologically unsophisticated humans like Eric.

Despite the name, which was a sardonic reference to some obscure twentieth-century fictional rodent, Ignatz's "personality" was entirely independent of the rat-brain meatware on which it ran.

Indeed, Ignatz did not have *a* "personality." Ignatz had a large menu of personalities to choose from. You could talk to everything from a flat affectless computer voice, to something that sounded like a duck on methamphetamine, to any number of show business personalities living and dead, or historical figures, or even to yourself, if you were narcissistic enough to try it, as Eric had done on several occasions.

But Ignatz was not in evidence as Eric gave Monique Calhoun the computer naif's tour of the control room. The computer boys had prepared what they called a "Potemkin interface." Ignatz would now emerge from behind the Potemkin interface only in response to a voice fitting Eric's voiceprint parameters uttering the key phrase "open sez me."

So Eric threw a series of manual switches to activate the twenty video screens.

"Every camera and microphone has its own number," he told Monique, "which is how we can display the feed from all of them on only these twenty screens."

He began typing number keys on an actual keyboard and the scenes on the screens began changing—a casino table, a toilet stall, a table on the upper promenade deck, boudoirs, staircase, flick, flick, flick.

"And if you hold down the control key when you type in a number, that camera and mike feed records until you do it again," Eric lied. In fact everything was being recorded all the time.

"But how in the world do you remember what number refers to the feed from where . . . ?" she asked dazedly.

"Oh, it becomes second nature after a while," Eric told her cavalierly.

For while Ignatz was now hiding behind the Potemkin interface, it was up and running and controlling this preprogrammed demonstration while Eric hit random keys. Otherwise, he would have been just as hopelessly confused as Monique Calhoun now looked.

"But for the novice, there's the help menu. . . ."

He hit "Control H" and six adjacent screens filled with schematic diagrams of the casino, the restaurant, the bars, the promenades, the belowdecks boudoirs, each camera and mike pair marked with a number.

"My God . . ." groaned Monique Calhoun.

"You can either type in the number of the camera and mike you want, or . . . use this trackpoint to point and click . . ." Eric said in what sounded to him suitably like a geek in a computer pub spot, "and . . . voilà!"

Monique slumped back in her swivel chair. "You . . . do this all by yourself, Eric?" she said, with a gratifying awe as she regarded him in this unexpected new technically proficient light.

"Of course not, only when I'm anticipating . . . something of significance, I leave it to a technical assistant to do the routine monitoring . . ." Eric told her.

This was a species of truthful lie, another aspect of the Potemkin interface, for the "technical assistant" was in reality the inhuman, tireless, sleepless, boredomless Ignatz. But when Monique was in the computer room without him, Eric would supply her with a human "techie" from the security department of Bad Boys.

"Well, I guess I'll have to hire one of my own. . . ."

Eric shook his head ruefully. "Not part of the deal, Monique," he said. "For obvious reasons, this is a secure area. The door lock is keyed to my retinas. I escort everyone in and out. You are the only outsider I'll risk giving access."

"But you can hardly expect me to—"

"No problem, Monique, when I'm not here with you, my technician will be," Eric told her airily. "You just tell him what you want, and he'll work the system for you." Or rather, Ignatz will be listening in and doing it while your minder tickles the computer ivories.

"But when I'm not down here—"

"You just use one of these," said Eric, reaching into a drawer filled with assorted cigarette lighters, and extracting the one with the Moonlight & Roses logo.

"Mobile mike," he said, handing it to her. "What I use to instruct the technician down here to record the scene wherever I might be on the boat."

Actually, of course, since Ignatz had access to every mike aboard, and could be keyed to her voiceprint parameters as well as his, such a silly gizmo was unnecessary. But to explain that would require him to reveal Ignatz's existence.

Somewhat dimly, Eric found himself appreciating the esthetic elegance of the completeness of the Potemkin interface's design.

Monique Calhoun eyed the device dubiously, then cocked her head at Eric himself, and gave him a similar fish-eyed stare.

"Moonlight & Roses?" she said. "Why the logo of a gigolo syndic?"

Eric mooned at her soulfully. "Call it a romantic notion, Monique," he said, "for with it you may also instantly call me to your side."

That much was true.

"And I remind you," he told her, transforming his expression into what he hoped was a charming parody of a lupine leer, "that this is one of the only two places aboard blind to electronic eyes."

That was of course a lie.

Who, after all, shall watch the watchmen?

The computer room was bugged too.

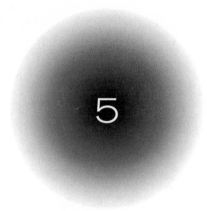

5

MONIQUE CALHOUN HAD NEVER HANDLED VIP
services for a major conference before, and as the said VIPs began to
arrive, Avi Posner's elusive clandestine agenda and Eric Esterhazy's
fatuous passes at seduction were put on hold by the donkey-work of
installing her charges at the Ritz and dealing with their "special requirements."

Her VIPs fell into four broad categories: chief representatives of
some of the major exhibitors, heads of delegations from sovereign and
semi-sovereign jurisdictions, speakers and presenters at the conference
itself, and the press.

Her list of speakers and governmental functionaires came from
Lars Bendsten and their needs were financed out of the official UN-
ACOCS budget. The list of trade delegation people to be favored by
her care came from Avi Posner, meaning the client, meaning the Big
Blue Machine of which their operations were components, meaning
they were self-financed. The press list came from Bread & Circuses'
Paris office and *their* lavish freebies came out of the B&C operational
budget.

The Ritz being the Ritz and Bread & Circuses' Paris branch providing her with a team of gophers, the hotel arrangements were the

least of Monique's problems. She herself was only called in to iron out a few delicate details. A Muslim delegate's prayer rug had disappeared in transit and a replacement had to be supplied. A Chinese climatologist had to be shown four rooms before finding one that she deemed possessed of the proper feng shui. The dos and don'ts of various peculiar dietary requirements—halal, kosher, Hindu, vegan, two different variants of macrobiotic—had to be carefully explained to the bemused and unamused hotel chef.

The real headaches were the "special requirements" and judging just how far VIP services should go to fulfill them.

The requests for professional sexual companionship were easy enough to meet, though Monique felt it prudent to get authorization from Ariel Mamoun before picking up the tabs from Ladies of the Evening or Moonlight & Roses for the press.

Drugs presented more difficulties. Ordinary marijuana, hashish, and cocaine were readily available from Bad Boys at reasonable prices, but theirs was basically a mass-market, not an artisanal, operation, and some of the special orders were expensive pains in the ass.

Lydia Maren, a formidable London press dragon, insisted on trying absinthe, a concoction that no one had made for over a century, and Monique had spent a whole day and a ridiculous amount of money ferreting out the chemical formula and having the stuff synthesized. John Sri Davinda, a climatologist from California, insisted that he had to have peyote, a wild cactus from the great Tex-Mex desert, in order to sufficiently "focus his consciousness" to make his presentation at the conference, and given the current incoherent state thereof, Monique was forced to agree that any alteration was likely to be an improvement. Chativan Kuritkul, the Thai Minister of Climate Control, insisted on a gourmet strain of Colombian marijuana, and Bernard Kutnik, CEO of Erdewerke, would only be satisfied with Thai stick.

By the time requests came in from several quarters for Cipriani, a red-wine-and-cannabis potation popular among the upper crust in the nineteenth century, Monique had gotten the message that ungrateful souls were bent on seeing how far she could be pushed.

So she bought four liters of the worst plonk she could find, dissolved a half kilo of hashish in foul Moldovan gin, mixed it all together, poured the mess into bottles with phony labels, and let them toast their greediness with that. The escalating requests for arcane psychotropics began to wane considerably the morning after.

But dealing with the ruffled feathers of those she had been forced to drop from the guest list for tonight's inaugural soiree aboard *La Reine de la Seine* was the lowest bridge she'd had to duck her head to pass under on her way to the conference's opening.

The riverboat comfortably accommodated 240 people, and Eric Esterhazy refused to take on more even for one night, citing some Syndique de la Seine regulation, nor could he be wheedled into giving her some of his own slots just this once.

This left Monique with a maximum guest list of 120. Cutting the UN's list of governmental VIPs was impossible since they were at least officially the client and the results would be a series of nasty diplomatic incidents. The major speakers could hardly be axed. This left Posner's trade delegation people and the press. Snubbing any major press figures would be public relations seppuku. And Posner's list represented the organizations footing the bill.

After she explained this to Avi Posner, a dozen of the people on his list turned out to "have other engagements." How this had been accomplished Monique did not at all feel a need to know. This still meant that twelve lesser lights had to be dropped from the press list.

This was not going to make her life easier. These people were going to have to be on *La Reine* lists for the next two nights if she had to bump Jesus Christ and the Twelve Apostles to do it.

But by the afternoon of the conference's opening ceremony, Monique was able to take a breather. Her VIPs were now all cozily installed at the Ritz, her gophers had loaded them into their limos and delivered them to the Grand Palais before she went over herself, so at least until evening, she could fade into the A-list crowd with her top-level pass and play VIP herself.

Though it was a partly cloudy afternoon outside, the smart glass of the greenhouse ceiling enclosing the great exhibition hall had been set to simulate a brilliant bright blue sky with a golden sun at the zenith, the better to glorify the climatech engineering displays for the benefit of the television cameras.

Fully set up now, except for something near the center of the exhibition space hidden by a makeshift box of canvas screening and apparently still under construction, the trade show, and that was certainly what it was, made an impressive demonstration of the wares of the Big Blue Machine.

Plankton-seeding barges, cloud-cover generators, cloud-seeding drones, various species of potted Qwik-grow trees. Scale-model mock-ups of orbital mirrors, launch vehicles, occluders. Screens and holos running loops of nuclear terrain-sculpting demos, orbital mirror weather adjustments, damming projects, reforestation schemes, and yes, the S&L for the Gardens of Allah prepared by Bread & Circuses at the Advanced Projects Associates pavilion.

All glorified and enhanced by multicolored strobes, flashing lights, halogen tubing, a cacophony of competing musical accompaniment.

And, since everyone on the trade show floor who wasn't press seemed to be an industrial presenter, all for the benefit of the multitude of microphones and cameras.

Although it was not her professional turf, it *was* the work of her syndic, and Monique felt a surge of patriotic pride as a citizen-shareholder thereof at how Bread & Circuses had turned out the coverage for an event the previous versions of which, in the words of Jean-Luc Tri, B&C's Paris press maven, had they been horse turds, would have been unable to draw flies.

They were all there, or so it seemed—Worldnet, StarNet, Sat One, BBC, NipponOrb, TeleFrance, Mundoticias, SiberWeb, as well as a horde of camera people from local stations and news sites, still photographers for the pix mags, freelancers covering for the indigent media of the Lands of the Lost—swarming around the exhibits shooting their visuals before the heads began to talk.

The talking heads in question were just about settled in as Monique passed through the blue fiberboard screening discreetly separating the unseemly trade show huckstering from the serious scientific raison d'être.

The amphitheater of temporary seating was just about full, but Monique's priority pass gained her access to B&C's own little reserved section ten rows back from the stage and only slightly left of center. Ariel Mamoun was already there, Tri was down at the cluster of cameras in front of the stage, there were several people from the Paris office that she didn't know, and her own little crew of gophers.

"Well, it's all over for the moment except for the speaking, as they say wherever it is they say it," Ariel said by way of greeting.

"Shouting," corrected Monique.

"Whichever. Either way, it will no doubt go on and on and on."

Jean-Luc Tri, an exaggeratedly dapper figure in a black silk pin-striped suit and ruffled white linen shirt, scuttled up the aisle and took a seat beside Monique. His sleek black mane was static-molded into a rakishly crested coiffure without a hair out of place; he might be panting a bit, but his smooth oriental skin did not deign to display a single bead of sweat.

"Great turnout, Jean-Luc, how did you pull it off?"

Tri gave her a characteristic cynical lidded smirk. "With B&C picking up the tabs for the stars, and the lower levels fighting each other for the assignment like the famished dog packs of Detroit, at-tracting the paperatti to an expense account junket to Paris is about as difficult as dumping a load of fresh fish in the Seine and waiting for the alligator feeding frenzy to start."

The reaction was somewhat more subdued than that as Lars Bend-sten led six people up onto the stage and launched the standard UN welcoming speech. These were supposedly the MIPs of the conference, that is the Most Important Persons, and they had all made it to both the Ritz and Monique's invitation list for tonight's opening party on the riverboat.

"Good afternoon, ladies and gentlemen, mesdames et messieurs, meine Damen und Herren, distinguished guests, and welcome to the sixth United Nations Annual Conference On Climate Stabiliza-tion. . . ."

But interestingly enough, all of the scientists had been on the VIP list handed to her by the General Secretary. None of them had been deemed worthy of Avi Posner's attention or the direct funding of Big Blue.

"Dr. Allison Larabee, whose Condition Venus climate model was the genesis of these conferences. . . ."

"Dr. Paolo Pereiro, whose climate model predicted the current breakup of the north polar ice cap, and which many now regard as the current state of the art. . . ."

"Hassan bin Mohammed, chairperson of the Committee of Concerned Climatologists . . ."

The scientists were *window dressing*, Monique realized, as Bendsten's introductions droned on. Window dressing from the point of view of what had become the real power here, the economic power that had financed this high-budget move to Paris in the first place. And was now calling the tunes.

Including, she was forced to admit, her own.

"Mary Cardinal N'Goru, Papal Legate to the United Nation. . . ."

"Dr. Bobby Braithwaite, winner of the Nobel Prize for Climatology for his modeling of the desiccation of Mars and the threshold theory of climate change . . ."

"Dr. Dieter Lambert, developer of the Qwik-grow tree, the carbon-dioxide-fixing coral, the photosynthetic fungus . . ."

Fancy window dressing to be sure, but window dressing still, just as whatever went on at the actual conference in here was no doubt going to be window dressing for the main event out there on the trade show floor.

A True Blue setup, as these conferences had always been—this time, however, financed by, and fronting for, the commercial interests of the Big Blue Machine.

That was the cynical professional analysis, and a bit of the Green in Monique doing the calculating. Larabee, Braithwaite, Pereiro, and Lambert were all climatological superstars of the True Blue persuasion, but they were no longer workers at the cutting edge; monstres sacrés, as the French would put it, or, as the Americans would say, famous long ago.

The speeches began with just the sort of yawners Monique had dreaded and expected. Pereiro delivered a numbing discourse on the mathematics of climate modeling incomprehensible to her layman's knowledge of the subject. Lambert presented an embarrassing paean to his own faded brilliance.

Braithwaite, a tall, courtly, black man with gray dreadlocks, a wistful Jamaican lilt to his voice, and an air of not quite knowing why he was there, at least was able to rouse Monique from her daze, if only because he was a better and more sympathetic speaker.

"What's an expert on the climatological history of Mars doin' at a conference about stabilizin' the climate of *this* here planet?" he said with a shrug after presenting the dry facts of Martian desiccation.

He grinned boyishly despite his years.

"Well, who could resist a free trip to Paris?" he said. "But long as I'm here, I *could* point out th' obvious. Earth is a planet. Mars is a planet. On Earth, life began t'evolve in the soup of a sea. Started likewise on Mars. Might've made it. Might've evolved into brilliant critters with a roomful of advanced degrees just like us."

He held up the thumb and forefinger of his right hand a millimeter or two apart.

"Came *this* close," he said. "Jus' a *little* more mass, and Mars has a *little* more gravity. Jus' a *little* more gravity, and Mars holds enough hydrogen and carbon dioxide to increase the vapor pressure *jus'* enough to hold its liquid water and give its infant biosphere the chance to photosynthesize oxygen and maybe those microbes get to evolve into thee and me."

He shrugged. "So what's that got to do with stabilizin' th' climate of *this* planet? Well, what we've been doin' to the chemistry of the atmosphere and the energy budget of *this* planet for th' past three hundred years or so is *orders of magnitude* greater than what made the difference between a warm wet Mars with a breathable atmosphere and a biosphere an' the dead desiccated Mars we see today. Was a close thing, and when Mars went, it went—"

He snapped his fingers. "*Jus' like that!*"

Braithwaite smiled ruefully. "In geological terms, of course. So what can we Earthlings learn about life on Earth from th' story of Mars?"

Another one of those engaging shrugs.

"Well, the evolution of a planetary biosphere may not be quick and easy come," Braithwaite said, "but it *sure is* quick and easy go."

And ambled away from the podium to not much more than a polite pro forma ration of applause, which left Monique feeling vaguely annoyed, a bit of a Martian herself, a naif among the sophisticates.

Or was it the other way around?

Hassan bin Mohammed followed with the sort of standard whining True Blue political screed that was soporific enough to ease whatever it was that Braithwaite had stirred within Monique back into its slumber and to bring the bulk of the audience, who had heard and probably said it all themselves a thousand times before, to fidgeting murmuring boredom.

But Mary Cardinal N'Goru managed to turn it to pregnant silence just by the way she walked ever so slowly and majestically to stage center, a tall regal black woman in middle years, her head turned to one side to maintain eye contact with the audience, or rather the cameras, bright red cloak swirling and then swept aside with a theatrical gesture as she reached the podium.

Bread & Circuses could still learn a trick or two from the Roman Catholic Church, Monique realized. They had always had the gear. They had always had the moves.

"I am here as a Princess of the Church to speak to you of sin!" she boomed out in a prophet's voice to the audible dismay of her secular audience.

"The Bible speaks out against the sin of killing a human and names it murder! And this was the worst sin known to man until the twentieth century invented a worse evil, the deliberate killing of whole peoples, and lo! we have named that sin genocide!"

The only sounds were the squirming of asses on hard seats and the subliminal hum of the massed television equipment.

Mary N'Goru leaned a tad closer to her audience, addressed those cameras a bit more intimately, spoke in another, slightly softer voice, a voice more of sorrow than anger.

"But I am also here as a daughter of Africa, and I must speak to you with the voice of that dying continent, with the voice out of the great central desert where nothing may live, with the voice of forests gone into dust, with the voice of a thousand species of animals and birds gone into that final night from which there is no returning, with the voice of a hundred peoples existing on bile and ashes for a while before they follow. . . ."

And it seemed to Monique that this woman had made herself that voice, the voice not only of dying Africa, but of all those Lands of the Lost, crying out not *in* the wilderness, but *from* that widening wilderness, here in the balmy green City of Light.

"And that too is a sin!" she declaimed, reverting to the posture and voice of the righteous prophet. "A century ago we began to commit a sin too terrible to be named! The sin of killing not a human or a people but whole lands, whole ecosystems. It began as a sin of careless ignorance and willful stupidity, but now it is a sin of knowing indifference and egoistic greed!"

Again Mary Cardinal N'Goru leaned forward and gazed directly into the cameras, but this time there was cruelty in her eyes as well as anger, a sardonic set to her mouth.

"But though we have not yet found a name worthy of a sin as terrible as *that*, now we must find a name foul and awful enough for the *ultimate* sin, the sin whose burden the soul of our species will bear to the grave and the Final Judgment beyond!"

She paused, she hooked her elbows under her red cloak so that it rose into a mantle about her as she raised her arms.

"And what shall we call the sin of murdering an entire biosphere?" she roared. "How do we name the slaying of a living world?"

And, swirling her cape around her, swept back to her seat to guttural murmurings, a scattering of nervous applause that swiftly died away into silence.

"Both ears and the tail . . ." Ariel Mamoun muttered beside Monique.

"Not quite the tail," said Jean-Luc Tri.

Monique heard these peculiar remarks with only half an ear, caught up in the moment with her heart, but also wondering who could possibly be shoved forward to do what after an act like that, as a Bread & Circuses professional.

And then she found out.

"Dr. Allison Larabee . . ." was all that Lars Bendsten said or had to.

And there was a mighty round of applause as the frail white-haired old woman shakily made her way to the podium.

And why not?

Allison Larabee was the Grand Old Lady of UNACOCS. The patron saint of these conferences. The woman who had spoken at all of them. The creator of the Condition Venus climate model. Which had been instrumental in creating the panic that had called the United Nations Annual Conferences On Climate Stabilization into being.

Without her, UNACOCS would not exist.

Without her, these people would not now be here.

Anyone who was here out of True Blue conviction or for academic credit or commercial gain or just for a free trip to Paris owed their presence to Allison Larabee. And they showed it with prolonged applause whose enthusiasm seemed entirely unfeigned.

But for some reason Dr. Larabee did not seem amused.

Not at all. She stood there scowling until the ovation finally died away.

"As all of my colleagues here today know," she said in a soft grandmotherly voice, "I've attended every one of these conferences since they started. . . ."

She paused for a bit, and when she spoke again, it was in a voice twice as loud and dripping acid. "Every damned last stupid one of them!"

She paused again to let her audience feel the shock.

"Well this is the last one of these things I'm attending!"

Stunned jaw-dropped silence.

"No, I'm not on my deathbed, I'm afraid I'd probably outlive our *planet* if that were somehow possible," she said, reverting to the little-old-lady voice.

She wagged an outraged granny's finger at her poleaxed audience. "Speaking as a scientist, there's a technical term for what's been going on here for six years. Do you know what that technical term is, my esteemed and learned colleagues?"

She allowed a long beat of dramatic silence.

"The word," she shouted at the top of her lungs, "is *bullshit!*"

Monique could hardly believe what she was hearing. What was going out live to the largest television audience these conferences had ever garnered. What was going to make headlines all over the world.

"Nero fiddled while Rome burned, the orchestra played traveling music as the *Titanic* went to the bottom, and you people have been bullshitting yourselves and the world while the Earth reels closer and closer to Condition Venus! And mea culpa, I've been one of you!"

Murmurs, looks of disbelief, groans, moans of anger.

"There's nothing left to talk about!" Larabee shouted. "There never was, but we've all wasted six years talking about it anyway! We cool down this planet and we do it fast, or all too soon there'll be no one left alive on it to engage in any more useless goddamn conferences! That is my contribution to this symposium! That's all I've got to say because that's all there *is* to say! Get it together this time, or do it without me!"

She stepped out from behind the podium with her hands on her hips.

"You may now throw dead cats and rotten eggs," she said sweetly, then stormed down off the stage to an uproar of shouts, applause, boos, and angry contumely, and the opening session of the conference broke up into pandemonium.

"And the tail . . ." said Jean-Luc Tri.

Groups of people were on their feet shouting at each other. Others sat there stunned. Some followed in Larabee's wake as she marched through the chaos, through the cluster of cameras before the stage, and right out of the auditorium. After a moment, the camera people exited after her, still shooting.

Perhaps half the audience remained clogging the seats and aisles of the makeshift amphitheater babbling to each other. The rest, drawn by the most recently evolved of human tropisms, tried to follow the media following Larabee out beyond the partitions and onto the trade show floor.

Monique, too, found herself kneeing and elbowing her way through the crush, going with the flow of the intellectual exodus out into the realm of commerce without really thinking about why, as stunned as any of them by what had happened.

By the time she was out there among the climatech displays and industrial sales exhibits, Dr. Allison Larabee was nowhere to be seen, and the news crews who had followed her were now indistinguishable from those who had been shooting visuals out here before the speeches began.

Monique stood there blinking in the strange disjunction.

Camera crews were crawling all over the exhibits. Crowds were milling about. There was something so insanely *normal* about it. As if the Cardinal hadn't made her fire-breathing speech. As if the godmother of UNACOCS had never screamed "bullshit" and stormed out of the conference.

As if it had all been forgotten.

As if it had never happened.

But of course it *had* happened.

And it wouldn't be forgotten.

Because it had happened live on television and the net and had been seen by perhaps a hundred million people. And because of *what* had happened, ten times that many people would tune in and log on to the recorded coverage.

Monique wondered how many of them would feel what she now felt. And she wondered just what this psychic dyspepsia was, this visceral malaise compounded of shame, and shock, and rude awakening.

Shame for what?

For her backstage role in promoting a conference whose spiritual founder had cursed it as useless bullshit and walked out?

Shock at what?

At witnessing live the sort of iconic news event—like a political assassination or major disaster—that transcends the bread and circuses of the media of transmission?

Awakening from what into what?

From doing her job as usual into the unbidden realization that she might *really be involved*, however tangentially, in however minor a role, in something upon which the very fate of life on Earth might conceivably depend?

Lost in the unaccustomed depths of these musings, Monique didn't notice that Jean-Luc Tri had come up beside her until he spoke.

"Well, did we spin news, or did we *spin news!*"

"What . . . ?"

B&C's Paris press maven grinned sly satisfaction at her. "What an opening! I *knew* I was right to go with that sin and bullshit script! Let them try and ignore the Paris UNACOCS after *that!*"

"Script . . . ?"

"The Cardinal was perfect, but then they're all pros. Larabee remembered her lines, but that 'dead cats and rotten eggs' bit was an ad lib. . . ."

Tri frowned, he eyed Monique speculatively.

"What do you think, Monique, professional opinion," he asked, "was that maybe a little over the top?"

Scant hours ago, this grandmotherly woman in the rakish white evening gown had been shouting "bullshit" in an apparent fury on the
news channels, but now it seemed it was all that Dr. Allison Larabee
could do to keep from blushing like a schoolgirl and curtsying as Eric
Esterhazy greeted her at the top of the gangway with the standard
Romanian hand-kiss.

"Welcome aboard *La Reine de la Seine*, Dr. Larabee. . . ."

"Thank you, Prince Esterhazy, uh, Your Highness. . . ."

Eric beamed her his best noblesse oblige smile. "Simply *Prince Eric*
to you, Dr. Larabee. . . ."

"*Allison* to you, Prince Eric."

Now she actually did blush as she moved on to allow the next
guest aboard.

"Ah, Sidney, I've been hearing rumors about some rather outré
cross-gender casting in your production of *Faust*. . . ."

It had long since ceased to surprise but not to amaze Eric how a
properly delivered kiss on the hand and warm smile from a handsome
prince, even a phony one, could have this effect on ladies of a certain
age, world figures or not, media stars of the hour or not, especially if
they came from a country, such as America, that had never had its
own tacky tribe of titled parasites.

"Nice piece on that nasty mess in Athens, Derek, maybe you'd
like a change of pace, like a bit of puffery on *La Reine* after you're
through covering this tedious climate conference. . . ."

It was a goodly part of his stock-in-trade, and beyond that, it gave
him a certain warm altruistic glow when applied to women he had no
intention of bedding for reasons of lust or commerce. Why not? It
gave them pleasure and it cost him nothing.

"Mr. General Secretary, an honor to have you aboard. . . ."

Of course, it didn't always work. It hadn't gone too well with
Cardinal N'Goru a few minutes ago. The heads-up display in the contact lens in his left eye might supply him with the curriculum vitae
of all the guests as they came aboard, but there was nothing on precisely where a prince was supposed to kiss the hand of a female cardinal. Eric had made for the proper fingertips, but Mary N'Goru, none
too charmed to begin with, had more or less shoved her ring in his

face, and scowled at him as if he had committed a faux pas by neglecting to kneel.

"The famous Dr. Davinda, I believe? Welcome aboard."

The tall, thin, slovenly dressed man with eyes deeply set in blackened sockets gave him the strangest haunted paranoid look, as if caught in some vile sexual act or under the influence of some even viler drug and possibly both.

"I do hope there's nothing but the famous local weather in that climate model you've brought for us from sunny northern California."

The fellow's eyes all but rolled like slot-machine tumblers, and came up as blankly vacant as well-polished cue balls. He skittered boorishly past Eric as if he didn't exist, or as if he wished Eric didn't exist, without so much as a return word of greeting.

What did I say? Eric wondered, covering his discomfort by quickly kissing the next available hand, which fortunately turned out to be feminine.

Could it be that Davinda didn't realize that a professional meeter and greeter on Prince Eric Esterhazy's exalted level would be accessing a database in the act thereof? Was he perhaps stoned and Californian enough to now be convinced that Eric was some vibrating Third Force psychic?

"Well, well, well, the famous Lydia Maren herself! Isn't scientific reporting a bit far from your usual purview . . . ?"

"Would I pass up ten days in Paris at the Ritz and the chance to party on your fabulous riverboat?"

"Would the sun fail to rise in the east? Would I serve Spanish Rioja with lobster Thermidor?"

"Not the last time I looked, but these days, quién sabe?"

And so it went and so it had been going, as Eric did his hostly duties wondering when, and as it went on even if, Monique Calhoun would finally come aboard.

And although he did not presently have a gun in his pocket, not just because he was looking forward to being glad to see her.

Word had come down from the board via Eduardo and thence through Mom that it was the opinion of Bad Boys that the chances of a fire-and-brimstone intro by a high diplomatic official of the Roman Catholic Church followed by an out-of-character speech and walk-out by the doyen of the conference being random bolides were about that of the dealer drawing two royal flushes in a row in an honest game of poker.

"Got Bread & Circuses written all over it, Eric," Mom had told him. "*Written*, like in *script*, get me?"

"Obviously they wanted to draw the sort of media attention to the opening that these boring things have never had. . . ."

"No shit, Sherlock! But why?"

"Why? Why not?"

"*Why not?* Why not shoot your wad on the first day of a ten-day conference? Use your head for something besides a pretty hat rack, Eric! Despite appearances, if B&C sets off a blast like that the first day, it *can't* be the capper! If they fire such big guns up front, it's got to be to have the lights and cameras around for something much bigger later."

"Like what?"

"Eduardo thinks that maybe that's for Monique Calhoun to know and you to find out. You fucked her yet, Eric?"

"*Mother!* A gentleman never tells!"

"I'm not asking a *gentleman*, I'm asking *you*."

Eric had been sourly constrained to tell the unflattering truth, and Mom had told him in no uncertain terms to get cracking, and it was hard for him to decide whether this maternal demand to get down to the business of mixing business with pleasure took something of an edge off his natural desire or was a kink that would turn it up a notch when the time came.

Eric went through the motions with growing annoyance, which became anxiety, and then perplexity, as *La Reine* took on its full nightly load of passengers, before Monique Calhoun finally sauntered out of the embarkation pavilion and up the gangway. She was appetizingly enough presented in a tight kelly-green pants suit, but the way she moved somehow wasn't quite flaunting what she manifestly had, and, strangely enough considering her syndic's professional triumph of this afternoon, she did not have the look on her face of a happy camper.

Eric made with the dreamy smile and the hand-kiss anyway. "I thought you'd never get here, Monique. . . ."

The distracted look in her eyes raised the question as to whether she yet had. "First the sheep, then the shepherdess," she said.

Eric gave her a perplexed look.

"I've been here all along checking the arrivals against my guest list," she told him. "Doing my job."

"Bread before circuses, as it were . . . ?"

"The circus had an early matinee today, or didn't you notice?" Monique said, in a tone of voice neither pleased nor amused.

"Ah you mean the sturm und drama at the conference," Eric ventured, fishing for he knew not quite what. "Marvelous theater!"

Monique Calhoun suddenly snapped out of her funk to give him a hard appraising look of the sort that said *maybe you're not just a pretty face.* Which, while a compliment and in accord with Eric's own opinion of himself, made him realize that he had made a tactical blunder he had better cover.

"One hardly has to be a major drama critic to recognize acting, Monique," he prattled in a tone of airheaded silkiness. "And after all, I just welcomed aboard this floating den of iniquity the very cardinal who spoke out so stirringly against sin and the climatologist who might have walked out of her own conference but only as far as the opening-night party."

He took her hand. "Shall we join them?"

"One . . . professional to another?" Monique said, favoring Eric with a tiny ironic smile.

Takes one to know one, he tactically refrained from rejoining.

Monique Calhoun might not be in much of a mood for a party, but she could appreciate how well Prince Eric put one on, *one professional to another.*

Anyone could have produced the magnificent food by hiring a world-class chef and getting out of the way. But the way he had squared the circle of a straight buffet, which would've been tacky on a boat famous for its restaurant, and the fact that the said restaurant could seat less than half of the guests at any one formal setting, had been quite clever.

A lavish hot and cold buffet had indeed been set up at one end of the restaurant, where people could be served their choices on cunning platters with holes in them to hold wineglasses. But those who wished to do so could seat themselves at the fully laid restaurant tables and be served from the buffet by waiters.

The music was just right too.

In the restaurant, an all-acoustic string and piano quartet quietly played jazz rearrangements of Baroque music, while in the casino, where something a bit more raucous was required, it was synth, electric guitars, sitar and tabla drums doing Hindu Hard but at a relatively low level.

That might be mere professional competence. But that neither band used a singer to interfere with conversation was a master touch all too unfortunately missing in so many soirees that Monique had attended.

And watching Eric Esterhazy work a room taught Monique that he was a lot more than an excellent caterer who looked good on the door.

"Good to see you back on board, been a while, hasn't it Dieter, back when you were still married to Maria, as I remember. . . ."

"Better than I do, Eric, it all seems like a dream now, and not a very pleasant one. . . ."

He was constantly on the move, but ever so slowly, languidly, seemingly randomly, never appearing to be table or conversation hopping while agilely doing it just the same.

"Personally, Gail, I thought those notices were brain-dead. I may not know much about haute couture, but I know what I like. . . ."

"And so do I, Eric—tits and ass, tits and ass!"

Your perfect host, not merely moving from group to group, but melding groups into each other, moving people between them en passant.

"Yes, this *is* sort of an unofficial official party for the climate conference, Jean-Pierre, and if you want to meet Dr. Larabee, come along with me. . . ."

That he seemed to know everyone on *his* guest list—which seemed to run to show business and infotainment movers and shapers, syndic heavyweights, patrons and practitioners of the arts, high-level bureaucrats, and the sort of celebrities who, like himself, were famous for being famous—was hardly surprising.

"Allison, if I'm not interrupting, this is my good friend Jean-Pierre Balfort, chairman of the Syndique de la Seine. Jean-Pierre, Dr. Allison Larabee, of Condition Venus fame, and, I believe, Dr. Franco Niri, who was short-listed for the Nobel a few years back, and Dr. Istavan Bukan, the fellow in charge of the smoke and mirrors that keeps the Gulf Stream going and our Parisian asses from freezing off. . . ."

But that he seemed to recognize everyone on *hers* and not only greeted them by name but dropped the sort of bits of knowledge that hinted he knew and had admired their careers had to mean that he had either an eidetic memory or psychic powers, or more likely was using the sort of contact lens dataprompt favored by campaigning politicians and private club bartenders.

"You're the cow fart man, aren't you, Dr. Collins? All that methane!"

"Not just cows, Prince Esterhazy, all ruminants contribute their fair share of greenhouse gases. *Billions* of cubic meters per annum."

"Which is why we should stop raising them and switch to getting our protein from beans instead. . . . ?"

"Bart was a confirmed vegetarian to begin with!"

"Well, I suppose I *could* give up tournedos Rossini and choucroute garni to save the biosphere if I had to, but on the other hand, beans make *me* fart, an all-too-common human condition, so wouldn't that just put us back to square one . . . ?"

Even the manner in which she had been allowed to spend the past two hours drifting about as a detached observer impressed her with Eric Esterhazy's professionalism. Knowing all too well that he had every intention of seducing her and that sooner or later in her own good time he was going to succeed, Monique had to admire the way he neither stooped to sidelong glances, nor attempted to squire her about, nor smarmily avoided her. She was one of the guests, and it was his job to make each and every one of them feel equally important.

Prince Eric was no mere professional bullshitter.

He was a true bullshit *artist*.

And only now, with the party well under way and their two guest lists thoroughly mixed, did Eric come sauntering over to her bearing two glasses of wine like the perfect host spying a nervous wallflower.

"You don't seem to be having all that good a time, Monique," he said, handing her one.

Monique shrugged. "I'm here as a working girl," she said.

"Oh? I thought you were a citizen-shareholder in Bread & Circuses, not Ladies of the Evening. . . ."

"There are times when the distinction seems a bit subtle. . . ." Monique found herself muttering.

Eric leaned closer, deep into her body-space by any cultural criterion. "Then this might be a good time for a quick trip belowdecks," he said.

"To do what?"

Eric beamed at her, took her hand. "Wouldn't you like to try out my equipment?"

"Getting a little crude, aren't we, Prince Charming?"

"The *surveillance* equipment," he hissed, without leaving the role of the seducer making his move to the eyes of any beholders. "Though of course, on the other hand, if you've got something better in mind . . ."

Monique could not help laughing.

Nor could she help realizing that in this moment she did.

"Loose zips sink spy ships, Eric," she told him, running a quick finger up through the air about a hand's breadth from his fly.

Eric led Monique Calhoun by the hand through the dining salon and down the stairs just as if they were one more couple on their merry way to one of the belowdecks boudoirs, and the gossip would make the obvious assumption when he returned to his hostly duties a half hour or so later.

It was part of the mystique. A gallant host did not refuse a lady. A good enough sophist might even contend it was in the line of duty.

Nor did Monique do anything to break the public illusion.

If that was what it was.

Eric had the feeling, by instinct and long experience, by the moist warmth of her palm, that warm moisture was gathering elsewhere, that if he suggested a detour, it would be an offer she would be hard put to refuse. But hard as *he* was to put that offer to her, as insistent as Mom was that he *do* it already, his sense of timing said, No, wait, she *will* come to you, so let her do it in her own time, and it will only be the sweeter.

Besides which she was playing the current game quite well, giving him a real match, and the prolonged frisson of arch frustration was not exactly unpleasant and in the end would only make the match point more enjoyable.

So Eric, true to his princely word, keyed them into the computer room with his retina-print. Although Ignatz was recording everything as usual, one of the security boys from Bad Boys was inside pretending to be a technician, the human component of the Potemkin interface hiding *La Reine*'s resident AI from Monique Calhoun.

Much of what he was whiling away the time watching was not what the conventional would deem fit for the eyes of a conventional lady, a dozen of the screens being filled with the feed from the boudoirs and toilets, and the sound system producing an unseemly cacophony of grunts, moans, gurgles, and splashes.

Eric dismissed him with a lidded scowl, but noted with interest that Monique seemed more amused than offended by the copulatory, excretory, and urinary live uncoverage.

"I can understand why you'd have sight and sound from the boudoirs and even the washrooms," she said, as they sat down in the swivel chairs, "but why the *toilet stalls*? What do you expect to happen there except . . . the usual?"

"You'd be surprised," Eric told her, though somehow he doubted it. "Nevertheless, let's kill the sound, and kill the toilet visuals," he said, typing random numbers on the keyboard and allowing Ignatz to create the illusion that he was actually controlling the mike and camera feeds in this primitive fashion.

"There," he said, "much more . . . stimulating."

Seven of the screens still showed couples—hetero, homo, and in one case an ambiguous threesome—having at it.

"Speak for yourself, Eric. If I want to watch porn, I'd prefer professional performers, decent lighting, and a director. The real thing just looks silly when you're watching it."

"Really? Haven't you ever done it with mirrors?"

"I'll bet *you* do all the time. And you probably don't even need a partner to enjoy it."

"Admittedly one does meet a better class of people."

Monique laughed. And Eric had to admit that this sort of repartee was more . . . stimulating than the action on the screens. Who was it who had said that the most sensitive erogenous zone was the human brain?

"Well, shall we have a quick tour of the less erotic aspects of the party?" Eric said somewhat reluctantly.

He hit 'Control H,' which automatically replaced the boudoir feed on six screens with the schematics of the boat and their plethora of camera and microphone numbers.

Moving the cursor over the numbers on the diagrams with the trackpoint and clicking the pickup equipment on was within the limits of Eric's modest computer expertise, and so he did it, more or less at random.

This filled the remaining fourteen video screens with a series of new visuals, but it also resulted in a screech of babble, as fourteen microphone feeds came gibbering out the sound system together.

"Uh, I think Control S also cuts the sound," Eric shouted for the benefit of Ignatz as he typed it, who, picking up on the voice command, made it so.

"And then . . . to hear the feed from a microphone, you just put the cursor on it, and type Control M. . . ."

Eric did so with a microphone picking up a table in the restaurant.

"—said that the only reason to be here at all was the food and drink—"

"Well, Esterhazy *does* know how to cater a party, but *some* of the people at *this* one—"

"Boring!" Eric said hastily and switched to Allison Larabee having a tête-à-tête with Paolo Pereiro out by the aft upper-deck rail.

"Embarrassing, you mean!" said Monique.

"—means necessary."

"Oh really, Allison, such cheap theatrics. . . ."

"Maybe, but this really *could* be our last chance."

"You know as well as I do that the Condition Venus model is full of unresolved variables. . . ."

"And whose climate model isn't?"

"Mine at least was eighty percent predictive in its time."

"In its *time frame*, Paolo, which was quite modest."

"Whereas yours is far too ambitious to be predictive of anything short-term at all."

"I hope I'm wrong, but I'm afraid I'm right."

"I'll believe it when I see one of your white—"

"Tedious climatech babble," said Eric, cutting to two stools at the forward bar, where Lydia Maren was attempting to pick up Geoff Gilden, the Lloyds ambassador to Paris. "*Much* more amusing."

"—in any of the boudoirs downstairs?"

"Oh, I've done the dungeon, once or twice, ma chérie."

"S or M?"

"Depends on my mood, the phase of the moon. . . ."

"What's so amusing about *this?*" Monique demanded.

"She seems to have no idea that Geoff is thoroughly gay."

Monique frowned at him. "If you're through peeping through keyholes, Eric," she said, "may I give it a try myself?"

And she reached for the trackpoint, placed the cursor on the feed from a table in the private aft bar, where Hassan bin Mohammed was having a hunched, hushed conversation with three other men, hit Control M.

"—but it's in their syndic charter—"

"—too risky—"

"Mmmm, the Chairman of the CCC," muttered Monique, "this might be interesting, *how* did you say I record?"

"Uh . . . you record by keeping the cursor where it is and hitting Control R." Eric said for the benefit of Ignatz.

"—sure the effects will be transient?"

"—define sure—"

"—certain—"

"—a mathematical impossibility as every failed attempt at a definitive model has proven—"

"Who are these guys, anyway?" Monique muttered.

Eric shrugged. His dataprompt identified them as Hideki Manimoto, a contract climatech engineer for an orbital mirror corp; bin Mohammed's deputy at the Committee of Concerned Climatologists, Aubrey Wright; and the chairman of Erdewerke, Bernard Kutnik— but telling *her* that would of course be giving too much away.

"—numbers then—"

"—ninety-three percent—"

"—minimal risk, I'd say—"

"—famous last words—"

"—precisely what we're trying to prevent—"

"—at a profit, of course, Bernie—"

"—a wise man does well by doing good—"

"Oh really!" Eric groaned, and he moved the cursor to another screen, where an unlikely threesome of the female captain of the sixteenth arrondissement's Force Flic and two males, one a Bad Boys importer, the other a not-all-that-well-known actor, were sashaying arm-in-arm-in-arm down the corridor past the boudoir doors.

"—the Sun King's?"

"—too retro—"

"I'll place my bet on the sauna, Monique, what about you?"

"—the tree house—?"

"—missing one Jane—"

"Don't you have *any* interests that aren't prurient, Eric?"

"—the dungeon—"

"—what kind of boys do you think we are—?"

Eric leered at her languidly. "Give me a week and I'll think of one," he told her. "Don't you have any that are?"

"—just a big enough overbid to stick them with the contract—"

It had taken Monique Calhoun less time to learn the simple command structure than it had to outlast Eric Esterhazy's smarmy attempts to seduce her via voyeurism; in fact, she supposed a reasonably intelligent chimpanzee wouldn't have taken much longer.

"—a smile like the Mona Lisa with nothing but hard vacuum behind it—"

"—cruel, Terry, really cruel—"

So the so-called technician Eric had summoned when he finally left her alone in the computer room was probably a minder who needed to know about as much about the equipment as she did about quantum mechanics to do the job.

"—tornadoes, more like superheated thermals, not a true atmospheric vortex—"

"—fits the model though—"

"—if no one's looking too closely—"

At first, Monique had played along with the charade, calling out locations on the boat, and letting the "tech" enter them with the keyboard.

"—think they're telling us everything—"

"—only what serves the *client's* interests, Jean-Luc—"

But it soon became obvious that she could do just as well or better with the boat schematics and the cursor herself. And if her suspicions needed any confirmation, she got it from the way Eric's minder raised no objection at all to handing over the controls, quite out of character for the techie type.

"—desperation, if you ask me, they've sucked the Lands of the Lost dry—"

"—still money to be made adjusting to the local adjustment, always will be—"

What was *not* obvious, upon reflection, was what she was supposed to be doing here, how she was supposed to do it, or why.

So she had learned to operate the surveillance equipment, but what was she supposed to be looking for? And even if she *knew* what she was looking for, how was she going to find and record it in this chaos of images and sound from hundreds of cameras and microphones?

And why me, anyway?

"—like dogs and cats, the nastiest backstage atmosphere I've ever seen—"

"—didn't seem to hurt the production, though—"

She was supposed to be here running Bread & Circuses VIP services, not playing Mata Hari for Mossad. What would happen if she told Avi Posner just that? To piss off and let her do her real job?

But Monique knew in the pit of her stomach that it would not be a smart career move to try to find out. Meaning she was *afraid* to find out. Meaning she was over her head in waters she had never had a desire to swim in. *Political* waters, her grandparents' waters, the Hot and Cold War.

"—a lot worse at the turn of the millennium, everything from flying saucer cults to the Second Coming—"

"—Jesus or Elvis—?"

"—both, and half of them didn't know which one played the guitar—"

Monique had never considered herself a political person, whatever that might still mean in this largely post-sovereign world. From what she had seen in her travels, patriotism, emotional allegiance to a geographical or ethnic identity, sovereign or semi-sovereign, living or dead, was the hobgoblin of mesmerized minds.

"—the central Sahara, Kansas, Australia, need deserts to make it work—"

"—and the hottest spots to make it plausible—"

Her only true allegiance was to Bread & Circuses, the syndic of which she was a citizen-shareholder, and that wasn't political in the bad old bug-brained sense. That was a confluence of her individual and its collective self-interest. That was enlightened syndicalism.

Never be a citizen of anything in which you would not want to hold shares.

"—most beautiful country left on the planet, and a climate to die for now that the rainfall's under control—"

"—for *who* to die for is the usual question, White Man—"

So her heart was not made of emerald-green stone. So she had seen far too much of the Lands of the Lost not to feel True Blue inside. But that was *conscience*, wasn't it, not politics? *Idealism*, if you wanted to get sloppy about it.

"—used by artists and scientists and mystics to enhance their consciousness—"

"—and brain-burn cases to get wasted—"

Something that was not an obvious feature of the revenant capitalist corporations displaying their climatech wares in the Grand Palais. Cool this place down, heat that one up, cloud-cover here, burn it away from orbit there—their only allegiance was to what they had called in the age of capitalism the sacred bottom line. They did it for the money.

"—never been so disgusted in all my life—"

"—de gustibus non vomitorium, my dear—"

Big Blue was a mercenary outfit.

Everyone knew that.

Didn't they?

So what does that make me?

Just a cog in the gearing of the Big Blue Machine. A pawn in some game I don't even understand. Upon which the fate of the Earth might hang. Or just a lot of fat contracts.

Do I really want to know?

Does it matter?

Not really, Monique realized sourly, because either way it leaves me right where I already am.

The choice had never been hers to make.

This was politics.

And like it or not she was in it.

"Summon Prince Eric to key me out of here," she told her faux-techie minder. "I do believe I need a breath of fresh air."

6

GIVEN THE MEDIA SPOTLIGHT TURNED ON THE
United Nations Annual Conference On Climate Stabilization by the
sudden advent of the so-called white tornadoes and the obvious self-
interest of Bread & Circuses and the client in turning it up even
higher than such a harbinger of planetary doom might naturally inspire, Monique Calhoun was prepared for the pandemonium that
greeted her as she arrived at the Grand Palais for the emergency plenary session of UNACOCS.

There was a large and raucous crowd of demonstrators on the
Avenue Churchill sidewalk across from the Grand Palais, held back
by Force Flic horsemen, and waving placards bearing such slogans as
COOL THE EARTH NOW!, STOP CONDITION VENUS!, and A BLUE
WORLD OR NONE! though mercifully neither REPENT NOW! nor THE
END IS NIGH!"

What Monique had not quite been prepared for was such *well-
organized* pandemonium.

Not only were the placards slickly printed, they seemed limited
to about half a dozen slogans, and although the color of the type
varied, the print font did not. There were even computer-enhanced
stills from the only extant TV footage of a white tornado.

The *same* still cloned dozens of times.

The entrance to the Grand Palais itself was being kept clear by a functional semicircle of flics on foot armed with electric wands, but the horsemen holding back the crowd across the street were Garde Républicain in full fancy kit—plumed steel helmets, cloaks, costume swords—available for ceremonial occasions only at a hefty premium.

The gutter itself was jammed with camera crews who threatened to outnumber the demonstrators, and although it was a bright sunny afternoon, they turned on brilliant white shooting lights to herald the entry of major players, cuing shouting, screaming, and pro forma surging against the Force Flic lines, and pro forma gooses with electric wands by the flics, who made a pro forma show of displeasure. Even Monique got her share of eye-killing glare and incoherent shouting as her pass got her inside.

The vast trade show floor, on the other hand, was eerily empty of people, even camera crews, except for those streaming through the exhibits toward the makeshift auditorium and the guards at the canvas enclosure hiding the mysterious whatever.

The atmosphere inside the Grand Palais was oppressively grim and electric. It took Monique a long moment to realize that this was at least in part due to a deliberately created visual special effect.

The smart glass panels of the roof had been adjusted so that the bright blue sky outside became the sinister luminescent gray of an impending thunderstorm in which the sun was bleached but undimmed to roughly simulate a schematic version of the furnace vortex of a white tornado.

And when you entered the makeshift auditorium itself, your eye was immediately drawn to a loop of video footage of the real thing cycling on the big screen behind the stage:

Mirage-shimmering desert that could've been the Sahara or central Australia or Nevada or the sere empty waste at any low-latitude continental heartland under a bleached-out cloudless sky. In the middle distance, a whirling white maelstrom abruptly rises from the desert floor, corkscrewing upward, sucking sand and rock with it, rising up into the stratosphere for all the camera eye can tell, persists for a minute or so, then like footage of the birth of a conventional tornado run backward, disappears *upward* into the empty sky.

And again, and again, and again, endlessly.

By all accounts, the white tornadoes were quite transient, at least so far, and occurred only in the hottest of hot spots long since all-but-abandoned by humans, so this brief footage shot by a scientific expedition who had chanced to be on the scene of one was all there was.

But there had been anecdotal accounts of distant sightings. And satellite instruments had picked up a few of the white tornadoes from on high. And measured their temperature and internal wind velocities.

The white tornadoes seemed to be superheated columns of air, monster thermal updrafts that developed a vortex whirl as they rose through the atmosphere, then, cooled by the upward expansion, de-stabilized at their base and disappeared skyward.

That was about as much as was known about the white tornadoes. As to what was causing them to appear now, how many there had been, whether the phenomenon might continue, what might happen next, there were a thousand theories, all of which when translated into screaming news headers came out: "CONDITION VENUS! END OF THE WORLD!"

"End of the World" or not, however, Jean-Luc Tri made no hyp-ocritical attempt to hide his glee when Monique reached the reserved Bread & Circuses seats in the otherwise standing-room-only audito-rium.

"Look at this crowd! What coverage! I only wish I had thought of it myself!"

"You mean you didn't?" Monique said dryly.

Jean-Luc laughed. "I'm good," he said. "I would not give you an argument if you said I was the greatest. I would love to take the credit." He shrugged. "But God, I am not."

Maybe not, but Monique had it from the source that it had been Ariel Mamoun who had broached the idea of an emergency plenary session of the conference to Lars Bendsten when the story broke. And Jean-Luc who had secured the only footage of a white tornado for UNACOCS and had probably suggested using this loop of it as the background visual for the emergency session. And probably had a word or two with the Grand Palais people about the smart glass effects too.

Bread & Circuses!

Of course B&C could not possibly have created this mysterious climatological phenomenon. But who but Bread & Circuses could have so quickly and thoroughly turned it to the client's advantage?

Monique should've been proud of her syndic. And on a professional level, she supposed she was. But there was another level on which the whole thing was elusively disturbing.

Okay, the organized crowd supplied with professional placards, the max coverage, the visual grace note of the Garde Républicain, the smart glass special effect—standard B&C technique, nothing to upset the conscience about a little scene setting like that, now was there?

But were these "white tornadoes" *really* the apocalyptic event that the coverage was making of them? Was it *really* time to panic?

After all, if you took a deep breath, and stood to one side of the hype, were a few hyperthyroid dust devils *really* major disasters?

On a planet that had seen a rise in temperature that turned farmland into wasteland and wasteland into deadland and the flooding of the littoral homelands of hundreds of millions and the breakup of at least one of its polar ice caps?

The impending advent of Condition Venus?

Was the sky *really* falling?

Was the End of the World *really* Nigh?

Or was Chicken Little a Bread & Circuses professional too?

"Open sez me."

"I hear and obey, Little Master of All the World."

Given the silly pun password, it seemed only appropriate to Eric Esterhazy to have Ignatz reply through the persona of a genie out of a hokey Arabian Nights pic.

Certainly better than having the AI talk through the persona of Mom, which was a menu option too. The real thing had been more than enough for one day.

It was afternoon, *La Reine de la Seine* was moored at the Quai Branly, and Eric had the boat and the computer room more or less to himself, besides which, if he wasn't quite master of all the world, he was for present practical purposes the master of this little part of it.

Much of the rest of the world might be flapping its arms and rushing about in front of television and net coverage of the emergency session of the UNACOCS conference, but Eric had more important things to do. If the world came to an end this afternoon, he'd just have to catch it on the late news playback.

Eric had been having lunch with Mom at a favorite Chinese restaurant when the subject of the so-called white tornadoes had arisen in the conversation as it must have at that moment in tens of thousands of such luncheon conversations all over Paris.

"Seems to me I've heard the term somewhere before . . ."

"Hardly surprising, Eric, seeing as how the white tornadoes've replaced the King Bobbie's sex-change operation as the hot media wank . . ."

"I mean *before* they made the news. . . ."

"What? You're *sure* about this, Eric?"

"Not really . . ."

"Where? When?"

"I don't really remember. . . ."

"*Think*, fer chrissakes, Eric! You *do* know how to think, don't you? It's not *really* as hard as it seems. You just forget about your pecker for five minutes and pretend your most important organ's located between your ears."

"I'm not even sure I heard the two words together in the same conversation . . . it was all rather jumbled together and cut up somehow, as I recall. . . ."

Mom had pounced on that like a mongoose.

"*Like a lot of random microphone feed over the surveillance equipment on the boat?*"

"Now that you mention it . . ."

"Hell's bells, Eric, I have to *mention* it before you take your head out of your rectum? Who? When?"

Eric had shrugged.

"Don't you think it would be sort of swift if you found out?"

Eric had indeed been constrained to agree.

"Phrase search, Ignatz. White and tornado or tornadoes."

"Time-frame, Master?"

Let's see, the story broke yesterday, so . . .

"Go back three days, then forward for forty-eight hours."

"Your wish is my voice command."

The stage was as packed as the auditorium, additional folding chairs shoehorned together to accommodate the crush. Every chair but one barely held the vibrating butt of an attending climatologist, nineteen of the heavyweights, each eager to get in the first and/or last word. If the individual mikes had been on, it would already have been a tower of media Babel; they were already arguing with each other. Such was the chaos that the return of Allison Larabee to the conference she had so recently stormed out of had created no drama at all.

In the center of the lion cage sat Lars Bendsten, pressed into service to preside over the emergency session. From the look on his face, it seemed to Monique that, provided merely with a mike and a mike control panel in lieu of the traditional whip and pistol, he was wondering how long it would be before he was forced to stand up and defend his ground with his chair.

"The emergency plenary session will now come to order," he began. When it didn't, the General Secretary turned up the gain on his microphone and commanded it by brute auditory force. "THE EMERGENCY PLENARY SESSION WILL NOW COME TO ORDER."

It did, more or less.

"We will conduct this session in a rational and civilized manner," Bendsten said, turning his volume back down to a more bearable level and proceeding in his standard UN diplomat's voice.

"Each of the participants will have five minutes to make an opening statement, and then the floor will be opened to discussion."

The mighty collective groan that arose at this came from the news crews massed in front of the stage. If everyone stuck to their time limit, an optimistic assumption indeed, it would be at least an hour and a half before the real show began.

"As it was written, so it has been done, Little Master," said Ignatz. "Search completed. Twenty-seven instances of 'white tornado' recorded within the time-frame of the search parameters."

"*Really?*" said Eric. Mom was right, he thought out of all-too-well-ingrained reflex.

"By the Beard of the Prophet, I swear it to be true, oh Little Master of All the World!"

Eric decided that the genie of the lamp had already gotten tedious. "Identify the speakers," he said, replacing it with the breathy purr of Marilyn Monroe.

"In alphabetical order, *Eric* . . . Dr. Jackson Belaview, Hans Cartwright, Chu Lun, Birgit Holmgren, Bernard Kutnik, Dr. Allison Larabee, Hideki Manimoto, Horace McPherson, Hassan bin Mohammed, Dr. Paolo Pereiro, Aubrey Wright."

"That many!"

"*Exactly* that many . . . *Eric*."

No question about it, "white tornadoes" had definitely been a hot topic of conversation before their advent. Curiouser and curiouser.

"Tag the speakers," Eric said, replacing the distraction of Marilyn with the flat neutral voice of the twentieth-century actor Leonard Nimoy playing the logical alien, Mr. Spock.

"Dr. Jackson Belaview, meteorologist. Hans Cartwright, President, Orbital Solutions, Incorporated. Chu Lun, Minister of Environment, Guangdong. Birgit Holmgren, Chairwoman of the Board, Environmental Imagineers S. A. Bernard Kutnik, Chairperson of the Board, Erdewerke, A. G. Dr. Allison Larabee, climatologist. Hideki Manimoto, engineer, Orbital Solutions, Incorporated. Horace McPherson, Chief of Public Relations, Committee of Concerned Climatologists. Hassanbin Mohammed, Chairperson, Committee of Concerned Climatologists. Dr. Paolo Pereiro, climatologist. Aubrey Wright, General Secretary, Committee of Concerned Climatologists."

Eric didn't need to be Machiavelli or even Mom to realize that most, if not all, of these personages were one way or another, on one level or another, associated with the Big Blue Machine.

And with the "white tornadoes."

Ergo, the white tornadoes were associated with Big Blue.

You didn't need the logic of Mr. Spock to figure that much out either.

But . . .

Why?

They couldn't . . .

Could they?

They wouldn't . . .

Would they?

Oh yes they would, if they could, and had a bottom-line reason why!

"Sequence the conversations and play them back in chronological order," he told Ignatz.

"Illogical command, Captain. Some of them took place simultaneously."

"Well then just give me those in alphabetical sub-order!" Eric snapped irritably.

"Illogical command, Captain. Alphabetize according to what parameter?"

"According to *whatever*," Eric groaned. "According to a random number program. According to the last name of whoever said the keywords first. According to the I-Ching."

Some twisted impulse made him replace Mr. Spock with Mom as he parroted one of her all-too-familiar lines at Ignatz.

"Use your noodle for a change, kiddo!"

"Now you're finally using yours, Eric!" the Artificial Intelligence said.

Surreal boredom was a concept that would have previously seemed self-contradictory to Monique Calhoun.

However the possibility of its existence was being amply demonstrated now, as one after another climatologist delivered learned discourses, most of which were puffs for the efficacy of their own climate models, while everyone else waited for Allison Larabee herself to have the last formal word.

While behind them, on the giant screen, the endless loop of the white tornado towered over the proceedings with the iconic menace of the previous century's mushroom pillar cloud.

Perhaps without the presence of the image of the impending apocalypse in question, Monique might have found this symposium moderately interesting. Certainly she had already learned more about the art of climate modeling than she had ever thought she wanted to know.

And first and foremost, though the participants would never own up to it themselves, was that climate modeling, at least in its current state, *was* as much an art as a science.

Since even if the data *were* sufficient, even if a definitive climate model program *could* be written, there existed no computer of sufficient power to run it on, all the malarkey about "indeterminacy," "plus or minus x percent," "insufficient data," "margin of error," "random factors," and the rest of it, seemed to be academic euphemisms for estimations, fudge factors, or just plain bullshit.

In the twentieth century, or so Monique had heard, they used to say that everyone talked about the weather, but nobody did anything about it. Now that everyone was doing something about it, the futile talk had shifted to the results thereof upon the planetary climate, but none of these savants had produced a climate model that had really proven predictive.

Except perhaps one.

Models were presented that had indeed in the past predicted the breakup of the north polar ice cap, the weakening of the Gulf Stream, the permanent El Niño, the rapid southward march of the Sahara, the rough rate of the sea-level rise, and all the rest of it. Indeed it was fair to say—and each partisan of their own model certainly did—that there wasn't a major aspect of the rapidly changing climate that *someone's* climate model hadn't predicted.

But it was also true that none of the climate models being put forth here as the latest state of the art hadn't missed predicting one or more of the major climatic events. And therefore, given their track records, none of them had much credibility when it came to forecasting what would happen next.

Except perhaps one.

Only Dr. Allison Larabee's Condition Venus model had yet to be discredited by conspicuous failure to predict a major climatic change, perhaps because it was more speculative than the others, broader, looking further ahead. Admittedly it hadn't yet got anything right that the others had gotten wrong either. . . .

Or had it?

The image glowering over the palaver ominously suggested otherwise. The video loop of the white tornado continually reminded the audience and the cameras, if not, it would seem, the speakers, that *it* was what this emergency plenary session of the United Nations Annual Conference On Climatic Stabilization was supposed to be about.

Meaning that the fidgeting and murmuring grew and grew as speaker after speaker droned on while everyone else waited in impatient and expectant boredom for Larabee.

"This is an excruciation," Ariel Mamoun groaned.

Jean-Luc Tri shrugged. "At least it's a build."

"But we've probably lost most of the live coverage," Mamoun said.

"Bendsten didn't really have much choice," Jean-Luc pointed out. "Anyone he put on after Larabee would be like shoving a dog act onstage after the magician pulls a live brontosaur out of his top hat."

"He could at least have limited the speakers to two minutes each," Monique suggested wearily.

Jean-Luc snorted. "And repealed the law of gravity while he was at it."

"Ready when you are, C.B.," said Ignatz's simulation of Mom's voice.

"Roll 'em," said Eric. "Screen one."

On the chosen screen, Hassan bin Mohammed, the Chairperson of the CCC, Bernard Kutnik, Chairperson of the Board of Erdewerke, Hideki Manimoto, the engineer from Orbital Solutions, and bin Mohammed's deputy Aubrey Wright, sat around a table in the aft bar.

"But why *not* let Bread & Circuses in on it?" said Wright. "We're their client. They're professionals. Their job is to promote our agenda."

"Can't really trust their discretion with something like *this*," bin Mohammed told him.

"But it's in their syndic charter."

"Hassan is right," said Kutnik. "It's too risky." He turned to Manimoto. "You're *sure* the effects will be transient?"

"Define sure."

"Certain. Beyond a doubt."

Manimoto shrugged. "When it comes to predicting the global climatic effects of local alterations, there's no such thing, it's a mathematical impossibility as every failed attempt at a definitive model has proven."

"Well give us numbers then," said Kutnik.

"Ninety-three percent chance that the effects will dissipate once the mirrors are no longer focused on the target areas."

There was a long moment of silence as Bernard Kutnik took a sip of his drink, and one by one the others followed suit, Kutnik, bin Mohammed, and Wright exchanging glances over the rims of their glasses. It seemed to Eric that this little cabal wasn't so much pausing to ponder some decision, but rather nerving themselves up to go ahead and act on a decision that had long since been made.

Kutnik finally shrugged and spoke. "A minimal risk, I'd say."

"Famous last words?" Wright suggested sardonically.

"That is precisely what we're trying to prevent."

"At a profit, of course, Bernie."

"A wise man does well by doing good."

"By any means necessary?"

Kutnik scowled. "You just heard Manimoto assure us that the white tornadoes will have no lasting effect."

"A ninety-three percent probability, Bernie."

"Considering the alternative, I'd say those are odds we can hardly afford not to accept."

"Pause," said Eric. "Well, what do you think of *that?*"

"*What do I think of that?* Jeez, Eric, I don't *think* anything of any-thing, I'm just an Artificial Intelligence, I'm not *really* your mother. And even if I were, I'd be telling you to use your own head."

Eric shook the cobwebs out of the said organ, replaced Mom with the neutral computer voice for the sake of clarity.

"Is there more on this engineer Manimoto?"

"Yes."

"Go to that."

On the screen, Hideki Manimoto stood with Hans Cartwright, President of Orbital Solutions, on the extreme prow-end of the upper deck promenade as *La Reine de la Seine* slowly cruised past the half-drowned and thoroughly overgrown abstract statuary of the Tino Rossi sculpture gardens, eerie ruins, somehow, of a future that never was.

"White tornadoes is a misnomer, Mr. Cartwright," he said. "What we're going to simulate won't be tornadoes, more like superheated thermals, not a true atmospheric vortex—"

"It fits the model though, doesn't it?"

"If no one's looking too closely. Or has a chance to study them for very long."

"*How* closely? *How* long?"

"A reciprocal relationship. From the surface, it would be hard to tell. If anyone's monitoring the mirrors—"

"Pause," said Eric.

And paused to think himself.

He didn't need to be a rocket scientist to know that Manimoto *was* a rocket scientist, or anyway was in the employ of Orbital Solutions, one of the outfits that maintained and rented out a string of orbital solar mirrors.

Or that these mirrors, ordinarily hired for such tasks as maintaining the Gulf Stream, burning off undesirable cloud cover in the monsoon latitudes, punching holes through temperature inversions, and undoing cooling effects for jurisdictions that didn't want them caused by the contracts of adjacent jurisdictions that did, probably had the power to produce these, what did he call them, superheated thermals.

And the head of Erdewerke had put out a contract with Orbital Solutions to do just that.

The white tornadoes were fakes.

And Bad Boys had the proof.

And this was surely a hot commodity.

How hot? How far did it go?

Follow the money, as the Wolves of Wall Street and the Gnomes of Zurich used to tell each other in the bad old days.

Besides Kutnik and Cartwright, Birgit Holmgren of Environmental Imagineers would seem to be in on it. And the Chairperson of the Committee of Concerned Climatologists. And his deputy. And his PR chief. And where was the UN getting the extra financing to hold this thing in Paris from in the first place?

Not just Erdewerke.

The collective slush fund of the Big Blue Machine.

Was the sainted *Allison Larabee* in on it too?

Perhaps there was a way to find out.

"Go to the Allison Larabee recording," he told Ignatz.

The white-haired savant in question leaned against the aft upperdeck railing talking with Paolo Pereiro.

"Do you really intend to sit out the rest of the conference, Allison?"

"That's not quite what I said," said Larabee. "I said *this* was the last one of these things I'm attending, and *that* I meant."

Pereiro eyed her narrowly. "So in other words, your dramatic walk-out was a piece of attention-getting sophistry, not sincere outrage."

"My outrage at six years' worth of useless talk that's gone nowhere is sincere all right, Paolo!" Larabee snapped back at him. "And I sincerely intend to do whatever I can to save the biosphere of this planet from the myopic stupidity of its top predator. By whatever means necessary."

"Oh really, Allison, such cheap theatrics do not exactly enhance your scientific credibility."

"Maybe, but this really *could* be our last chance."

"You know as well as I do that the Condition Venus model is full of unresolved variables."

"And whose climate model isn't?"

"Mine at least was eighty percent predictive in its time."

"In its *time-frame*, Paolo, which was quite modest."

"Whereas yours is far too ambitious to be predictive of anything short-term at all."

"I hope I'm wrong, but I'm afraid I'm right."

"I'll believe it when I see one of your white tornadoes."

"Will you, Paolo? Or will you shrug that off as one of my model's 'unresolved variables' too?"

Pereiro gave her a rueful but ameliorative little smile. "At least if the phenomenon occurs, we'll all have to admit that your model supersedes all of ours." His smile broadened and lightened. "And when can we hope to see one, Allison?" he said. "The time-frame's always been a bit vague."

Dr. Allison Larabee was not amused. "Hope to see one? Believe me, I hope we *never* see one! Because if we start seeing white tornadoes, it just might be too late."

"Pause," said Eric. Ignatz paused the tape, and Eric pondered.

The Larabee recording was ambiguous. Someone who wished to believe she was not in on the white tornado fakery could easily enough convince herself of her own innocence.

But spinmeisters could easily enough make the point that Larabee had probably been following a Bread & Circuses script when she walked out of the conference, since this conversation with Pereiro had taken place *before* Big Blue faked the white tornadoes.

And if a case could be made that Larabee was in on it, a case could also be made that so was *the Roman Catholic Church*, that Cardinal N'Goru's fire-breathing sermon had been a deliberate lead-in to Larabee's act, scripted by B&C too.

In a trial by justice syndic, the Larabee recording would prove nothing. But in a trial by media, it could be made to suggest anything.

How hot was this material?

Hot enough to melt down the UNACOCS conference into slag, maybe take the Big Blue Machine and the United Nations with it, and have enough heat left over to take care of what was left of both polar ice caps too.

Hot enough to get a phony prince taken as a man of consequence within his syndic. Hot enough to take directly to Eduardo Ramirez.

Monique realized that she had been staring vacantly at the white tornado for several speakers now. The endlessly repeating video loop seemed to function as an animated mandala, drawing the focus of her attention into its depths as the only escape from the boredom of the proceedings short of nodding off.

As several people in the audience had actually done, one of whom had produced snores of sufficient volume to garner him an elbow in the ribs from a neighbor.

Most of the speakers were Blue, as they had always been at these things, most of the climate models they presented were therefore similar, most of them concluded that the mean planetary temperature should be stabilized at a lower level than at present, and what differences there were were over the means of achieving this, which boiled down pretty much to pub for what was being hawked in the trade show outside by the financial sponsors of the conference.

It was like being forced to endure the screening of endless dull amateurish television commercials one after another.

Like?

This event, after all, *was* being put on for the benefit of what world television and net audience hadn't yet tuned it out. The speeches *were* commercials, for the climate models of the speakers, for the services of the Big Blue Machine.

It was television from hell—all bad commercials and no program.

". . . John Sri Davinda."

"At last," groaned Ariel Mamoun. "There's no one left but Larabee after this."

Davinda wore a faux-African dashiki-shirt and authentically threadbare antique American jeans. His mousy brown hair was done in a buzz cut. His eyes . . .

His eyes . . .

His eyes reminded Monique that Davinda was the Californian climatologist for whom she had had to procure that obscure hallucinogenic cactus, at no little hassle, all the way from the Tex-Mex desert.

Those bloodshot sclera, those enormous pupils, that vacant stare, seemed to indicate that Davinda had not let her efforts be in vain.

"Are we become Shiva, Breaker of Worlds?" he began in a loud but quavery and somehow haunted voice.

"Insufficient realtime processing capacity," he said in quite another voice, this one flat and affectless.

Uneasy murmurs swept in waves through the audience.

"Are all our climate models written on the wind blowing through Maya's tattered veils?" Davinda declaimed.

Again, a schizoid alter ego seemed to answer in that mechanical parody of a synthesized software voice: "No deterministic outcome is inherent in the data."

"Mon Dieu," groaned Ariel Mamoun, "he's up there *talking to himself!*"

"To be or not to be, is that the operative algorithm of the question?"

"The algorithmic time-frame has not been specified."

Davinda's blink rate went sky-high when he spoke in what seemed to be his natural voice, dropped suddenly when he answered his own crypticisms in what to Monique's mercifully untrained ear seemed like nerdish computer babble.

"Are these the Last Days? Is this the Great Wheel's final turning?"

"Insufficient realtime processing capacity."

"Merde!" exclaimed Ariel. "Speaking in tongues! Next will he produce a basket of snakes and proceed to handle them?"

"Condition Venus? Condition Terminal?"

"No deterministic outcome is inherent in the data."

"The man is drunk!" exclaimed Ariel Mamoun.

"*Stoned* is probably a more accurate description," Monique muttered guiltily.

"But literate," said Jean-Luc Tri.

"Is Chaos the condition of Lao's Tao?"

"Third Force gibberish!" someone shouted from the audience, to general cries of agreement.

This seemed to bring Davinda back from somewhere.

"The . . . the results were not anticipated," he stammered. "The initial iteration was only partial."

"Get off!"

"The full implementation will not be demonstrated until—"

"Get him off!"

"Get him out of there!"

The learned audience now began to stamp its feet like a boorish soccer crowd. Lars Bendsten moved to the podium, put a gentle hand on Davinda's shoulder.

"I didn't know!" Davinda shouted.

Bendsten pulled at him rather less gently. And Davinda fairly roared, his voice now an eerie amalgam of his own and that of his strange computer-like alter-non-ego.

"All will be known when I become the Whirlwind's Voice!"

And with that, John Sri Davinda, or whatever peyote demon from a fractured id had been seeking to possess him, or both, seemed to deflate like a collapsing balloon, leaving a gaunt, pathetic, and de-energized figure standing there facing the boos and catcalls, all too eager now to let the General Secretary lead him away.

Once again, Allison Larabee was called upon to speak after a lead-in that had galvanized a dozing audience and probably brought back much of the lost live coverage too.

Monique cast a suspicious eye at Jean-Luc Tri.

"Was *that* one of your scripts too?" she asked half-seriously.

Jean-Luc shook his head. "Don't I wish!" he said.

"You can't say I didn't warn you," Allison Larabee began unceremoniously. "My climate model predicted the onset of Condition Venus in roughly this time-frame and you responded with these conferences which only served to keep the world asleep. After all, Larabee's climate model hasn't discredited itself like all the others by failing to predict the usual microchanges only because it doesn't try to. And nothing in the Condition Venus scenario's happened yet. . . ."

Dr. Larabee turned to gaze up at the white tornado whirling behind her.

"Yet?" she repeated sardonically. "You wanted *yet?*" She gestured at the vortex. "Well here's your *yet!*" she said.

She turned to regard the audience, or rather the cameras.

"For all you folks out there who haven't been paying rapt attention to these conferences all these years or read the journals or downloaded my climate model and run it, I will tell you just what these so-called white tornadoes are," she said.

Without taking her eyes off the cameras, she pointed up and back at the screen. "*That* is a transient superthermal updraft. Under certain newly natural conditions, where and when the surface reaches a superheated threshold, a vortex of superheated air rises upward until the cooling of its expansion destabilizes it."

Larabee lowered her arm and leaned forward slightly.

"At present, they are transient and they occur only above the hottest spots on Earth," she said. "Locales that were furnaces *before* the greenhouse warming even began. Locales which are now far hotter than the geological record for any place on this planet before *we* in our infinite wisdom began pumping carbon dioxide and nitrous oxide and heat into its atmosphere. Death Valley. The deep Australian Outback. The central Sahara. And so forth. Where the biomass approaches zero. Where the biochemistry with which the biosphere of the Earth evolved is no longer viable. Places which by any previous climatological criteria *are no longer part of this planet.*"

Monique shuddered, remembering that Libyan blimp ride.

Been there. Felt that.

"Am I saying that these places now resemble conditions on Venus? Of course not! The Venusian surface is still over five times hotter. So what's the problem? We're nowhere near approaching the conditions of Venus, now are we?"

She looked away from the cameras at her fellow climatologists for a beat. "*Condition Venus* made a nice news header, didn't it?" she said. "But they got the meaning wrong, now didn't they?"

She turned back to the camera. "Condition Venus doesn't really mean that the surface temperature of the Earth will rise to five hundred degrees centigrade by next Tuesday, or ever," she said. "Condition Venus refers to what *happened* to Venus. A planet just about the size of the Earth, and certainly not six times closer to the sun, reputable astronomers used to imagine swamps and oceans beneath those clouds. But closer enough to the sun so that the temperature rose above a certain threshold, creating a natural greenhouse effect, and then . . ."

She suddenly slapped her palms together. "Wham!" she shouted. "It fed on itself, went exponential, and shot up to where it is now in a relative planetological eyeblink."

She paused for a long moment of silence, then gazed back up at the vortex. "So what are these so-called white tornadoes telling us?"

She looked back at the camera and seemed to Monique to be attempting to put on, not too successfully, a folksy face.

"I'll put it simply, so that anyone who's ever boiled water to cook spaghetti in can understand it," she said in a similar attempt at a grandmotherly voice.

"You know how nothing at all seems to be happening as the water heats up? You know how finally a few streams of bubbles start drifting up to the surface? And you watch, and you wait, and then you turn away in boredom. . . . And then when you turn around, the whole thing's foaming and bubbling up and if you don't turn it down it's going to overflow and turn into steam!"

Dr. Allison Larabee cocked her head at the camera, no more foxy grandma now. "They say a watched pot never boils?" she said.

Once again, she turned to look up at the white tornado. "Well, we've been watching ours for quite a while now. And it's starting to. Don't you think it's damn well time we turned down the stove?"

———

"Fakes, and what you've just seen proves it," said Eric Esterhazy. "The white tornadoes are *disneys*. Literally done with mirrors."

He turned off the monitor and the video deck, then slid the false bookshelf over the equipment to convert his office back into the faux library of a faux nineteenth-century British nobleman, hoping that the clubby effect would give him more weight in this rare direct man-to-man with Eduardo Ramirez in the absence of Mom.

"Can I get you a drink, Eduardo?" he said, moving toward the bar. He fantasized offering sherry or brandy, but that would be going way over the top. Besides which, he lacked the traditional cigars to go with it.

"Tequila in the Mexican style if you can manage that," Eduardo said, as if changing the mode to match his white linen suit, so reminiscent of Mom's cherished Floridian retro gangster chic.

Eric poured him his tequila, put it on a plate with a lemon slice and a saltcellar, took a snifter of old Calvados himself, put the drinks down on the little round coffee table between two big leather armchairs, sat down across from Eduardo, and waited for him to react to what he had seen.

And waited.

"Well, Eduardo . . . ?" he finally said.

"Well, Eric, I certainly agree that these recordings are valuable material," Eduardo Ramirez said. "The operative question is, to whom?"

"To whom?" said Eric. "To us, who else? To Bad Boys."

"Then what do you recommend we do with them?"

"Sell them, what else?"

"To be sure, but to whom?" Eduardo wagged a cautionary finger. "Think carefully before you advise the obvious. Consider the larger ramifications. Yes, there are news organizations and scandal sites who would pay well for this, but by *their* modest standards, not by ours. Not nearly enough to cover what we would lose by selling it to them."

"Lose?" said Eric. "What would we lose?"

"Give your brain some isometric exercise, Eric," Eduardo said, softening it with an urbane little smile. "As your mother might somewhat less gently say."

Eric thought.

The first thing that he thought, and sourly, was that going directly to Eduardo with this coup had not kept Mom, even in her physical absence, entirely out of the loop.

Eric had never really felt uncomfortable dealing with his mother's lover as his superior in the syndic, or at least so he told himself, and he knew that if it hadn't been for Mom's connections with Eduardo and unnamed others like him, he wouldn't be where he was today.

But he *was* where he was today.

While it might have been Mom who had made him a Bad Boy, he was also a big boy now. He had made his bones. He was master of *La Reine de la Seine*, if perhaps in name only. And now he believed he had contributed something major to the fortunes of the syndic. The making of another set of bones, and perhaps a more important one. One that would establish him as more than a front man. More than his mother's son. As a real player.

And it would seem that Eduardo was challenging him to think like one.

Well then . . .

"If these recordings were broadcast, everyone would know they were made on *La Reine de la Seine* . . ." Eric said slowly. "Meaning that everyone would know that the boat was wired. Meaning we'd lose the whole operation. . . ."

Eduardo merely nodded, smiled, salted the back of his hand.

"So the recordings are worthless to us . . . ?"

Eduardo shook his head, licked his hand, knocked back the tequila, bit into the lemon slice.

"Selling to any syndic that would make them public would be a loser then . . . ?"

"You are beginning to comprehend, Eric. . . ."

"But *threatening* to sell them to the media . . ."

Eduardo put on an exaggerated show of moral outrage. "Why Eric, that would be . . . *blackmail* . . . " he said. "You're a . . . Bad Boy."

Eric grinned. Then frowned.

"But it would be a bluff," he said. "And Big Blue would have to know it . . . so . . . so . . . ?"

Eric realized, in no little confusion and consternation, that he appeared to have taken this train of logic to its inevitable unfortunate conclusion. "So we can't do that either . . . ?" he said unhappily.

"Not necessarily," said Eduardo. "Consider what Bad Boys loses if we bluff and Big Blue calls. To preserve our honor and credibility, we are constrained to sell the recordings to the media at the cost of losing *La Reine* as a data sponge. A net loss, true, but less than catastrophic . . . to *us*."

He smiled, and this time Eric could see the gleam of the predatory teeth behind it.

"Now consider what *Big Blue* loses if that happens. The conference they desperately financed to revive their sagging fortunes turns into a fiasco. Having faked the white tornadoes and been exposed, they can never credibly cry wolf again, even with a real one at the door. The True Blue cause itself is discredited and the Hot and Cold war is decided in favor of the Greens. If you were playing their hand, would you dare to call?"

"No way," said Eric.

"And how much would you say they'd pay to prevent such a terminal outcome?"

Now it was Eric's turn to make with the feral grin, one top predator to another. "Just about anything short of everything they have."

"You're learning, Eric," Eduardo Ramirez said, and Eric felt a boyish glow of pride.

"So we go ahead and do it!" he said. "Send them a copy of the recordings!"

Eduardo Ramirez sighed. "Your mother's son," he said. "A woman of many virtues. But patience is not among them, as you may have noticed from time to time."

The flush that Eric now felt was far from pleasant.

"Being young is nothing to be ashamed of, Eric," Eduardo said gently. "We all must endure it, after all."

This did not exactly tranquilify Eric's mood.

"I don't see what *patience* has to do with any of this," he said irritably.

"So I've noticed," Eduardo said. "But consider. Is the value of these recordings likely to deteriorate with time? Might not their value *increase* if we *didn't* use them to thwart Big Blue's schemes and they somehow succeeded in using the UNACOCS to gain major new financing? The more money they have, the more money they have to lose, the more money they would be willing and able to pay to avoid losing it."

"Oh," said Eric.

Eduardo Ramirez nodded and favored him with a smile. "Some assets appreciate with time," he said. "And all assets appreciate with knowledge."

"Knowledge . . . ? Of what?"

"In this case, of what is really behind the moves the Big Blue Machine has been making. They spend money they cannot really afford to move UNACOCS to Paris and hire Bread & Circuses to promote it. They perhaps enlist Dr. Larabee and the Papal Legate in their scheme. They simulate the white tornadoes. But why?"

"*Why?* To create a panic and trick Green money into financing their Blue operations."

"So it would seem. But why then do they have this Monique Calhoun hire *La Reine de la Seine* as a data sponge targeting the conference participants—"

"—knowing that we're running it!" Eric exclaimed. "They've been fools to take the risk, and these recordings prove it!"

"Never assume that your adversaries are fools, Eric," Eduardo told him. "They may *be* fools, but making the assumption is never an advantage. So assuming they're not fools . . ."

"There's something they have a major need to know. . . ."

"Very good, Eric. And therefore . . . ?"

"The white tornado disneys aren't their capper. They've got something else up their sleeve. But whatever it is, it's not something they believe they have under control, at least not yet . . ."

"Excellent, Eric. And we must . . . ?"

"Find out what it is before we make our next move."

Eduardo Ramirez nodded. "And how do we do that?" he asked.

But this time Eric felt that the question wasn't rhetorical, that Eduardo was no longer playing sensei, that he was finally asking a question to which he did not have the answer, man-to-man.

"Through Monique Calhoun," he told Eduardo. "After all, they *have* put her on *La Reine* to find out something, and if we can find out what—"

"Then we know what it is. But how—"

Eric found himself speaking as fast as he thought, or perhaps even a bit faster, and if Mom would say he was thinking with his dick, then so be it.

"I let her seduce me. . . ."

"I am truly touched by the sacrifices you are willing to make for the syndic, Eric."

"I don't make it easy, but under enormous sexual pressure, I finally admit that I lied, that all the data feeds on the boat *are* recorded—"

"We cannot compromise Ignatz," Eduardo said firmly.

"We don't. All I allow her to get out of me is the existence of the raw recordings, thousands of hours of them. So which ones she takes will probably tell us something itself. And just maybe, she seduces me into helping her with the tedious task of rooting through it all. Which allows me to monitor what she's searching *for*."

"Another disney," Eduardo said. "Nice. It even gives us a credible way to leak the existence of the white tornado recordings to her handlers if and when the time comes. . . ."

Eric nodding knowingly, as if he had thought of that angle too, which he hadn't.

Eduardo Ramirez smiled.

Eric smiled back.

There was a long moment of satisfied silence.

"Another tequila, Eduardo?" Eric finally said.

"I do believe I will," Eduardo said. "But let's go outside."

It was quite warm for the season, and the air was unpleasantly and uncharacteristically muggy, but the view from the terrace garden was still lovely at this hour, made even more dramatic by a rather unusual weather condition.

The sky over Paris was a clear royal blue not quite yet deepening to purple at the zenith, but on the western horizon, a pearly fog bank seemed to be moving in like an enormous slow-motion breaker of cloud, turning the sun in the process of descending into it into a glowing disc of fiery orange that cast long mauve-tinted shadows over the streets of the city below, glazed the waters of the Seine with a golden sheen. The deeply shadowed vegetation encrusting the quais

152 ° GREENHOUSE SUMMER

now seemed reminiscent of the lost reefs of tropic coral or a verdantly green human brain.

Eduardo Ramirez sipped thoughtfully at his tequila as he gazed out over this tropical urban vista.

"Paris is a fortunate city," he said softly. "It was always a beautiful city, but before the warming, the climate was foul. The skies were gray and the weather was cool and dank for more of the year than not. Doubly fortunate to be situated in these rich climes."

"Doubly fortunate?"

"Doubly fortunate that northwestern Europe can afford to pay the price to maintain the Gulf Stream with orbital mirrors. Without which . . . who knows, or wants to find out?"

Eric had never observed Eduardo in such a mood before. But then, he had seldom had a real conversation with him in the absence of Mom.

"Yes, a fortunate city, Eric. Almost as fortunate as Siberia the Golden. . . ."

He turned to face Eric, and Eric saw that he was frowning now.

"To maintain this balmy climate, the Gulf Stream must be maintained, and to do that, tropic waters must be heated thousands of miles away, which only adds more heat to the planet, and who knows, perhaps causes the north polar ice cap to melt faster than it otherwise might. . . ."

"I didn't know you were an amateur climatologist, Eduardo."

Eduardo Ramirez laughed softly, ruefully so it seemed. "I may not know much about climatology," he said, "but I know what I like. And I know we would lose these long sweet Parisian summer seasons should Big Blue succeed in its schemes to cool the planet back down. As Siberia the Golden would once more be locked in snow and ice."

"But they won't," Eric said him. "We have what it takes to stop them whenever we want to."

"But *should* we?" said Eduardo.

"*Should we?*"

"The Big Blue Machine may be a collection of revenant capitalist corporations out to turn a profit above all else, they may have faked the white tornadoes, but . . ."

"But . . . ?"

Eduardo shrugged. "But none of that necessarily prevents them from being *right*," he said. "Perhaps Condition Venus *is* imminent. Perhaps the biosphere *is* in mortal danger. In which case . . ."

He sighed. "In which case, we would not do right by stopping them, now would we? In which case, must we not sacrifice the lovely climate of this beautiful city, Siberia the Golden, and all the rest?"

"Must we?" said Eric. Eduardo was unexpectedly floating out into waters a bit too deep for him.

"If that should *really* be what it takes to preserve the biosphere itself, what choice would there be?"

This was an Eduardo Ramirez that Eric had never known, and he was beginning to show Eric levels within himself that he had never known either, starting with the revelation that Eduardo owed his elevated position in the syndic to an elusive something more than cunning.

"Your mother so enjoys Bad Boys' gangster mystique," Eduardo said, "and it's certainly true that we evolved from mafias and triads. By certain definitions in certain jurisdictions we may even still be a 'criminal organization.' But we are *not* capitalists, never forget that, Eric. Do you know what *really* destroyed the capitalist global order?"

Eric shook his head, never having given such matters any thought.

"The economic historians speak of the bursting of the Great Bubble, the Markowitzians speak of the entropy created by the disjunction between the virtual and the productive economies, the Third Force mystics claim it was the despiritualization of capitalist man, and no doubt all that is true," Eduardo told him. "But in the end, the capitalist world global order was destroyed by the very thing it worshipped. . . ."

"The so-called sacred bottom line . . . ?" Eric ventured, and was rewarded with a nod and a rueful smile.

"If capitalists had to choose between their own short-term economic self-interest and the survival of a larger common good, even one that included themselves, they would take the money and run. Even if there was no place to run *to*. It was said they would sell you the rope to hang themselves if they could do it at a profit."

Eduardo laughed. "And that's essentially what they did."

"I don't understand," Eric said with utter sincerity.

"Someone also once said that you have to be honest to live outside the law."

Eduardo turned to look out once more over balmy beautiful Paris and Eric too turned to stand beside him, surveying from on high the City of Light of which he was at least an ersatz prince.

"Just what are you trying to tell me?"

Eduardo did a fair imitation of Mom.

"We're Bad Boys, but we wouldn't flush the world down the toilet just to make a fast buck in the process, kiddo! That's the difference between predatory capitalist pigs and the bastard sons and daughters of romantic buccaneers and honest gangsters like ourselves!"

Prince Eric Esterhazy struggled to fully understand what Eduardo Ramirez was trying to tell him, but it remained elusive.

But somehow, as the heady floral fragrances of the city drifted up to mingle with the winey perfumes of the potted plants closer to hand, his rooftop garden seemed to transform itself into a disney of the tropical city below.

As Paris itself too, in that moment, seemed to him a disney.

But of what, he could not tell.

GLASS HOUSES

PART TWO

7

WHAT IS THE LEVEL BEYOND VIP?
Stella and Ivan Marenko.

The only thing missing is the "Ode to Joy" over the speakers and a twenty-one-gun salute, and I'm liable to catch shit for not providing them, Monique Calhoun thought as she stood outside the Hotel Ritz watching the clattering Force Flic helicopter descend to the Place Vendôme perilously close to the central column in a fearful whirlwind of dust and debris and noise against all conventional rules and rational safety reason.

"Do you know who these people *are?*" Avi Posner had asked when he called to inform her that the Marenkos were already on their way by private jet from Zekograd.

"The names are familiar . . ." Monique had said slowly, pretending to be searching her protoplasmic memory while running a quick net-search on the fly. "The honcha and honcho of Meat & Potatoes, aren't they?"

She didn't need to be told that the co-chairs of the largest Siberian agricultural syndic were just the sort of bears that the client had laid on the UNACOCS honey pot to attract, but Posner did it anyway.

"That makes them important enough. But they are a lot more than that. They are . . . shamans, as the Siberians have it."

"Shamans . . . ? *Witch doctors?*"

"Siberian hyperbole, of which they are major exporters. Powers. Influences. Weighty personages."

Posner's image on the vidphone screen shrugged.

"I am not a doctor of political philosophy from the Sorbonne, so please do not expect me to explain the politics of the Siberians, who claim not to have any," he said. "Suffice it to say that Stella and Ivan Marenko have influence beyond their official positions of the sort that can open or close the Siberian purse strings. They are now your number-one priority. I want daily reports from you on everything they do and say, everything they *think*, if you can manage it. And they are to be afforded *every* courtesy, no matter how expensive, no matter how extravagant, no matter how bizarre. Without limit."

"*Without limit?*"

"They are to be treated as the Second Coming of Santa Claus. What they request, you *will* obtain for them. If God Himself is occupying the suite they require, you will eject Him forthwith."

The extent to which *this* was or was not hyperbole was demonstrated less than half an hour later when some Force Flic functionaire called to tell Monique not to bother to send any limo to the airport.

Somehow, while still in flight from Zekograd, the Marenkos had rented or commandeered one of their helicopters and had done the considerable whatever it took to circumvent any number of rules and regulations to have it take them directly from their plane and deposit them conveniently in front of the hotel.

The Force Flic pilot managed to put the helicopter down without damage to life, limb, or property, and a couple debarked before the engine had completely powered down. No helicopter actually required the ducking of heads to pass under its still-turning vanes, but Monique had never seen anyone resist the reflex to do so.

There was a first time for everything.

Stella and Ivan Marenko walked unflinchingly under the turning rotors with posture erect and heads held high as if the mere ruffling of their hair thereby was perilously close to an excess of lèse-majesté.

Stella Marenko was a tall, robust, big-breasted woman in middle age, of the sort to appear on poster art of the mid-Bolshevik period heroically driving a tractor, or, by the look of her, picking it up and throwing it into a ditch.

She had a broad high-cheekboned Slavic face and eyes like sapphire lasers. Her long blond hair was secured above her ears by a silver tiara encrusted with black pearls. She wore a red silk pants suit secured by a sash crafted of lapis-lazuli beads and silver chain mail, high black boots, and a high-collared black silk cloak liberally trimmed in ermine.

Ivan Marenko was of roughly the same age, half a head shorter, and burly not quite to the point of being fat. His sleek black hair was artfully cut into a medium-length mane to blend with a full but neatly trimmed beard to create the impression of an expensively barbered Rasputin. His lips were full and expansive and there seemed to be laugh lines around his deep-set brown eyes.

He wore a black velvet take on a twentieth-century business suit without a shirt, the better to display his hirsute chest and the enormous gold medallion depending thereon, and, of all things, gold lamé boots.

And as they approached, Monique realized that both of them were dripping with jewelry, she in silver, he in gold. Every finger save the thumbs. Bracelets on both wrists. Pendants. Earrings in his left ear and both of hers. Heavy and rough-hewn for him, finely wrought and bejeweled for her.

Monique found herself wondering how much of it they were wearing under their clothes and on which body parts, then decided she really didn't want to know.

"I'm Monique Calhoun, of Bread & Circuses VIP services—"

"And we are your Very Important Potentates!" Ivan Marenko boomed out at her, then grabbed Monique in a bear hug and kissed her on both cheeks before she could even catch her breath.

"Nikulturni, Ivan!" Stella Marenko said.

She smiled ruefully at Monique as Ivan Marenko released her.

"He is again being . . . what is the word . . . ?"

"Asshole!" proclaimed Ivan Marenko proudly. "I am again being an asshole. Yes, Ms. Calhoun, this is correct?"

"Uh . . ."

"You are embarrassing the girl, Ivan. Ms. Calhoun, feel free to tell this nikulturni asshole he is behaving like . . . like . . ."

"Like an asshole!" said Ivan Marenko and burst into laughter.

And his wife joined in.

"Uh, perhaps you'd like to choose your accommodations now . . . ?" Monique suggested in a bit of a daze.

"Perhaps," said Ivan Marenko, eyeing the ornate grand entrance of the top hotel in Paris like a three-star chef perusing yesterday's leftover goods at the fish market.

"Or perhaps not," Stella Marenko said dubiously as Monique led them up the stairs and into the entrance lobby, where, as per her instructions, they were met by the hotel manager, and a tuxedoed waiter bearing two glasses of champagne and caviar canapés on a silver tray.

The Marenkos slurped down the champagne in a few quick gulps, then sampled the canapés. They exchanged disdainful glances.

"Russian crap," Stella Marenko muttered.

Ivan Marenko held up his empty glass.

"Where is bottle?" he demanded.

The manager quickly dispatched the waiter to fetch it. It only took a couple of minutes, but Russian crap or not, the Marenkos managed to gobble up the caviar canapés before he returned.

After which, trailed by the fawning hotel manager and the champagne-pouring waiter, Monique took the Marenkos on a tour of the best accommodations the Hotel Ritz had to offer, immense bedrooms, more immense parlors, suites featuring libraries, dining rooms, grand pianos, even one with a harpsichord. Suites furnished with millions of wu's worth of antiques. Suites with huge terraces looking south over the Seine, westward into an Eiffel Tower sunset. Suites that had accommodated CEOs and heads of state, cine stars and royalty.

The Marenkos were mostly silent during all this, except for muttered exchanges in Russian, and the occasional demand for more champagne when the waiter was slow enough to let their glasses go dry.

By the time they had seen it all, the champagne bottle was empty, and steam was all but coming out of the hotel manager's ears. Monique, the Marenkos, and the manager descended to the lobby in the fancy elevator in stony silence.

"I have a *few* other things to attend to," the manager said, as stiffly as if someone had shoved a curtain rod up his rectum. "*Do* let me know as soon as you've made your choice." And made his exit, leaving Monique and the Marenkos standing there by the elevator bank.

Ivan Marenko stared at his wife.

Stella Marenko stared back, nodded.

"Shithole," she said.

"Da."

"Rent us a town house, Ms. Calhoun," Stella Marenko said. "Three, four floors. Left Bank. Nice view of the Seine. Sauna."

"Maybe a swimming pool?" suggested Ivan Marenko.

"Ivan! Don't make the girl crazy! If it doesn't have a swimming pool, you'll just have to live with it."

Ivan Marenko gave Monique a warm apologetic smile.

"Take your time," he said. "We wait in the bar."

"You want what?" exclaimed Eric Esterhazy.

"Rent bar," said Stella Marenko.

"*La Reine de la Seine* does not rent out its salons for private parties," Eric Esterhazy told these comic-opera Siberians. Least of all when we've sold half the guest-list rights to Bread & Circuses already, he refrained from adding.

"Only small bar," said Ivan Marenko. "For big money."

Eric was going to have an unpleasant word or two with the security guards in the embarkation pavilion for letting these arrogant clowns on board in the first place.

The best casting director in the world could not have done better than Ivan and Stella Marenko for super-rich Siberians, she wearing a flowing dress sewn together out of python hide and cut low in the bodice to display the huge ruby pendant hung upon her mighty breasts and a tall leopard-skin hat and matching cloak, he sporting a chamois-colored suit tailored out of actual chamois pelts and trimmed with gold braid, the both of them tastelessly festooned with enough expensive jewelry to open a major branch of Cartier.

Eric had been on the forward upper deck when they made their entrance, affording him the pleasure of watching them storm up the gangway as if they owned *his* boat, or soon would, if they felt like it.

Eric had dashed down to the lower deck to confront this apparition, and by the time he was descending the interior staircase to the restaurant, the Marenkos were already inside, opening the door to the stern bar, peering inside like real-estate agents.

"Who do you think you are?" Eric had demanded angrily.

"I think we are Stella and Ivan Marenko," said the woman. "Is this not so, Ivan?"

"I am sure of it. It is not yet late enough in the day for me to be drunk enough to have forgotten my own name."

"Later, it may be different."

"How did you get on my boat?" Eric snarled.

"*Your* boat?" said Stella Marenko. "Ah, then you must be the famous Prince Eric Esterhazy!" She held out a paw so laden with rings that it must've been a considerable athletic feat to hold it horizontal. "Shouldn't you be kissing my hand?"

Eric managed to remain enough of a gentleman not to tell the woman what part of *his* anatomy *she* could kiss, but not by much. "How the hell did you get past the guards?" he demanded.

Ivan Marenko had given him a broad wink.

"We are *very* big tippers," he had said.

Rent them the stern bar for the duration of the UNACOCS conference? Au contraire, the Marenkos had earned themselves a permanent eighty-six from the guest list.

"Perhaps I do not make myself clear?" Ivan Marenko said. "English is not my first language. We want to rent big table in bar to entertain guests. All nights of UNACOCS conference. We buy drinks. We buy drugs. We pay you regular bar prices. We ask no discount for volume."

"Where is problem?" said his wife.

"I say who the guests on this boat will be," Eric said, temporarily half-truthfully and not put in a better mood for it.

"So, as Stella says, where is problem? We buy *your* guests drinks and drugs from *you* with *our* money. This is your idea of a bad deal?"

You are my idea of an arrogant boor was what Eric wanted to tell him.

"I maintain a highly selective guest list, and thus far, I must say, you have done little to convince me that you even have a place on it," he said instead, which amounted to a more elegant phrasing of much the same thing.

"You should now consult your principal," Ivan Marenko said.

"What?"

"Call your principal, Prince Potemkin," said Stella Marenko.

Suddenly the theatricality had been turned down and something else had been turned up. Suddenly they were speaking better English.

"I don't know what you're talking about," Eric said, not sounding very convincing even to himself.

"So have Eduardo Ramirez explain it to you," Ivan Marenko said evenly.

Eric locked eyes with him for a long silent moment without being able to fathom what was behind them. But it was enough to convince him that it would be prudent to do what the Siberian suggested.

Stella Marenko had stepped into the stern bar and apparently inspected the stock. "Ivan!" she called out. "Come here! Let the boy make his call in private! They have pepper vodka!"

"In freezer?" Ivan Marenko boomed back at her without changing gaze or expression. "Real stuff?"

"In refrigerator! Russian!"

"Vodka you keep in freezer compartment," Ivan Marenko told Eric. "Best pepper vodka is Ukrainian. Russian stuff is knockoff for export."

He winked. "You will remember this, yes, Prince Potemkin?" He clapped Eric heartily on the shoulder. "Now go be a good Bad Boy and call Ramirez."

There was a phone behind the bar of the main saloon at the other end of the restaurant, sound only, and Eric went there to call Eduardo.

"There's a couple of Siberians on the boat slurping up our vodka even as I speak and demanding I rent them a permanent table for the duration," he said, after passing through several layers of intermediaries.

"Ah, so you've met the Marenkos," Eduardo said, sounding rather amused.

"I've endured the dubious pleasure. Who in hell are they?"

"Important clients, Eric."

"Clients?"

"Movers and shapers in the upper realms of the Siberian syndics."

"Those buffoons?"

"*Those buffoons* paid a handsome price just for a *look* at the recordings that prove the white tornadoes are disneys," Eduardo Ramirez told him. "They're here to decide whether to put together a consortium to buy the reproduction and distribution rights and use them against the Big Blue Machine. If they do, we are talking *hundreds of millions* of wu. Need I tell you that they are therefore to be afforded every conceivable courtesy?"

"They seem so . . . so . . . ."

Eduardo laughed. "Indeed they do," he said.

"Why didn't you tell me?"

"And have you miss such an amusing experience?" Eduardo said, and laughed again. "And a lesson as well, Eric," he said quite seriously. "Remember what I said about assuming your adversaries are fools . . . ?"

"It's never an advantage to assume that your adversaries are fools, even if they are. . . ?"

"Just so," said Eduardo. "Now consider the advantage in persuading potential adversaries that *you* are."

Stella Marenko did not seem impressed as she gazed at the formidable displays of climatech machineries laid out on the floor of the Grand Palais for the perusal of just such potential patrons as herself.

"So this is famous Crystal Palace," she said dubiously.

"*Grand Palais*, Mrs. Marenko," Monique Calhoun told her.

"Whatever. Looks like flea market in old Baikonur cosmodrome."

Her husband seemed more interested in the overarching glass and iron framework ceiling than what was under it.

"Smart glass, da?"

"That's right."

"So why is smart glass faking crappy gray day with storm when it's blue skies and sunshine outside?"

"Supposed to be *white tornado*, Ivan."

"They put whole conference inside commercial for itself?" Ivan Marenko said sardonically. "This is what your syndic calls *deep sell*, Monique? Deep as what's left of Aral Sea. Subtle as Socialist Realist metrostation mural."

Monique found herself giving him a sudden sharp look. The Marenkos were the biggest ass-pains she had ever experienced in her career in VIP services, totally and unreasonably demanding, entirely unself-conscious of their own arrogance, crude, boorish, and in their own terms, nikulturni.

But sometimes a native shrewdness broke through to remind her that these people couldn't have gotten to the position where they could get away with behaving as they did by being as thick as they generally seemed.

And Ivan Marenko had a good point.

Having spent yesterday miraculously securing the Marenkos their town house close enough behind the Musée d'Orsay to give them their required view of the Seine, finding and moving in the portable sauna that it unfortunately lacked, renting them additional furniture and more agreeable paintings, and stocking the place with food and drink, Monique hadn't been to the Grand Palais at all.

But as she had learned from the news coverage, after Allison Larabee's passionate plea to turn down the planetary heat, the conference sessions had degenerated, and she suspected according to plan, from a scientific symposium into a series of sales presentations by representatives of the climatech companies sponsoring UNACOCS for expensive schemes to do just that.

Create and maintain a vast orbital ring of finely divided dust to reduce incoming sunlight. Or do it with gigantic mylar occluders. Use cloud-cover generators on an unprecedented massive scale to create permanent blizzards to rebuild the crumbling ice caps. Use orbital mirrors to change ocean currents to somehow bury excess calories in the abyssal oceanic heat sink.

Suck carbon dioxide out of the atmosphere by reforesting every available meter with Qwik-grow trees. Or with a new gene-tweaked hemp supposedly able to thrive in desert extremes. Or by enriching oceanic nutrient upwellings with iron to increase photosynthetic plankton.

Would you buy a used planet from these people?

Because Monique lacked the financial means to do so, making such decisions was not her problem. But since, according to Posner, the Marenkos were here as representatives of interests who did, it apparently *was* a decision they were here to consider.

Yet despite the fact that she now found herself working for the Big Blue Machine in the service of a campaign to separate these fools from huge amounts of Siberian money, Monique was not displeased to see that they were not swallowing it whole.

"Would you like to attend the conference session now?" Monique suggested not very enthusiastically.

"Better than sitting through Christmas performance of *Nutcracker Suite* danced by badly trained bears with audience of bored snot-nosed brats," Stella Marenko admitted. "But not by much."

Monique had to choke back laughter. There were even odd moments when she caught herself *liking* the Siberians.

"Better to inspect the goods than listen to advertisements," her husband said.

"Da."

So Monique tagged along in the background while the Marenkos wandered among the kiosks and industrial pavilions, the cloud-cover generators and plankton-seeding barges, the models of launch vehicles, orbital mirrors and occluders, the nuclear terrain-sculpting charges and the before-and-after dioramas.

The Marenkos did not seem to be entirely ignorant of climatech as far as Monique could tell, or at least knew enough to fake it with the industrial reps when one of them caught them kicking the metaphorical tires.

"Covers how many square kilometers. . . ?"

"Is guaranteed no residual rads . . . ?"

"What is scale of model? How much area is deployed. . . ?"

Monique found it amusing that while their English was good enough to ask apparently intelligent technical questions, every time the reps sidled up to the subject of cost or money, they shrugged, threw up their hands, and reverted to Russian.

It seemed that the Marenkos were only at the Grand Palais to put in their usual conspicuous appearance. The only time they showed real interest in anything was when they were confronted with a rare something they couldn't have.

Namely a peek at whatever was inside that big enclosure of canvas screening near the center of the exhibition floor. There was no sign, no banner, no rep, just blank green canvas and two armed guards flanking the only entrance flap.

"What are they guarding?" Stella Marenko asked Monique.

Monique shrugged.

"We look inside," said Ivan Marenko, barging up to the entrance. The guards took single side steps to bar his way.

Ivan was not pleased. Nor used to being obstructed.

"Out of way, please," he demanded. "We look inside."

"No you don't. This is a restricted area."

"What's the big secret?"

"Who wants to know?

"I am *Ivan Marenko!*"

"And I am Jared, your security guard for today, and I'm telling you you're gonna have to wait till Sunday to find out like everyone else."

"Is only doing his job, Ivan," Stella Marenko said, coming up behind him, and trying her version of a charm offensive, which was to reach into a pocket, pull out a fistful of Siberian gold wu coins, and shove them under the guards' noses. "So, nice boys, you tell us what is big secret, we give you big tip."

The guards eyed each other greedily but, it seemed to Monique, forlornly.

"We don't know."

"They don't tell us."

"We play game. You guess. We like, you win."

"Bunch of computer stuff, I think."

"Not climatech?"

"Don't look like it."

The Marenkos looked at each other, exchanged a few words in Russian.

"Okay boys," Stella Marenko said, handing over the money, "have a nice day."

"So what you think, Monique?" Stella said as Ivan wandered over to inspect a plankton-seeding barge.

"About what?"

"Mystery item."

Monique shrugged.

"You have conference program? Anything interesting Sunday?"

Monique fished the program booklet out of her bag, scanned it. "Presentation of ocean current modification proposal by Orbital Mechanix. Presentation of climate model by John Sri Davinda. Presentation of albedo-increasing forest cover by Qwik-grow. Summing up by General Secretary Lars Bendsten. Closing ceremony. Usual stuff."

Shit, she realized, *I'm* lapsing into Russified English!

She vowed to watch her sentence structure for the duration of the Marenkos' tour of the climatech exhibitions, which fortunately did not prove difficult, since the Siberians seemed to lose interest after another twenty minutes or so during which they mostly conversed with each other in Russian.

"Okay, we see enough," Ivan Marenko finally said as their brownian trajectory took them near the entrance to the makeshift auditorium from which the drone of the proceedings could be dimly heard.

"You want to catch some of the conference?" Monique asked.

"So, Ivan?" Stella Marenko asked.

"Better to catch up on drinking," her husband said. "Is bullshit in there. Answers only one question . . ."

Stella Marenko eyed him warily. "This is going to be joke, Ivan?"

"Da."

Stella glanced at Monique. "*Dirty* joke," she told her. "Knows no other kind." Monique noticed that half a dozen people on the way into the conference, drawn, no doubt, by the visual spectacle of the Marenkos, had paused within earshot to listen.

"Why is planet like nymphomaniac?" Ivan Marenko said.

Stella Marenko rolled her eyes. "Okay, so why is planet like nymphomaniac, Ivan?"

"*You* should know, Stella!"

Ivan Marenko grabbed his wife squarely by the crotch as Monique goggled in disbelief.

"Much easier to heat up than cool down!"

The restaurant band was playing Dixieland Bach, the tables were full of chattering diners, but the raucous noise leaking from the aft bar was still audible over the general buzz of the far larger salon even from the foot of the spiral staircase.

Eric Esterhazy smiled, waved, chatted, did his professional hostly duty as he meandered through the restaurant toward the stern, but inside he was seething as he made his way to the Marenkos' lair.

For two nights now the Siberians had held court back there. He had been constrained, that is all but ordered, to remove a third of the tables in the aft bar to make room for one that the Marenkos appeared to have acquired at one of those larcenous antique boutiques specializing in fobbing off flea-market junk on tourists at ridiculous prices, an oversized round wrought-iron dreko-deco monstrosity that looked as if it had been fabricated from an outsized manhole cover and a defunct nineteenth-century Métro kiosk.

And there they sat, drinking like Road Warrior mercenaries back from a bone-dry six-month tour guarding the Ka'bah in Mecca, ordering whole smoked Scottish salmon and baked sturgeon by the school, wild boar, venison, and pheasant by the meat locker, fruits de mer by the boatload, and caviar by the ice bucket delivered to their table, and floating it all on a continuous flood of the most expensive champagne and wine and exotic vodkas swilled down as if they were supermarket plonk as they invited all comers to partake of their largesse in loud beer-hall voices.

Eric wondered why he was even drawn to visit this unseemly permanent brouhaha, since there was nothing he could do to impose any measure of civilized restraint, Eduardo Ramirez having made it clear that if the Marenkos chose to bite the heads off live chickens and spit them across the room, he was to supply the poultry and spittoons.

Perhaps it was the same outraged instinct that caused baboons to display their flaming red buttocks in the face of intruders. The Siberians had usurped a portion of *his boat* as their own, and if he was powerless to drive them off, the least he could do was establish his own right to invade it with impunity, without, of course, going so far as dropping his pants.

The Marenkos' table and surrounding environs were crowded as usual. As many chairs as was geometrically possible had been pulled up to the table and filled, most of these with climatologists, including Pereiro, Braithwaite, and even Allison Larabee, plus Aubrey Wright, and some lower-rank climatech-corp people.

A second-tier standing-room crowd consisting mostly of press, show people, professional celebrities, and assorted hangers-on reached greedily over the shoulders of the fortunate seated for the huge iced mountain of fruits de mer, the caviar-and-sour-cream-filled blinis, the contents of the caviar bucket itself, the charcuterie platter, the tranches of smoked salmon and smoked freshwater eel.

Ivan and Stella Marenko poured drinks with one hand almost as fast as empty glasses were shoved under the bottles they held, he vodka, she champagne, while belting it down themselves with the other. There was a mound of designer dust on a Tiffany mirror that guests were vacuuming up through rolled and taped hundred-wu notes that had been thoughtfully supplied.

"Aha, so Sweet Prince Potemkin arrives!" Stella Marenko shouted by way of greeting. "But sober as Saturday night in downtown Kabul and tush as tight as my dress!"

This item was a silver sheath that seemed spray-painted on, the paint having given out just north of her nipples and south of her ass. Her long blond hair was cornrowed with beads of emeralds and rubies. A gem-encrusted golden dagger depended on a heavy chain between her bulging breasts.

She shoved away the forest of empty glasses supplicating her like the ravening beaks of baby birds with her bottle, grabbed her husband's, and filled a champagne glass with vodka. Her bloodshot eyes glowed like whorehouse neon.

"Loosen rectum and join very serious intellectual party!" she barbled boozily. "I learn English verb form! You drink till you stink, he drank till he stank, I'm drunk as a skunk!"

She handed the glass to Eric, who did not need to approach within range of her breath to verify that that exalted state had indeed long since been achieved.

"Is everything all right, Madam Marenko?" he said frostily. "Is there anything I can do for you?"

"You think you're up to it, do you, boy?"

"I *meant* is there anything you need?"

"Need to pee!" Stella Marenko woozed, attempting to rise to her feet, and, on the second try, barely making it.

She reached out for Eric's right forearm to more or less hold herself upright. "Be a good boy and help me!"

Eric gave Ivan Marenko a sour not-my-job look; Ivan shot back a shit-faced shrug that said, Oh yes it is. At which point, Stella Marenko tugged heavily at his arm, or perhaps lost her balance and teetered backward, the result in any case being that Eric found himself being dragged out of the bar and into the salon by a reeling drunk.

Once in the restaurant however, Stella Marenko's balance suddenly improved at least to the point where she could walk more or less steadily by holding his arm and leaning up against him while nuzzling his ear.

In this state, but with much more physical force than seemed apparent or that Eric could easily resist without creating an even more unseemly scene, she steered him like a tug pushing a river barge not toward the nearest toilet, but out onto the promenade that ran around the lower deck.

There she threw her arms around his neck, pressing her body against him, pulling his head into her embrace, and for all the world seemingly whispering dirty sweet nothings in his ear.

"Must be someplace on this boat that isn't bugged," she said quite clearly. "You take me there now."

Monique Calhoun had circled the lower promenade, wandered through the restaurant, peered into both lower-deck bars, subjected herself to the noise and babble of the upper-deck casino, mingled with the guests on the upper-deck promenade, then reversed course and did it all again backward, but, like the proverbial cop, just when she needed him, Prince Eric Esterhazy was nowhere to be found.

Or rather, no doubt, since Prince Eric was constantly in hostly motion and so was she, their trajectories had failed to intersect in the same place at the same time. There was probably a mathematical equation to explain it, the Heisenberg Uncertainty Principle or something, but Monique, being no mathematician, preferred the characterological interpretation, namely that the karmic logic of a character like Prince Eric would of course impel his random motion along a path of least resistance to pissing her off.

Not that she had boarded *La Reine de la Seine* tonight in the best of moods to begin with. Avi Posner had made his displeasure plain after her report this morning.

"What you've given me so far is virtually useless. The Marenkos examine the climatech equipment and seem to understand what they're looking at. They try to bribe their way into an unfinished exhibit out of piqued curiosity. They talk to a lot of climatologists on *La Reine de la Seine* where they seem permanently drunk. Low-grade, Monique, low-grade! Talk about *what?* Where's the pattern? Didn't I tell you that your priority assignment was to find out what *they're* trying to find out?"

"You also told me, as I remember, that I was to obtain for them whatever they require, Avi, and believe me that alone is a full-time job! How am I supposed to cater to the every wish of people who seem to have one a minute, run the rest of Bread & Circuses' VIP operation, which just happens to be my day job, and vet their drunken table-talk babble all at the same time?"

"Amateurs, amateurs . . ." Posner had grumbled. "You get copies of all of their table-talk recordings since they arrived out of Esterhazy and review them in your spare time!"

"Spare time? I heard you say *spare time?* And what *recordings* are you going on about?"

"The automatic recordings that Esterhazy's surveillance equipment makes of everything that's said on board the boat, what else!"

"Esterhazy didn't mention anything about his equipment automatically recording everything. . . ."

"*Of course* it does! It has to! *The Secret Service of Lower Moronia* wouldn't install surveillance equipment that didn't!"

"But how am I supposed to get Esterhazy to admit it and hand over copies?"

"I . . . suggest . . . you . . . use . . . your . . . feminine . . . charm," Posner had told her very very slowly as if indeed explaining it to one of the aforementioned morons.

This had not exactly piped Monique aboard *La Reine* tonight in a lighthearted mood, and fruitlessly trying to track down Eric Esterhazy in order to accomplish this moronically modest task was not improving it.

And while she was ignorant of the mathematical raison d'être for her current state of frustration, she now recalled a semimathematical method for resolving it that she had once heard, the lazy woman's way out, namely that if you sat in one place long enough, anyone you were looking for would sooner or later come to you.

Nor did she need to be a mathematician to figure out that *where* she planted her ass would likely exert a non-random influence on the time-frame thereof.

Monique sighed, then made her way across the restaurant to the aft bar, and what even a certified agent of the Lower Moronia Secret Service could not fail to perceive as the logical nexus even if she wanted to—the table of Stella and Ivan Marenko.

The only places on *La Reine de la Seine* deaf to the surveillance equipment were the wheelhouse, hardly suitable for a private conversation, the interior of the fuel tank, not exactly practical, and Eric's own dressing room, so the forced choice was obvious.

This had an upside and a downside and they were one and the same. The downside was that it required Eric to squire Stella Marenko down the corridor past the private boudoirs and for her to do her amorous drunk act when several people to-ing and fro-ing from their own assignations observed them en passant.

The upside was that it provided a sufficiently lubricious cover for their somewhat prolonged disappearance from public view.

Once inside the dressing room, however, Stella Marenko was all business. She parked herself on the bed, but sat upright on the edge, and made no protest when Eric, somewhat relieved, sat down on the single chair rather than romantically close beside her.

"What do you know about Davinda?" she said, in a voice that betrayed no hint of drunkenness, quite impressive considering how much she had been slugging down.

"This is what?" asked Eric. "An obscure branch of Hinduism? Some new flavor of Third Force psychic energy?"

"This is *John Sri* Davinda. This is a human."

"Oh yes, the name is vaguely familiar . . ."

"A climatologist from California. He presents climate model on last day of conference. What can you tell me about him?"

Eric shrugged. "Not much more than you've just told me," he said. "I remember meeting him once, I think, the opening night of the conference. Dressed and barbered like the Ancient Mariner."

"He is not aboard tonight?"

"He had the poor taste to appear drunk or stoned or insane on-stage at the conference. In the absence of a proper classic vaudeville hook, Bendsten had to drag him off himself. For obvious reasons, he hasn't been on Calhoun's guest list since."

"Put him on yours. Get him here."

"May I ask why?"

"We want to talk with him, Ivan and me."

"About what?"

Stella Marenko shrugged, a motion that came perilously close to popping her breasts out of her dress.

"There is mysterious something in Grand Palais under guard," she said. "Secret is to be revealed on Sunday. Sunday program has closing ceremony, speech by Bendsten, something about Qwik-grow forest, something about playing with ocean currents from orbit, and presentation of climate model by Davinda. Closing ceremony, General Secretary, forest, orbital mirrors, these cannot be hidden inside canvas tent. Must be something to do with Davinda climate model, da?"

"Da," said Eric, actually impressed by this woman for the first time; despite all appearances, obviously not just another stupid face. "But what?"

"What we must find out, Prince Potemkin," Stella Marenko told him. "You know what means 'Lao'? This is a word in English?"

"Not that I know of."

"Not Russian either. Maybe Chinese, but—"

"What does this have to do—?"

"I hear Kutnik say this word to Aubrey Wright, he looks at me as if to see if I heard it, I do not think they speak Chinese, so . . ."

"So . . . ?"

"So maybe is code, how do call it, acronym?"

"For what?"

"Maybe for Sunday surprise package?" said Stella Marenko. "Maybe you better find out before they open it?"

"He takes Stella to the toilet," Ivan Marenko informed Monique when she inquired after Eric Esterhazy.

"He took your wife to the toilet?"

Marenko laughed, shrugged, knocked back another slug of vodka. "Stella's face, how you say, shitted?"

"Shit-faced," corrected Dr. Bobby Braithwaite to a general round of less-than-sober laughter.

"Take load off feet, Monique," Marenko said, patting the seat apparently temporarily vacated by his wife. "Tie load on," he said, pouring her a glass of vodka.

Gingerly, Monique took her seat at the crowded table. The sit-and-wait theory, it would seem, would soon pay off. If Stella Marenko was so drunk that she required the services of Prince Eric to get her to the ladies', then simple logic would seem to indicate that when she was finished with her business within, Eric would have to bring her back.

"What's so important about knowing what the Sunday surprise is anyway?" Eric Esterhazy asked Stella Marenko. "If you're right, it's probably just Davinda's climate model."

"Nyet, climate model is *software*, software you don't hide behind screening. Must be something else in there."

"So what?" said Eric. "After the panic they've created with their fake white tornadoes, how can whatever it is be anything but an anticlimax?"

"Bad theater. Very stupid, da?"

"Da. Very."

"*Too* stupid. Only assholes assume other players are assholes. No one ever tells you this, Prince Potemkin?"

Eric couldn't help smiling. "Not quite as elegantly," he said dryly.

"So not to be assholes, we must assume Big Blue Machine thinks their move will be smart, da?"

"Da," Eric found himself muttering, and rather stupidly by his own lights. The quality of Stella Marenko's English seemed to vary like a faucet she turned up and down at random, but the more she talked, the sharper she seemed.

"Ramirez tells you why we are here, da?"

"To decide whether to buy the recordings that prove the white tornadoes are fakes and expose the whole thing . . ."

"More than that, Prince Potemkin," Stella Marenko said. "You ever ask yourself why?"

"*Why?* Why what?"

"Why do we even *think* of paying Bad Boys hundreds of millions of wu for recordings?"

"To use them to destroy UNACOCS and Big Blue. . . ."

"What for?"

"*What for?*"

"Why bother when we *already know* white tornadoes are fakes?" Stella Marenko said. "Why not just stay home, drink vodka, make love, and sit on our money?"

Eric could do nothing but stare at her with a mind as blank as the expression on his face. The expression on Stella Marenko's face, however, revealed a frightening intensity.

"Because what Big Blue Machine *seems* to be doing is *too stupid*," she said. "They pour last big money they have down rathole of UNACOCS. Take terminal gamble with faked white tornadoes, gamble they lose if we want to expose it. Why?"

"Because they're desperate. Because they've sucked all the money out of the Lands of the Lost that there is to suck."

"Da, maybe," said Stella Marenko. "And if we find out they want to turn Siberia the Golden back into Siberia the Ice Box *just to make money*, we buy the recordings and use them to pound those capitalist bastards into mincemeat filling for pilmenyi!"

Now Stella Marenko actually grew pensive. "But . . ."

"But . . . ?"

"But what if something more important than money makes them so desperate?"

"More . . . important . . . than . . . money . . . ?" Eric said very slowly, rolling this novel morsel around in his mouth to see how it tasted. "What's more important than money?"

"*Life*, Prince Potemkin," Stella Marenko said. "Life on Earth. Not so easy to enjoy your money if you and everyone else and whole biosphere are dead. Da, white tornadoes are fakes. But this does not prove *Condition Venus* cannot be real. Maybe *is* real. Maybe *is* really starting to happen. Maybe Big Blue knows this. Maybe *this* is what makes them so desperate. Might be enough to have even unreconstructed capitalist bastards desperate for more reason than profit— especially if is big profit in selling awful truth anyway!"

"Da," said Eric. "Da," he repeated, remembering that Eduardo Ramirez had presented him with more or less this very train of logic. Apparently just before showing the white tornado recordings to *these very people*.

And now Eric actually saw an expression of sadness form on this formerly clownish woman's face.

"*This* is what we are here to find out," she said almost softly. "Because if this *is* true, and we prove to world that white tornadoes are fakes, we do terrible thing, worse than Stalin, worse than gulag, worse than . . . worse than . . ."

She shrugged, throwing up her hands. "All-time-Olympic-record atrocity. Because then no one will believe that it *is* true. No one pays to cool planet. And *we all die*. Syndicalists. Capitalists. Saints. Assholes. Birds and trees. Fishes and flowers."

Stella Marenko leaned forward, almost teary-eyed now, or so to Eric it seemed.

"So, Prince Potemkin," she said, "if this is *really* true, we must eat as big pile of shit as is necessary to prevent it, da? Must eat shit and let Big Blue Machine get away with evil capitalist fakery. Must eat shit and let Big Blue plot succeed. Siberian syndics must eat all-time-Olympic-record pile of shit and lead the way to finance the cooling of the planet."

"But—"

Now there definitely *were* tears misting Stella Marenko's formerly hard blue eyes.

"But is a lot of shit to eat, da," she said in a voice barely above a whisper. "But if we don't, no one else will. And if we who have most to lose lead, world will follow, da. . . ."

"But—"

"Da, Siberia the Golden pays to destroy its own days of wine and roses. . . . Da. . . ."

A single teardrop formed in the corner of Stella Marenko's left eye, and hung there, perhaps only by dint of her iron will, nor would she deign to notice it by brushing it away.

"But we are *Siberians!*" she said, her voice hardening. "Great-grandchildren of zeks Russian czars sent east to freeze to death for centuries. Grandchildren of Uncle Joe's gulag. Children of the capitalist collapse. We know long long winter before this greenhouse summer comes. We are tough bastards, Prince Potemkin. We are Siberians. We survive. We are not Soviets, we are not Russians, we are Siberians! We are not communists, we are not capitalists, we are syndicalists! And we are not the kind of assholes who let building burn down with ourselves inside it because it is cold outside! We are *Siberians!* And if Siberian summer must die so the world can live, well . . ."

She managed an ironic little smile. "If world *dies*, Siberia the Golden dies with it anyway, da, Prince Potemkin? We can always go back to furs and thermal underwear, and I get to wear mink and ermine all year round."

She laughed then, and Eric found the bravado of it quite touching.

"More stylish at least than raggy prison uniforms and newspapers stuffed in boots!"

". . . okay, Dr. Larabee, so after white tornadoes come on stage, how long we have before planet turns into broasting oven?"

". . . before the biosphere is terminally damaged? Or before the greenhouse runaway becomes irreversible?"

". . . is not the same?"

". . . the runaway may become irreversible before the biosphere becomes terminal, if we start seeing measurable rises in atmospheric pressure, if the superheated thermals increase in number, if they persist longer, if we start to see them over the equatorial oceans, if the overall humidity increases along with the temperature . . ."

". . . we're all climatologists on this here bus, not biospheric ecologists . . ."

". . . so before is too late to do anything but stay drunk . . ."

". . . is there's anyone at this table who hasn't reached that state already . . . ?"

". . . forty years, plus or minus a margin of error of twenty-five percent . . ."

Monique Calhoun tried not to find herself idly visualizing what Stella Marenko must be doing in the toilet to have been gone so long.

". . . is awful big margin for error . . ."

"Not in predictive climatology . . ."

Boring!

". . . we start now, we can see a full degree drop within a decade . . ."

It wasn't so easy to keep the scatological and barfological images from flitting through her mind as she sat there sipping tentatively at her vodka enduring this tedious climatological table talk that seemed little more than a woozy face-to-face reprise of the whole damned conference itself.

The climatologists, who had obviously been prepped, kept trying to convince Ivan Marenko that the white tornadoes meant The End Was Near. Aubrey Wright and the climatech executives kept trying to turn this into an unsubtle sell for their planet-cooling services.

Marenko, the object of this ham-handed amateur-night pub, seemed to have his wits together at least well enough to see through it, admittedly not a major intellectual feat, and took rude pleasure in rattling the bars of their cages while refilling their glasses almost, if not quite, as fast as he kept draining his own.

". . . mylar shits . . . ah *sheets* . . . a few molecules thick, you'd be shurprised at the area we can occlude per throw-weight . . ."

". . . trees, y'see, sequester th' charbon dioxide . . ."

". . . better marijuana, da, grows even faster, valuable cash crop . . ."

". . . but you release what you've sequestered when you burn it . . ."

Marenko, it seemed, was being a lot more successful in getting these eminent scientists and climatech corp execs blotted than they were at selling him Condition Venus.

". . . flower gardens, then, da, on rooftops, window boxes, everywhere, carpet all city space with roses, tulips, peonies, poppies, da, let a million million flowers bloom, as says famous Chinese Communist . . . Bao? Chao . . . ? Lao . . . ?"

"*Lao?*"

"Mao!"

". . . not such a crazy idea, worldwide campaign, cover lots an' lots of unused shurface area . . ."

". . . Qwik-grow flowers . . . make 'em white t'increase th' albedo too . . ."

On the other hand, Marenko wasn't failing to get himself blotted either. He was, after all, drunk enough to be blithely ignoring the fact that his wife had disappeared toward the toilet with a character like Eric Esterhazy at least fifteen minutes ago.

If that was *really* where they were.

Somehow Monique suddenly found herself doubting it.

". . . crow shits on little chicken's head, and Chicken Little runs around screaming sky is falling, da, famous proverb . . ."

". . . point of which is . . . ?"

". . . do not listen to birdbrain running around like chicken with head cut off, da . . . hah, hah, hah . . ."

Now the images that Monique could not keep from swimming through her mind's eye involved both Eric Esterhazy and Stella Marenko, they did not involve urinary, excretory, or vomitory functions, and the set was Prince Eric's private dressing room, rather than the ladies'.

And she was bemused to find that these images infuriated her.

Not that *jealousy* had anything to do with it.

What was there to be jealous about?

But Eric Esterhazy had some nerve!

While she sat here waiting for him to return through a subjective eternity of boring blather *he* was probably belowdecks in his dressing room bonking Stella Marenko!

———

Stella Marenko placed her palms on the bed behind her, leaned back, arching her breasts in Eric's direction, and while in a strictly physical sense this moved her farther away from the chair on which he sat, in some other subtle sense she seemed closer.

He found himself admiring this woman. Even liking her.

Nor, he discovered in some surprise, was his penile alter ego in disagreement.

"You are right about one thing, Prince Potemkin," she said. "Only thing we know for sure is that Big Blue capitalists *are* desperate to get Siberian money for planet-cooling schemes. Maybe to save the world. Maybe just to save financial asses. We must know. We have big decision to make. We must be very careful."

"You and Ivan don't exactly impress me as the careful types," Eric told her.

Stella Marenko laughed. "*Careful*, not . . . timid," she said. "This means we take care to do right thing, da, not that we are cowards. We are loud, we are brave, but we . . . take care."

She smiled at Eric, she stretched like a cat, upward and outward, looked directly at him with those bright blue eyes.

"For instance, Sweet Prince, we have been gone from table a long time, we must . . . *take care* that people do not think this conversation happened," she said.

Eric found himself moving forward to the edge of his chair, leaning toward her. Was what he sensed was beginning to happen really beginning to happen? Did he want it to?

"By convincing them we were doing something more . . . innocent?" he ventured.

Stella Marenko lifted her hands off the bed, slowly pulled herself upright using the muscles of her back alone, an unexpectedly fluid and athletic motion, and one which Eric found suddenly and acutely stimulating.

"Who would believe that?" she said.

"You have . . . something better in mind?"

Stella Marenko leaned deeply forward, toward him, with that same athletic fluidity, and held that difficult position like a yogic adept, affording him an excellent and not at all uninviting vista down the majestic slopes of her cleavage.

"Something . . . *more credible*," she said.

And then, amazingly, she ran her hands through her bejeweled cornrowed hairdo, disarranging it into dishabille. She ran the back of one hand across her mouth, smearing lipstick. She reached down, popped her left breast out of her bodice, the nipple of which was erect, Eric could not fail to notice as she all but shoved it in his face.

"Wha—"

She bounded off the bed, and stood there towering over Eric where he sat, hiking up her short skirt, yanking down her black silk panties, deliberately ripping them in the process, and stood over him, a mighty blond amazon looking for all the world as if he had had his way with her already.

Or rather, realistically, vice versa.

She ran both hands through his long blond hair, thoroughly tangling it. She stuck a hand down his shirt to feel his chest, popping the top two buttons. She withdrew it. She cupped his face in both hands, pulled him upright, kissed him everywhere but on the mouth, wetly and messily. She reached down, pulled open his velcro fly, and—

Stood back, while Eric stood there with a throbbing erection half out of his pants, all but panting and drooling.

She shoved her breast most of the way back into her bodice, pulled her ripped panties up to half-mast, rearranged her short crumpled dress so that just a hint of torn black silk showed if she bent a little too far over.

She reflected a moment, then bit Eric just under the left ear hard enough to create a little bloody bruise, unceremoniously and with some difficulty stuffed his prick back into his pants, artfully resealed the fly halfway up and crooked.

"Da," she said, observing her handiwork critically. "Now when we leave, no one who sees us will think we were doing anything in here but fucking."

Monique found making a graceful exit from the Marenko table ridiculously easy. She had not been taking part in the conversation, there were a dozen people waiting to squeeze into any momentarily empty chair at the feast, and Ivan Marenko, too drunk to notice that his wife had gone missing, didn't even notice her departure.

Getting the recordings of all the Marenkos' past drunken table talk out of Eric Esterhazy tonight, though, was not going to be as easy.

It would probably take some arduous exercise of her feminine wiles to even get him to admit they existed, though admittedly, if Posner hadn't all but ordered her to do just that and she weren't so pissed off at Eric, that wouldn't exactly be the most onerous task she had ever confronted.

But first she had to find him. And while she now had an unpleasant idea of *where* to find him, it didn't seem like such a smart move to go banging on his dressing-room door to roust him out of bed with Stella Marenko.

Still, she didn't see what else she could do, so she made her way belowdecks to boudoir country, passing a couple on their way in to one of the chambers, and another on the way out of one, on her way to Eric Esterhazy's dressing room.

Now what?

Mercifully the corridor remained empty for several minutes, so there was no one to observe her standing there like a fool trying to decide whether to knock or wait.

If she knocked and got no answer, it could mean either that they weren't in there, or that they were, and naturally didn't want to be discovered. If she waited, and they *did* eventually emerge, it would be just as awkward, and if she was wrong, and they weren't in there, she could wait forever.

Fortunately there was no keyhole, or no doubt she would have been caught bent over with her ass in the air peering through it like the foil in some moldy old French bedroom farce by the two couples who came sauntering down the corridor as—

—the door opened.

And out staggered Prince Eric Esterhazy and Stella Marenko in a state hardly more fit for public consumption.

Her hair was a mess. Lipstick was smeared all over her face. Her short skirt was hiked halfway up one buttock. One of her enormous tits was just about hanging out.

His hair was also a rats' nest. The top two buttons of his shirt were missing. His face was smeared with lipstick too, and there was a bloody bruise under one ear. And his *fly* was half open, though at least his cock wasn't hanging out.

What a spectacle! Couldn't they have at least washed their faces, combed their hair, and pulled up their drawers properly afterward?

"I hope I haven't interrupted anything important," Monique Calhoun said in a voice like a cryogenic stiletto.

Eric stood there grinning stupidly like . . . like someone caught with his pants down.

As Stella Marenko had intended.

"Oh we jus' having little philosophy talk about state of world and ethical structure of universe," Stella woozed, giving Monique a broad wink that didn't seem to improve her current opinion thereof.

"But we're finished now," Eric told her.

"You're *sure?*" said Monique, glancing portentously down at his crotch.

Stella laughed. "Whoops!" she said, reaching down to reseal his fly.

Eric shrugged weakly and gave Monique a vapid smile. Like it or not, and he wasn't quite sure why he didn't, he was going to have to go along with this bedroom farce to cover the true nature of his tête-à-tête with Stella.

As Stella Marenko had intended.

"And your, ah, slip is showing, Mrs. Marenko," Monique said with poisonous sweetness. "Not to mention your tit and your ass."

"Thank you," Stella said blithely, smoothing down her dress, pulling up her bodice.

"Would not want to upset Ivan, da?" She gave Monique a conspiratorial one-of-the-girls look. "Men are such jealous beasts, da? No need to know."

"My lips are sealed," Monique told her with Saharan dryness.

Stella Marenko regarded Eric like a prime cut of meat, gave Monique yet another stage wink, ran her tongue slowly around her mouth like a cat licking cream.

"No need to go *that* far," she said.

A sentiment which in that moment Eric amply shared.

"Do you think you can . . . navigate by yourself, Mrs. Marenko?"

Monique said. "Prince Esterhazy and I have a bit of business to discuss."

"No problem," Stella told her. "Exercise clears head. Handsome prince is finished doing *my* business, now is turn for him to do *yours.*"

She walked away slowly up the corridor a few paces, turned, gave Monique Calhoun one last juicy wink. "Have fun," she said, "but don't do anything I haven't done already," and exited, stage left.

"What was that woman doing with you in there?" Monique said acidly after Eric Esterhazy had dismissed the tech and they were alone in the computer room. "Showing you what made Catherine the Great great? Something to do with screwing horses, wasn't it?"

"You're jealous!" Prince Eric said in what seemed like genuine surprise as he stood there looking as if he had just played overmatched stand-in for the said equine stud service, which he probably had.

"I am not!" Monique snapped back.

Eric gave her a warm winning boyish smile. "Relax," he said, "I find it charming."

Monique did not know what to say to that.

His smile was so innocent, *pure*, she would have had to say if he hadn't so obviously come straight from a heavy horizontal wrestling match.

Why, after all, *was* she angry? Who Eric Esterhazy went to bed with, assuming they had gotten that far, was none of her business. What was more, he had made it abundantly clear almost every time they had met that *she* could enjoy his considerable physical charms whenever she chose to. And the main thing that had kept her from taking him up on it was that his own opinion of his animal allure was manifestly higher than even her own.

Was she jealous?

But of whom and why and of what?

Jealousy, after all, is not a rational logical reaction, she told herself. And you're here on business. So get professional.

"I am not jealous," she said very evenly. "But I *am* annoyed with you."

Eric draped himself languidly over one of the chairs in front of the wall of computer screens like a fashion model, legs akimbo, so as to display, no doubt deliberately, the still-or-perhaps-once-more formidable bulge in his pants.

Which, considering the circumstances, Monique had to admit was a feat she could only consider impressive.

Or quite flattering.

And either way or both, therefore exciting.

Infuriatingly so.

"Why?" he said, teasingly, all-too-knowingly. "Because I didn't save my virginity for you?"

"Because you were off playing hanky-panky with Stella Marenko while I needed you here for serious business," Monique Calhoun told him.

Eric spread his arms, leaned back, manfully refrained from uttering the horrid cliché about how anger enhanced her attractiveness, which it didn't.

But the way the images planted in her mind by false appearances aroused her lustful jealousy against her will, and his almost painful state of fiery unfulfilled arousal, certainly did.

"Well I'm here now," he said instead, "and I'm all yours and open for business, serious or monkey."

"You certainly have a high opinion of yourself, Eric Esterhazy!"

"My only flaw," Eric said dryly, "is an unfortunate tendency to false modesty. But I *am* working on it."

It amused him to see her choking back laughter. Eric was not accustomed to being left achingly horny by the sort of masterful cocktease Stella Marenko had worked on him, though watching a woman making an ultimately futile attempt to pretend she found him physically resistible was something with which he was very familiar.

The combination of both at the same time was a unique pleasure and he found himself quite enjoying it.

Well all right, Prince Handsome, though lightweight, *was* charming, and the source of his charm was that he acknowledged his lack of seriousness without taking it seriously, which, Monique supposed, was what it took to make a successful gigolo or phony prince.

"Seriously, Eric—"

"Seriously? Are you sure you wouldn't prefer a little monkey business?"

"Not now, maybe later," Monique found herself blurting.

"Business before pleasure..." Eric said agreeably, but without changing his spread-legged posture or removing that inviting bedroom smile from his face. "On the other hand..."

On the other hand, maybe we should just get it over with now was the clear implication. And Monique accepted that they were not going to leave this room without doing it.

After all, she reminded herself, that was what she had come here to do for *tactical* reasons in the first place, to literally screw the Marenko table talk recordings out of him.

Business before pleasure?

Here was one of those all too rare moments when they were going to coincide.

Eric Esterhazy was one attractive male animal. Prince Eric was also a famous lady-killer whose looks and attitude clearly indicated that his reputation was not unjustified. Eric could have his choice of hundreds of women and just had.

Yet this handsome male creature, who had apparently come straight from a session with a hungry amazon which should have left him limp as an overcooked cannelloni, was ready, willing, and eager to rip off *her* clothes this very minute and fuck her on the floor.

Perverse or not, it was the ultimate compliment.

And the ultimate turn-on.

But why not enjoy that sweet perverse tension a while longer and turn it to advantage in the pragmatic matter at hand...?

"I want something from you," Monique Calhoun told Eric. She still hadn't taken the other seat in front of the monitors, which Eric found promising, yet hadn't approached him any closer, which he found amusing in the manner of a cobra patiently awaiting the approach of a mesmerized bird.

"Who am I to thwart your desires?" he said.

Now she did approach his chair, standing over him, looking down, giving him a nicely complex smile back. "Who am I to thwart yours?" she said in an insinuating tone.

She reached down and ran a finger through the air about five centimeters from his fly. "But I want a quid before you get your pro quo. . . ."

"I'm all ears . . ." Eric said.

Monique Calhoun stared frankly down into his crotch. "Not from where I'm standing," she said.

Eric laughed. So did she.

He sat up somewhat straighter, spread his legs even wider, moved his right hand toward his inner thigh. "Have a seat then," he invited.

"Not so fast," Monique said.

"Take it as slow as you want," purred Prince Eric.

"Let's just see how slow *you* can stand to take it," Monique said, reaching down and undoing his fly. There was nothing particularly huge or unusual about what emerged eagerly from its restraints, but the way Eric simply maintained eye contact without moving, without showing surprise or impatience, as she slowly ran just a fingernail up its length, was something very special indeed.

"Now then," Monique Calhoun said, hiking up her dress and pulling down her panties, "the matter of quid pro quo . . ."

She reached down again, and this time just flicked the head of Eric's cock playfully. Eric suppressed a moan of agonized delight.

"Your wish is my command," he said.

"Is it?" said Monique. She bent over, kissed him lightly on the lips with just a flick of tongue, but at the same time clutched him quite firmly down below.

"Try me," said Eric.

Monique massaged him to within a tasty millimeter of causing him to lose it, which, under the prolonged circumstances, did not take very long, and then held him there, right on the edge.

"Find this . . . *trying* enough?" she said.

"You'll have to try me a bit harder than that, Mata Hari," Eric declared heroically.

"Ve haff our vays," Monique said, moving forward to straddle Eric Esterhazy, positioning herself just short of impaling herself sweetly upon him. It was a difficult position to hold in more ways than one, but as with a less erotic gymnastic posture in a competition routine, the degree of difficulty perversely made it more enjoyable.

"So what do I have to do to . . . get you to reach the bottom line?" Eric said.

"I want copies of all the recordings you've automatically been making of the Marenkos' table talk," Monique said.

Now Eric almost *did* lose it.

What was that old American folktale about Brer Rabbit and the briar patch? The rabbit pleads with the fox to do anything but throw him into that nasty old briar patch, which, being his home and escape route, is of course precisely what he wants the fox to do.

And leaking those recordings to Monique and hopefully allowing her to wheedle him into assisting in her inquiries to see what she was after was likewise precisely what Eduardo wanted *him* to do!

Should he surrender at once?

Oh no, much more credible to play hard to get!

"Automatic recording . . . ?" he said innocently.

"Don't tell me your . . . equipment can't handle it!" Monique said, giving it a squeeze.

And ever so much more enjoyable.

"You're about to discover just how much my equipment *can* handle. . . ."

"Not until you admit you've got what I want."

"All right, all right," Eric told her. "I've got what you want . . . I've got . . . *everything* that you want."

"The recordings . . . ?"

"That too."

Monique Calhoun smiled, seated herself upon him, then began a deliberate, languid rotation.

"Now then," she purred, "the name of this game is *you* don't get to come until you agree that I get what I came for."

"Fair enough," Eric told her. "But I should warn you, I'm a slow deliberate player. It might take some time to reach the endgame."

"Getting there is half the fun. . . ."

"At least," said Eric, and he relaxed into it, and sighed, and favored her with a low moan of pleasure.

And they sealed the bargain with a deep open-mouthed kiss.

How slowly could he stand to play this game?

Very slowly indeed.

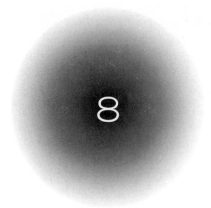

8

MONIQUE CALHOUN HAD NEVER BEFORE HAD
the dubious honor of being summoned to Avi Posner's apartment, but
Posner had insisted on vetting the material in a secure venue, not her
suite at the Ritz, or the Bread & Circuses office.

The weather had turned strangely humid and hot not only for this
time of the year but for any time of the year in Paris. New Orleans in
August her grandparents had proclaimed; a steambath in a microwave
oven according to others; a secondary sign of the onset of Condition
Venus according to those with a vested interest in promoting it.

Whatever was producing this hot foggy overcast, the effect upon
Parisian tempers had not been sweet. The cab ride from the Ritz to
Rue Dominique had been a curse-punctuated zigzag through horn-
blaring traffic, the Place de la Concorde a chaotic bumper-car ride at
a not-so-fun fun fair, and by the time Monique reached the address
Posner had given her, her nerves were as frayed as the pavement was
fried.

The address in question turned out to be one of those perpetually
graying apartment houses that all seemed to have been designed by
the same architect and thrown up in the same month in the late

nineteenth century, and had formed the backbone of the Parisian housing stock ever since.

There was the usual doorcode and the usual cramped twentieth-century retrofit elevator shoehorned into a wire cage in the center of the stairwell. The name on the mailbox and directory of the fourth-floor apartment, Israel Dupont, seemed like some kind of elusive Mossad joke.

Posner answered the door in a tan short-sleeved shirt and matching jungle shorts. All-too-characteristically of this vintage of Parisian apartment, built with living room windows in the form of doors that opened out onto a balcony, only the bedroom was air-conditioned, the main room making do with the open windows and an overhead fan-cum-water-device known for some arcane reason as a "swamp cooler."

The "living room" didn't look as if anyone really lived in it and Monique suspected that the bedroom would be more of the same, though she had no particular interest in finding out. The generic Scandinavian couch, chairs, lamps, and tables had probably been rented en suite. There were no plants, rugs, paintings, or bookcases.

The electronic equipment, however, was not standard. A multi-screen computer console with assorted decks and docking stations. Two video phones, four voice-onlys. A steel rack of stuff Monique didn't recognize but which she doubted was a fanatic's state-of-the-art music system. A stand-alone high-rez TV. Scanners. Printers. A portable sat-dish.

Obviously Mossad's Paris spook shop, not Avi Posner's cozy bachelor pad. Nor did he offer convivial hospitality.

"What've you got?" he said instead when Monique parked herself in one of the faux-Bauhaus sling chairs.

Monique extracted a handful of recording chips from her purse and proffered them to Posner.

"What's this," he said dubiously, "the raw recordings?"

"What else did you expect?"

Posner sank down onto the couch, holding up the chips and shaking them at her. "None of these is an edited summary?" he groaned.

"How am I supposed to prepare an edited summary if I don't have the faintest idea of what I'm editing for?" Monique demanded.

"*Amateurs*," Posner moaned, rolling his eyes toward the ceiling. "So this is an unedited mess of Marenko table talk?"

Monique nodded.

"You have at least reviewed this material?"

Monique nodded again.

"So perhaps you can at least provide a *verbal* description?"

"Climatech babble. Wine- and vodka-snob babble. White tornado babble. Condition Venus babble. Dirty joke babble. Basically a lot of drunken babble getting less and less coherent as everyone concerned gets more and more blotted."

Posner seemed to be making an effort not to grind his teeth and not entirely succeeding. "You *did* say you reviewed this material?" he said. "Thoroughly? While actually conscious?"

"I've, uh, scanned through it."

"You've . . . scanned . . . through . . . . it. . . ?"

"It's hours and hours of recordings!" Monique snapped irritably. "What was I supposed to do?"

"*What were you supposed to do!*" Posner shouted.

Then he abruptly calmed himself. "I'm sorry," he said in quite another voice. "This weather must be getting to me. I forget that you are not a professional, nor do you have access to professional-level equipment." He shrugged. "Not that you'd know what to do with it if you did."

He got up, went to the computer, Monique trailing behind, sat down, and began loading the chip recordings into its memory.

"Not the latest generation hardware maybe," Posner told her as they loaded, "but the software's first-rate."

By the time Monique had pulled up a chair, the loading process was just about finished.

"Word frequency, level one filter . . ." Posner told the computer.

The computer began muttering electronically to itself.

"What's it doing?" Monique said.

"Ranking all the words spoken on the recordings by frequency, eliminating the hundred most common words in the language."

A column of words followed by numbers began scrolling vertically down the screen.

"Stop," said Posner.

The scrolling halted.

"Word frequency, level three filter."

The scrolling began again, then stopped.

"Eliminates the five hundred most common," Posner said. "Let's see . . ." He thought for a moment. "Word frequency, level four filter, nouns only."

More scrolling, shorter this time.

"Now we're getting somewhere. . . . Word frequency, level four filter, proper nouns only . . ."

The list of words was much shorter this time, and all of them were capitalized.

"Word frequency, level four filter, proper nouns only, place-name filter, filter Paris, filter France, filter Siberia, option filter, filter Marenko, filter Ivan, filter Stella . . . top fifty only . . ."

The computer did its thing in less time that it took Posner to issue the command.

"Venus" was at the top of the list, followed by "UNACOCS," "Larabee," "Mohammed," "Bendsten," "Pereiro," "Davinda," "Wright," "Lao" . . . on down to "Esterhazy," way at the bottom.

Monique was somewhat piqued to see that she hadn't made it.

For some reason, Avi Posner did not seem pleased either.

"Shit," he observed, scowling at the screen, more in agitation than anger.

"Sequence and record. Chronological. Voice only. Follow Davinda. Follow Sri. Follow Sri Davinda."

More computer noises, then a "sequence and record completed" message on the screen.

"Playback," said Avi Posner.

". . . Davinda's crazy speech even in Zekograd," said the voice of Stella Marenko.

". . . Davinda was drunk at big ceremony," said the voice of Ivan Marenko.

". . . Davinda's brilliant in his way . . ." said a male voice that sounded like Paolo Pereiro.

". . . Davinda a few drinks . . ." said the voice of Ivan Marenko.

". . . Sri Davinda's not very sociable, hardly *socialized* these days . . ." said the male voice.

"...Sri Davinda!" boomed the voice of Ivan Marenko. "Anyone gives speech dead drunk I want to meet!"

"...Sri Davinda's done reputable work, but gotten involved with some strange people in the past few years..." said a female voice Monique couldn't place.

"...Davinda aboard..."

"...Davinda's Hindu name, like Lao, da...?"

"...Sri Davinda's climate model on Sunday..."

"...Davinda sort of disappeared into the woods after that..."

"...Davinda and Lao, Lao and Davinda, is code, maybe..."

"...Davinda and those Third Force rumors..."

"...Davinda's hardly first-rank, Mrs. Marenko..."

"...Davinda's *monk*, or something, da, follower of gurus, Hubbard, Bodhidharma, Lao..."

"...Sri Davinda so interesting...?"

"...Davinda's a man I like to meet..."

"Stop," said Avi Posner.

For some reason that Monique couldn't fathom from listening to these seemingly meaningless recordings, Posner had grown more and more agitated as he listened.

"What's the—"

Avi Posner held up a peremptory hand for silence.

"Word search, proper noun and/or acronym, multilingual, global, word Lao."

After about thirty seconds, four entries appeared on the screen:

Lao—person of Laotian nationality.

Pathet *Lao*—Laotian Communist Party cum guerrilla army of mid-twentieth century, ally of Viet Cong in Vietnam War.

Lao Tze—putative author of Tao Te Ching, hence legendary founder of Taoism, possibly historical personage.

THE CIRCUS OF DR. *LAO*—twentieth-century fantasy novel by Charles Finney.

Posner shook his head in bewilderment; it seemed to Monique that he was making an effort to avoid the cliché of scratching it.

"Search word Lao," he said. "Sequence and record. Chronological. Follow Lao. Voice only. Playback."

". . . Lao, Mao's blood brother, da, Kutnik . . . ?"

". . . Lao, Marenko . . . (laughter)"

". . . Lao, da . . . ? He is Indian, or Californian mystic . . ."

". . . Lao, is Chinese Minister of Environment? Haven't met yet . . ."

". . . Lao, *Chu Lun*, Ivan . . ."

". . . Lao and Davinda, Davinda and Lao, is code maybe . . ."

"*Maybe?*" Avi Posner snarled sardonically. "Stop!" he fairly shouted.

He turned off the computer with an angry gesture, stood up looking quite worried, began pacing in small circles.

"What is it?" Monique asked. "What's the matter?"

Posner stopped pacing. He stared at her. He seemed to be *studying* her. "Do you have a need to know?" he muttered in a tone of voice that seemed to indicate that he wasn't really asking her, but himself.

"Know what?"

"Can I tell you . . . ?" he muttered. "Can I not . . . ?"

Avi Posner sighed. "Outside," he said.

"You think *this place* is bugged?"

"Assume that *every* place is bugged, Monique. I believe I've told you that."

"But the only people who could be bugging this apartment are your—"

"I'm bending the contract a bit. I'm doing this on my own authority. There's no choice. You now have a need to know."

"Know what?"

"*Outside.*"

Outside on the narrow balcony, it was hot and muggy and the graying of the sky by an alien atmospheric condition not quite coherent enough to be called cloudy but too high to be called fog not only contributed to a sense of psychic oppression but somehow *did* have Monique wondering uneasily about its possible connection to Condition Venus. Posner went to the iron railing, leaned over, motioned for Monique to do likewise.

"The reason you have a need to know, the reason I'm telling you this," he said sotto voce, "is that you must *keep John Sri Davinda away from the Marenkos.*"

"May I ask why?"

"I suppose so, not that they tell *me* everything," Posner muttered unhappily. "What I *have* had a need to know, according to the client, is that the climate model Davinda is demonstrating on Sunday is their whole raison d'être for the conference."

"What! How is that possible?"

Avi Posner shrugged. "This they do not believe I have a need to know," he said. "But this is why they are guarding whatever it is behind that canvas screening in the Grand Palais like an old-fashioned state secret."

"Just another climate model . . . ? It makes no sense."

"I *am* given to understand that the client financed whatever it is, and that the client believes that whatever it is will convince even the Siberians that Condition Venus is an inevitability unless they finance the client's projects to stop it against their own class self-interest."

"Our . . . client poured all that money it really can't afford into a crap-shoot bet that Davinda's climate model can do that?" Monique exclaimed.

Posner pressed a finger to her lips, leaned closer.

"*He's* crazy?" Monique whispered. "Sounds to me like *the client's* been taken in by a pretty clever con artist."

"Maybe . . ." Posner whispered. "But maybe not . . ."

"But how?"

Posner fidgeted. He positively squirmed. "This they do not believe I have a need to know either. And maybe they are right. Maybe this is something I do not *want* to know . . ."

Monique took him by the shoulder, turned him toward her rather gently. The look on his face was not that of the tough professional Mossad operative. Avi Posner looked . . . haunted.

"This is only deduction, Monique, there is no corroboration, but, well . . ."

"Spit it out, Avi. . . ."

Posner sighed. "A climate model, no matter how advanced, no matter how sophisticated, is software," he told her. "So what they are hiding under guard can only be the hardware it runs on. . . ."

"Obviously . . ."

No breath of wind disturbed the heavy muggy air. But Monique felt a chill anyway.

Avi Posner wrung his hands together. "Well, if it used a polymerized human brain as a central processing unit . . ." he muttered furtively.

"They *couldn't!*" Monique exclaimed.

"Of course they could," Posner whispered softly. "Polymerized rat brains are commonly used as parallel meatware processors in top-end equipment, and pig brains are winked at in a few Muslim and Jewish jurisdictions. From a technical point of view, a mammalian brain is a mammalian brain. And that chimp brain affair . . ."

A few years back, the Chinese *had* cloned a chimpanzee brain, polymerized it, and installed it as a central processing unit in a computer. But the worldwide shrieks of rage and horror when they boasted publicly about it without so much as a poll or a focus group first had made it politically and ethically impossible to go beyond the brains of rats, a universally unpopular mammal with no significant sentimental constituency.

"They *wouldn't!*" Monique exclaimed. "Would they?" she added in a much less certain tone of voice.

"It would certainly be the most powerful computer ever constructed. . . ."

"But public relations suicide!"

"So it would seem," Posner said. "At first glance. To an operative of Bread & Circuses. But . . ."

"But?"

"But from a more ruthlessly sophisticated realpolitik point of view, what you call the 'deep sell' might be the reverse. Precisely *because* it would break such a strong taboo, *because* it would seem to be such a public relations disaster, *because* it would seem to be so politically counterproductive, would it not be the ultimate proof of sincere desperation beyond mere economics? Would not even the Siberians be therefore convinced that even capitalist monsters would only do such a thing to save the planet itself?"

"I think I'm going to puke," Monique said.

It wasn't true, but she wished it were, she wished she could disgorge this morsel of tainted knowledge, for Posner's theory had a dreadful and slimy credibility. Such a twisted deep sell strategy might very well work.

Worse still, much worse, if in fact the Big Blue Machine *was* in possession of self-convincing knowledge that Condition Venus was imminent, would not such a horrid act be *morally justified?*

Wouldn't she herself do her professional duty and use such a deep sell if she knew that the alternative was the death of the biosphere?

Indeed, hadn't she been unknowingly been involved in doing so all along? Would she back out now? Could she?

Should she?

"Lao is the code name for . . . for *that*, Avi?" she said.

"Lao . . . ?" Posner muttered distractedly. "Lao?"

Then, more forcefully, as if returning from a distant somewhere else: "I have no idea who or what Lao is."

He frowned, he turned back toward the apartment, toward his business-as-usual persona. "But the Marenkos dropped this seemingly meaningless word into their general conversation no less than half a dozen times. So we had damn well better find out."

Eric Esterhazy was not surprised that the dining room of the Marenkos' rented town house was furnished like a cross between the Versailles palace and a five-star bordello in Monaco.

The Marenkos had summoned Eric and invited Eduardo Ramirez— no one could *summon* Eduardo—and Eduardo had brought along Mom—no one could presume to refuse Eduardo a choice of dining companion either. Eduardo had arrived costumed as a twentieth-century banker in a severe black pin-striped suit. Mom wore a loosely flowing rose pantsuit and a matching derby hat with a veil that reached down just past her eyes. Eric was accoutered in a lime-green linen suit and black silk shirt.

This gear somehow went with the room that the retro-English butler escorted them into with much bowing and flourishing: a huge eighteenth-century formal salon, with massive crystal chandeliers, a high paneled ceiling painted sky-blue with clouds, floral and fruit sconce-work in full color, nineteenth-century landscape paintings in massive gilt frames, rose and blue flocked silk wallpaper, a huge antique dining table with white napery, and service of blue Delft china, Venetian crystal goblets, solid gold dinnerware.

It *was* a surprise therefore when the Marenkos entered in matching plain black jumpsuits, no jewelry, no gold braid, no decoration of any kind, like Brigade Ninja Ronin operatives prepared for a drop behind enemy lines.

It was an even bigger surprise that while the lavish lunch was served by five waiters in full black formal, one for each diner, nothing stronger than white wine was served with it and Stella and Ivan Marenko sipped abstemiously even at that.

Over an entree of raw oysters piled high with caviar, Ivan Marenko laid it all out succinctly. His English might not have become perfect, but the borscht and bullshit had pretty much gone with the drunk act and the tacky flash.

"We can assume that Sunday surprise will be this Davinda climate model. Logical to assume that secret under guard in Grand Palais has something to do with it. That Big Blue Machine believes it opens our wallets. So . . . we must make Davinda talk, get look at what is being hidden in Grand Palais, all before Sunday. And we know Monique Calhoun is monitoring our table talk, but *she* doesn't know *we* know, could be advantage. Questions?"

Mom had one, but it was for Eric.

"You fucked her yet?" she inquired genteelly.

"Mom!"

"Spare us the gallant knight act, Eric, we all know you're not, we're all adults who've consented to acts that would make a pederastic pirate blush, and we have a need to know."

"Your mother has a point," Eduardo said.

"Yes, I have *fucked her*, Mom," Eric said crossly. And then, unable to resist the supercilious addendum: "Or rather, I have allowed her to fuck me."

"Noblesse oblige . . ." said Eduardo dryly.

"Dirty job, but someone gets to do it!" Ivan Marenko observed somewhat less suavely.

"I fail to see what this has to do with—"

"She in love with you, kiddo?"

"Get real, Mom!" Eric snapped back without thinking.

"In lust, at least, I hope?"

This both required and inspired more thoughtful consideration. Who had seduced whom? In a perverse manner, it had been Stella Marenko who had seduced Eric, by dropping him into the computer room with Monique in a state of frustrated tumescence in which he would've fucked almost anyone even minimally presentable who made herself available. In which state, he had indeed worked his wiles on Monique, according to both plan and erect inclination. And she had indeed responded.

But on the other hand, Monique had run that tasty Mata Hari tease on *him*, to which *he* had responded at least as enthusiastically, even though, or perhaps *because*, it was quite openly a stratagem.

From one point of view, it had all been quite humorous, from another, deliciously perverse, and be that as it may, when push, as it were, had finally come down to prolonged shove, he had quite enjoyed it, and was far too experienced to believe that either her enjoyment or her orgasm had been faked.

"Let's just say the chemistry is there," Eric concluded.

"This is your professional judgment, or your dick talking, Eric?"

"In certain instances, Mom, they are one and the same. But what is the point?"

"The point," said Eduardo, "is point of entry, Eric. We need a point of entry into the strategy of the Big Blue Machine, the only available one would seem to be Monique Calhoun, and the only point of entry to her would seem to be—"

"—the point of your prick!"

Eduardo glared at Mom. Mom actually looked chastened; an effect that, in Eric's experience, no one but Eduardo Ramirez had ever been capable of achieving.

"*The point being,*" Eduardo said, "that it would seem that Monique Calhoun regards *you* in a similar manner. Do you think you can—"

"—stay on top of her?"

This time Eduardo did nothing, and the Marenkos laughed.

"I think I can manage," Eric said, though admittedly it hadn't quite turned out that way the first time around.

Fortunately, this train of conversation was interrupted by the arrival of the homard en son nid de truffe, lobster in saffron cream sauce served over huge mounds of sautéed truffles—a delicacy whose cuisinary might commanded a certain period of respectfully silent gustatory appreciation, and when the table talk resumed, the subject mercifully shifted to John Sri Davinda.

"Except for the opening night, he's never been on the guest lists Calhoun has given Eric," Eduardo said.

"Proof she wants to keep him away from us, da Ivan?" said Stella Marenko.

"Reason to put him on *your* list, Prince Potemkin," said Ivan.

"As I have already . . . recommended," said Eduardo.

"Doesn't look suspicious?" said Stella.

"Da. But only of what they already know but don't know *we* know they know. That we are very interested in this John Sri Davinda."

"So if Calhoun tries to complain, *how* she complains maybe tells us something?"

"Is that why you kept dropping this word 'Lao'?" said Eric. "To try and get a reaction that would give us a hint of what it means?"

"Da," said Stella. "Interesting to rattle bars of cage to see what monkeys do."

"Unless what they do is throw shit in your face!"

"Ivan! This is *lunch*!"

She *couldn't* have made such a ghastly mistake.

The thin man with the close-cropped hair in the grimy white blouson and loose pantaloons approaching the dock end of the gangway was no down-on-his-luck karate master or indigent sensei of Third Force arcana or mendicant Buddhist monk lacking even a begging bowl.

He was John Sri Davinda.

In a panic, Monique Calhoun scooted up toward the bow end of *La Reine de la Seine*'s promenade, out of sight of Davinda as he boarded, to double-check her guest list.

No, Davinda's name *wasn't* on it.

But he *had* gotten past the people checking the invitations in the embarkation pavilion. Meaning he had one. Meaning he could only have gotten it from Prince Eric Esterhazy.

But why?

Had Eric done it just to torment her?

But Eric *couldn't* know about Avi Posner's order that she keep Davinda away from the Marenkos.

Could he?

Order?

That thought was a wake-up call. She *was* taking orders from a Mossad operative in the service of an umbrella organization of revenant capitalists whom Posner himself believed ruthless enough to install a human brain in a computer to further an agenda that might be the saving of the biosphere or just their own threadbare economic asses.

In the service of which, more or less under the orders of whom, she had had sex with a man for strategic gain. True, it had not exactly been cold-blooded, true too she had enjoyed it, but it still made her a whore from a certain viewpoint, albeit an enthusiastic one.

It was a long way from New York. It was even a long way from that tacky Gardens of Allah deal in Libya. It was no longer just Bread & Circuses.

As one of those sourceless Third Force epigrams had it: "Wherever you go, there you are."

There was another one that went: "The way out is the way through."

Ambiguous persiflage as the Third Force versions might be, the B&C version reduced it to pragmatic operative terms: "Deal with it first, and figure it out later."

The crew *was* lifting the gangway, the Marenkos *were* on board *La Reine*, and now so was John Sri Davinda, and her task, however problematic, however she had managed or rather *been* managed to find herself stuck with it, was to keep the one from the other.

There seemed to be only one chance.

In for a dime, in for a dollar, as they still said anachronistically in New York long after that currency had gone out of circulation.

Now that we've established what you are, it's just a question of price.

That was one New York line that Monique doubted would ever lose currency.

———

As was his expected custom, Prince Eric Esterhazy was up in the wheelhouse as the lines were cast off and Captain Klein warped *La Reine de la Seine* away from the dock, but he was not taking his usual prideful pleasure in the departure spectacle.

Instead, he was peering down at the forward promenade, where Monique Calhoun was trotting purposefully up behind John Sri Davinda, who stood leaning against the forward railing staring out across the Seine at the lights of the Trocadéro or perhaps just into space.

"Eric . . . ? *Eric!*"

Eddie Warburton was shouting at him to utter the next pro forma command.

"Oh . . . right . . ." Eric muttered. "Light her up, Eddie!"

"Rock and roll!"

Bah-*bah*-BAH! *BAH-BAH!!*

The familiar orchestral fanfare sounded. The halogen tubes lit up *La Reine*. The big holographic smokestacks sprang into virtual being spouting twin phantom plumes of black smoke and clouds of white steam. The riverboat's lasers exploded virtual star shells and Roman candles and rockets across the Parisian sky. The great paddle wheels began to turn. "When the Saints Go Marching In" resounded over the Seine.

The Queen of the River was under way.

But the princely master thereof was peering down at Monique Calhoun talking to John Sri Davinda with all the lordly dignity of a jealous husband peeking through a keyhole.

Not that sexual jealousy had anything to do with it. That would be laughable. Nor was it a matter of curiosity. The promenade was miked and he could always play back the conversation later.

But the way Monique had glommed onto Davinda as soon as he was aboard, while interesting on an informational level, was not a pleasant operational omen. It obviously meant that she intended to do her best to keep him occupied.

To keep him away from the very people Eric was commissioned to lead him to, Stella and Ivan Marenko.

La Reine de la Seine reached the center of the channel, and, on cue, the band broke into the blithe tune of "Rollin' on the River." But somehow Eric doubted this was going to be an easy rollin' voyage.

"Strange weather we've been having lately . . ." Monique Calhoun ventured, trying to hide her exasperation.

True enough, even though what had been described as a "freak saturation high" generated by "transient jet-stream anomalies" by the Green spinmeisters and "a symptom of long-term increase in planetary atmospheric humidity levels" by the Blue had rolled out as precipitously as it had rolled in.

She had approached Davinda via her professional capacity, which, by now, she had almost come to think of as her cover.

Hello, I'm Monique Calhoun, your VIP services representative, is everything all right, are you having a good time, is there anything at all I can do for you? *Anything at all?*

All the while trying to whip entendre on it with an intrusion into the penumbra of his body space.

But John Sri Davinda had not only been oblivious to such flirtatious subtleties, he had not even turned around to acknowledge her presence.

"I have no current requirements," had been the extent of his reply.

Monique would've taken it as an insult to her feminine charms had not Davinda given off such a strong anti-erotic anti-vibration, something that went far beyond what every woman experienced from time to time mistakenly flirting with a confirmed homosexual. She sensed a void in this man beyond the sexual. As someone or other had said about some place or other, there was no there there.

And so, since this guy *was* a climatologist and had about as much small talk as a zombie, what *else* was left but to try the weather?

"Define the time-frame," John Sri Davinda now replied in that flat robotic voice.

"The last couple of days," Monique snapped peevishly.

"Within the limits of predictive extremes."

"And your forecast for the rest of the week, Dr. Davinda?" Monique said sarcastically.

"In so short a time-frame, chaotic uncertainty makes meaningful prediction impossible."

"Great! You're a big-time climatologist, but you can't even tell me if it's going to rain on Sunday so I know whether to carry an umbrella or not!"

"A hard rain will fall," said John Sri Davinda.

He said it in quite another voice, this one all too colored with some extremity of human emotion that Monique could not quite parse. And perhaps didn't want to. For now, Davinda did finally turn to face her, and his visage was a deeply disturbing sight.

The pupils of his heavily bloodshot eyes were hugely dilated. There was a blankness there that seemed both affectless and haunted. As if something had been . . . washed away. Or washed over.

Yet the muscles of his lips were trembling as if in concentration, as if in *desperate* concentration, as if he were struggling to control them, as if there were something trapped behind those eyes trying to . . . get out.

And not quite making it.

Monique had secured some hallucinogenic cactus for Davinda, and to judge from his abortive performance at the UNACOCS emergency session, he had attempted to speak under the influence of either the peyote or some other drug, perhaps not unmixed with alcohol.

Was he stoned now?

Or worse, had permanent damage been done to the neurons or biochemistry of his brain?

"Hello in there?" Monique said, half sarcastically, half in genuine human concern. "Is there anyone at home?"

The idea of keeping Davinda away from the Marenkos via sexual dalliance now seemed about as practical as arousing the phallic ardor of a corpse and only marginally more appetizing.

"Am I interrupting something . . . personal?"

"Hardly," Monique found herself blurting truthfully as she turned to the sound of Eric Esterhazy's voice, so nuanced with all the bantering slyness, the testeronic overtones, the masculine humanity, that Davinda's lacked.

Merde! Shit! Damn!

There Eric stood, big, blond, and handsome, every gram and smirk of him exuding erotic innuendo, the hunky cocksman image of everything John Sri Davinda was not. Even the ways he had of pissing her off, and they were legion, were the mirror image of Davinda's dead-fish inhumanity.

On a cellular and hormonal level, she was all too glad to see him. What her body wanted to do was get rid of Davinda and stick with Eric. But her brain reminded her that her professional duty was to do exactly the opposite.

"Good," said Eric in his oleaginous phony-prince voice, "it's always such a charming pleasure to see you again, Ms. Calhoun," and true to his official persona, made with the hand-kissing act.

"No offense," he said, "but it's Dr. Davinda I've been asked to find." He turned to John Sri Davinda. "And now that I have, Dr. Davinda, I'd like you to accompany me inside to meet some very interesting people who are just *dying* to offer you their most generous hospitality."

"And who might that be?" Monique asked.

As if she didn't know.

From a strictly physiognomic standpoint the smile that Eric gave her might appear to be as bland as the affectless expression of John Sri Davinda. But what lay behind it was anything but.

"Our magnanimous friends from Siberia," he said, "Stella and Ivan Marenko."

Don't be cruel to a heart that's true, the sainted Elvis had sung, as Eric remembered, but Monique's wasn't exactly, and this bit of cruelty was no worse than the teasing foreplay she had run on him, so . . .

"Perhaps you'd care to come along, Ms. Calhoun?" he said. "If you've got nothing more entertaining to do?"

Monique Calhoun gave him a long lingering look, half drop dead, half professional control over what must be seething within that Eric found quite admirable.

"I'd be delighted," she lied through invisibly clenched teeth.

What else could she say?

It was obvious that her mission was to prevent from happening exactly what was going to happen, no doubt to the extent of entertaining Davinda in one of the boudoirs to keep him away from the Marenkos. But she was not going to be able to prevent it. And to show pique now would only make matters worse. Her best course was to tag along like a good little minder and attempt to exercise what damage control she could.

Though what she or her handlers imagined might now be damaged remained elusive. And there might be tactical advantage in finding out.

The Marenkos had kept a seat empty between them, and that, of course, was where Eric Esterhazy had to plant John Sri Davinda. The nightly soiree at the Marenkos' table had only begun to get under way when they arrived; there were several empty seats, and Monique took one as close to Davinda as she could get, which was two chairs away, that of Ivan Marenko, and that of Chu Lun, the Guangdong Minister of Environment. Unbidden, certainly by her, Prince Eric slid in beside her.

Also at the table were Allison Larabee and Paolo Pereiro, whom Monique had seen together so often that she was beginning to think they were an item, Dr. Braithwaite, who seemed to be a regular, the Qwik-grow biologist Dieter Lambert, three journalists covering UN-ACOCS for StarNet, NovaNews, and Public Eye, and several other people she didn't recognize.

As usual, the table talk was mostly climatological, this being a conference where everyone *was* trying to do something about the weather at a time when the weather seemed to be suddenly getting ominously stranger, what with the white tornadoes, the hot humid murk that had enrobed much of France and the Low Countries, the wave of Saharan heat that had rolled over the Midi, the so-called Indian Ocean El Niño, the unconfirmed rumors of monster waterspouts over the equatorial Pacific.

Ordinarily, such dire disaster talk among the so-called experts would have held Monique's attention, but now she found herself tuning it out in favor of a dumbfounded personal fascination with the object of her current professional mission—John Sri Davinda.

Davinda wasn't taking part in the climatological gloom-and-doom talk. He wasn't talking at all. The Marenkos were keeping him occupied with other matters.

Davinda might have all the masculine presence of a human disney, but that didn't prevent him from guzzling the Marenkos' vodka like a camel tanking up at an oasis or snorting up their designer dust like a vacuum cleaner.

His capacity was amazing. Stella stuck the dust-laden mirror under his face every few minutes and Davinda never turned it down. While he snorted, Ivan would refill his glass; when Davinda was finished with the dust, Ivan would clink glasses with him, and Davinda would dutifully empty it.

There was something bizarrely machinelike about it. The Marenkos were doing their considerable best to get him thoroughly smashed and Davinda offered no resistance. But he didn't seem to be enjoying himself either. Monique could detect no change in his demeanor, probably because his brain had somewhere somehow been permanently gelatinized already.

Monique was beginning to have hope that while she had failed in her Posner-given mission to keep Davinda from the Marenkos, the evening might just pass without them being able to grill him, which was to say that Davinda might pass out before he even passed into the conversation.

No such luck.

". . . haven't said a thing all night, Dr. Davinda," said the Public Eye reporter.

"Come to think of it, I don't think I've seen a paper by you in years and years," said Pereiro.

"What ever happened to publish or perish?" said Dieter Lambert.

"He hasn't published, but he don't seem t'have perished," said Dr. Bobby Braithwaite, fixing his gaze on Davinda, snorting up another line of dust. "But at least y'can't say he's not tryin'," he added to less than kindly laughter.

This at last seemed to return John Sri Davinda to the land of the living. He put down his rolled bill with half a line of dust still before him and looked across the table at Braithwaite. Or at least turned those empty eyes in his direction like twin sat dishes.

Again that trembling of the lips before he was able to speak in a more or less human voice. "Trying very hard," he managed to say.

"T'do what, John, finish a paper, or fry your brain?"

This seemed to agitate Davinda, to incite him to make an effort to speak more forcefully if not to make more sense.

"To make it dance," he said.

"*It?* What's *it?*"

"It's in the bits and bytes," Davinda said.

"*What's* in the bits and bytes?"

"The dance."

"*Dance?*"

"The dance of the bits and bytes."

"What are you trying to say, Dr. Davinda?" said NovaNews.

Davinda seemed to be struggling to say something, or struggling with something, maybe both, and not quite making it.

"I . . . I . . . say I say . . . I say . . . nothing . . ." he said. He snorted up the rest of the dust.

And then he spoke in that eerily affectless voice, far flatter than any but the most primitive vocal emulation software.

"I am nothing."

"You're *nothing*, Dr. Davinda?" said StarNet. "Can we quote you on that?"

"It is the voice that speaks from the dance."

Merde!

John Sri Davinda had now become the center of attention. If the three journalists hadn't been recording before, they certainly were now. Braithwaite looked humanly concerned. Most of the rest of them seemed merely curious. Chu Lun, for some reason, looked worried, but concern for the state of Davinda's sanity didn't seem to be it.

Stella Marenko was studying Davinda intently. Ivan was doing likewise, but, practiced at it as he must be, this did not prevent him from refilling Davinda's glass with vodka without looking, without spilling a single drop.

"It, what?" said Stella Marenko.

"It is real."

"*What* is real?" said Ivan Marenko.

"Only it is real."

"Ah, is riddle!" Ivan Marenko said enthusiastically. "Only it is real. . . ? Dance of bits and bytes . . . ? Speaks from dance . . . ?"

He pondered thoughtfully for a moment, or at least pretended to; then a metaphorical lightbulb seemed to go on over his head. "Ah!" he exclaimed. "Must be . . . *program*! Must be . . . your *climate model*, da?"

Oh shit.

Davinda turned his empty eyes on Ivan Marenko, blinked rapidly, spoke in what passed for his human voice. "The interface between matter and energy—"

"—is *pattern*, da?" said Ivan. "Is neither and both! Dance of bits and bytes!"

Davinda's eyes seemed to widen in surprise, no mean feat under their dilated circumstances. Ivan stared back unwaveringly for a moment. Then he broke into the innocent beaming smile of a small boy.

"Love riddles!" he said.

"Is very good at them," said Stella. "Why not? Ivan is one big hairy riddle himself!"

Ivan Marenko laughed. "I'll drink to that!" he exclaimed, and clinked glasses with Stella, then Davinda.

"You'll drink to anything!" Stella proclaimed, and downed her vodka in a single gulp.

Ivan did likewise, then nudged Davinda. Without looking away from Ivan, Davinda brought his glass to his lips and drank it down.

"This climate model of yours is big riddle itself, da . . . ?" Ivan Marenko said.

"What do you know about climate models, Mr. Marenko?" Chu Lun broke in with suspicious haste, as if trying to do Monique's work for her by breaking this up before it went any further.

"I don't know much about climate models," Ivan said, "but I know what I like. And freezing ass off in new Siberian winter is not it!"

"And being stuck with bill for privilege in the bargain!" added Stella.

"So, Herr Doktor Professor John Sri Davinda, what is big secret hidden behind screens in Grand Palais?" Ivan Marenko said. "Is *your* secret, da . . . ?" He held up his hand. "Wait! Don't tell. Is good riddle. We get three guesses first. Stella . . . ?"

"Is . . . computer, da? Must be some kind of *very* special computer . . ."

Davinda turned sharply to stare at Stella Marenko. Other than the speed of his reaction, no emotion showed. But that was enough to elicit a knowing smile from Ivan, to make Chu Lun squirm.

"So . . ." said Ivan, "what makes a computer special . . . ?"

"Nothing, it's not the hardware, it's the software!" Monique blurted quickly, hoping to deflect the speculation before it could come to the question of the species of any installed cerebral meatware. "The, uh, dance of the bits and bytes. The climate model itself."

Chu Lun looked relieved. John Sri Davinda turned to look in her direction but neither spoke nor reacted. Sweat had broken out on his brow. His eyes showed little but giant black pupils floating in marbled pink sclera.

Maybe the dust and vodka were finally catching up to him. Monique willed Ivan Marenko to pour him another shot. Probably no telepathy was involved or needed, but Ivan complied, and poured himself one too.

"Two guesses," Ivan said. "Last one is mine." He picked up his glass, sipped at it thoughtfully, clinked glasses with Davinda, nodded. "Special climate model program, okay, da, runs on special computer, must be . . . what?"

Drink it! Monique telepathed.

John Sri Davinda lifted his glass slowly and mechanically like a good little robot and slugged down his vodka. Definitely approaching condition terminal.

Stella Marenko laid out another line of dust, handed Davinda the rolled-up bill. Yes, yes, Monique prayed hopefully, another line, another shot, and maybe he passes out.

"Is maybe not digital program, is why it needs special secret machine . . . ?" Ivan Marenko said. "Is *analog*? Is maybe *quantum*? Has *uncertainty program* to roll the bones . . . ?"

Ivan Marenko paused, refilled Davinda's glass.

"Or robot hand to toss the stones for famous LAO TE CHING . . . ?"

"*TAO TE CHING*, Ivan," corrected Stella Marenko, "not *Lao*."

"Ah, is famous *I-CHING* of *Dr. Lao* . . ."

What I tell you three times is true?

Maybe not true, but not random either, the utterance of the mystery word three times in rapid succession by the Marenkos did not seem like an accident to Monique. Particularly since they had managed to stress it twice.

All the more so considering the effect it had on John Sri Davinda. "Lao is the Tao of the Chao," he babbled so woozily that it was difficult for Monique to decide which of his schizoid voices was doing it. "The Tao of the Chao is Lao . . ."

He snorted up the line of dust convulsively. "The Chao of the Tao is Lao . . ." He began to vibrate. No, he was shaking. He slugged down the vodka. It didn't help. His blink rate went sky-high.

The vodka, the dust, some sort of engrammatic reaction to a keyword, whatever, sweat was pouring down John Sri Davinda's forehead now, he had turned an almost greenish pale. Monique had been hoping for the drugs and drink to take effect, but not like this.

"Dr. Davinda!" she cried, rising clumsily from her seat.

"Lao is the Tao of the Chao . . . the Tao of the Chao is Lao . . . the Chao of the Tao is Lao . . . Lao is the Tao of the Chao . . ."

Davinda was chanting this gibberish like a mantra now, as if trying to enter a trance state, or perhaps chant his way out of one which he had already entered . . .

Monique reached Davinda, put her hands on his shoulders, shook him, tried to raise him—

". . . the Tao of the Chao is Lao . . . the Chao of the Tao is Lao . . . Lao is the Tao of the Chao . . ."

"Will you please help me get him out of here to someplace quiet instead of just sitting there?" Monique shouted at Eric Esterhazy.

Eric rose from his chair, went to her.

"Well, I can see why you left this guy off your guest list, Ms. Calhoun," he said suavely, as he grabbed hold of Davinda's right arm. Monique grabbed the left, and together they managed to hoist John Sri Davinda to his feet.

Whether he had achieved nirvana or just passed into a deeper state of intoxication, Davinda stopped chanting and hung there limply between them, barely conscious enough to keep his eyes open and his feet moving one after the other as they began to walk him out of the bar.

Prince Charming, in the act thereof, managed to turn his head, and shrug at the Marenkos' table, where the reaction varied between the usual shock and the usual lugubrious amusement such unseemly scenes elicited.

"Sorry about this, ladies and gentleman," he said, "the poor fellow doesn't seem to be able to hold his vodka."

"Is not *his* vodka he cannot hold!" said Stella Marenko.

"Is *ours!*" shouted Ivan.

And they removed their victim from the scene under the cover of the usual nervously boorish laughter.

The only empty boudoir had been the Kama Sutra room, and after Eric helped Monique Calhoun drag Davinda into it, he could hardly resist repairing to the computer room, dismissing the guard, and peeking, as it were, through the video keyhole.

"Open sez me," Eric said, activating Ignatz, and taking a perverse pleasure in choosing Mom from the personality menu, for in some way he figured she virtually deserved this.

"Let's see the Kama Sutra room, Mom."

"Your prurient interest is my command, kiddo."

This boudoir's walls were covered with life-size pseudo-Hindu erotic stone statuary, as many positions of the Kama Sutra as could be squeezed into such a confined space; not enough to satisfy a completist, perhaps, but more than one might think. The ceiling simulated rosy twilight. The floor was a continuous nest of cushioning liberally scattered with large pillows, not authentic, maybe, but a lot more practical than doing it on a stone floor.

The effect was that of being the centerpiece of an energetic and imaginative orgy frozen in stone and time. Monique had built up a kind of bedstead out of pillows in the midst of this erotic profusion and propped the supine Davinda up against it. Davinda's eyes were open, but that was the only obvious evidence of consciousness. She kneeled before him in a posture that, given their surroundings, suggested imminent fellatio, but the look on her face as she studied Davinda hardly suggested arousal, and oddly enough, not so much well-justified disgust as a grim species of relief.

"Sound," said Eric.

". . . all right?" said Monique. "You're not going to vomit?"

Davinda stared straight ahead. He might conceivably have lost consciousness with his eyes open. He might even be dead.

This thought had apparently occurred to Monique too.

She leaned closer to Davinda, putting a palm on his chest to feel for his heartbeat, hesitantly attempting to bring her face close enough to his to visually observe his breath without being constrained to smell it.

Eric couldn't help himself. The temptation was just too great.

The erotic ambiance of the boudoirs could be enhanced by music, either prearranged or piped in from the computer room.

"Let's give them that instrumental Hindu Hard version of 'I Can't Get No Satisfaction,' but just at the subliminal edge . . ."

"Low, Eric, really low."

"Takes one to know one, Mom."

The mike in the Kama Sutra room was not sensitive enough to relay such subtle music back to the computer room, nor did the Hindu Hard version of the ancient Rolling Stones classic raise the dead in any manner that Eric had imagined or intended.

Davinda's head began to sway back and forth a bit, a clear enough sign of life. He belched quite loudly, causing Monique to yank her head backward, and, considering all that he had consumed, causing Eric to be thankful that the surveillance gear was not equipped for smell.

His lips began to move.

"What?" said Monique, understandably reluctant to lean closer to hear what he was muttering.

The technology, however, left Eric under no such esthetic constraints. "Turn up the microphone gain," he told Ignatz.

". . . is the Tao of the Chao . . . Lao is the Tao of the Chao . . . the Tao of the Chao is Lao . . ."

That mantric Third Force babblement again, and Eric needed neither a guru nor Ignatz to tell him that the magic word upon which it was centered was "Lao."

Perhaps it was merely the meaningless automatic playback of what might have been implanted in some island of recording cells in the climatologist's besotted brain by the Marenkos. But just maybe it was that which they had sought to evoke bubbling up, via the booze and the dust and the subliminal music—the code word or acronym for whatever lay within that mysterious enclosure in the Grand Palais.

For whatever surprise Davinda was going to spring on Sunday, assuming he survived tomorrow morning's heroic hangover to do it.

"... Lao is the Tao of the Chao ... Lao is ..."

"You're not making any sense, Dr. Davinda," Monique said.

"A brilliant deduction," muttered Eric.

"Elementary, my dear Watson," said Ignatz.

"*What* is the Tao? What is the Chao? What is Lao?"

"Lao is the Tao of the Chao ... the Chao of the Tao is Lao ..."

"*Lao*, Dr. Davinda, what is *Lao*?" Monique repeated, grabbing him by the shoulders and trying to shake some sense out of him.

Interesting, thought Eric. Maybe *very* interesting. Monique was making a strenuous effort to find out what the word "Lao" hid.

Ergo, she didn't know. That in itself was already a useful piece of information. . . .

"... the Tao of the Chao is Lao ..."

But it seemed clear to Eric that she was going to get nowhere this way. And despite her shaking, Davinda's voice was getting weaker, his terminally bloodshot eyes lidding over.

It was Eric's considered professional opinion as someone who had observed and dealt with many people who had consumed far less dust and booze than the Californian climatologist that he was about to pass out for the night. Nothing was going to keep him awake much longer, let alone restore some sort of useful level of coherence.

Nothing?

Well . . .

There *was* another way to heat things up in the boudoirs. The erotic atmosphere within could be augmented by a menu of pheremonically tailored vapors released into the ventilating system.

From where Eric sat.

This was getting nowhere. John Sri Davinda's lips were still moving but nothing was coming out except a sickening green tornado of acetone-laden breath.

As far as using the occasion to extract anything coherent from the Californian climatologist, Monique was ready to give up. But she was frozen in place. It would be imprudent to leave him alone in the thoroughly bugged bowels of *La Reine de la Seine* until he had become comatose for the night.

Monique had experienced men, even straight men, entirely oblivious to her charms, and had been in the presence of men too blotted to move, let alone in an erotically purposeful manner. She had been in the presence of men who fell below the porcine level of sexual attractiveness. Upon a few occasions in the professional line of duty, she had found herself hopefully waiting for a drunk to pass out.

But never before all at once.

And certainly not in the center of a stone forest of copulating, cunnilingating, fellating, and analizing figures giving a whole new meaning to the concept of statuetory rape.

Whoever had designed this boudoir of assignation had done a masterful job. There she was, with perhaps the sorriest specimen of carnal masculinity she had ever had the misfortune to be closeted with, out of his mind to begin with and stinkingly stoned, and . . . and *the room* was turning her on.

It *had* to be the room. It certainly couldn't be John Sri Davinda stirring this irrational warmth in her loins. It was said, mostly by men, that women were not generally aroused by pornography, but what this *really* meant, Monique was now itchily beginning to realize, was that most pornography, at least in the Occident, had always been produced with phallic arousal in mind.

This work of the pornographer's art however, and art it surely was, would seem to have been crafted as an equal-opportunity turn-on. Indeed, Monique was hard put to imagine a sexual opportunity not on offer in the full-circle sexual tableau that surrounded her, bathed in rosy light that seemed selected down to the last angstrom to illumine and inflame her sexual desire.

Desire for whom?

Desire for what?

It didn't seem to matter.

Monique had never experienced anything quite like this pure sexual hunger. It was delicious, terrifying, frustrating. What did she want?

She wanted the rosy naked stone figures surrounding her to come to life, she wanted to become one of them, to join their eternal orgy, to be penetrated in every orifice, to . . . to . . .

I've got to get out of here! Monique realized when she found her hand inside her panties. *I've got to get off or get out of here!*

Or both.

Davinda's eyes, though heavily lidded, were still marginally open, and his lips were still moving.

Fucking a man into unconsciousness might be the female equivalent of the male sexual power fantasy, but in this case it would be easy.

If he came in this state, Monique reasoned, or managed to convince herself that she reasoned, he would surely pass out.

It shouldn't take long. There wouldn't have to be anything personal about it. Scratching this lovely and terrible itch would secure her escape. Just get him ready and straddle him.

As she pulled off her underwear and crawled purposefully toward Davinda's crotch, the vision came to her of Eric Esterhazy watching her right now, which, given that this chamber was bugged, might be closer to fact than to fantasy.

But in her current state, this proved to be a sexual aid. There was nothing whatever sexually appealing about John Sri Davinda, but Eric was a man for whom she had a strong animal attraction, and the thought that he was going to be watching just about drove her wild.

Wild enough at least to open Davinda's pants and extract his pathetically limp prick and impatiently begin to rub it.

She might as well have been massaging an over-boiled carrot.

Closing her eyes, she slid this mushy tuber into her mouth, and found herself imagining that it was Eric Esterhazy's princely member.

But while this fantasy enabled Monique to endure, even to enjoy, her prolonged and determined ministrations, it accomplished nothing at all by way of imbuing the object in fleshly question with the sexual puissance thereof.

And when the fantasy that kept her fruitlessly going was shattered rudely, in every sense of the word, by the advent of loud and deep snoring, and her eyes popped open to reveal that the unsavory reality on the other end of the fantasy handle had fallen dead asleep during her heroic attempt, her frustration was exceeded only by her insulted outrage, as she spit this doubly unsavory morsel out.

"I'm coming, I'm coming!" Eric Esterhazy replied to the frantic hammering on the computer room door.

Well, not yet!

Eric made a great effort to straighten his face as he went to open it, though his phallic alter ego was quite uprightly linear already, thank you very much. He had never before achieved a mighty erection in the process of laughing uncontrollably, but there was a first time for everything.

And there might just be strategic as well as sexual advantage in it too.

He paused.

"We have an empty boudoir available?" he asked Ignatz as Monique, and it had to be her, continued to hammer on the door.

"Only the dungeon, kiddo."

"Karma . . ." Eric muttered, then, louder: "Turn on the happy gas. Love potion sixty-nine."

"It's people like you who make this emulation disgusting," said Ignatz.

Eric frowned. Ignatz's Mom personality program needed some tweaking. The real thing would be enjoying this.

The real thing would probably have also enjoyed the sight that greeted Eric when he opened the door, if not with quite the same masculine enthusiasm.

Monique Calhoun's clothes were in disarray, and of course, though it didn't show, Eric knew that she now wore no underwear. Her hair was tangled. Her fair face was flushed red—with lust, with frustration, and, to judge from the set of her brows and the curl of her lips, with anger at she-was-not-quite-sure-what-and-had-better-not-find out.

"You were watching, weren't you, Eric Esterhazy?" she snarled.

"A gentleman never tells," Eric said smarmily.

"A gentleman doesn't peek through keyholes!"

Monique Calhoun's hands balled into fists. She was still panting. "Do you know what I'd like to do right now!"

Eric grinned at her. "Chain me to a dungeon wall and take it all out on my helpless body?" he suggested.

Monique gaped at him.

Eric looked deep into her eyes as he wiped the smile off his face, leaned closer into the steamy heat of her body-space. "You don't have to be ashamed," he said softly. "I'd enjoy being your sex slave. I'd be glad to put myself entirely in your power."

Monique stared at him in wonder. In lust. In outrage.

"You're . . . you're serious!" she exclaimed.

Eric nodded. "A *true* gentleman," he said, "never tells, might peek through the occasional keyhole, but would never ever dream of leaving a damsel in sexual distress so desperately hot and bothered."

"Of all the—"

Eric stepped forward, threw his arms around her, pressed their bodies together, and kissed her ever so softly and genteelly on the lips.

There was a momentary pro forma resistance, and then all pretense was gone, and she kissed him savagely and hungrily back, nipping him a bit harder than playfully on the upper lip to widen his mouth to accept her tongue as she wriggled her body against him.

This was all happening like a dream, but no dream Monique had ever dreamed she would ever have.

A stone-walled dungeon cell? A straw-covered floor? Manacles and chains?

Eric Esterhazy doing a slow striptease before her?

Then lying down in the straw with a throbbing erection, spreading his arms and legs and . . .

"Go ahead," he whispered throatily, "chain me to the dungeon walls! Make me your slave! Torture me with pleasure!

And she manacling him in this spread-eagled position and standing over him fully dressed and just watching for a long contemplative moment before deciding to undress herself.

And thoroughly enjoying it . . . ?

Eric Esterhazy was no devotee of sadomasochism or bondage, but unlike Monique, he was willingly and knowingly giving himself over to the pheremonal vapors, meaning that he knew that this could be a first time for *anything* and he could relax and enjoy it.

Moreover, despite the illusion of being chained to the wall of Torquemada's torture chamber, it was all perfectly safe, since Ignatz monitored everything that went on in the boudoirs and would intervene if things got out of hand other than pleasantly.

Not that Eric believed that they would. His main difficulty was going to be keeping at least enough of his wits about him to make strategic use of his "helplessness."

For, Monique having revealed that she knew no more about what lay behind the code word "Lao" than the Marenkos did, it had occurred to him that his knowledge of this ignorance could be used to extract information from her.

And in a most delightful manner.

Monique was in no coquettish mood, nor, while she was avidly hungry for his body, was she in any mood to unselfishly provide pleasure to Prince Peeping Tom. In fact, perversely enough, the heat of the volcano between her legs was actually turned up a notch by the realization that she was about to quench it by impaling herself on the only aspect of Eric Esterhazy that she *wasn't* pissed off at.

Torture me with pleasure, was it?

With pleasure, Eric!

And, she realized through the bright red fog as she slid down upon him with an enormous sigh of impending relief, maybe learn something useful in the process too, which, after all, was what you were supposed to do in the castle dungeon, now wasn't it. . . .

Monique, like most women, had from time to time been displeased by men who by ineptitude or sheer piggish selfishness, or admittedly perhaps because of the differential design of the apparatus, came too quickly, leaving her hot and bothered.

Now was her chance to return this disfavor.

For now she had been so hot and bothered for so long and at such a level of intensity that a half a dozen long deep strokes were enough to bring her to a fine orgasm.

A lesser man than Eric might have released himself at that moment, but Prince Eric, prideful master cocksman that he was, had of course paced himself for a marathon, not a sprint, and so was left panting in frustration when, having scratched her own itch, she sat there astride him in the rosy afterglow not moving a muscle.

"Well . . . ?" he finally demanded, wriggling beneath her in frustration as much as his spread-eagled bondage would allow, which was hardly enough to let him take charge of matters.

"Well, you made three wishes, Aladdin," Monique told him. "Chain you to the dungeon walls, make you my slave, and torture you with pleasure." She grinned down at him. "And you've had your first two. . . ."

She rotated her hips a teeny little bit, just enough to tease him, somewhat amazed to find that her animal lust did not yet seem quite sated.

"And now it's time for the third," she said.

"I want information," Monique Calhoun said, grinding ever so slowly and tantalizingly, "and you don't get to come till I get it."

"I'll never talk!" Eric declaimed in the best over-the-top cine hero voice he could muster. "You can't make me!"

"Then you won't mind if I give it a good long try," Monique purred, and she slid herself slowly up the core of his aching pleasure, and paused there without granting him a downstroke.

"Do your worst!" Eric declared mock-heroically. "I cannot be broken!"

But it was true, for despite the physical configuration, his knowledge that they were both breathing the pheremonic vapors and his desire to *appear* to be "broken" under prolonged sexual torture actually put him in command of the situation.

Monique slid slowly down. And halted. And around. And halted. And up. And halted. And down. And halted. And around.

She was good. She knew just what she was doing, applying an agonizingly slow and intermittent rhythm that brought Eric right to the edge and could hold him there indefinitely.

But Eric, cocksman that he was and often enough in the line of semi-professional duty, had often enough sustained just this situation willingly himself in the name of prowess and had long since learned to enjoy it.

He could always come.

He would come later.

But best to make his resistance credible. Best not to seem to give up too soon. No indeed. A hard job, but Eric had reason to believe he was definitely up for it.

Monique found Eric Esterhazy's controlled endurance impressive as he lay there supine and helpless beneath her ministrations grinning up at her as if he wouldn't mind at all if she tortured him like this for hours or possibly decades.

Was it an act? Was it ego? Was it sheer enjoyment of the endless tantalization?

Or, she began to wonder, might Eric be taking this bedroom game a bit more seriously that he pretended? Might he really be hiding a secret?

Be that as it may, Monique found, rather to her surprise, that as it went on and on and on, she was building up a more and more urgent need in *herself* for a second release. It was taking more and more discipline and control to keep her rhythm slow and intermittent rather than climactically urgent, while the son of a bitch beneath her by comparison seemed to be taking it all as cool as stiffly frozen cucumber.

It seemed to Monique that she had better give it a try while she could. With no little psychic effort, she paused panting on the upstroke and held it, managing to pulse her nether muscles slightly.

"You know what 'Lao' is, don't you?" she said.

"I might . . ." Eric sighed, looking up at Monique, sweaty, panting, obviously moving toward the urgency of another orgasm under the influence of the pheremonics, but not knowing it.

Time for the next move.

"And you know what's inside the mysterious tent, don't you . . . ?"

"I might . . ." said Monique, but it seemed that even under the influence of lust and pheremonic vapors, a dark cloud passed across her visage.

Eric used what limited penile prehensibility he had attained to wriggle the organ in question enough to hopefully recenter her attention.

"And I might tell you mine if you tell me yours. . . ."

It seemed to work.

"Who's torturing whom here?" Monique said, sliding down, and returning to her tantalizing rhythm.

"That remains to be seen, Mata Hari," Eric told her.

But he then granted her a rolling of his eyes in pleasurable agony, a groan, a sigh. It was approaching the moment when he must appear to lose control.

After which, he could allow himself the pleasure of actually doing so.

Eric was finally writhing and rolling beneath her and against his bonds in agonized ecstasy, but Monique doubted that she could endure this sexual torture much longer herself, and if this was turning into a perverse endurance contest, she was at a disadvantage, since she was the one in control, the one who must hold back her body's burning desire for fleshly apotheosis by act of swiftly eroding will.

A little while longer, a little while longer. . . .

"All right, all right," Eric moaned, judging by the increasing frenzy of Monique's accelerating rhythm that the time had arrived. "Let me come, and I'll tell you what I know about Lao."

"Tell me first!" Monique said raggedly.

"Why should I trust you?"

Monique looked him directly in the eyes.

"Because you know damn well that I want to come as much as you do, Eric Esterhazy," she said.

Eric laughed.

"Takes one to know one," he admitted. "But since you want to reach the climax of this little sexual theater piece as much as I do, it's only fair I get my quid pro quo. You have to tell me what you know about what's in the tent."

"You first!"

"*You* first!"

"Why should I trust you?"

"Why should *I* trust *you?*"

"Damn it Eric, can't you at least be a bit of a gentleman *now!*"

Eric made a great show of sighing.

"Lao is the reference code for some kind of operation the Siberians are running against Big Blue here," he lied. "Something to do with Davinda and his climate model."

Monique's rhythm began to increase, her breath was coming in pants, but she still was making an effort to hold back.

"What kind of operation?" she demanded. "Was Ivan maybe repeating the word to Davinda as some kind of posthypnotic key or something?"

"You think the Marenkos tell the hired help stuff like that?" Eric moaned. "That's all I know!"

Her rhythm was picking up. Eric's show of impatience was becoming genuine.

"Come on, Monique," he groaned, "isn't that enough?"

She didn't reply in words. She didn't have to. Eric didn't want her to. Not yet, anyway. She just moaned, and sighed, and let herself go. It didn't take long for Eric to come along with her. After all that twisted psychic foreplay, finally letting his body do what came naturally didn't take long at all.

"Well . . . ?" Eric said as Monique lay catching her breath atop him in the rosy sweaty afterglow.

"Well what . . . ?" Monique muttered, physically exhausted, sexually satisfied, but dumbfounded to discover that she *still* didn't quite feel sated.

"Well we had a deal. What's hidden under guard in the Grand Palais?" Eric said, and Monique was equally amazed to feel what should've been thoroughly deflated beginning to stir beneath her.

"Oh . . . the computer that they're going to run Davinda's climate model on," she said dreamily, reaching down to affirm this formidable fact, and sliding herself into position to take carnal advantage.

"Oh really?" Eric said snidely. "That's hardly the point now, is it?"

"*This* is the point," said Monique, slipping the tip of the organ in question into her, "and it *does* seem to be hard enough for now, now doesn't it?"

"This is your idea of a fair trade of information?" Eric said angrily as she began a slow smoky rotation. "You're hiding something, I know you are, what is it?"

Her sexual fires on the rise yet again, Monique was nevertheless brought up short by that, for yes, she was hiding something, had been hiding something, from herself as much as from him, something she had been constrained to push below the level of emotional awareness to be able to continue her professional services to the client at all.

And now, here she was, in the midst of the most profound sexual experience of her life, and the man who was giving it to her was asking for the truth that in this passionate moment she realized she wanted to shout from the media rooftops.

Eric Esterhazy looked up at her. Perhaps it was an illusion of the sexual afterglow through which they were moving toward yet another round of lovemaking, but it seemed to Monique that she had never seen such a look of concerned sincerity on this phony prince's the-atrically handsome face, a face which, in that moment, she could almost imagine herself loving.

"What's the matter, Monique?" Eric said softly. "Don't be afraid. You can tell me."

So she did.

"There is . . . reason to believe that there's a polymerized human brain installed as a processor. . . ."

"*What!*" Eric found himself shouting.

"Just a supposition . . ." Monique whined defensively.

"That's . . . that's . . ."

"Horrible? Disgusting? Illegal in any jurisdiction . . . ?"

Eric could only nod numbly, having just learned something about himself the hard way. He had no particular regard for the laws, rules, or regulations of any jurisdiction save those of the syndic of which he was a citizen-shareholder, and Bad Boys' charter specifically mandated its citizen-shareholders to violate any of them in the syndic's service if necessary.

He had certainly committed acts which the majority of the planet's population would consider reprehensible. Including removal operations which the bluntly punctilious might be so tasteless as to style "murder."

But apparently imprisoning a human brain, polymerized or not, in a machine to serve as the core of the operating system was enough to arouse even a confirmed Bad Boy's moral outrage. Who, after all, could say if it would be "conscious" or not, and in what horrible manner, except the hapless meatware chip itself?

"Why . . . ? What could they possibly hope to—?"

"Credibility," said Monique. "*Because* it'll be seen as such an unacceptable atrocity, the Siberians and the world will *believe* a climate model that proves Condition Venus is under way with a human brain in the computer running it. Because the Big Blue Machine would never risk doing such a thing unless *they* sincerely believed it . . . and so . . . so I believe it too . . ."

This was more than enough to wilt Eric's erection psychically, but the aphrogas wouldn't let the flesh succumb to the detumescent will of the spirit.

Monique gazed down at him, miserably, longingly, pathetically. "A necessary evil, Eric, isn't it?" she said imploringly. "Your syndic specializes in that, doesn't it? A terrible evil, but if it's the only way to save the world from Condition Venus . . . and the white tornadoes—"

Eric quite lost it.

"Are a fucking fraud!" he shouted.

"Turn off the aphrogas!" Eric Esterhazy shouted.

"What . . . ? What . . . ?" Monique stammered in confusion.

"Purge the room with forty percent oxygen!"

"Do *what?*"

Now Monique began to realize that Eric hadn't been ordering *her* to do the incomprehensible, as he looked more directly at her, and said in quite another voice, "Unchain me, Monique."

Monique sat there immobile athwart him as she felt him detumesce out of her, as her own fires began to cool, as the rosy fog began to clear from her head, as she found herself feeling used and ridiculous, straddling a manacled man in a tacky disney of a medieval torture chamber. . . .

"Come on, let me loose!"

Aphrogas? Purge the room with oxygen?

She leapt rather shakily off of him.

"Let you loose, you son of a bitch!" she screamed.

Her eyes scanned the torture chamber disney for anything that might serve as an appropriate instrument—an ax, a sword, even a baseball bat would do!

"Oh, *I'm* a son of a bitch for playing a little harmless prank which you can't tell me you didn't enjoy, but of course *you*, and the capitalist slime you're working, for are as pure as the uncut Bolivian snow!"

"It isn't like that . . ." Monique said, unconvincingly even to herself.

"Oh, of course not," Eric said insinuatingly. "What's using a human brain as a computer chip and faking the end of the world to turn a profit, after all, just . . . Bread & Circuses as usual, right?"

"But . . . but if Condition Venus is beginning—"

"Didn't you hear what I said, Monique?" Eric said somewhat less sardonically. "Condition Venus isn't happening. *The white tornadoes are fakes.* We've got recordings that prove it!"

"And the humidity waves and the heat waves and the Indian Ocean El Niño—"

"Probably more smoke and orbital mirrors too!"

"They wouldn't—"

"*Right*," said Eric. "People who would stick a human brain into a computer would never *dream* of faking the beginning of Condition Venus."

"Shit," said Monique.

What was that punch line to Ivan Marenko's dumb joke?

Why is a planet like a nymphomaniac?

Much easier to heat up than cool down.

"Now will you please let me loose, Monique?" Eric said gently. "We have to talk. And I don't think you really want to continue the conversation here."

———

Fresh air seemed to be a good idea, and so once they were dressed, Eric took Monique up through the main salon and along the prome-nade to the bow, where they secured a bubble of privacy by, ironically enough, pretending to be in the process of seducing each other.

This took some glad-handing and small talk en passant, and by the time they were standing side by side in the bow of La Reine with the river breeze in their faces as it rounded the Ile St. Louis, Eric's head had quite cleared and he fully realized the perilous magnitude of what he had done under the influence.

Eduardo would not be pleased. Nor would the Marenkos.

On his own initiative, or to be more embarrassingly precise, under the influence of aphrogas and sex as much as moral outrage, he had made a major policy decision without syndic authorization. He had revealed the existence of the white tornado recordings to Monique Calhoun.

To an operative of Bread & Circuses under contract to the Big Blue Machine.

He had been a bad Bad Boy. His big mouth—or, as Mom would no doubt say, his big dumb dick—might have landed him in deep dark shit.

"These recordings . . ." Monique Calhoun said coldly, "they really prove that the white tornadoes are being faked?"

Eric nodded. "Maybe not legal proof in most jurisdictions, but in the court of public opinion where it counts," Eric told her. "And any halfway conscious spinmeister could use that to convince even the True Blue that they've been faking the rest of the recent weird weather too, true or not."

"Faking Condition Venus . . ." Monique muttered. "Heating up the planet even further to get fat contracts to cool it back down. . . ."

"Those recordings get released to the media, and the Big Blue Machine, UNACOCS, any further talk of Condition Venus, is as dead as . . . as dead as . . ."

"A human body after its brain has been ripped out and installed in a computer?" Monique suggested sardonically. "You know what I think?"

They were leaning against the rail, bodies touching, faces turned close together like a couple soon to become lovers for the sake of cover, but the eye contact was not exactly romantic.

"That I am an egotistical shallow ruthless phallocratic son of a bitch for pumping aphrogas into the boudoir and taking shameless advantage of your sweet innocence?"

Monique Calhoun did not seem to be amused. But she did seem to have passed beyond her anger at him.

"That too," she said. "But you're right. What you've done is just some stupid schoolboy prank compared to what the . . . capitalist slime I've somehow found myself working for have done. *If* they've really done it."

"I told you, we have proof that the white—"

"But I don't *know* if there's *really* a human brain in the Davinda climate model computer, it's just a deduction from—"

"You don't *want* to believe it!"

"Do you?"

Eric shrugged. "Who would?"

"What are you going to do with those recordings?" Monique said slowly.

"Not my decision to make," Eric told her all too truthfully.

"Your . . . syndic, then."

How much more could he tell her?

Only what she could figure out for herself.

"Sell them," he said. "For quite a lot of money."

"To the media?"

"Or . . . the highest bidder . . ."

"Like the Marenkos? Who'd use them to destroy UNACOCS and Big Blue and discredit the Condition Venus hypothesis forever . . . or until it's too late?"

"You might think that," said Eric. "I couldn't possibly comment."

"You can't *do* that, Eric," Monique said. "What if we *are* about to slide into Condition Venus even if the white tornadoes *are* fakes? What if the Davinda climate model *does* prove it, human brain or not? You really want to discredit the truth because the messengers happen to be unprincipled capitalist liars? Without being sure? Without knowing?"

"So let's find out!" Eric blurted.

Of course.

Eric looked directly into Monique Calhoun's eyes, all superciliousness purged from his expression, or so he hoped.

"When you want to pry open an oyster," he said, "you use a big
tough knife. Do you know what I'm thinking?"

Monique just shook her head.

"I'm thinking you're going to report what you've learned up some
chain of command. . . ."

"You might think that. I couldn't possibly comment."

"So the . . . people at the top of that chain of command are going
to know we can blow the whole scam open with the white tornado
recordings anyway . . ."

"So . . . ?"

Eric paused. He expanded his chest with a deep breath of river
air as his boat rode the current westward past the klieg-lit glory of
Notre Dame cathedral. Was he not the master of *La Reine de la Seine*?
Did that not make him a Prince of the City? Or was he just a fancy
doorman?

Eric knew he was about to cross another river, not the Seine, but
a personal Rubicon. Could he do it? Could he not? If he succeeded,
he would redeem himself with Eduardo Ramirez and his syndic. If he
presumed such authority and failed, the alligators of the Seine might
enjoy a princely dinner.

"So you tell your chain of command that unless I am allowed to
inspect what's hidden in that tent in the Grand Palais before Sunday,
the white tornado tape recordings get released to the media on Saturday."

"*We*," blurted Monique Calhoun. "We're in this together, sweet
prince."

"So be it," said Eric.

Monique Calhoun eyed him more narrowly now, as if studying a
new Eric Esterhazy, a man she had never really seen before.

And, thought Eric, maybe she's right.

"You don't really have the authority to make a threat like that,
do you, Eric?" she said softly. Admiringly, he was flattered to think.
"You're taking a big personal chance, aren't you? You don't know that

your . . . chain of command would really back it up, or . . . or . . ."

Eric gave her the great big stoic hero smile, half-convinced in that moment himself.

"*Your* chain of command might just think that," he said. "But would they dare to take the chance?"

For the first time since they had come up on deck, Monique smiled at him. It wasn't a lustful smile, it wasn't a loving smile, it might not even be a friendly smile, but it seemed quite sincere.

"You know what I'm thinking, Eric?" she said.

Eric shook his head.

"Let's find out who and what we're really working for, you and me, Prince Valiant," she said. "That's what I'm thinking."

She didn't kiss him, she didn't embrace him, but she did take his hand and squeeze it quite hard, like a comrade-in-arms.

Which to Eric, in that moment, seemed quite enough, quite right, quite appropriate.

9

"SO, MOM . . . ?"

"So, Eric?" said mom, taking a long slow sip of her Mimosa.

"So what do you think Eduardo will say?"

Rather than deal directly with Eduardo, Eric had decided that much the best course was to use Mom as a buffer, at least initially.

He had told her to meet him for brunch—Mom seldom arose early enough to eat anything that could properly be called breakfast— aboard the *Café du Monde.*

This was a converted river barge anchored behind the Ile de la Cité where a branch of the Seine separated it from the Ile St. Louis. It was done up as a disney of a famous café by the same name in the French Quarter in sunken New Orleans, which, in turn, had been a disney of a "typical" café in the Latin Quarter of "gay Paree."

It served coffee with chicory, sugar-dusted doughnuts it styled "beignets," eggs bienville, and an assortment of other faux-Louisianne brunch fare; decently cooked, but most of it disney, sometimes, like the restaurant itself, twice removed.

"I think Eduardo will be pissed off," Mom told him, unsurprisingly.

Eric nodded grimly.

When choosing a restaurant for this brunch, Eric had forgotten,

234 o GREENHOUSE SUMMER

at least on a conscious level, that the *Café du Monde* was anchored close by the Monument to the Deportation, built to commemorate one of the many ghastly events of the ghastly twentieth century's most ghastly war.

Be that as it may, the river view thereof was an iron grille in a stonework quai resembling nothing so much as the Thames-side prison gate to the Tower of London through which prisoners of state were once taken to be beheaded.

Somehow this did not now seem like favorable feng shui.

Worse still, the Parisian version was overgrown with vines, often semi-submerged, and, given its proximity to a restaurant boat that tossed its scraps into the river to attract them as local color, was a favorite hangout of the Seine alligators. If these creatures yet retained too much dignity to beg tidbits from the diners, they were cruising slowly back and forth below the railing table where Eric and his mother sat in dim reptilian hope that someone might fall overboard.

Or be thrown their way, perhaps, in a fit of ire.

"That's why I want him to hear it from you first, Mom," Eric told her.

Mom shook her head. "That would *really* piss him off," she said. "He'd be insulted."

"*Insulted?*"

"You take it upon yourself to tell Little Mary Sunshine that the white tornadoes are fakes and Bad Boys has the stuff to prove it, and then you go ahead and use the recordings that *maybe* the Siberians will buy as your own little offer the Big Blue Machine can't refuse, and maybe blow an eight-figure deal in the process," said Mom.

She took another sip of Mimosa.

"I'd say you had some nerve, wouldn't you, Eric?" she said.

Eric nodded morosely.

"You've got the nerve to do all of that," said Mom, "but you don't have the balls to tell him yourself? Insulting, Eric, *insulting.* I mean, what does that make Eduardo?"

"Well, when you put it that way, Mom . . ."

"Be a man, kiddo!" Mom told him. "I don't know how pissed off Eduardo will be at what you've done, but sure as shit, he'll detest you for the craven pussy you'd be if he has to hear about it first from your *mother!*"

She leered at him toothily.

"Anyway, kiddo," she said, "what's the worst thing that can happen?"

She flipped a forkful of Cajun blood sausage over the side.

An alligator snapped it up before it hit the water.

Monique Calhoun found herself "getting professional." She called Avi Posner and told him to meet her by the southwest pillar of the Eiffel Tower at noon; that is, outdoors at a randomly chosen location, where there could be no possibility of bugging. For the same professionally paranoiac reason, she refused to tell him why.

Another wall of hot saturated air had moved in on northwestern Europe, or, Monique suspected, given what she knew now, had been shepherded in from on high by the loathsome "clients' " orbital mirrors, and the noontime clime this Paris day was a fair disney of Lost Louisianne or the equatorial coast of Africa, whence this condition might just have been deliberately exported.

But the pillars of the Tower had long since become great iron trellises overgrown with honeysuckle, ivy, bougainvillea, and morning-glory vines all the way up to the first-level platform, so that the area beneath it, thronged with tourists, vendors, and buskers, was an immense shaded and perfumed arbor that at least afforded some respite.

Avi Posner was already seated on a wooden bench when Monique arrived. "So?" he said without bothering with the courtesy of rising to greet her.

"What do you want first, the good news, the bad news, the worse news, or the worst news?" Monique said, sitting down without bothering with the niceties either.

Posner just gave her a glacial impatient stare.

"The good news is that I've found out that 'Lao' is the code word for some kind of Siberian operation against our . . . client's interests at UNACOCS."

She held up her hand for silence. "And *don't* ask me how!" she told him.

"May I ask if it involves Davinda?"

"You may ask, but the best answer I can give you is probably."

Posner did not look tremendously pleased. And *that* had been the good news.

"And the bad news?"

"Very bad indeed," Monique said.

Avi Posner tapped his foot impatiently.

Monique frowned, paused, hesitated, glanced around. She realized on a rational level that she really *was* being paranoid, but, well . . .

"You once told me to assume that *everywhere* was bugged . . ." she said.

Now Posner's impatient demeanor became one of worry, of professional concern. "*That* bad?"

"Worse," Monique said.

"Let's walk.

Southeast from the Tower to the École Militaire, the long oblong park of the Champ-de-Mars ran through a corridor of immense live oaks, another canopy of shady greenery.

A "natural" disney, Monique thought sourly as they ambled slowly down a path through the leafy tunnel toward the incongruous square shape of the École Militaire. Lost Louisianne re-created in a Paris that was itself the product of climate change and sustained by climatech. Climatech which was now perhaps being turned against it. The same climatech which was at least temporarily turning the world into a disney of Condition Venus. Disneys within disneys within disneys.

"The white tornadoes are fakes, Avi," Monique finally said. "It's being done with orbital mirrors."

Posner froze in his tracks. "How do you know this?" he said sharply.

"Esterhazy told me."

"*Esterhazy!* You expect me to believe anything he tells you isn't disinformation?"

"They have proof. They have recordings of conversations."

Posner sat down on a nearby bench. It seemed like a involuntary action. He seemed quite stunned. Even more stunned, or so it seemed to Monique, than the revelation warranted.

"Our *client* is creating the white tornadoes with orbital mirrors . . . ?" he said softly.

"And they could just as easily be creating the rest of this so-called Condition Venus weather, couldn't they?" Monique said, sitting down beside him.

"Adjust some mirrors, move some jet stream, fiddle with the ocean currents . . . no one would spot it unless they were monitoring their orbital mirrors very closely . . . from orbit . . . and only the Big Blue Machine itself has that kind of gear. . . ."

Posner had descended into muttering to himself, and the frowning set of his brows grew deeper and deeper. "Human brains . . . faked tornadoes . . . Condition Venus disneys . . ."

"That's not all . . ." Monique told him tentatively.

"There's *more?*" Posner groaned.

Monique nodded nervously.

"Well?"

"Well . . . I had to trade information to find all that out . . ."

"This is supposed to be a surprise?" Posner snapped. "You told Esterhazy what?"

Monique hesitated. "That the Davinda climate model may be run on a computer with human meatware in the circuit," she blurted quickly.

"*And?*" Posner demanded.

"Look, Avi, I'm no professional at this, and I don't want to be, so you can't blame me," Monique said, adopting a strategically defensive whine. "I didn't know they'd . . . I mean . . ."

Another set of disneys within disneys within disneys, for that very disclaimer was a calculated move itself, masking her collusion with Eric, her betrayal of B&C's client, Mossad's client, in the service of Bad Boys' client, to find out the truth about what *her* client was hiding.

No professional? It seemed to Monique that she was becoming more of a professional at this moment by moment. But just what her profession had now become and whether it was any younger than the oldest did not at the moment bear close contemplation.

"And, well, Esterhazy, Bad Boys . . ."

"Out with it, will you!"

Me thinks the lady has protested long enough, Monique decided.

"Bad Boys intends to find out what's being hidden under guard," she said breathily, making her final show of reluctance. "And, well—"

"Spit it out!"

"And they're using the recordings to do it. I'm to deliver their ultimatum. Esterhazy is given access to the computer that's going to run Davinda's climate model on Sunday, or they release the recordings that prove the white tornadoes are fakes to the media on Saturday."

Monique shrugged, smiled wanly. "And now I have."

Avi Posner took a moment to digest this. Then, unexpectedly, he favored her with a grim little smile. "Good," he said.

"Good?" Of all the reactions she had imagined, this certainly had not been among them.

"You have done well. And you have also done right. And so have Bad Boys."

"I have? You're not angry?"

"Oh, I'm quite furious, at least provisionally," Avi Posner told her. "But not at you. And not at Esterhazy or his syndic."

"At . . . our client?" Monique said, beginning to get his drift.

Posner nodded. "Let's walk," he said, getting up from the bench, reversing course and leading Monique slowly through the overarching glade back in the direction of the Eiffel Tower.

"What do you know about Mossad?" he said after a few silent moments.

"It began as the Israeli secret service?" Monique said. "It became a syndic when the Israeli government shed most of its sovereign functions? It provides security and intelligence services to its clients?"

And does dirty work and wet work when the price is right, she found it impolitic to add.

Posner nodded. "The operative point is that Mossad is a *syndic* with a charter and citizen-shareholders. We are *not* the dedicated security service of any entity, corporate or sovereign. We work under contract. And under our charter, there are limits on the contract terms we will accept."

"What are you trying to tell me, Avi?"

Avi Posner seemed somehow elsewhere. He made direct eye contact with her, but he didn't answer directly.

"Israel itself was partially founded by kibbutzniks," he told her. "The kibbutzes were one of the direct ancestors of modern syndics. They had charters, they were collectively owned by citizen-shareholders who elected their governing boards, this even in the era of capitalism and absolute national sovereignty."

"I don't get it, Avi, what's the point . . . ?"

"The point, Monique, is that Mossad's syndicalist roots go back deep into the capitalist era, and the organizations our syndic has indirectly evolved from were not corporate capitalist ones, but collectives of utopian idealists."

"So okay, Mossad is a respectable syndic, so—"

"So our client is *not*, Monique!" Posner snapped. "Do you know who really runs the Big Blue Machine?"

"Kutnik? Hassan bin Mohammed?"

"*No one*, Monique. There are no citizen-shareholders for the boards of its constituent corporations to be responsible to. And no syndic charters setting forth a moral philosophy. It's a loose collection of capitalist revenants, each a corporation whose default and only value is the maximization of profit. The Big Blue Machine is . . . *a machine*. A mechanism for generating profit with no human moral responsibility in the circuit, individual or collective. *This* was why the capitalist world order could blindly destabilize the planetary climate in the process of destroying itself. It wasn't evil. It didn't recognize evil *or* good. In that sense, in a moral sense, it had no soul."

"So . . . ?"

"So *we* are not capitalists!" Posner declared with a passion that quite took Monique aback. "Not Bread & Circuses, not Bad Boys, and certainly not Mossad! Your syndic, and mine, and even Esterhazy's, may have *different* moral philosophies, but unlike Big Blue *we have them*. And our charters agree on one thing—no contract binds us to aid capitalist clients in committing moral atrocities for no higher cause than their own profit!"

"Such as using human brains as meatware processors in computers? Such as faking the onset of Condition Venus?"

"It depends . . ." said Posner, suddenly pensive.

"On what?"

"On the ends to which they are the means. You have surely been subjected to the asinine aphorism that claims that the ends do not justify the means. But of course, the reverse is true. *Nothing* but the ends justify the means."

"What ends can possibly justify means like using human brains as computer processors and faking the onset of the end of the world?"

"Saving the planet from the *real* end of the world, of course," Avi Posner said. "If we were convinced that it was indeed necessary to save the biosphere, Mossad would commit atrocities that would make Hitler himself cringe if we had to."

They were back under the Eiffel Tower now, surrounded by the tourists and the vendors and the buskers, shaded by the vines overgrowing the pillars of the tower, breathing the rich floral perfumes.

Even in the shade, the humid air was still sweltering, but foul though the current weather might be, disney though this sweet arbor might be, this was still, at the moment at least, part of the tender biosphere of a living world.

Would *I* commit atrocities that would make Hitler cringe to save it? Monique wondered.

That she didn't know, and hoped to never have to find out.

But she did believe that she understood what Avi Posner was trying to tell her. She understood his hard and ruthless moral logic, and could only agree with it in her own hardest heart of hearts.

She knew that whether she would do evil to save her living breathing world was not a question of whether it was right or wrong but of courage.

For the first time in her life, Monique was confronted with the cruel realization that greater than the courage to do right in the face of danger or adversity was the courage to commit a lesser evil to prevent a greater.

And that if the evil that needed preventing was the ultimate one, the death of all living things, then Avi Posner was right. *Any* means were justified to accomplish that end. Anything at all.

"You're right, Avi," Monique said quietly. "Some ends do justify any means."

"But merely turning a profit is not one of them!" Posner said savagely. "And if those capitalist sons of bitches are committing such evils for no higher cause than profit, any contract they had with Mossad is null and void!"

He made a visible effort to calm himself. "And so . . ."

"And so?"

"And so *I* have *more* need to know whether my client has installed a human brain in that computer that you and Esterhazy do," Posner said. "Because, now that we know they've lied to us about faking the white tornadoes and probably this stinking Condition Venus weather too, if they've installed a human brain in the Davinda climate model computer and hidden it from us, Mossad is not about to continue to honor its contract without at least extracting the full truth. By whatever means necessary."

"Then you'll transmit Esterhazy's blackmail threat up the line?"

"Oh indeed I will," Posner told her. "And on behalf of my syndic I will add one of my own—there will be no further provision of the contracted services by Mossad until *I* see what they are hiding myself!"

One did not *summon* Eduardo Ramirez, and certainly not to a meeting within hours, so despite his trepidation at walking into the lion's den under these circumstances, Eric Esterhazy was constrained to show up at Eduardo's office unannounced.

Bad Boys did not maintain a suite of syndic offices as such, each citizen-shareholder who needed one rented his own with syndic funds, and Eduardo had chosen one high up the old Tour Montparnasse, a somewhat déclassé business address which afforded him a measure of anonymity, along with a magnificent view northward across the city.

The office was small by design—just an entrance foyer, an outer office for a receptionist and a computer operator, a modest inner office for Eduardo's executive assistant, and Eduardo's own lair itself.

This was more of a lounge than an office and done in an Italianate retro-deco mode. No desk as such, rather an enormous free-form ebony table thing at dining-room height, with an inset swirl to accommodate Eduardo's favorite chaise—an antique dentist's chair which could be pneumatically arranged to almost any configuration and position—and lesser seats for lesser folk.

The window with its sweeping view of Paris was the main item of the decor and had been framed in sleek silver paneling as if it were a painting, though there were a couple of small Mondrians and a Modigliani on the walls.

Eduardo, in true Bad Boys style, maintained minimal bureaucratic protocol, and so there was no problem for a citizen-shareholder on Eric's level to show up and gain almost immediate access.

The trouble, Eric knew, as he entered the office, would begin now that he had.

Eduardo did not bother rising to greet him, or shaking hands, or making with an embrasso, or any such stuff, nor had Eric expected it.

"I gather you have something urgently important to tell me, Eric?" he simply said.

"I do," Eric replied in similar style, and he sat down and laid it out as succinctly and quickly as possible in words of one syllable, leaving nothing at all out, not even his use of the aphrogas, nor the supine posture in which he had secured most of the information he was relaying, nor even his collusion with Monique Calhoun, wanting to get it all out in one piece before he lost his courage on the one hand, and figuring that he at least owed that much to Eduardo and his syndic on the other.

When he had finished, Eduardo Ramirez just sat there silently regarding him over steepled fingers for at least a full minute, displaying no emotion, giving nothing away, making Eric sweat.

"You've been rather venturesome, haven't you, Eric?" he finally said.

"It was necessary . . . under the conditions."

"Interesting conditions," said Eduardo, still stone-faced. "Created by you."

"I gained a piece of valuable knowledge," Eric told him.

"Did you?"

"We now know that a human brain—"

"A supposition," Eduardo said coldly. "But we did learn something else." He granted Eric a frosty smile. "Do you know what it is?"

Eric felt he was being tested in a way he did not quite understand. He thought very carefully before he spoke.

"That . . . that if Monique Calhoun swallowed my lie about Lao being the code word for an operation of ours, it isn't one of theirs."

"Perhaps," said Eduardo. "Or . . . ?" He cocked an inquisitive eyebrow.

"Or . . . if it is, Calhoun didn't know . . . any more than she knew they're faking the white tornadoes. . . ."

Eduardo nodded. But he did not smile approvingly. Not at all.

"But she knows now," he said. "And much more importantly, Big Blue will know that *we* know, by dispensation of a major policy decision you made without prior authorization from the syndic. Wouldn't you say you've taken quite a bit on yourself, Eric?"

"I wasn't exactly in a position to make a phone call first," Eric said, and, despite the dire circumstances, couldn't entirely suppress his grin.

"True," said Eduardo, the corners of his lips merely twitching. "I would've done the same in your . . . position."

"Then I did the right thing?"

"You certainly did a dangerous thing," said Eduardo.

"Dangerous?" said Eric.

Eduardo Ramirez let him sweat for a good thirty seconds.

"Dare I suppose that, given the circumstances, you might not have been calculating the ramifications with cold logical clarity?" Eduardo finally suggested dryly. "That you might not have been fully cognizant of the bet you were, ah, laying down, or the stakes?"

"Uh . . . maybe not . . ." Eric said uneasily.

"True that nothing has been lost by letting Big Blue know we are in possession of material that could destroy them, and we do indeed have a need to know if they're using human brains as central processing units, but . . ."

Eduardo let that "but" hang and made a palm-forward gesture inviting or daring or perhaps requiring Eric to complete his sentence.

And of course now Eric did realize what he had more or less known all along, even then.

"But if Big Blue calls my bluff—"

"No bluff, Eric!" Eduardo said sharply. "You didn't make a *personal* threat, you made a threat on behalf of *Bad Boys*. And as a matter of both honor and practical credibility, Bad Boys can never be seen to have in retrospect bluffed. If Big Blue is so self-destructive as to believe we have, we *must* sell the recordings to the media, even if—"

"Even if it means blowing a much more lucrative sale to the Marenkos," Eric said.

Eduardo nodded. "Now you *do* understand what you've done," he said. "And the personal consequences. Because if that happens—"

"It will not have been a very good career move?" Eric said wanly, not really caring to contemplate, let alone ask, just how bad a career move it might turn out to be.

"Not at all," Eduardo said.

And then, unexpectedly, his whole demeanor changed.

He smiled, he rose, he went to a small bar and poured two snifters of cognac, and motioned for Eric to join him before the big picture window, where a travel poster vision of Paris spread out before Eric, lush and green and fair from this air-conditioned vantage, despite the sweaty reality beyond the glass.

Disneys everywhere you looked.

He wondered uneasily if Eduardo Ramirez's abrupt lightening of manner was more of the same, and when Eduardo handed him his glass, it took a bit of discipline for Eric to content himself with a gentlemanly sip rather than bolt down a big gulp for courage.

"On the other hand, Eric," Eduardo said, as if continuing the same conversation, but in an entirely altered mode, "if that *doesn't* happen, you will have earned the right to be considered a man of serious respect within Bad Boys. *Because* you took such a personal risk to do the right thing on the syndic's behalf."

"The right thing? But if it turns out wrong—"

"The *morally* right thing," Eduardo said. "Which is not a matter of profit or loss. Bad Boys are neither capitalists indifferent to any values beyond the economic, nor the rough gangsters of your mother's nostalgic fantasies. You did the right thing. I say without false modesty that I would've done the same thing. Or I wouldn't be where I am today. I can't protect you from the consequences, nor would I if I could, but win or lose, you *did* do the right thing, and I admire you for it."

"I did the right thing, but I have to suffer the consequences if it turns out wrong?" Eric said.

"Who else would you suggest bear the consequences of your actions?"

"It doesn't seem fair."

"Life isn't fair," Eduardo said. "Perhaps you've noticed? And if it turns out that your misjudgment cost the syndic a large amount of money . . ."

He shrugged. "We are not capitalists, Eric. Personal decisions on the behalf of the collectivity require the acceptance of personal responsibility for the results. The buck, as the Americans never quite managed to understand, stops with each and every citizen-shareholder."

Eric took a longer sip of cognac, but still a controlled one. He felt fear, he knew that he had put himself in this situation without being fully aware of what he had really been doing.

Yet he also felt he had unwittingly gained something thereby. Not just the warm glow of have done "the right thing" nor the adrenal rush of bravery, but the sense of having gained entry into an exclusive company, of having in some way beyond position in the syndic pecking order become the equal of Eduardo and been accepted as such.

Perhaps simply—though there was really nothing simple about it—having finally ceased to be merely his mother's son in the eyes of Eduardo Ramirez and indeed perhaps even in his own, and become fully a man.

"Understood, Eduardo," he said. He clinked glasses. "Understood and accepted."

Eduardo clinked glasses back, and the two men drank to it.

As Monique Calhoun approached the café she had arranged for the rendezvous, she saw that Avi Posner and Eric Esterhazy had already arrived and were seated outside eyeing each other cautiously like two tomcats.

Checking her watch, she saw that she was a few minutes late and wondered whether this had been by unconscious instinctual design, for now, in retrospect, she thought that it wasn't such a bad idea. For although the men were the principals in this little inspection tour and she was just a supernumerary, keeping them waiting for her for a bit altered the geometry somewhat, made the triangle more equilateral.

Avi Posner had been rather bemused when he called to tell her that the client had readily agreed to allow Esterhazy, himself, and

Monique to inspect what they now admitted was indeed the computer on which they would run John Sri Davinda's climate model on the final day of the conference.

Too readily by Posner's lights.

"They came right out and admitted they were faking the white tornadoes when I confronted them with it, but they told me I wouldn't be sorry if I reserved judgment," he had told her. "They made a mere pro forma show of shock and dismay when I told them that Bad Boys had recordings to prove it before they caved in to the blackmail."

"What's the problem, Avi?"

"The problem is there's no problem. And there should be. It's too easy. I don't understand it. And I don't like what I don't understand."

"Professional paranoia, Avi."

"Perhaps," Posner had said, coming as close to cracking a joke as he ever had, which was not very, "but in my profession, it pays to never leave home without it."

If Posner had been less enthusiastic about Big Blue's swift capitulation to Eric's ultimatum that he should've been in Monique's opinion, Eric himself had been more relieved than the situation would have seemed to warrant when she told him.

His normally suave and supercilious persona had vanished from the nervous face on her phone screen when she called, and he had leaned forward eagerly.

"*Well?*" he had demanded without his customary niceties.

"Well what . . . ?" Monique could not refrain from teasing coyly.

"*Please. . . .*"

"Please what . . . ?"

"Please stop playing games and tell me whether it's yes or no!"

"Oh *that* . . ." Monique had purred, letting it and him hang.

"Yes that!"

"It's a yes," Monique finally told him mercifully. "Five o'clock."

It was as if a balloon had been emptied of a heavy gas and reinflated with helium. The edgy tension went whooshing out of Eric's demeanor with a nearly audible sigh of relief and the familiar Prince Smarming came surging back.

"Excellent," he said. "Why don't we meet at say, three? That should give us sufficient time to . . . relax beforehand. My apartment? Or perhaps your suite at the Ritz?"

Only then did it dawn on Monique that Eric, being an operative of Bad Boys and not Bread & Circuses, might have something a lot more personally vital riding on pulling off this blackmail scheme than she did.

And only realizing that, did it then seem to her that behind that supercilious persona there might be something admirable that had not been there before. And that made him more attractive because it was.

Nevertheless . . .

"We'll have to meet at a café," she had told him. "We're going to have a third. . . ."

"Sorry I'm late," Monique said, as she walked up to the table. "Avi, this is Prince Eric Esterhazy of, er, *La Reine de la Seine*, Eric, this is Avi Posner of, ah . . . er . . ."

"Mossad," said Posner.

Monique cocked an eyebrow, at which of them she wasn't sure.

"We've already introduced ourselves," Eric told her with a smile.

"Up to a point," Posner amended cautiously.

Eric Esterhazy felt more in command than ever he had from the wheelhouse of *La Reine* entering the Grand Palais with Monique Calhoun and Avi Posner.

This was no disney and he was no front man. This was *his* operation. He had taken it upon himself to conceive it, he had bet everything on it, perhaps even his life, and he had won. He was now, as Eduardo had said, a man of serious respect within Bad Boys.

And treated as such by this older and obviously hardened professional from Mossad.

That Big Blue would insist on sending its own minder along was no surprise and it was already known that they had hired Mossad. But Avi Posner's attitude had not been what Eric had expected.

Monique had flashed him Posner's photo at the end of her call, and Posner could not help but be familiar with the face of the famous Prince of the City, so they had recognized each other immediately when Posner approached the café table that Eric had already taken.

"Avi Posner, I presume?" Eric had ventured with the habitual superciliousness of his princely persona. Then, catching himself, and establishing his weight. "Of Mossad?"

"Eric Esterhazy?" Posner had replied, dispensing with the title, which Eric found himself taking more as a compliment than a slight. "Of Bad Boys?"

With that, Posner seated himself, and they ordered coffees. Eric, not used to this sort of thing, broke an awkward silence.

"About the, ah, methods we've employed—"

"A nice piece of work."

"No hard feelings then?"

"Between Mossad and Bad Boys? We're cousins are we not? Our menus of methods are not that different. Our syndic charters are not that dissimilar. The main difference is that you undertake certain free-lance commercial activities on your own and we stick to our contract work."

"But we're representing the interests of a client we believe your client may be running a scam on, and you're representing the scammer in question. . . ."

Posner frowned. "Let's get one thing straight between us, Ester-hazy," he said quite vehemently. "For the duration of this inspection at least, I represent *my syndic* and not any cabal of capitalist bastards who would play Frankenstein games with human brains merely for profit!"

Both Posner's angry intensity and his frankness had startled Eric, but he believed he had managed to cover his surprise. "Guilty until proven innocent?"

"Come off it, Esterhazy! You know as well as I do that neither Bad Boys nor Mossad would honor a contract with creatures like that. Man to man, either of us would eagerly enough accept a contract to terminate the decision makers, would we not . . . ?"

Posner had grimaced. "In the unlikely event that any individual responsibility could be sorted out of the corporate dung heap," he had added sourly.

At which point, Monique Calhoun had arrived, they had paid the check, and walked over to the Grand Palais, where Monique, as Bread & Circuses' VIP services chief, had VIP passed them inside.

And now here they were, at least for the duration with a united purpose—Monique, himself, and Posner; Bread & Circuses, Bad Boys, and Mossad.

And in deadly earnest though that purpose was, Eric could not help amusing himself with the thought that someone should have composed a syndical anthem and a big brass band should be playing it behind them now as they strode together righteously through the massed climatech displays of the Big Blue Machine toward the dark secret that the capitalist miscreants held under guard.

Eric's first sight of their objective, however, was something of an anticlimax, being a simple enclosure of green canvas screening, the gap in which was presided over by two slightly overweight guards, discreetly armed with ordinary pistols, and wearing the rumpled and ill-fitting gray uniforms of Keystone Kops, a syndic not noted for providing anything more sophisticated than routine physical security.

The guards did not seem to have the thespian talent to fake the blank looks they gave Posner as he approached them, meaning that the chances that they were actually Mossad operatives in drag were minimal.

Instead of speaking, Posner palmed a small photo ID card, and passed it quickly under their noses.

"Right," grunted one guard. "Horst, the peeper . . ."

Horst went through the gap and emerged a few moments later with a device that looked something like a pair of antique opera glasses on a thick stalk, which Eric recognized as a retina reader.

The other guard, who seemed to be in charge, took it and held it up to Posner's eyes briefly, regarded a readout on the stalk.

"Right, you're Avi Posner," he said. "Orders are you and your party have a maximum of twenty minutes inside, no weapons, no cameras, no recording devices. Right?"

"Right," Posner mimicked humorlessly, and the guard led them inside the enclosure to a small antechamber, just more canvas screening and two open gateways leading into the main area, one after the other, that resembled standard metal and explosive detection equipment.

"No weapons, cameras, explosives, electronic equipment, medical implants, phones, metallic objects bigger than belt buckles," the guard droned mechanically. "If you got 'em, drop 'em. The first gate detects 'em, the second will fry any and all circuitry."

He glanced at Eric's wrist, then Monique's. "Including those watches." They removed them and laid them on the floor. Posner, who seemed to know this drill, hadn't been wearing one.

With an "after you" gesture, the guard ushered them one by one through the double security gates and into the main enclosure, following close behind.

The interior was illumined by harsh overhead halogens strung on temporary wiring. There was a computer console with an assortment of standard keyboards, microphones, and speakers, and a single screen; a rig which impressed Eric as not only ordinary-looking, but, considering Ignatz and its multiscreen setup, even cheesy.

There were two ordinary swivel chairs in front of the computer, plus a third seat which reminded Eric of Eduardo's antique dentist's chair, or, fitted as it was with a clunky virtuality hood on a flexible stalk, more of an equally antique lounger from an old-fashioned public cyber arcade.

Beyond the computer console was a large rack of sat-link equipment and assorted electronic bric-a-brac. An untidy spaghetti bowl of wiring and cables taped to the floor linked everything to everything.

"This is it?" Monique muttered in a tone of disappointment.

And Eric fully sympathized with her.

He didn't know quite what he had expected—a naked human brain in a jar of bubbling green goo? towering electrodes sparking away madly? Dr. Frankenstein and Igor?—but this wasn't it.

This installation didn't even seem to be up to what he had in *La Reine*. On the other hand, Eric knew that he was hardly an expert.

"Can you explain what this gear is?" he asked the guard.

The guard looked at him as if he had just arrived via transporter beam from the planet Mongo.

Avi Posner, though, was already poring over the equipment. He examined the keyboards, the front panel of the computer console. He stepped behind it, peered through a series of ventilation grilles at the interior, while Eric stood there like a display window mannequin wondering what to do.

Monique Calhoun seemed to be in the same quandary. She locked eyes with him. She raised her eyebrows. She shrugged.

Eric shrugged back, and went over to the front of the computer console, doing a disney of Posner's inspection routine just to keep from looking stupid.

Monique went over to the virtuality lounger, apparently doing likewise, poking at the cushioning, peering up the hood, as if she were a customer in an antique shop contemplating buying the thing. Eric joined her for a bit, giving it the jaundiced and uncomprehending once-over of the twentieth-century husband likely to be stuck footing the bill.

Posner, meanwhile, had moved over to the rack of electronic equipment, peering closely at this and that, frowning, muttering to himself, all but scratching his head.

Eric moved behind the computer console, looked through the ventilation grilles as Posner had done. All solid-state circuitry and a couple of fans as near as his unschooled eye could tell. Certainly no object in there remotely large enough to contain a human brain, polymerized or otherwise.

Posner paced the floor following wiring. Eric and Monique pretended to do the same. On and on, seemingly to no purpose, as the guard stood athwart the entrance with his arms folded across his paunch, looking as bored, if not as puzzled, as Eric felt.

Finally, after a good deal less than their allotted twenty minutes, Avi Posner walked up to Eric, grimacing in puzzlement, shaking his head. Monique joined them.

"Well?" she said softly enough not to be overheard by the guard.

"Well nothing," said Posner. It was hard to tell whether he was angry, puzzled, or relieved, and Eric suspected that he didn't know either.

"A CJC 756 computer with no organic elements that I could detect, and certainly no human meatware central processing unit. Ordinary sat-link equipment. The whole thing seems designed to merely run software and broadcast the output. And maybe slave the display screen in the auditorium to it."

He cocked an inquisitive, even imploring look at Eric. "Anything to add, Esterhazy?"

Eric shrugged.

"If there's a human brain anywhere in here, it's been sliced into tasty bite-size pieces," he said. "It's the Night Before Christmas, and all through this house, not a creature's been circuited, not even a mouse."

10

"MEET ME ON THE PONT DES ARTS AT ELEVEN,"
was all that Avi Posner had said over the phone but the agitated tone
of his voice and the fact that he was setting up another outdoor rendezvous away from possible bugging told Monique that the absence of
a human brain in the Davinda climate model computer had not entirely restored his trust in the client.

The Pont des Arts was an old footbridge over the Seine between
the upscale end of the Latin Quarter and the Louvre; wooden planking
on a metal framework, the only bridge over the river that was pedes-
trian only.

It commanded a magisterial view of the Louvre, the stone-bound
prow of the Ile de la Cité, the tropical gardens of the Tuileries, the
Eiffel Tower beyond, and it had therefore been turned into a linear
sidewalk café with tiny tables along both railings, the better to milk
the considerable tourist traffic.

So it was crowded and noisy, ideal for secure conversation, and
Posner had already taken a table and ordered two frosty mint juleps
by the time Monique had arrived.

Though yesterday's humidity was in the process of being burned
off by the sun—or an orbital mirror adjustment—it was still turning

into a scorcher of a day and there was no room on the narrow bridge for table umbrellas.

Nevertheless, to judge by his demeanor, something more than the heat and the fact that he had gone through half of his drink already was causing Posner to sweat profusely.

"It makes no sense, Monique," were his first words to her as she sat down.

"Life, the universe, and everything?"

"That too, I'm beginning to believe," Posner said morosely.

Monique took a sip of her julep. The sun was nowhere near its zenith and she too was starting to sweat.

"So my fears about human meatware in the computer were mistaken, paranoid perhaps, even," Posner babbled as if this were already the middle of a conversation. "So ersatz white tornadoes seemed what the Catholics would term merely a venal sin under the circumstances, the contract with the client was still valid, and as a matter of course I passed along your information that I had withheld—"

"That Lao was the code designation of some Siberian operation against Davinda?"

Avi Posner didn't even bother to nod. He just went on as if he were talking to himself. Perhaps in effect he was.

"And it was like poking a stick in a wasps' nest! Screams! Howls! Find out what it is! Put a stop to it! By whatever means necessary! Do it yesterday!"

"I don't get it, Avi," Monique said calmly. "Why the agitation? Isn't that the sort of thing they hired Mossad for in the first place?"

"Think, Monique, *think!*"

"About what?"

Posner took a long sip of his julep, then a slow deep breath, and seemed to have succeeded in calming himself.

"That Bad Boys is in possession of recordings that can prove they've faked the white tornadoes, they take *too* calmly," he said. "As if they know they are holding a card which can trump it. I am led to believe, or perhaps I lead myself to believe, that the trump is a human brain in the computer. But that turns out not to be so. So it can only be—"

"Davinda's climate model itself."

Posner nodded, and his expression, if it did not relax, at least expressed a reassurance at the acknowledgment that she was now following his logic.

"So you *do* see?" he said.

"Uh . . . look Avi, I appreciate the compliment, but I really *am* an amateur at this stuff. . . ."

"*What are they afraid of?*" Posner exclaimed in exasperation.

Monique squinted at him uncomprehendingly.

Posner made a visible effort to truly calm himself, to get professional, and didn't speak again until he had succeeded.

"What do they *have* to be afraid of?" he said evenly. "Davinda's climate model has already been loaded into the computer, and the computer is under guard."

"So . . . ?"

"So what harm can the Siberians do by eliminating Davinda now, or even turning him?"

"Nothing," said Monique. "Unless . . ."

"*Unless?*" Posner said eagerly. He leaned forward and peered across the table at Monique intently, hopefully, or so she thought. "You have an *unless?*"

"Unless they got to Davinda a long time ago," Monique told him.

"My god!" Posner exclaimed. He looked as if he had been bonged on the head with a mallet. "He's a *mole*! And Lao isn't just a designation, it's an *activation signal*!"

He frowned. "But to do *what?*"

Monique shrugged. "Don't ask me, Avi, I'm an amateur," she said. But then an obvious and unsettling thought *did* pass through her mind. "Unless . . ."

"You have *another* unless?" Posner asked avidly.

"Unless the Marenkos were prompting Davinda for confirmation of something he's *already* done," Monique told him.

"Already done? Like what?"

"What's all of this been leading up to?" Monique said. "Isn't it obvious?"

"The demonstration of Davinda's climate model. . . ."

Monique nodded.

"*There's* your Siberian mole, Avi," she said. "Not John Sri Davinda, *his climate model.*"

"Merde!" Posner exclaimed, whacking his forehead quite hard with the heel of his hand.

And then he actually reached across the table, grabbed her hand, and kissed it.

Eric Esterhazy had never pondered the technical prowess of his syndic beyond his appreciation of its manifestation in Ignatz, had never even imagined that Bad Boys maintained facilities like this or that there were citizen-shareholders who worked in white lab coats.

But when he had informed Eduardo Ramirez of what he had apparently *not* seen in the Davinda climate model computer, Eduardo had not been satisfied by his inexpert verbal report or even the confirmation by an experienced Mossad operative.

"It wouldn't have been possible to slip inside with a camera," Eric had pointed out.

"Yes and no," Eduardo had replied enigmatically, and Eric had found himself being whisked out here into the suburbs northeast of Paris in Eduardo's limo.

Here being a little late-twentieth-century faux-Bauhaus factory building indistinguishable from the half-dozen other such rusty aluminum and faded glass boxes in a crumbling so-called industrial park inside the chain-link fence of which not so much as a blade of grass was evident.

The sign on the side of this "factory" read BOUTIQUE SPECTRE, S.A., and it double-took Eric a few moments to get the joke, which, like the operation, was hidden in plain sight, "Boutique Spectre" being an awkward literal French translation of "Spook Shop," the initials of which, appropriately enough, were generally understood to indicate "bullshit" in English.

Eduardo pressed a buzzer at the outer door. What had appeared to be a simple old digicode pad slid upward and a peeper extruded itself. Eduardo looked into the eyepieces for a moment. The peeper retreated, the panel slid shut, and a minute or two later the door opened and they were met by a gray-haired black woman in a white lab coat.

"Monsieur Ramirez . . ."

"Dr. Duvond . . ."

No further greetings, no introduction, as Dr. Duvond led them down a series of climatized pastel-green corridors far cleaner than the grimy exterior past mostly closed and peeper-locked doors to one that seemed no different than the others.

If the inside of the Davinda climate model enclosure had disappointed Eric in terms of proper mad scientist decor, this room went a ways toward making up for it.

There was a wall of slick-looking computer equipment. There was a cabinet full of glass vials and syringes and an autoclave. There was what looked unsettlingly like an operating table surrounded by electroencephalography gear, gas tank with face mask, some kind of virtuality helmet, a large video monitor, though at least no surgical instruments were in evidence.

There were two male technicians in the room—or doctors, or nurses, or whatever they were—and Dr. Duvond didn't bother to introduce them to Eric either.

"You will now please lie down supine on the table, Prince Esterhazy," she said instead. "No need to undress."

"How kind of you," Eric smarmed, then turned to Eduardo. "*Now* would you mind telling me what's going on?"

"There's a twentieth-century literary work called *I Am a Camera*," Eduardo said. He laughed. "Well you have been."

"We all are," Duvond said. "Human visual memories, like all memories, are, after all, stored in the meatware of the brain. Much the same technology that allows us to use rat brains as processing and storage components allows us to read them."

"But those are *polymerized* brains!" Eric protested. "You have to *kill* the animal to use them, don't you?"

"Only to use a mammalian brain as a RAM chip," Duvond told him. "But using it as ROM, as read-only memory, is a physiologically and psychologically nondestructive process. It's not like using your brain as a processing unit. It's simply the reverse of using computer input to generate a virtual reality sensorium in the brain in question. No need to remove it from the body. No danger of cerebral overload because your brain isn't installed as a circuit component. We've tested this device with living rats, even dogs, and the personalities of the animals survive with no significant observable deterioration. To the extent they may be said to have personalities."

"*I* am not a rodent or a dog, Dr. Duvond, perhaps you've noticed?"

"But I do believe you are a mammal," Duvond said, "and the operating system is not species-specific."

If this was some sort of dim medical humor, Eric did not at all appreciate it.

"Lie down, please," Duvond repeated impatiently. "I assure you, this will not be significantly unpleasant."

"*Significantly?*" said Eric. But he bowed to the inevitable.

As one of the technicians went around turning things on, the other went to the medicine cabinet, extracted a vial of something, and, thankfully, loaded it into a pneumatic injector rather than some hideous old hypodermic needle, so that it was painless when he injected whatever it was into the pit of Eric's left elbow.

Duvond then fitted the "virtuality helmet" over Eric's head. But there were no visuals, 3D or otherwise, just complete blackness and the feeling of a wire mesh pressed close against his skull. Then another painless injection.

After a few moments, Eric felt his bodily sensations beginning to dwindle, a sense of his flesh dissolving. He tried to say something, but the muscles of his mouth and tongue didn't seem to be working.

"Don't worry, Prince Esterhazy," said a disembodied voice that began to fade away even as it spoke, "we're merely putting your non-visual sensory and non-autonomic motor functions off-line the better to . . ."

Then silence.

Darkness.

Panic.

And not a damn thing he could do about it. He couldn't move. He couldn't scream. He couldn't feel. All he could do was think.

And what he was thinking was that this must be what it would be like to be a disembodied human brain installed in a computer. This was what it would be like to be one of the rat brains in Ignatz if the polymerized brain of a rodent had sufficient consciousness to ponder its horrid condition.

Wrong.

Not quite.

That, he learned a few moments later, had been the *resting state* of computer brainware, for then he was "booted up."

Suddenly the darkness was flooded with silent visual images. Flashing before him with unnatural washed-out brightness, faster than his consciousness could assimilate, in no coherent order, as if a lifetime of visual memories had been transferred to old-fashioned celluloid film, cut into individual frames, shuffled like a deck of cards, and then blasted into his eyeballs with a laser-driven stroboscope.

On and on and on it went until—

—he was looking through a ventilation grille at boards of solid-state circuitry—

The image froze.

It grew larger and larger, as if he were a zoom lens on a camera, until it faded away into an indistinctness the reverse of video pixelation—

—then the image-strobing began again and—

—froze on the interior of a green canvas enclosure lit by overhead halogens—

—became jerky slow motion as he moved into the enclosure, looking around, which—

—froze on the computer console, zoomed in—

—to a slow motion pan, which became normal motion, which became high-speed stop motion, as he scanned standard video screen, microphone, speakers, chairs—

—and froze on the "virtuality arcade lounger." Zoomed in. Moved along it in extreme slow motion up its length to the helmet-hood on its flexible stalk—

—pulled back to a still image of the hood itself—

—zoomed in and in and in until the image lost detail and definition. Repeated the process from different angles on different parts of the hood four times: the surface, the stalk, a part of the interior which seemed to be a mosaic of tiny blunt metal pins, another part of the surface—

—more speeded-up motion as he skittered randomly about the enclosure—

—freezing on an image of the rack of sat-link and assorted other electronic components—

—panning across it in the medium distance very slowly, freezing to zoom in on every component before continuing, pan, freeze, zoom, pan, freeze, zoom, pan, freeze, zoom . . .

—a sudden blindingly fast shuffle of the whole sequence backward to the virtuality lounger—

—the pan along it again, this time in agonizingly slow motion, seeming to stop every few centimeters for a zoom—

—the same tedious process applied to the hood alone—

—and reversed—

—and again—

—and reversed—

—and again—

—freezing on the interior of the hood. Zooming in on the field of blunt metal pins that seemed to line its interior. Zooming in further and further into a vista of dull gray dots dissolving into grayness it-self . . .

Suddenly becoming blackness. Nothingness.

Into which faraway voices began to blissfully intrude . . .

". . . to him now . . ."

". . . not unlike this equipment . . ."

And slowly Eric felt bodily sensations returning . . .

The first of which were a pounding headache and a queasy greenness in his guts.

"It's your theory, and you deserve to take the credit for it directly," Avi Posner told Monique Calhoun. "But security must be maintained, and you have no need to know."

Or desire, Monique Calhoun thought.

It was the most bizarre communications set-up she had ever experienced. She and Posner sat side by side in the so-called living room of his so-called apartment. Each of them had a voice-only telephone handset. The phones were plugged through the computer in some arcane manner which allowed Posner to speak and hear but Monique only to speak.

Monique would be able to speak directly to Posner's nebulous contact with "the client" without hearing the "contact's" voice even through a distortion algorithm.

Posner hit a function key on which a telephone number was stored. The phone apparently rang on the other end, but Monique couldn't hear it. Someone had apparently picked up because Posner started speaking into his phone.

"Posner, Avi, shalom," he said flatly, as if identifying himself to voice-recognition circuitry, which he probably was.

A long minute or two of silence as Posner listened to something obviously not to his liking.

"Yes, yes . . ."

Silence.

"Well Calhoun has come up with a theory that makes sense to me . . ."

A short beat of silence.

"Of course!"

More silence.

"You had better listen to what she has to say!"

A shorter silence.

"*Of course* send only! What kind of rank amateur do you think you're dealing with?"

Silence.

"Then hire another syndic, damn it!"

A very short beat of silence.

"All right then . . ."

Posner glanced at Monique, nodded.

"What am I supposed to do?" Monique asked.

"Just speak into the phone. Tell . . . them what you told me."

"I believe I've figured out the . . . ah general nature of the . . . operation against . . . you under the designation Lao . . ." Monique said, and paused for the reaction, as she naturally would have at this point in any conversation she had ever had, live or electronic.

But of course there wasn't any. Except for Avi Posner impatiently waving his hand for her to go on.

"Since there is ... uh ... strong reason to believe that it's ... uh ... a Siberian operation targeting John Sri Davinda, and ... er ... or his climate model, and ... ah ... since ... the climate model is already completed and in place in the computer ..."

Monique paused, covered the mouthpiece with her hand. How was she supposed to do this without any feedback at all? How could she even know there was anyone on the other end of the phone?

"How am I doing, Avi?" she whispered.

"Go, go, go!"

Monique spit it out quickly, anything to get this over with. "So Davinda or his climate model or both can't be the *targets* of the operation, they have to be *part* of it. He's got to be, what do you call it ...?"

"A mole," Posner stage-whispered.

"A mole. And since the Marenkos kept repeating the word 'Lao' to Davinda, it must be either an activation signal or a confirmation code, and ... and ... and that's all I have to say ..."

Monique put down her phone with no little relief, cocked an inquisitive look at Posner. Posner made a circle with his thumb and forefinger.

But then he spent at least two minutes time just listening, shaking his head, grimacing. "Understood, I'll wait for your call," he finally said, and hung up.

"Well?" demanded Monique.

"I said I had poked a stick in a wasps' nest?" Avi Posner said. "Well, you just cracked it open like a piñata!"

After an injection of something-or-other and a good snort of high-quality designer dust, Eric Esterhazy felt restored to a state approximating human existence. He had even managed not to puke when he sat up, though not by much.

Trying to get up off the "operating table" and walk, however, was something his shaky equilibrium told him might prudently wait for a bit later. Finding out whether anything had been learned which could in any way justify the ordeal he had been put through could not. The techs had left the room sometime before the hood had been taken off his head, leaving only Dr. Duvond and Eduardo, and Eric was in no mood to converse with the Marquess de Sade.

"Well, Eduardo," he demanded peckishly, "did you find out anything we didn't know already?"

"Oh yes," Eduardo told him. "It was well worth it."

"*Oh really?*" Eric snarled. "To whom?"

Eduardo glanced at Duvond.

"We cannot be certain without actually inspecting the device in question itself," Duvond said, "but it's a conservative hypothesis to assume that the 'virtuality hood' circuited into their computer is no more a virtuality hood than what we've just applied to you. It's a similar device, but probably more sensitive, and almost certainly not read-only."

"More simply put for a lowly mammal, Doctor?" said Eric.

"In basic layman's terms, it is likely a socket for a human meatware processor. A central processing unit of unprecedented power."

This had Eric starting bolt upright. The sudden movement sent a wave of vertigo and nausea surging through him.

"It would appear than they've found a way to do it without removing the brain from the body," Eduardo said. "The Davinda climate-model computer *will* have a human brain in the circuit," Eduardo said.

"Davinda's?" said Eric.

"Who else?"

"Could anyone survive that?" he said dubiously.

"Since the brain is not being removed from its original biological matrix, there should be no physical damage to the meatware processor or the organism itself," Dr. Duvond said.

"But what about the *inhabitant* of the biological matrix and the meatware processor?" Eric demanded.

"I don't quite follow your terminology . . ."

"The poor bastard with his head stuck in the socket! *Davinda!* What happens to the *person?*"

"I would imagine that a subject experiencing even brief usage as a meatware central processing unit would emerge with his psyche severely fragmented. More prolonged usage and he would probably not retain an integrated human consciousness at all."

Eric nodded.

Bad move. His cranium felt like a glass fishbowl that had been cracked with a hammer. And *he* had only been subject to a few minutes of the read-only version.

"Take it from someone who's been there," he groaned. "If he does, he'll wish he hadn't."

Neither of them were in any mood for small talk, so Monique had spent about a half an hour staring at Avi Posner, the ceiling, the wall, anything, nothing, waiting for the phone to ring.

When it finally did, she found herself doing likewise for another ten minutes while whoever was on the other end delivered a monologue that had Posner's expression slowly and then not so slowly turning graver and graver.

By the time he hung up, he was quite ashen. "I need a drink," he said woodenly. "And I need someone to have one with me." He went into the kitchen and came back with two water glasses a quarter full of what looked like vodka.

He handed Monique one glass and slugged the contents of the other down. Monique took a sip for the sake of solidarity. It *was* vodka. *Warm* vodka, and quite horrible.

"I am not authorized to tell you this," Posner said, "but I am going to tell you anyway. Because I don't know what to do and I must talk to somebody."

"What *is* it, Avi?" Monique said softly. She had never seen him quite like this. It wasn't at all . . . professional.

"That thing that looked like a virtuality helmet?" he said. "It's a socket for a processing unit."

"You mean . . . a *human* processing unit . . . ?"

Posner nodded. "A human brain still inside a living body . . ."

"Davinda?"

"Davinda came to them for the financing to implement climate model software he claimed was not only the state of the art but *definitive*."

"Definitive?"

"A one-for-one real-time model of the planetary climate and everything inputting into it: satellite data, individual climatech mods, atmospheric patterns, ocean temperatures, the works. A complete virtual Earth in software running in real-time. Or speeded-up. Input your climatech mods or natural factors and see the effects beforehand. The best climate model even theoretically possible."

"But that would be an *enormous* program, wouldn't it?" Monique said. "And there's no computer that could run such a thing in—"

She paused.

She swallowed hard.

"Oh," she said.

Posner nodded. "Davinda's tribe or commune or whatever they call it out there in Third Force Wonderland had also provided him with the schematics for a computer that would be able to run the model—"

"Using a human brain as the central processor—"

"Big Blue's software people couldn't run the whole thing, but when they ran bits and pieces and partial versions on partial data they got Condition Venus or something like it most of the time. The hardware people were confident they could build his human meatware computer at reasonable cost. Big Blue was very interested...."

Posner shrugged. "That much, I can readily believe." He grimaced. "The rest . . . ?" He shrugged again. "According to what I have just been told, the Big Blue Machine still hesitated to finance the project out of tender moral concern for the welfare of the human component. So Davinda—"

"Volunteered!" Monique exclaimed.

"If you believe in the tooth fairy," Posner said. "A cynic might suppose that they made it a condition for closing the deal." He shrugged once more. "Operationally, it amounted to the same thing. They came up with the money and built the thing. And when they tested it—"

"They've already run it? With Davinda in the circuit?"

"Only for five minutes, or so I have been told," Posner said. "Davinda came out of it shall we say somewhat less coherent than when he went in, but that was to be expected, sanity is not a required specification for a human central processing unit, and the results were so golden, or rather True Blue, that the Big Blue Machine conceived the present scheme to take over UNACOCS, and move it to a Green media capital—"

"But faking the white tornadoes? And this suddenly weirder weather?"

"This I am not supposed to have a need to know," Posner said sourly. "But given that Davinda's mental state would seem to have gravely deteriorated, probably after they bet the farm as it were on UNACOCS, and given that many elements of the Big Blue Machine originated as corporate constituents of the old national military-industrial complexes much given to a paranoid predilection for 'over-kill' . . ."

"Insurance, in other words?" said Monique.

"One can imagine the cost-benefit analysis," Avi Posner said. "All we have to do is readjust and reposition mirrors we already have in orbit, the cost will be negligible, so . . ."

"Which is why they were less than terrified about having the white tornadoes exposed as frauds—"

"They were still confident things would work on Sunday even after Davinda had to be led off the stage gibbering because the computer doesn't need a sane brain to work—"

"And they'd have their definitive climate model running on the most powerful computer ever constructed with its creator willingly risking death by putting his own brain in the circuit. Live on world television and the net! The ultimate deep sell!"

Posner nodded. "*But* if Davinda's been a Siberian mole all along, if the climate model demonstration has been programmed to fail in some highly counterproductive manner, the Condition Venus hypothesis will be discredited along with UNACOCS and conceivably the United Nations itself, and the Big Blue Machine will have bankrupted itself financing the fiasco. And so . . . and so . . ."

"*And so?*"

"If you don't mind . . . ?" Posner said, hoisting his empty glass. Then, muttering to himself, "Or even if you do." And he went back into the kitchen, emerging a moment later sipping from a quarter-filled glass.

"And so a negative option clause in the contract with Mossad has been invoked," he said. "Big Blue has prudently decided not to risk terminal destruction. If I cannot verify that Davinda is *not* a mole before Sunday, I am required to terminate him."

Monique squinted at Posner. "And you've got moral qualms about that, Avi?" she said skeptically. "It's something you've never done in the . . . line of professional duty?"

"Hardly," said Posner. "That's no moral dilemma *if* Davinda is a mole." He paused for more liquid fortification.

"But what if he isn't? What if Condition Venus is really beginning and Davinda's climate model would prove it? What if John Sri Davinda really *is* a dedicated idealist willing to risk death to save the biosphere? And I terminate him. And the proof is lost. Moral responsibility for one death, even if the reasoning for its requirement later turns out to be flawed, is something one accepts as a professional. But that . . . *that!*"

Avi Posner slugged down the rest of his disgustingly warm vodka. "And the worst of it is that it's a negative option. Unless I can verify that Davinda *isn't* a mole, I am required to terminate him. *Without knowing!* And I haven't the faintest idea of how to even try to find out!"

This hardened Mossad professional looked positively haunted, and Monique understood all too well by what, for that ghost of ultimate holocaust future was leering down at her too, with dead empty eye sockets like the lunar craters of a moribund planet.

Whose big mouth, after all, had created this situation? Was not she just as morally responsible for what came out the other side as Avi Posner?

Or more so?

She choked down a swallow of warm vodka for courage, or rather, perhaps, merely to wash away personal vanity, modesty, shame, which seemed like pretty picayune stuff under the circumstances.

"Maybe *I* do . . ." Monique said softly. "I never told you how I extracted the information for Eric Esterhazy that . . . that . . . that created this situation and you never asked. . . ."

"I didn't think I had a need to know."

"Well, Avi, you have a need to know now."

So she gulped down a larger slug of vodka and told him. All that had transpired in the Kama Sutra room and the ersatz dungeon. In clinical but graphic detail. Leaving nothing relevant out. By the time she had finished, Posner was staring at her in slack-jawed wonder. And confusion.

"Why . . . why are you *telling me* this . . . ?"

"Because you have a need to know, Avi . . ." Monique told him tremulously. "Because if Esterhazy can pump aphrogas into those boudoirs, he can pump in other things as well, and I think we can assume that Bad Boys are pretty sophisticated in the arts of chemical interrogation, can't we . . . ?"

"And you're willing to . . . ?"

"Tell your principals that I'm willing to tell Esterhazy some fairy story that will get me into one of those boudoirs with Davinda and the best cocktail of cock-and-tongue-looseners he's got. . . ."

"Knowing that he'll be watching and listening?"

"Knowing that he'll be watching and listening."

"It could be dangerous. . . ."

Monique gave him a little shrug of bravado, but after all, it was hard to imagine the likes of Prince Eric endangering much beyond her sexual judgment or emotional tranquility.

And emotional tranquility was something she knew she must do this to restore.

"Why are you doing this, Monique?" Avi Posner said in the most tender tone of voice she had ever heard emerge from his lips.

"You're not the only one with a need to know, Avi," Monique replied in kind.

Hardened Mossad operative or not, Avi Posner seemed near tears as he raised his glass and clinked it with hers in a toast.

"Here's to you, Monique Calhoun," he said. "Should you choose to change your citizen-shareholdership, there will always be a place for you in Mossad."

Monique laughed softly. "Have I made it, then, Avi?" she said. "Have I finally gotten professional?"

"Oh no," Posner told her with sincere but well-lubricated gravity. "That is something you've gone beyond."

"And you're another, Avi Posner," she said.

It had been decided between Eduardo Ramirez and the Marenkos to hold this meeting on *La Reine de la Seine*, in the midafternoon, and Eduardo had told Eric not to have anything more than snacks prepared, though of course when inviting Stella and Ivan Marenko to anything, a liberal supply of vodka, wine, and champagne was de rigueur.

But as it turned out the Siberians were as abstemious as Eric had ever seen them, merely sipping at pepper vodka as they sat at a table out in the hot muggy open air on the fantail while Eduardo, with only an occasional word edgewise from Eric, brought them up to speed on what Bad Boys had learned about the Davinda climate model and the machinations of Big Blue.

They were not pleased.

"Why you keep us out of circuit so long?" Ivan demanded when Eduardo had finished.

"Is because they think we pay more for white tornado recordings if we know computer uses human brain, Ivan! Or maybe don't buy at all if we know it doesn't, da?"

"So if you find brain, you tell us, if you don't, you shut up, hah, Ramirez?"

Eric had never seen Eduardo Ramirez so discomfited. He sat there stonily under the angry glares of the Siberians saying nothing, no doubt because he could think of nothing to say.

The staring contest was broken by Ivan Marenko's laughter.

"Smart strategy!" he said. "No hard feelings."

"As godfathers say in old gangster movies, 'just business'!" said Stella, and she broke up too.

What people! thought Eric. What people to have on your side! Whatever side that might turn out to be.

Eduardo having imparted his information, the Marenkos, as was their wont, took over.

"Okay," said Stella, "so *is* brain . . ."

"But *live* brain, maybe inside volunteer," said Ivan. "Not as bad as Frankenstein games . . ."

"I beg to differ," Eric found himself saying. "Speaking as someone who's been there—"

"Not the point, Eric," Eduardo said, cutting him off sharply.

"Da," said Stella Marenko. "Point is, does not *look* as bad as using cloned brain or brain ripped out of body. Much easier to . . . how would Calhoun say it . . . ?"

"Deep sell," said Ivan.

"Spin," said Eric simultaneously.

"Whatever," said Eduardo. "The point is that you can't *rely* on what happens when Davinda puts on that helmet and runs his climate model to discredit Condition Venus or anything else. . . ."

"Your argument for buying the tornado recordings from you for a lot of money and using them, da, Ramirez?" said Ivan.

"Da," said Eduardo.

"Is *good* argument," said Stella Marenko.

"But asking price is too high."

"Asking prices are *always* too high," said Eduardo. "That's why they're asking prices."

"You come down?"

"A little . . ."

"How much?"

"Wait," said Eric, his mouth running away from his brain again. "We had better think carefully before we close the deal. Something here just doesn't add up."

Eduardo glowered at him. "If you don't mind, Eric—"

"Let him talk!" said Ivan Marenko. It came perilously close to sounding like an order. And no one gave orders to Eduardo Ramirez. Eduardo was far too urbane to show it overtly but Eric could easily enough feel the heat of his ire.

And realize that he was perilously close to a brink whose full nature he did not care to contemplate. And it was too late to step back.

"What I mean to say, Eduardo," he said soothingly, "is we're forgetting I've got Big Blue convinced that the mysterious Lao is some operation *we're* running against them. . . ."

"So . . . ?" said Eduardo.

"So that they've bought it means that Lao can't be some operation of *theirs*. . . ."

"*So?*" said Eduardo in quite a different tone of voice, his anger forgotten, his curiosity piqued.

Eric's train of logic was running out fast. "So . . . er . . . if it isn't our operation . . . and it isn't theirs. . . ."

"Third Force?" said Ivan Marenko.

"Does not exist," said Stella. "Not exactly."

"Does not *not* exist, Stella. Not exactly."

"Da . . ."

Although any number of personages and organizations owned to a belief in the vague constellation of even more elusive concepts referred to as "Third Force," no syndic, corporation, or religious hierarchy had ever emerged from the virtual woodwork to claim philosophical trademark or corporate copyright of the free-floating aphorisms that were about all that Eric knew about this non-existent non-organization.

As such common sayings as "it ain't over till the fat lady sings" or "it's déjà vu all over again" were attributed to a legendary yogi called Berra, so were these crypticisms attributed to "Third Force," the self-defining central doctrine of which was "Whenever two forces oppose, the Third Force emerges."

All sorts of obscure cults left over from the twentieth century— Scientology, Sufism, Marxism, Social Entropists, Zen Vegetarians, whatever—claimed to be the ancestral roots of Third Force, and there was no reason Eric could see that they couldn't all be right, since the central doctrine thereof could be interpreted to imply anything from the mystic notion that the interaction between matter and energy produced a Third Force variously called "spirit," "soul," "god," "chi," "prana," "tao," or "chaos," to the proven culinary principle that the oversweet and the oversour combined to make an excellent sauce for Chinese food.

Or that the Hot and Cold War between the Blues and the Greens produced an intermediate state, namely the current planetary condition.

Or that any conflict between two opposing players would somehow conjure up a third player out of the smoke and mirrors of contention.

Which Eric had to admit seemed to apply to the current situation. "So what are you saying?" Eduardo scoffed to no one in particular and/or everyone in general. "That disinformation that Eric fed to Monique Calhoun has somehow manifested a real 'Lao conspiracy' out of nothingness?"

Ivan and Stella Marenko eyed each other nervously.

"Stranger things can happen," said Ivan somberly.

"With enough good vodka and bad mushrooms!" said Stella.

"You're forgetting the obvious," said Eric.

"Oh are we?" snapped Eduardo.

"Something called Lao was out there all along to begin with," Eric pointed out. "We never knew what it was, and we don't know now. The other side didn't know what it was, and only *thinks* it knows it's us now."

"Da . . ."

"Da!"

"So, Eric, what are you saying that implies?" Eduardo Ramirez asked. And when Eric hesitated, he smiled encouragingly. "Go ahead," he said, "you've been doing well so far."

"It means *we* don't know what's going to happen when they run Davinda's model with him in the circuit, and now *they* don't think they know either," Eric said. "And . . ."

"And?"

Eric shrugged, his brilliant deductions having reached their end point.

"The operational implications of which are . . . ?"

Eric shrugged again.

"We had better be very, very careful."

"About what?"

Eric thought he knew the answer, but this time he also knew he had better think very, very carefully himself before he dared to utter it.

He thought about Monique Calhoun telling him that even if the white tornadoes *were* fakes, even if there *was* a disembodied brain in the computer it could be a terminal mistake to destroy the Big Blue Machine, unprincipled capitalist liars though they were, if the Davinda climate model nevertheless *did* prove that Condition Venus was inevitable without the swift application of their planet-cooling technology.

Or to do it without knowing one way or the other.

He thought about what he had felt when he had summoned up the manhood to make common cause with her in trying to find out. Which was not that unlike what he had felt when he had gained Eduardo's admiration, had become a man of serious respect in the eyes of his syndic, by taking a grave personal risk to do the morally right thing.

And he remembered that, after all, it had been Eduardo himself who had told him that Bad Boys weren't capitalists indifferent to all but the bottom line.

Of course Eduardo had also told him that if he guessed wrong and cost the syndic a large amount of money, moral righteousness would not allow him to escape the personal consequences.

"The buck stops with each and every citizen-shareholder," Eduardo had told him.

Eric sighed, for in this moment he was all too keenly aware that it did.

"We had better be very, very careful about releasing the white tornado recordings to the media under *any* conditions," he said.

"Oh had we?" Eduardo said darkly.

"Why?" said Stella Marenko.

"Because we might destroy the Big Blue Machine."

"This is bad thing? To discredit capitalist liars who would turn Siberia back into winter wonderland to fill their own pockets?"

"It is if John Sri Davinda's climate model really *does* prove the Earth and everything on it, us included, dies if we don't let them get away with it."

"Da!"

"Da!"

Eduardo Ramirez stared across the table at Eric, poker-faced, giving nothing away. "You *do* realize what you've just done, Eric?" he said evenly.

Eric met his gaze. "Yes, Eduardo," he said.

"You have just given our Siberian friends here a most convincing argument for not buying the white tornado recordings. . . ."

"Da!"

"Thus costing Bad Boys a very large amount of money."

Eduardo stared stonily at Eric. Eric gave it right back to him. What else was there for him to do now?

"I know, Eduardo," he said.

"An argument so convincing that I believe it too," said Eduardo Ramirez. "An argument I would hope I would have had the courage to make myself."

Under the circumstances, it would have been asking far too much for him to crack a smile, but his glacial expression did melt, and that was enough to have Eric sighing in relief.

"And so," Eduardo told the Marenkos, "I must withdraw our offer to sell you the recordings."

"Oh no," said Stella, "we buy!"

"But for reduced price," said Ivan.

"I can't let you—"

"What's the matter, you don't trust us?" said Ivan Marenko.

"It's not that I don't trust you—"

"Is good deal, Ramirez," said Ivan. "We buy recordings now at big discount. Bad Boys gets a lot less money, but what did it cost you to make recordings, nothing, da, is still profit."

"I don't think I understand," said Eduardo. "What do you intend to do with the recordings?"

"Depends," said Ivan Marenko.

"On what?" asked Eduardo.

"If Davinda proves Condition Venus is real on Sunday, planet *must* be cooled, and we must shut up, hold noses, sit on recordings, pay lying unprincipled capitalist bastards to save collective planetary asses. But if is bullshit and he makes monkeys of Big Blue—"

"Ivan! If he makes monkeys of Big Blue Machine, is same thing as if we do! And if later, it turns out planet must be cooled anyway—"

"Stella!" shouted Ivan Marenko. "Shut up!"

Stella Marenko glared at her husband for a moment, as much in surprise as in anger, or so it seemed to Eric. But the desired effect *was* achieved. Stella *did* shut up.

"Now you will please let me finish?" Ivan Marenko said in as close an approximation of a conciliatory tone as Eric had ever heard him use. He paused to take the largest swallow of vodka he had taken all afternoon.

"Okay," he said, "if Davinda's climate model proves Condition Venus, is not good, but *is* simple, no choice, we do nothing. But if not, we use recordings as blackmail threat to make Big Blue turn off white tornado machines and behave like good little capitalist bastards or else. But *not* to pound them into filling for pilmenyi!"

"Ah!" exclaimed Stella. "Because maybe next week or next year or next century maybe we find we need Big Blue climatech after all!"

"Da," said Ivan. "We must preserve Big Blue Machine like last polar bears in Siberia or remaining bits of Amazon rain forest or quaint folk music of Urals."

"Even from own evil assholery!"

"*Especially* from own evil assholery. Considering that evil assholes are not so good at preserving *themselves*. Considering that is main thing that makes them assholes."

"And how do you expect to do this?" asked Eduardo.

"*We* don't do it, Ramirez, *you* do," Ivan told him. "Is fair Bad Boys must do *some* little service to earn money."

"Indeed," agreed Eduardo, "but how do you propose we earn it?"

"Maybe we ask handsome prince?" Stella Marenko suggested. "Maybe today he proves he is not just another pretty face?"

And all at once, Eric was the center of attention. The Marenkos turned away from Eduardo to focus on him. And Eduardo himself was smiling thinly, as if he saw what was coming and found it both amusing and just.

And so did Eric. It was obvious.

"A contract?" he said. "On Davinda?"

The Marenkos nodded.

"A negative option contract? I verify that Davinda's climate model will prove that Big Blue's Condition Venus disney hides the real thing or I prevent the full catastrophe from happening by canceling the Sunday demonstration by . . . permanently removing their human central processing unit from the circuit?"

"Da," said Ivan. "Either Condition Venus is proved on Sunday or demonstration is canceled and *nothing* happens. Big Blue looks stupid, but survives and we keep them on short leash like nice dancing bear. Next year, maybe even another UNACOCS. And we pay for contract either way. Better than poke in eye with sharp stick, eh, Ramirez?"

Eduardo pondered this. But not for very long.

"It's your contract to accept or refuse, Eric," he said.

"I made it, I'll take it," Eric said immediately.

After all, *he* had talked the syndic into this situation. And by making it a free choice rather than an order, Eduardo Ramirez had given him the opportunity to redeem himself. It was more than the right career move. It was doing well by doing good.

"Thank you, Eduardo," he added upon this reflection.

Eduardo acknowledged his understanding with a mere nod of his head and a wave of his hand. But it was enough.

"Oobla di, oobla da," Stella Marenko sang off-key, popping her fingers, "life goes on."

And she poured them all big shots of pepper vodka.

What people! Eric thought again as they raised their glasses in a silent toast. What people to have on your side!

And now Eric Esterhazy was beginning to understand what side it really was. And that they *were* all on it together.

The fiery vodka slid down his gullet and ignited a warm glow of comradeship in his stomach.

Which did not sour until after the Marenkos had left, leaving him sitting there alone with Eduardo Ramirez, indeed not until Eduardo also got up to leave, and hit him with it as a casual parting afterthought.

"Oh, one more thing, Eric, should it come to pass that you must indeed remove Davinda, we obviously cannot afford to have the good deed credited to our account or that of the Marenkos . . ."

"Obviously," agreed Eric blithely.

"So we should, as your mother would put it, pin it on a fall guy . . . or in this case *girl*, since no one else is available."

Then it was that the pepper vodka, like Eduardo's words, gave Eric a hard sour sock in the stomach.

"*Monique Calhoun?*" he exclaimed. "You're ordering me to pin it on Monique Calhoun?"

Eduardo gave him one of those expressionless stone-faced looks that could mean anything. "Call it . . . an operational suggestion," he said. "A personal decision, Eric, not an order."

"With personal responsibility for the results . . ."

"Exactly," said Eduardo, and left it at that.

Nor did Eric wish to press him further as to exactly *what* would be the personal results if he . . . opted to ignore such an operational suggestion.

When Avi Posner showed up unbidden at the Ritz instead of calling, Monique Calhoun did not expect him to be the bearer of happy tidings. She had been in the shower when he called from downstairs, and while she told him she needed ten minutes to get herself presentable, his unexpected advent left her too apprehensively curious to do anything more than dry her hair, slip on a dress, and step into a pair of shoes.

When she opened the door to the suite, Posner barged in without a greeting, and sat down heavily on a sofa in the parlor. Only when she had seated herself in a plush velvet armchair across the coffee table from him did she notice, to her astonishment, that he had arrived bearing a large gilded cardboard box of fancy chocolates.

Posner? About to get romantic? At a time like this?

But the look on Avi Posner's face was anything but hearts and flowers.

"First the good news," he said grimly. "The principals have accepted your proposal. Tonight you take Davinda to *La Reine de la Seine*, you enlist Esterhazy's aid, you get him into one of those bordello boudoirs, and you . . . ah, pump him. If you succeed in verifying that he is not a Siberian mole, your reward will be promotion to head of the Bread & Circuses' Paris office after Mamoun retires next year. . . ."

"And the bad news . . . ?"

"I'm not through with the good news," Posner said, though neither his expression nor his tone of voice made that contention credible. "The rest of the good news is that even if it turns out that you cannot exonerate Davinda, you still get Paris. Provided . . . provided you accept the bad news."

And, fidgeting with downcast eyes like a shy teenage boy tremulously courting his heart-throb, he handed her the box of chocolates.

"But Avi," Monique exclaimed in total perplexity, "I *love* good chocolates!"

"Open it," said Avi Posner.

Monique did.

No chocolates.

Inside the chocolate box was a gun.

A gunmetal-gray carbon-fiber automatic pistol with a fat barrel heavily perforated at the muzzle end.

Monique stared woodenly at the gun, then at Posner.

"The bad news," said Avi Posner, "is that they've given *you* the contract."

"Avi! You know I can't—"

"Yes you can," Posner said in a voice that seemed made deliberately robotic as he fixed his gaze on a spot somewhere above her head. "This weapon fires a high-velocity cloud of spent-uranium flechettes. With it, a rank amateur such as yourself can blow the head off a bull elephant at any range within twenty meters."

"You know damn well that's not what I mean!"

Posner sighed, nodded, shrugged.

"They *do* have an operational point," he said. "If Davinda is found in a boudoir on *La Reine de la Seine* shot with just the sort of weapon a Bad Boys operative might use for the purpose, who would believe that anyone but a Bad Boys operative performed the removal operation? Let alone someone like you. You have access and deniability Quite clever, really."

"*Clever!*"

"If Davinda *does* have to be taken out because they can't trust what his climate model might do, this provides the best damage control for the client," Posner said. "They loudly claim that Davinda was killed by Greens to prevent his climate model from proving that Condition Venus was inevitable. And if the Siberians then try to counter with those recordings, they won't be believed because the client will then sound a lot more credible claiming the *recordings* and not the white tornadoes are the frauds."

"I can't do it, Avi. I'm no killer. I've never even held a gun in my life."

"That's why you're perfect."

"No!"

Posner sat there silently regarding Monique for a moment, seemingly not studying her, but pondering something else. And then shaking his head as if rejecting it.

"Obviously this reaction was not unanticipated," he said, "and having offered you the carrot, this is where I'm supposed to brandish the stick."

"Which is?" Monique snapped, more angrily than fearfully.

Posner shrugged, shrugging it *off*, or so it seemed. "Severe career consequences. Expulsion from Bread & Circuses on charges of defrauding the syndic."

"Bullshit!" said Monique. "They expect me to commit murder over stuff like that!"

"Also a reaction that was not unanticipated," Posner said. "So this is where I'm supposed to intimate that if you don't accept the contract on Davinda, they put one on *you*."

He held up his hand before Monique could utter a protest.

"But I'm not going to do that," Posner said. "I'm going to do something worse."

"*Worse?*"

Avi Posner nodded. "I'm going to appeal to your conscience," he said. "I'm going to try to convince you that it would be immoral for you *not* to take this contract." His eyes hardened. "And I am going to succeed."

"I doubt it."

"You volunteered for this mission because—"

"I didn't volunteer to kill anyone!"

"You volunteered to do your utmost to find out the truth about Davinda, did you not? And you were willing to abandon all personal modesty and shame to do it? Why?"

"You know why! Because I couldn't countenance your killing Davinda without finding out. . . ."

Monique caught herself short, sensing the yawning trap opening up before her.

"Because you knew *you* had a chance to find out and I didn't. . . ?" Avi Posner said softly.

Monique just sat there numbly, seeing it coming at her with an awful inevitability now, but unable to do anything to stop it.

Posner took the box with the gun from her slack hands. "You are going to have to ask for this back, Monique," he said. "If you don't, it will be given to me, or to someone else, who, unlike you, has no chance to find out whether John Sri Davinda is a Siberian mole or the potential savior of an otherwise doomed biosphere. Whose contract will simply be to take no chances."

Posner smiled ruefully at her. "So you see, Monique, you have no escape. If you refuse to take up the gun, you will be just as responsible for Davinda's death as if you did. More so, because then it will be certain."

"S-s-sophistry . . ." Monique stammered.

"If you refuse and Davinda is *not* a Siberian mole, someone else will certainly kill him," Posner said coldly. "And that will be the end of a climate model that might save the biosphere of this planet from certain destruction."

"I never said I wasn't willing to go along with trying to find out the truth," Monique told him. "I volunteered, remember? But—"

"But if you learn that Davinda *is* a mole and Lao *is* a plot to destroy the only organization with the climatech to save the biosphere from possible destruction, and you are too pure to do what the situation requires, then what . . . ?"

Monique just stared at him.

She knew.

But she was unable to voice it. Even to herself.

So Avi Posner did it for her. And perhaps in the brutal moral calculus he was applying, that was the closest she could expect to come to receiving mercy.

"Then to avoid committing the crime of murder, you might become guilty of a crime worse than genocide, a crime too awful to even have a name."

He took the gun out of the box, offered it to her like a poisoned valentine.

"No good deed goes unpunished," he said.

"You bastard . . ." Monique whispered, and took it.

11

"LIGHT HER UP, EDDIE!" SAID PRINCE ERIC
Esterhazy as *La Reine de la Seine* warped away from the dock.

"Rock and Roll!"

Bah-*bah*-BAH! BAH! BAH!

The familiar orchestral fanfare sounded as the virtual smokestacks
sprang into being amidships puffing phantom gouts of black smoke
and clouds of white steam, and the paddle wheels began to churn up
foam, and the halogens came on, and the band began to play "When
the Saints Go Marching In," and her lasers saluted her with virtual
fireworks as *The Queen of the River* moved out into the main channel,
a soul-stirring scene of son-et-lumière glory.

But the mind's eye of the Prince of the City presiding over tonight's fateful departure from his customary station in the wheelhouse
was elsewhere. Nor was his soul being stirred by images of cakewalking
sainthood.

Eric Esterhazy was remembering a scene from an old war pic from
the twentieth century he had once seen. A journalist is up in a helicopter that's strafing fleeing refugees.

"How can you shoot women and children?" he demands.

"Easy," says the gunner. "You just lead them by about ten feet less."

How can you pin a murder on a woman you've made love to and common cause with?

Easy, though Eric. All it takes is two guns.

In a shoulder holster, Eric carried a carbon-fiber spent-uranium flechette pistol, a serious professional weapon. In his left-hand jacket pocket, he had a pearl-handled piece-of-crap revolver, the sort of pistol a female amateur would secrete in her purse to do the job, its grip taped.

And Monique Calhoun herself had made it even easier. Not only had she volunteered to provide the ideal opportunity, if he tried hard enough Eric might just be able to convince himself that she had provided a moral justification.

She had, after all, called *him*. She had, after all, enlisted his collusion in conducting an interrogation of John Sri Davinda in a below-decks boudoir filled with an assortment of persuasive vapors.

And fed him an insultingly preposterous cover story.

"Why would it be in my interest to help you interrogate Davinda?"

"Because you'll be looking over my shoulder. Because we both have the same need to know . . ."

"We do? Know what?"

"Whether Davinda is a . . . whether his . . . climate model . . . is a fake . . . like the white tornadoes . . ."

Monique might be a Bread & Circuses professional whose job it was to put spin on the truth, but she was an amateur when it came to forthright lying. Eric doubted whether she had rehearsed this cover story at all. She had almost tripped over her own tongue and let slip what Eric already knew, that her true purpose was to find out whether Davinda was a Siberian mole.

But since that was the result of disinformation *he* had fed to her, Eric had to play the naif himself. Up to a credible point.

"Your client wants you to find out whether *they themselves* are going to run another scam?"

"No, no, of course not, it's . . . ah . . . uh . . ."

"Posner . . . ?" Eric said, gallantly giving her a helping hand with this pathetic charade.

Monique almost gave a sigh of relief. "Mossad is pissed off," she said. "They feel they've been fed disinformation all along, and if the Davinda climate model is another disney, they'll construe it as breach of contract, and pull out, maybe even change sides."

This was a cover story that no one would even pretend to believe unless they had a need to pretend to believe it. As Eric did.

But it wouldn't do to let it seem too easy.

"Whose side are *you* on, anyway?" he had demanded. "Big Blue? Mossad? Bread & Circuses? Or just whichever side seems to be winning?"

Monique Calhoun's nostrils had flared at that one, but she otherwise did a good job of masking her ire, lowering her voice instead, and putting a reasonably credible fearful catch into it.

"The side of my own enlightened self-interest," she had said. "Let's just say that . . . Posner has made it clear that not getting this job done might be . . . worse than a bad career move. *How* much worse is something he didn't feel he had a need to tell me and I sure don't feel I have a need to find out. . . ."

"Well, in that case . . ."

Pretty thin, maybe, but good enough to let him pretend to swallow it like a gallant gentleman. And allow Monique Calhoun to set herself up perfectly.

All he had to do was go along, install her and Davinda in one of the boudoirs—the virtuality room might be best—observe, and wait for the opportune moment.

At which point, he could barge in and hold the flechette pistol on Monique Calhoun while he made a messy and obviously unprofessional job of dispatching John Sri Davinda with the amateur-night revolver, untape the grip, and then force her to handle the gun.

He could then literally scream bloody murder, summon Force Flic, and when they arrived, the master of *La Reine de la Seine* would be holding the murderer at gunpoint over the corpse of the deceased.

With the lady whose fingerprints were all over the murder weapon caught standing over the body by the outraged proprietor, who would believe than anyone else had done the deed, who would believe that anyone but *her* client had commissioned the hit?

If it came to that.

Was it perverse of him to wish that it wouldn't?

Was it perverse of him to wish that it would?

Whether the last few days' ominous weather had naturally sweetened or whether the Big Blue Machine had turned down its Condition Venus disney effects in preparation for cutting its possible losses, it was a golden balmy Paris evening, and here he was, riding high, wide, and handsome atop *The Queen of the River* as *La Reine* promenaded up the Seine through the heart of the tropical City of Light.

It was good to be a Prince of the City. Eric had no ambition beyond the life he had already achieved. He certainly did not want to lose it. He certainly did not want to see the dank, cold, gray skies of winter return to Paris.

And for all this to continue, it seemed he must kill John Sri Davinda. Because his contract was to remove Davinda unless he could verify the certainty of impending Condition Venus.

Meaning that if he did not eliminate Davinda, it could only be because this endless Parisian summer must die that the Earth itself might live.

Davinda or the good life.

The emotional logic *should* have been simple.

Eric *should* have been hoping that his contract on Davinda would have to be carried out, since that would mean the preservation of the clime and style of life he held dear.

But the addition of Monique Calhoun as a factor royally screwed up what should have been the self-interested simplicity of the moral equation.

Not just because he had had sex with her, Eric was not as romantic as all that. But because, despite representing different clients, despite the little lies, despite the professional fencing match, he sensed that, in some way he could not quite define, they were on the same side.

Eliminating Davinda in the service of enlightened self-interest would be an act he could perform with clean moral clarity. But pinning it on Monique Calhoun would not sit well with his conscience.

And sourly contemplating the truth of this made Eric realize, to his unpleasant surprise, that he was indeed burdened with one.

"What's right is what you feel good after," had been a moral compass offered up in simpler times.

Who could argue with that?

But Eric could not imagine any outcome that was likely to make him feel good after tonight.

Monique Calhoun supposed it was standard psychological operating procedure for assassins to depersonalize their victims before the act. But in this case, the prospective victim seemed to have depersonalized himself already.

John Sri Davinda might be able to locomote by himself and utter the occasionally coherent sentence, but most of his personality seemed to have already departed his corpus, as if in morally convenient anticipation, leaving this affectless disney behind.

Five minutes as a human central processing unit would seem not only to have inflicted permanent damage at the time, but left his brain, or at least the previous entity inhabiting the meatware, in a continuing state of deterioration.

Rather than walk this unseemly golemized creature through the public hubbub of the main restaurant salon to the Marenkos' table, where word was that Eric was currently to be found, she was taking him around the main-deck promenade toward the stern, stealing up on the aft bar from behind.

Not that Davinda cared.

John Sri Davinda didn't seem to care about anything.

She had phoned his room with some cock-and-bull story about Prince Esterhazy personally inviting him to La Reine de la Seine to make amends for the other night's unseemly events by affording him the use of a special meditative chamber access to which was granted only to his most favorite guests.

Davinda hadn't replied to this at all.

When she strenuously suggested it would be politic to accept such an invitation, Davinda had simply said "Affirmative."

Monique had the feeling that had she invited him for a swim in the alligator-infested waters of the Seine, his reaction would have been much the same.

When she came to collect him, he was unshaven, odorously un-washed, wearing these rumpled gray slacks and dirty blue shirt, and unshod. Under the pressure of time and circumstances, the most Mo-nique could bother to do was get his shoes on before stuffing him into a limo.

Like leading a lamb to the slaughter, she thought somberly.

But which of us is the lamb?

And who is leading whom to what?

Monique felt that she too was running on rails like an empty disney of herself. It was all too damn easy and yet all beyond her control.

Too damn easy for one step to lead to the next once Avi Posner had trapped her with the moral necessity of committing this evil deed.

Too damn easy to convince Eric Esterhazy of the half-truth that Mossad was forcing her to interrogate Davinda. Too damn easy to get him to supply what was required.

Too damned easy to persuade the prospective victim to return to *La Reine de la Seine*.

Too damned easy to slip a loaded gun into her purse.

And now, here she was, and the notion that within the hour she might be faced with the necessary task of killing a man still had no reality.

Once Posner's dreadful moral trap had been sprung, she had run on automatic one step after the other, hoping that something would intervene to derail this implacable train of events.

That Eric would not believe her story, and after he did, that he would have some reason for not supplying a boudoir, and when he went along with that, that Davinda would refuse to leave the hotel, and in the limo, that she would forget her purse, or maybe the riverboat would sink, or . . . or . . .

Or it would turn out at the eleventh hour that her interrogation of John Sri Davinda would prove that he was *not* a mole, that his climate model *would* prove it was a necessity to begin cooling down the planet at once to evade Condition Venus. . . .

And that was the most bitter pill of all.

For that was the only thing that Monique could now imagine

rescuing her from her own moment of terrible personal truth.

Could she have ever imagined, let alone ever sought to be, where she found herself now?

Perversely hoping that the Earth itself really *was* in mortal danger?

"*That's* the target for tonight?" Mom muttered sotto voce to Eric as Monique Calhoun led John Sri Davinda up to the Marenkos' table. "Looks like something that's been sleeping under a bridge."

And smells like it too, Eric thought, nevertheless fetching Mom a warning kick to the shin under the table as Monique brought Davinda within auditory and olfactory range.

Mom was almost as infrequent a visitor to *La Reine* as Eduardo Ramirez, but while Eduardo had prudently eschewed being present at the scene of the prospective crime, Mom, being Mom, could not resist giving in to her morbid dramatic curiosity.

"C'mon, Eric, I want to see this guy before he's iced, and at least get to meet Ms. Mata Hari from B&C before Force Flic hauls her away to the guillotine."

"There's no capital punishment in this jurisdiction," Eric had reminded her unhappily, but Mom's gun-moll-mode whims were still beyond his powers to refuse.

The deal was that she was at least supposed to fade into the woodwork once Monique and Davinda appeared.

Fat chance.

"Eric, Ivan, Stella, Dr. Braithwaite, Dr. Larabee, Dr. Pereiro, you and Dr. Davinda all know each other ..." Monique began as she pressed Davinda down into an empty seat beside Allison Larabee, then cocked an inquisitive eyebrow at Mom.

"My mother," said Eric. "Mom, Monique Calhoun."

"Ah, the one, the only, Eric's told me all about you! But I'll bet he hasn't told you a damn thing about me."

Eric gave Mom a harder kick.

"And I probably wouldn't believe it if he did," Monique shot back rather woodenly and sat down beside her.

"Takes one to know one, hon," said Mom.

Eric groaned inwardly, already feeling the tense ennui of the blah-

blah to come and wishing it over before it had ever begun, the weight of the two pistols somehow having become both insistent and strangely comforting.

Wasn't it some American president who had said, upon sending in the riot troops with the truncheons and tear gas, "If we're going to have a bloodbath, let's have it *now*"?

". . . you're the white tornado lady, aincha?"

". . . it's my climate model that predicted it, if that's what you mean, Mrs. . . . er . . . Princess . . . what *do* you call a Prince's mother?"

"Countess, hon!"

"Well, then Countess Esterhazy—"

"Countess No-Accountess, hah, hah, hah!"

Monique found the banality of the table talk horridly surreal under the circumstances.

". . . you're the one that walked out of the conference, right Allie?"

". . . she made an important statement . . ."

". . . and then walked right back in!"

". . . only as far as parties!"

Monique found herself wanting to make a quick exit with Eric and Davinda so that she could get it all over with, yet at the same time unwilling or unable to do anything to effect it, perversely wishing this boring blather would go on forever so she would never have to.

". . . I did not come here for the parties, Mr. Marenko."

Monique noticed that Eric had been keeping his mouth shut during these endless few minutes, and now he was trying to send her exit signals with his eyebrows and glances in the direction of Davinda, who, equally out of the conversation and then some, was passing the time mechanically slurping up vodka, though fortunately the Marenkos had not yet laid out the designer dust.

". . . but as long as you are, huh . . . ?"

". . . nothing wrong with free drink and food!"

"Despite current appearances, UNACOCS is a serious conference," Allison Larabee said frostily.

"That you walked out of, Allison," said Dr. Braithwaite.

"And returned to when the lateness of the planetary hour became evident!"

"Famous white tornadoes again!"

"A little convenient, da . . . ?" said Stella Marenko.

"What do you mean by that?" Larabee said ingenuously.

"Walkout, tornadoes, return," said Ivan Marenko. "Like script."

"Or coincidence," said Dr. Braithwaite, gallantly coming to her defense.

"One is event, two is coincidence," said Ivan. "Three is—"

"Pattern," said John Sri Davinda in a loud toneless voice.

It was the first word he had said, and the effect was to freeze the conversation.

"When two forces oppose . . ." Davinda went on in that flat voice. And then paused, as his blink rate went way up, and something flickered wanly behind his dead eyes, and he completed the moldy old aphorism in a voice that at least hinted at humanity. "A . . . a Third Force emerges. . . ."

"Third Force claptrap!" Pereiro groaned.

Eric caught Monique's eye and mimed even more insistently with his eyebrows for an egress.

"What *are* you on about, John?" Allison Larabee said.

"Chaos," Davinda said hollowly.

"You've incorporated chaos theory into your climate model?"

"Chaos is not a theory," Davinda said. "Chaos is real."

"So I've noticed," said Eric's mother.

"But useless as a predictive parameter," Larabee said. "By definition."

"I do not predict."

"Your climate model isn't predictive? Then what—"

"I am."

"You stink, therefore you am?" cracked Eric's mother.

Everyone groaned but John Sri Davinda.

"Or not," he said.

"What next, Hamlet, alas poor Yorick, perchance to dream, to be or not to be, that is the question?"

The effect on Davinda was startling. For about thirty seconds, his blink rate went way up again and his face writhed through a series of contortions that Monique could not identify as any recognizable human expressions.

Then it abruptly stopped.

His face smoothed out into an expressionless mask. His blink rate dropped. He stared straight ahead, stopped talking entirely, and began drinking vodka again as if nothing at all had happened. It was as if someone had abruptly changed the control program in an audioanimatronic robot.

It was utterly weird. It was certainly a total conversation stopper.

It was also, Monique knew, the perfect exit cue.

But the weight of the gun in her purse made her reluctant to take it.

"I do believe Dr. Davinda has had a bit too much again," Eric said suavely, gently removing the vodka glass from Davinda's hand. "If you'll give me a hand, Monique, we'd better take him to someplace quiet."

Davinda made no resistance as Eric helped him to his feet, nor could Monique as she rose to assist him. Each of them holding the climatologist lightly by an elbow, they walked Davinda out of the bar.

John Sri Davinda moved unknowingly and to all appearances uncaringly toward his fate like a good little amusement-park robot running on destiny's rails.

And so, it seemed to her, or so perhaps she was merely trying to convince herself, did Monique Calhoun.

"Open sez me," said Eric Esterhazy, activating Ignatz. When the interface personality menu came up, Eric hesitated.

He needed Ignatz to control the machineries but he really didn't want a virtual kibitzer watching over his shoulder as *he* watched over Monique Calhoun's shoulder.

So he did what he rarely did and chose the neutral computer voice and affectless AI personality.

Nor did he want any distractions, so he blanked all the video screens save the one displaying the interior of the virtuality boudoir and another to display menus.

And come to think of it . . .

"Can you cancel the automatic recording?" he asked Ignatz, something he had never done or thought to. But making a recording of a prospective hit did not seem like sane procedure.

"Affirmative."

"Cancel recording."

"Recording canceled."

The virtuality boudoir was a single englobing softscreen. The smooth texture of the liquid-crystal plastic couldn't be changed nor the pillowlike kinesthetics, but since the visuals could be any mix of images in any database or real-time feed in the world and likewise for sound, the choices were for all practical purposes unlimited.

Of course the boudoir's use was usually limited to *one* practical purpose, and for those clients whose imaginations were also limited or intimidated by such a surfeit of choice, there was an extensive menu of preprogrammed erotic venues and scenarios.

But since erotic arousal was hardly the purpose of the current exercise, Eric was going to have to wing it.

The default value for the virtuality boudoir was a verdant green lawn under a cloudless schematic tropical sky the color of impending sunset, with soft faraway breakers, and occasional grace notes of mellifluous birdsong.

That was where Monique Calhoun and John Sri Davinda were now, seated facing each other in a padded depression in the lawn quite like the so-called conversation pits which had been à la mode around the sixth decade or so of the previous century.

And indeed, for once, conversation *was* what was intended.

Though not occurring.

Davinda sat there gazing blankly at Monique in what appeared to be either yogic meditation or an attempt to engage her in a schoolyard staring contest. And although the cameras were hidden, Monique kept looking around with an impatient expression as if trying to find one to play to.

This seemed to Eric to be a clear request to get on with it already, which he himself was eager enough to do. The first order of business was obviously to rouse Davinda from his stupor. But how?

"Stimulant menu," he told Ignatz.

A long list of chemical names began to scroll down the menu

screen in alphabetical order. Eric knew next to nothing of organic chemistry or psychopharmacology; just enough to know that, thanks to a skin-contact carrier called DMSO, he could introduce just about anything into the bloodstreams of whoever was in any of the boudoirs via the ventilation system.

This would not do.

"Rank in order of mental stimulation."

The names on the menu rearranged themselves but remained incomprehensible.

"Eliminate everything with hallucinogenic properties."

More electronic card shuffling.

Eric shrugged. "Pump in the top three on the list, optimum dosage," he said.

And now for the visuals and sound . . . something a bit more stimulating too . . .

The tropical sunset sky swiftly darkened as a front of towering black clouds moved in with surreal speed to a drumroll of approaching thunder, and though Monique Calhoun knew that the virtuality effects in the boudoir were limited to sight and sound, it seemed she could smell an ozone keenness in the air, feel her senses heightened, a tension building within her, as if at any moment blue sparks might shoot out from her fingertips.

FLASH!

CRACK!

An impossibly mighty bolt of lightning lit up the sky like a thermonuclear klieg light, followed by an earsplitting blast of thunder fit to wake the dead.

"Jesus Christ!"

"I am not him."

Or even John Sri Davinda.

The climatologist's eyes now blazed with a cold electric fire and he seemed to have been jolted out of his nonverbal daze to the point where he was at least capable of spouting gibberish.

But Monique found herself terminally out of patience with this shit. "Oh really?" she shot back, her nerves twanging. "Why I'll bet you're not Buddha or Vishnu or Elvis either!"

Beats of thunder became a crazy rhythm track as the black thunderheads above strobed with stuttery flashes of lightning, turning this disney of a storm into a mad meteorological discotheque.

"I don't give a bayou rat's ass who you think you are, you asshole," Monique found herself gabbling with a crazed energy and passion to match the unnatural elements, "and I'm up to the eyeballs with mystical bullshit and Third Force obfuscation! You tell me what's going to happen when you plug what's left of your deep-fried brain into that climate model right now! Or . . . Or else . . . or else . . ."

Monique found her hands balled into furious fists, and clean out of "or elses" save the ultimate one throbbing heavily in the purse beside her.

"Condition Chaos," said John Sri Davinda.

"SHIT!" Monique bellowed into the storm in red-hot outrage.

Eric was forcefully reminded that whatever he pumped into the boudoir affected both Davinda and Monique Calhoun by observing how the stuff that had done no better than minimally rouse the climatologist from his semicomatose funk had turned Monique into a raving rug-chewing monster.

Now what?

If he turned Monique *down*, he'd likely turn Davinda *off* again.

He needed help.

And if the only help he could get was virtual, well . . .

Sighing, Eric pumped up Ignatz's personality interface menu, and booted up "Mom."

"What do I do now?" he demanded.

"Me you're asking, kiddo? I'm not even here. The only advice available from this simulation is operational."

"Then how do I keep Monique Calhoun from going over the top without having Davinda drop back down through the bottom? I can't cut the stimulants, can I?"

"Take the edge off with a hit of mescaline doped with psilocybin. Ditch the storm und drang effects and play 'em a Himalayan high."

Eric was rather vague on just what Ignatz was suggesting through the cryptic interface of Mom, but whatever it was, he didn't have a better idea.

"Do it," he said.

Abruptly the sky cleared to a perfect cerulean blue subtly purpled by lofty altitude. Monique found herself surrounded by the snowcapped peaks of a range of mighty rugged mountains that rose from verdant valleys far below but failed to attain her even loftier altitude.

She sat facing John Sri Davinda upon an oriental rug that magically insulated them from the cold of the icy ultimate pinnacle upon which they perched. Or not-so-magically, considering that the air temperature inside the boudoir had not been altered. In the background, a sitar and tabla played, backed by an acoustic bass and sampled surf-sound.

Welcome to the Hindu Kitsch! Monique thought sardonically.

Still, kitsch or not, she had to admit that the effect was clarifying. At least to the point where she was able to realize that one would not be likely to extract anything coherent from a lunatic by raving at him like one yourself.

"Condition Chaos . . . ?" she forced herself to say evenly. "When they run your climate model with your brain in the circuit, the predictive output *won't* be Condition Venus?"

John Sri Davinda's eyes shone with all the inhuman illumination of a pair of polished steel ball bearings.

"All iterations produce the same output."

"Condition Chaos . . . ?"

"Condition Chaos."

Davinda's face was as calm and affectless as that of a golden Buddha, and whether it was the synergy of the music with the lighting, or some other effect, a palpable aura seemed to pulse off of him. But in spite of this, or perhaps because of it, it took an effort of the will for Monique to retain the clarity to refrain from slugging him.

To realize that the only way to get anything out of Davinda would be to enter *his* image system rather than fruitlessly attempt to dragoon him back into what *hers* told her was the "real world."

"*What* is Condition Chaos, John Sri Davinda?" she intoned in a portentous guru voice.

"I am Condition Chaos," said John Sri Davinda. "I model the Chao of the Tao."

"*You* model the Chao of the Tao . . . ?"

Monique struggled to make *some* sense of this or at least, now that she had Davinda talking, to question this oracular presence along a line that might elicit useful information. *Enter his image system,* she reminded herself again, *don't expect him to enter yours.*

"Okay, John Sri Davinda, we are all part of the Great Whole, the Wheel of Karma, and all that good Third Force stuff, the Dance of the Bits and the Bytes—"

And then the White Light hit her.

Then it was that two disjunctive image systems converged on an interface which was the Third.

Davinda had *already* interfaced his brain with the computer briefly. And it had turned him into . . . *this.*

Whatever this was.

A human climatologist with the better part of his neurons burned out and his personality destroyed? The software golem now occupying the vacant meatware? Some arcane amalgam?

Stay in the image system.

Stay in *its* image system.

Because whatever this . . . entity *really* was, it seemed to believe that it was John Sri Davinda's climate model itself, not the human creator thereof.

"Okay, so I'm talking to a climate model," Monique said. "So whyfor are you different from all other climate models?"

Was that a smile of perfect serenity or an expression of perfect acceptance of terrible fate on the face of John Sri Davinda? Was there anything human left in there at all?

"I am the last climate model."

"The . . . *last* climate model . . . ?"

"No more definitive climate model is mathematically possible."

"You're the . . . *perfect* climate model . . . ?" Monique said softly. "You've got all the answers . . . ?"

The effect was unexpected and cataclysmic.

The serene indifference on the face of John Sri Davinda morphed into an expression of agonized horror.

"What did I say?" Monique groaned.

There was no reply. The twisted look of horror remained, but it was as if she had pulled the plug on whatever light had been shining through those inhuman eyes.

"Shit, shit, *now* what?" Eric observed as he watched Monique Calhoun trying to shake Davinda out of whatever fugue state he had suddenly fallen back into just as she seemed to have at least been getting *somewhere*.

"Is that an operational question, kiddo, or are you just unhappy to see me?" replied Ignatz.

"What do I do now, *that's* the operational question!" Eric snapped back irritably. "Flush out the drugs? Change the prescription?"

"Remove Mohammed from the Mountain," said Ignatz.

"Words of one syllable, goddamn it, Mom, don't you start with that Third Force babble too!" said Eric, forgetting who, or rather what, he was really talking to.

"In *one* word of one syllable, *cut*, kiddo! Change the scene."

"To what?"

"A blast from his past."

"California?"

"You wanna bring the boy out, bring the boy back home."

The virtual hour didn't change, nor the blue clarity of the sky above, but the hue had become glorified with a subtle hint of gold, and now the background sound was that of the surge of breakers through the boulders and stony wave-etched tide pools of a rocky beach below.

Monique sat facing John Sri Davinda on the rough-planked porch of a neo-rustic redwood chalet. The peaked roof was a solar-panel array from which sprouted an impressive assortment of dish antennae.

The chalet was cantilevered out over a deep ravine or modest canyon descending from a coastal mountain range, and a river ran through its bottom to the sea. Palms and palmettos and succulents choked its depths and climbed its slopes, festooned with more chalets, cabins, domes, low-lying small factories, all unpainted wood, stone, green-tinted glass, weathered bronze, at one, somehow, with the tropical landscape.

And should Monique fail to recognize this as the idealized coast of central California, homeland of John Sri Davinda's roots, a syrupy orchestral remix of classic twentieth-century surfing music murmured in the background as a helpful hint.

California kitsch this time, Monique thought.

But if *this* doesn't work, I don't know what will. . . .

"John . . ." she purred gently. "You're back home now . . . back in California . . . back where it all began . . . remember . . . remember when . . . ?"

The musculature of Davinda's face, frozen into a horrified mask, began to slowly relax. . . .

"Yes, John Sri Davinda, that's who you are now, back when, way back when . . ."

Davinda's face smoothed out, but not into anything Monique could recognize as an expression of human emotion. Rather it became another mask, this a tranquil one, but with nothing behind the eyes but an empty void.

"Come on, John, I know you're in there, so come on out," Monique said in a rather harsher tone of voice, fighting against her rising exasperation, and beginning to lose.

Nothing.

Damn!

Or damned.

For Monique was running out of ideas as well as patience, and she found her eyes being drawn downward to the purse beside her. Felt the invisible presence of the gun pulsing inside it.

Or not?

Might that not be another illusion?

If she just reached down and palpated the purse, might she not happily discover that there *was* no flechette pistol inside it?

Her hand started to move toward the purse. She yanked it back, and convulsively shook Davinda by the shoulder instead.

"Talk to me, talk to me, will you!" she shouted. "Before it's too late."

"It's not working," said Eric.

"No shit, Sherlock," said Ignatz.

"Any more bright ideas?"

"Is that an operational question?"

"Yes, Mom, it's an operational question," Eric said testily, "and I'd appreciate an operational answer."

"Maybe it's time to *terminate* the operation, kiddo," Ignatz suggested.

Eric pondered this for a long moment.

Sooner or later, if Monique failed to get any more information out of Davinda, he *was* going to have to go in there and terminate the operation. Was it now later than sooner? Was unprofessional sentimental romanticism the only thing preventing him from doing it?

"That's the only operational advice you have?" Eric asked plaintively.

"What's preventing you from taking it, kiddo? Why don't you just ice him and get it over with?"

"Because I don't want to make a terrible mistake that could end up maybe *frying* the whole world, damn it!" Eric snapped.

"That's all, Eric?"

"That isn't *enough?*"

"Come on, kiddo, you can't bullshit a simulation of a bullshitter!"

"All right, all right," Eric whined, "so the idea of framing Monique Calhoun for the hit turns my stomach! There, I've said it, are you satisfied, Mom?"

Mom?

Eric abruptly realized he was trying to justify himself to this . . . this *program* as if he really *were* arguing with his mother.

And losing as usual.

"Well, kiddo, there *is* one thing you *could* try," Ignatz said. "You gotta remember, I'm only a simulation, and a female one at that, so it's kind of hard for me to model how you're gonna take this. . . ."

"I'm a big bad boy, Mom . . . I mean . . . jeez!"

"You got the place pumped full of *brain* stimulants, and the guy's still tranced out," said Ignatz. "So maybe you're . . . playing the wrong organ. According to the database this simulation is supplied with kiddo, you wanna raise a male zombie from the dead, you gotta . . . grab him by the handle."

When Monique felt the heat of her frustrated ire moving southward from her brain to her loins and becoming another form of warmth in the process, having no rational, emotional, or esthetic raison d'être for the transmutation and having experienced this illogical sexual arousal in similar circumstances before, she was certain that the effect had to be biochemical.

But while her first reaction was feminine outrage at Eric Esterhazy, this time around she knew exactly what he was doing, and found it difficult to argue with the why.

The why being the libidinal activation of John Sri Davinda and the effect on her being merely an unavoidable consequence, friendly fire as it were.

It hadn't worked on Davinda the last time around, but the last time around, Davinda had been blotted on booze and dust to begin with. And this time around, the aphrogas in the atmosphere could be augmented with brain and somatic stimulants.

And thinking that very thought quite clearly with her loins afire, Monique realized that it probably was already. Which explained her mood swings and the sharpening of her insight.

Which also explained the logical clarity of her present thought under these extreme and unlikely circumstances. And even made her somewhat glad that she was under the influence of the aphrogas too.

It wasn't going to make this fun.

But it might make it bearable.

"The climate model, John, this is where you created your climate model, tell me about the *climate model. . . .*"

Surely the queasy feeling Eric felt in the region between his stomach and his testicles wasn't *jealousy.* He liked Monique Calhoun well enough, he found her sexually attractive, he had enjoyed their sexual fun and down-and-dirty games, but he certainly wasn't *in love* with her.

Nor was the gruesome spectacle on the screen sexually arousing or anything to be jealous about. Monique had opened Davinda's fly, withdrawn a semi-flaccid organ, and managed to massage it to a more-or-less erect state, thanks mainly, no doubt, to the aphrogas, given that the still-vacant expression on Davinda's face gave little evidence of the involvement of his cerebral centers in the proceedings.

Now she was working his phallic pump handle forcefully and mechanically. It was about as erotic as watching a machine milking a cow.

"Come on, John, I *know* you're in there, come on out . . ." Monique wheedled, working her hand without looking, and trying unsuccessfully to force the ludicrously obscene visual image of what she was doing from the screen of her mind by focusing on the face, on the eyes, of John Sri Davinda.

Who seemed to be slowly coming to show some semblance of human life, a parting of the lips, a soundless moan, another, a rapid flickering of the eyelids . . .

And then Monique had a small satori.

If Davinda *was* a mole, then, to judge from the way the Marenkos kept repeating it to him, "Lao" was probably some kind of activation command.

And an activation command was certainly what she needed now.

"Lao . . . John . . . Lao . . . Lao . . . Lao . . ."

She moved her hand in time to the chant, took more care to halt teasingly on the upstroke, and bring it half-satisfyingly down on the beat. . . .

"Lao . . . Lao . . . Lao . . ."

"Lao . . ." Davinda finally muttered.

"Yes, John, Lao!"

Monique ceased her stroking and held her hand in place, clenching and releasing, clenching and releasing, trying, as it were, to squeeze it out of him.

"Lao, John, Lao . . ."

"Lao . . ."

"Lao is *what?*"

"Lao is the Chao of the Tao. . . ."

"Shit!" Monique snapped, giving him a convulsive yank.

Then she caught herself.

And took a long deep breath.

Enter his image system. Don't expect him to enter yours.

"Lao is the Chao of the Tao," she repeated, now trying to ease it out of him with gentle agreement and soft strokes. "Lao is the Chao of the Tao. . . ."

And then she had another little inspiration.

"Is Lao . . . the *model* of the Tao . . . ?"

"Lao models the condition of the Tao . . ." said Davinda.

An actual coherent sentence! Perhaps it was whatever cerebral enhancers Eric was pumping into this greenhouse California atmosphere, but Monique was beginning to believe that she was not only entering into Davinda's image system, but starting to decode it.

"Lao" was Davinda's climate model.

The Tao, from her dim knowledge of such Third Force mumbo-jumbo, was the non-material, non-energetic, spiritual force underlying the universe of matter and energy, aka chi, prana, karma, whatever.

Codewise, in this image system, it probably stood for the planetary karma of the Earth.

"Chao" was all-too-unsettlingly obvious, the simple dropping of an "s" to make Chaos rhyme with "Lao" and "Tao."

Davinda's climate model was the Chaos of the planetary karma?

That appeared to be the message in this madness.

But it didn't make any sense that Monique could fathom even from within this Third Force image system.

Unless . . .

"Lao models the condition of the Earth's Tao . . . ?" she suggested, priming Davinda's pump handle encouragingly. "And the condition of the Earth's Tao is—"

"Chaos!" Davinda shouted.

"*Condition* Chaos?"

And before Monique could frame the next question, it all came gushing out in a torrent.

"Condition Chaos! Should I have known? How could I! No one suspected, not Braithwaite, not Pereiro, not Manning, not even the great Allison Larabee, how was I to know, yes, it was implicit in the data, but no program was powerful enough, not before Lao, and even the early iterations of Lao couldn't show it, the hardware wasn't good

304 o GREENHOUSE SUMMER

enough, what was I supposed to do then, *tell them*, they would've canceled the program, Lao would *never* have been fully implemented, and—"

"Wait, wait, what are you trying—"

"Caused by a century of the climatech mods themselves! Too late to reverse it, the climate of the Earth has become a chaotic system, and Lao proves it, Lao is definitive, no more complete simulation is mathematically possible. Causality breaks down entirely past a ten-year time frame in *any* iteration!"

Davinda had been making frantically blinking eye contact with her as he gabbled this stuff and the haunted horrified expression on his face was all too human, so this was obviously what was left of the climatologist in there speaking.

But Monique was beyond her technical depth. Implicit in the data? Iterations? Chaotic system? Definitive simulation? Causality breakdown?

This was an image system she just didn't know enough mathematics to enter. She had to cozen him into translating it into something she could understand. But how?

Well, if there *was* anything human still inside that brain pan, it was male. And if it was male, the very last bit of humanity it was likely to surrender to the void would be its ego, said essence of maleness being directly circuited to the priapic organ she had firmly in hand.

So . . .

"You're very proud of your climate model, aren't you, John Sri Davinda," she said, pumping him gently but more insistently. "You're very proud of Lao, it's such a *wonderful* climate model, it's the *best* there is, it's—

"It's *more* than a climate model!" Davinda proclaimed. "I am the Tao incarnate in software!"

"It's *what*? You're *who*?"

Monique moved her hand up behind the very tip of his cock and applied upward pressure, as if to pull him right up out of himself by the handle.

Whether it was the sexual pressure, or her words, or the mix of vapors, or a synergy of all three, Davinda groaned, and began to babble a less technical brand of gibberish.

"Lao is a one-for-one model of the Tao of the Earth in software. Lao can . . . can steer the geosphere. Lao is pure pattern, the Third Force created by the interfacing of mind and matter. Lao is Gaia made manifest. Lao is . . . the Way."

"Deus ex machismo . . ." Monique groaned.

When she sought to drag what was left of John Sri Davinda back into the land of the living by the phallic ego, she certainly hadn't expected him to emerge from the cranial void proclaiming he had become a self-created god.

It was admittedly a pretty good trick by most standards.

But extracting the money to do it from the bottom-line capitalist pragmatists of the Big Blue Machine went it one better!

"Surely you didn't tell the Big Blue Machine that they were funding the birth of the Gaian Godhead of the bits and bytes . . . ?"

"They had no need to know."

"You mean *you* had no need for them to know."

"The software was mathematically definitive. That was verifiable. The partial iterations they ran pleased them very much."

"Sure, because they came up Condition Venus, didn't they . . . ? Or you made sure they did. But you needed the human meatware computer to summon up your Lao of the Tao, didn't you? And they weren't about to fork over without a guarantee of a human central processing unit, right? So the bastards blackmailed you into it, right?"

"Oh no," Davinda proclaimed, his eyes glowing with a sickly and unwholesome glory, "I gladly volunteered!"

"You *gladly volunteered!* To burn your brain out?"

"To become Lao! To become the Steersman of the Planetary Tao!"

Monique dropped Davinda's prick as if it had suddenly turned into a loathsome slug, which, from a certain perspective, as far as she was concerned, it had.

It was almost enough to make her a Third Force believer.

Whenever two forces oppose, the Third Force emerges?

Oppose Davinda's definitive climate model with Big Blue's bottom-line need to sell Condition Venus. Oppose phallic ego and capitalist greed.

And *this* is what emerges.

You can't bullshit a bullshitter?

As even the rawest Bread & Circuses recruit speedily learned, it was easy enough if the bullshittees had a strong enough self-interest in allowing themselves to be bullshitted.

But . . .

But the presence of the pistol in the purse beside her reminded Monique that none of this had answered her operational question.

To . . . kill or not to kill, *that* was the question.

And nothing she had heard thus far had enabled her to evade or resolve it.

"And when they plug your brain back into the computer tomorrow and run . . . the climate model . . . through you?" Monique Calhoun demanded, rather wanly, Eric thought. "What happens then?"

As Eric watched, John Sri Davinda's blink rate went sky-high, sweat broke out on his face, and, despite the aphrogas, his erection wilted.

"I . . . I . . . I . . . I . . ." he stammered weakly.

And then he abruptly went through yet another eerie transformation. His furious blinking ceased abruptly. He seemed to stop blinking entirely. His stare became fixed. His eyes became as glazed and implacable and inhumanly indifferent as a sleazoid generalissimo's silvered sunglasses.

And when he spoke again, the voice was firm and flat and devoid of affect, not unlike the default voice of Ignatz behind the interface personality masks.

"I am become Lao," it said.

Not unlike it at all.

"And that's what I'm speaking to now, is it?" Monique Calhoun snapped angrily, but with a strangely plaintive catch in her voice. "And what will . . . Lao tell the waiting world about . . . the condition of . . . the Earth's climatological Tao?"

"Condition Chaos," said the meatware voice, perfectly emulating a naked software emulation.

Monique Calhoun finally lost it. She threw up her hands in angry frustration. "Fuck Condition Chaos!" she shouted. "I need to know about Condition *Venus!*"

"All iterations converge on Condition Chaos within a ten-year time-frame."

"Condition *Venus*, damn you!" Monique screamed. "I need to know, I mean I *really* need to know what Lao, what you, whatever, will tell the world about *Condition Venus*. Real or disney? Yes or no?"

"All iterations converge on Condition Chaos within a ten-year time-frame. No other predictive outcome is mathematically possible."

"That's a no, isn't it?" Monique Calhoun said in a tiny voice, and began kneading her purse compulsively like a lost little girl's security blanket.

The interrogation phase of this operation would seem to have dead-ended in failure. Beneath the obscure mathematics and Third Force crypticism, John Sri Davinda, or Lao, or whatever might be said to inhabit that meatware corpus, would certainly seem to at least be saying that this so-called definitive climate model would *not* verify the impending reality of Condition Venus.

Therefore, according to the contract, Eric must now remove Davinda. He would have to do it with no assurances as to the ultimate planetary consequences, without knowing whether he would be doing the right thing.

That at least would be the fulfillment of a contract he had accepted but others had issued, so he could at least try to persuade himself that the responsibility was collective.

But the responsibility for setting up Monique Calhoun to take the fall for it would be his alone. Because framing Monique for the hit would be a deed done merely to evade his own personal consequences.

And that Eric *knew* would be wrong.

In that moment he could've blown John Sri Davinda away just for confronting him with this entirely unwelcome crisis of the conscience he hadn't known he had. Or wanted to.

"Any bright ideas, Mom?" Eric snapped angrily.

"Use your noodle, kiddo," Ignatz told him.

"Brilliant!"

But upon a moment's less than cool reflection, Eric did.

Or rather, in the time-honored human manner, allowed his emotions to run through his brain, and thence through his mouth:

"All right, Voice, eat Whirlwind!" he commanded.

A mighty white vortex came whipping in off the sea at unreal speed, growing larger and larger as it came, blowing the sea into waves, and the waves into breakers, and the breakers into a foam that broke up into pixels, tearing the serene blue Californian sky into shards, ripping away the verdant veneer of the landscape to reveal the bare rock beneath and the pixelation beneath that, rending the very mountains electronic dust to become the world entire.

"The white tornado!" Monique shouted over a rumbling roar not quite loud enough to prevent her from hearing herself. "Condition Venus! It's the end of the world!"

John Sri Davinda, or that which he had become, sat there in the eye of the storm with as much emotion showing on his face as in the utterly detached voice in which he spoke.

"This is not a white tornado. This is an emulation of a white tornado. This is not Condition Venus. This is an emulation of Condition Venus. This is not the end of the world. This is a modeling of the end of the world."

"And what are you, you son of a bitch," Monique shouted at him, "a computer program emulating a human being, or a human being modeling a computer program?"

Davinda's blank expression did not change. His eyes were turned in Monique's direction but she did not at all sense that he was looking *at* her. He didn't answer. A slight increase in his blink rate was the scant and only evidence that there might still be some remnant of a human being in there.

And Monique knew that this was her very last chance to reach it.

"Please, please, please, John, talk to me now," she begged forthrightly, "because if you don't . . . if you don't . . ."

Nothing.

Her hand found her purse and opened it. And slid inside. And found the grip of the flechette pistol.

Nada.

And closed around it.

Rien de tout.

And there in the pitiless heart of the white tornado, Monique began to cry.

Not the Whirlwind, not the tears of the woman crying within it, nothing was going to rescue Eric from the fulfillment of his contract.

He drew the flechette pistol from its shoulder holster, checked the magazine, flipped off the safety, started to rise, then hesitated, caught short by the leaden weight of the second pistol in his jacket pocket.

"Any more . . . operational suggestions . . . *Mom?*" he asked bleakly, all too aware in that moment that he was talking to a mask over a vacuum.

"No way around it, you gotta go in there now and ice him," Mom's voice told him.

"That's for Bad Boys, that's for the biosphere, that's for the Gipper, whatever. But you're either gonna be able to walk out of there like a man, Eric, or end up crawling out on your belly like a reptile. And that one's for you, kiddo."

With tears sliding down her cheek, Monique drew the flechette pistol from her purse and pointed it at Davinda's head with a shaky hand.

"If . . . you don't talk to me right now . . . I'm . . . going to have to blow your head off . . ." she shouted over the white tornado's roar. "Really I am! I mean it! Really!"

It came out sounding more to her own ears like a desperate plea than a credible threat. And John Sri Davinda just sat there like a stone buddha.

I am going to have to do this, Monique told herself. I am going to have to do this, she repeated silently, trying to turn it into a mantra. I am going to have to do this.

She reached up with her other hand to steady her aim.

I am going to have to do this because it is right. I am going to have to do this because I must. I am going to have to do this because if I don't—

There was a sudden sound behind her.

She whirled reflexively—

Eric Esterhazy strode through the maelstrom toward her like a god of doom, a gun in either hand.

Eric's jaw dropped in poleaxed amazement as he found himself staring at the muzzle of a pistol pointed squarely at his chest, held in a shaky double-handed grip by Monique Calhoun.

A spent-uranium flechette pistol that was the clone of his own. A weapon that he knew could not fail to be deadly at this range even in the trembling hands of an amateur as rank as Monique.

"Don't get the wrong idea, Eric!" Monique said hastily. "This is for *him*, not you!"

Nevertheless it did not seem too clever an idea to prove it by lowering her gun just yet.

Even when Eric Esterhazy broke into manic laughter.

Seeing as how even then, he didn't lower *either* of his.

"What's so damned funny?" demanded Monique Calhoun. "This is your idea of situation comedy?"

Eric broke up again.

Only Mom would fully get the joke.

There he was, in the howling of a raging virtual white tornado, pointing a pair of pistols at a woman who was pointing one at him. The woman he was about to frame for the hit he was about to perform. And it was not inconceivable that the fate of the Earth might hang in the balance.

Yet thanks to the vapors with which he had filled the chamber, he was facing this most dire existential moment of his life with a raging hard-on.

"It does have its humorous aspects," Eric said.

"Hah . . . hah . . . hah . . ." said Monique Calhoun. "Would you mind letting me in on the joke?"

Her voice caught. Her bravado broke. She sobbed, once, twice. "I could use a little comic relief long about now," she said plaintively.

Was it the aphrogas?

Was it the way Monique Calhoun stood there sobbing with a gun bravely pointed at his chest in her trembling hands?

Was it what Ignatz's simulation of Mom had told him—*you're either gonna be able to walk out of there like a man, Eric, or end up crawling out on your belly like a reptile?*

Was it because he knew the genuine item would've said the same thing?

Whatever. The synergy had touched and clarified his heart.

Could he act on a probability, not a certainty? Could he kill John Sri Davinda under the supposition that it might be necessary to preserve the Big Blue Machine from the results of its own machinations? To preserve a cabal of cynical revenant capitalist liars from the just consequences of their own assholery?

Yes, he could do that.

Yes, he *should* do that.

The Marenkos believed that under these very circumstances it would be necessary, Eduardo Ramirez believed it, and Eric had accepted the contract because he believed it too.

He could do his honorable duty and fulfill his contract and walk out of here afterward like a man with his head held high.

But could he lay the deed off on Monique Calhoun?

No, he couldn't.

No, he *shouldn't.*

No matter the personal consequences.

Because if he did, he would indeed be constrained to crawl out of here on his belly like the reptile it would make him.

Eric laughed again.

"Would you believe," he said, "that under these strange circumstances, a Bad Boy's best friend is his virtual mother?"

And tossed away the grip-taped pearl-handled revolver.

"What's that supposed to mean?" Monique said. "And . . . and what did you just do?"

Throwing away his *little* gun made no sense, since his *big* flechette pistol was still pointed straight at her.

"It means today I am a man," Eric Esterhazy said in a tone of smarmy insincerity that seemed to mask something deep and real. "And what I just did was . . . what I feel good after."

"Can we cut the crap for once?" Monique pleaded. "Can we please get real, Eric?"

"I thought you'd never ask," said Prince Eric Esterhazy.

"Ground zero," Eric commanded Ignatz. "Flush with forty percent oxygen. Turn off the bubble machine."

The white tornado abruptly vanished. The only sounds were their breathing and the hum of the pump purging the boudoir atmosphere.

And then there they were, just two people in a plain and featureless pearlescent chamber pointing pistols at each other.

"It doesn't get much realer than this, does it, Monique?" Eric told her softly.

"We have to talk, Eric," Monique said, followed by a bark of a laugh that Eric found strangely touching.

"What's the gun for, Monique?"

Monique nodded backward in the general direction of Davinda, who sat there as motionless and indifferent as a well-watered houseplant.

"*You* have a contract on him?"

Monique nodded.

"From whom, if I may be so crude as to ask?"

"From the Big Blue Machine. Unless I have proof he's no Siberian mole programmed to turn tomorrow's climate model demonstration into their fiasco I have—"

Eric laughed.

"What's so damned funny about that?"

"Same contract," he told her. "More or less. From the Marenkos."

"*The Marenkos?* The Marenkos want *their own mole* eliminated?"

"He may be *someone's* mole, but not the Siberians'. The Marenkos don't want to see the Big Blue Machine destroyed."

"*They don't?* Even though they faked the white tornadoes to bilk the Siberian syndics?"

"Not if their climatech is going to be needed to save the world from Condition Venus."

"Even if it means the end of Siberia the Golden?"

"Even if it means the end of Siberia the Golden."

Monique nodded in the direction of the discarded pearl-handled revolver.

Eric shrugged. "I was supposed to use *that*, get your fingerprints all over it, and pin the . . . removal on you."

"And you threw it away . . . ?" Monique gaped at him. "But won't they . . . ?"

Her lower lip trembled.

"Oh, I think I can finesse the situation if Mr. Davinda just disappears," Eric said, emulating cavalier insouciance. "The Seine is full of alligators who do not at all believe there is no such thing as a free lunch."

He gave her his best heroic hunk smile.

"So you see, Monique, we don't *really* have to shoot each other," Eric said, and lowered his gun. "On the other hand, we *do* have our contractual obligations."

He took a step toward John Sri Davinda.

"And since *I'm* the professional here," Eric said suavely, with a little bow, "do allow me. . . ."

In some ultimately mad but ultimately touching way, this was the single most gallant thing any man had ever proposed to do for Monique in her entire life.

"I can't let you *murder* a man for me, Eric," she told him, lowering her own gun.

"We *do* prefer the term *removal* in the profession."

"Do either of us *really* have to kill him?" Monique asked him all too rhetorically. "I mean, if he's not a Siberian mole—"

"A narrow interpretation of *your* contract might remove *your* obligation, but mine calls for a removal to protect the Big Blue Machine from its own self-created public relations catastrophe, and if they install this brain-burn case in their computer and run their climate model expecting Condition Venus to come out the other end . . ."

Eric shrugged. "You're Bread & Circuses," he said. "You tell me."

Monique sighed. "Goodbye, UNACOCS. Goodbye UN, maybe. Goodbye, any remaining credibility for the Big Blue Machine."

"Goodbye Earth, if it turns out later we're going to need their climatech to save it from Condition Venus after all. . . ."

"But we *still* don't really know, not for sure!"

Monique whirled around in a desperate fury to face Davinda, who, bereft of whatever benefits he might have had from the chemical augments previously in the atmosphere, now sat there blank-faced, vacant-eyed, his cock hanging ludicrously limp from his still open fly.

Dropping to her knees, she yanked him as hard as she could by the phallic handle, *hoping* it would hurt. Hard enough at least to get a good yelp out of him.

"Haven't you been *listening* to all this?" she shouted in his face. "Won't you at least *try* to talk us out of killing you? Don't you even *care?*"

No human reaction was in evidence.

All right then, Monique decided in what she knew was her final desperation, try *its* image system.

"Lao!" she shouted, yanking his cock once more, and quite brutally. "I know *you're* at least in there."

The yelp she extracted this time did not seem quite human. Less still the voice that finally deigned to speak.

"I am Lao."

"Do you realize the full program . . . will be run tomorrow, unless . . . unless . . ."

"I await complete and definitive iteration."

One final question, framed properly.

"Will your . . . definitive iteration demonstrate that Condition Venus is inevitable?" Monique said. "Yes or no?"

The *terminal* question, in *binary* terms, so that the answer would have to be . . . definitive.

"No," said John Sri Davinda. "Condition Venus is not inevitable."

"It . . . it isn't? You're . . . you're sure?"

"Full iteration will definitively demonstrate that no existing or theoretically possible climate model can or ever will produce a reliable prediction of climatological conditions beyond a ten-year time frame from any dataset. The geosphere of this planet has become a chaotic system. This is Condition Chaos. Condition Chaos cannot be re-versed."

"Not even *Lao* can tell us whether Condition Venus is inevitable?" Monique whispered. "No climate model ever can?"

But neither the man who had been John Sri Davinda or what he had become would speak again.

Yet Monique knew that she had had her terminal answer. Chaos mathematics and climate modeling might be image systems beyond her fathoming. But it translated easily enough into an image system she could all too well understand.

No climate model could produce any certainty now. Not because the program wasn't good enough or the hardware powerful enough but because that which it sought to model, the future climate of the Earth itself and the effects of humanity's endless alterations thereof, had gone beyond the limits of causal knowability.

Thanks to human climatech itself.

"Did you understand all that, Eric?" asked Monique Calhoun, rising slowly to her feet.

Eric thought about it.

All of it?

No, he didn't fully understand all of it. But he understood enough of the mathematics to know that what they ultimately, definitively, and paradoxically proved was that no one and nothing would *ever* be able to mathematically predict what further climatech mods would finally do to the climatological destiny of the planet.

The Big Blue Machine's planet-cooling climatech might be needed to save the biosphere now or ten years from now or a century from now or never. And there was no way of knowing.

Nor was "allowing the planetary climate to follow its natural course" an option. Because thanks to the wonders of science and technology, "the natural course" no longer existed.

Condition Disney had produced Condition Chaos.

"The lunatics have taken over the asylum," Eric said. "The passengers have hijacked the flight, and now like it or not, *we're* flying the planet."

"And like it or not," said Monique Calhoun, "we're going to have to fly it blind. Unless . . ."

She nodded in the direction of Davinda. "Unless . . ."

"Unless we try to weasel our way out of it by turning the controls over to the latest self-proclaimed version of Mr. I Am?" Eric said. "Seems to me, we've been trying that one for a few thousand years, and where, need I ask, has it gotten us?"

Monique Calhoun sighed.

"Where we are now," she admitted.

"And so . . ."

"And so, sweet Prince . . . ?"

Eric shrugged. "I can tell you what my mother would say," he told her, and switched over to an emulation of Mom, if not quite up to Ignatz's version.

"Know the one about how people in glass houses shouldn't throw stones, kiddo? Well setting off a nuke inside a planetary aquarium don't seem like such a swift idea either."

"Meaning what?"

"Meaning that if we both welch on our contracts, Big Blue will trot out Davinda as their heroic volunteer risking death to save the world by providing definitive proof of the onset of Condition Venus while there's still time to do something about it," Eric told her. "And they plug him into the computer before the horrified eyes of the world and boot it up and out comes—"

"An atrocity!" said Monique. "A public relations catastrophe! A raving psychotic proclaiming himself the Steersman of the Planetary Tao. Not even Bread & Circuses could spin Big Blue out of that. And if he *dies* during the process—"

"Hope he does," Eric told her. "Because there'll be plenty of people out there grateful to be able to bow down to Lao and turn things over to the Steersman of the Planetary Tao. Speaking of the lunatics taking over the asylum."

"And so, to save a bunch of lying capitalist bastards from the justly earned deserts of their misdeeds, we have to . . . we have to . . ."

"A wise man told me that the buck stops with every citizen-shareholder," Eric said. "Well, this one stops here. This one's ours."

"I was always advised never to be a citizen of anything in which I wouldn't want to hold shares," Monique said.

And then, in a small voice, with forlorn bravery: "But I suppose when it's the Earth, there's really no choice, huh?"

"We both accepted our contracts, Monique," Eric said, doing a last minute recheck of the magazine of his flechette pistol in the approved professional manner. "We're honor-bound."

"Just like that? How can you . . . how can you kill a man?"

"It's easy," Eric told her, making sure the safety was off, "especially with a weapon like this. You just aim, take a deep breath, hold it, and squeeze, don't pull, the trigger. The recoil isn't that bad at all."

"You've . . . done this before. . . ?"

Eric nodded. He raised the pistol. Monique scrambled out of the line of fire.

"And you *really* believe that you're doing the right thing?"

Eric took two steps backward. The pistol would fire a cloud of flechettes that would send quite a bit of blood and flesh flying and this *was* a good suit.

"Don't you, Monique? If the Marenkos would sacrifice Siberia the Golden if they knew it was the right thing to do, would it really make us pure as the returning snow to turn up our righteous noses at a little necessary wetwork?"

Eric took aim at the indifferent head of John Sri Davinda.

"Well . . . it's . . . it's not as if I'm the Virgin Mary, is it, Eric?" said Monique.

She bit down on her lower lip. She went to Eric's side. She put her left arm around his waist. She raised her pistol and took aim.

"Deep breath . . . ?" she said in a tremulous voice. "Hold it. . . ?" And inhaled.

"Squeeze, don't pull," Eric said gently. "On the count of three . . . one . . . two . . ."